THE
ARCHITECT

A NOVEL

by R. J. Linteau

DORRANCE
PUBLISHING CO
EST. 1920
PITTSBURGH, PENNSYLVANIA 15238

Dorrance Publishing Co
585 Alpha Drive
Pittsburgh, PA 15238
Visit our website at www.dorrancebookstore.com

ISBN: 978-1-6491-3790-6
EISBN: 978-1-6491-3978-8

THE
ARCHITECT

A NOVEL

Dedicated to:

My good friend,
Taylor Freeman
For his encouragement, support, and for putting
up with all my badgering.

Many thanks to Kay Olsen for a great job
editing this manuscript.

THE
ARCHITECT

This is a work of fiction. Any relationship to actual individuals, places, and circumstances is purely coincidental.

Printed by Dorrance Publishing Co.
In the United States of America.

Author e-mail: RJLinteau.author@gmail.com

Part One

THE LAND
APRIL 1973

Chapter 1

The brief note on executive stationery was enough. Connor Jones West read the words over and over again from the confines of the cold and cramped apartment above a garage off Harvard Square.

Dear Mr. West,

Call me.
We are interested in meeting you.

J

J. Vance Jefferson, FAIA
Director of Architecture
Nolan, Jefferson and Marlow
Architects and Engineers

He nervously made the call the next day. J. Vance Jefferson answered after what seemed like an eternity. He spoke in bright, clipped sentences.

"Mr. West, we are most interested in meeting with you about a position with the firm."

"Yes, sir, that would be great," hoping that his tone wasn't too eager.

"Wonderful, I'll make arrangements for you. Will next week work?"

"Uh, yeah, I mean yes, sure. Thank you." *"Shit,"* he thought, *"I'm at the end of my thesis and every day is precious."* But this was his future.

"My assistant will call you. We will pay for your flight and hotel. Her name is Marilyn. She'll be in touch."

The call ended as quickly as it started.

Connor bound up the stairs to the bright morning sun, and the cold air of this late April day stung his face. In excitement and anticipation, he took the steps two at a time with his lean but muscular 6'1" frame. His long, dark tussle of brown hair that was combed back fell across his face. *"Damn, I should have gotten a haircut,"* he thought, but it had all happened so fast and he had spent the last week working on his thesis. If it didn't get done, he wouldn't graduate. Up from the depths of the subway station below, his deep brown eyes surveyed the street scene.

He had slept on the flight from Boston to O'Hare. A private car picked him up at the airport; a sign held by the black-jacketed driver stated "Connor West." No one had ever held a sign wanting him. He checked in to a somewhat tired room at the famous Allerton Hotel, a dark, aging brick dowager from the 1920s. His mini-suite looked down onto Michigan Avenue, which was filled with throngs of people. *"All this for me?"* thought Connor. He unpacked and returned to the lobby, two stories tall, richly appointed in newer furniture. It was large and bustling, the check–in counter on one end and the lobby bar and restaurant on the other. After a beer and a steak dinner courtesy of NJ&M, Connor took a brisk walk up to the Water Tower, down Michigan Avenue and back to his hotel room. He collapsed on his bed and slept soundly until the wakeup call came at 6:30 A.M.

Many other firms had expressed interest; such was the prestige and pedigree of a Harvard degree. Firms in New York said: "We want you and you'll start as an apprentice. By 50, you'll be a partner." Bullshit to that. Boston firms had wanted him too, but he was sick of Bean Town and the pay was crap. Connor West had been poor too long to accept that. Hell, even with scholarships he would still owe over twenty-five thousand dollars in student loans after graduation.

He had only two criteria: he would work for whatever firm would pay him the most for his efforts, and he wanted to design buildings— great buildings.

Nolan, Jefferson and Marlow was different. It was known nationally, and it was in Chicago, home of American architecture. His career in architecture was finally about to start. He believed in himself and his abilities, though right now there was the inevitable queasiness in his stomach. But his sheepskin would state magna cum laude directly under the conferring degree, Master of Architecture. He had accomplished that after all.

With his design portfolio under his arm, Connor proceeded east on Monroe as he read the directions provided by Marilyn, and then arrived at Michigan Avenue. The canyon of buildings ceased, and in front of him laid the vast expanse of Grant Park, Buckingham Fountain and then Lake Michigan. Looking south he could make out the neo-classical façade of the Chicago Art Institute. Turning the corner, he headed in that direction. Finally, he reached the majestic terra cotta behemoth known as the Railway Exchange Building with huge letters atop the building proclaiming "Santa Fe," the great railroad being a major tenant there.

This 1904 edifice was the home of Nolan, Jefferson & Marlow, Chicago's largest and most distinguished architectural firm. In Chicago it was known as the "connected" firm, garnering big city contracts from the mayor, John "Big Jack" Malone to his lifelong friend, Francis Daniel Nolan, Sr., FAIA, the firm's founder, and once secretary to the great architect and planner Daniel Burnham, who once proclaimed, "Make no little plans; they have no magic to stir men's blood."

He entered the gilded beaux arts lobby of the building with its carved wood pediments and grand staircase that led to the second-floor mezzanine. It was topped by a majestic skylight roof, revealing the light-well open to the dark azure sky fifteen floors above. Connor managed to squeeze into one of the ornate neoclassical elevators with many other office workers trying to get to their desks by 8:30 A.M. He pressed 14. This was the same floor where the famous Daniel Burnham had once practiced and where the firm had finally evolved into NJ&M, led by Francis Nolan.

All of the building elevators opened to the large lobby on the 14th floor, where an attractive receptionist sat behind a desk at least twenty feet long. He asked for Mr. Jefferson and she directed him to the seating area off to the side while speaking in hushed tones into the phone. On one wall was a Mark Rothko painting, a Claes Oldenburg on the other. He sat in an original Mies van der Rohe Barcelona chair. Its dictate of style over comfort had always annoyed him.

Connor shifted from one position to another, and the butterflies in his stomach were making him want to take a crap. He brushed his tweed coat and looked down at his pressed khaki pants, just purchased with money waiting tables at a pizza joint off Harvard Square. It was the best outfit he had, but one that wasn't impressive. Nonetheless, with his height and long, dark brown hair, deep brown eyes and chiseled features, he cut an impressive figure.

Another "10" secretary summoned him with a warm smile.

"Welcome to Chicago, Mr. West. I hope your hotel room is satisfactory?"

Struck with her beauty, all he could muster was, "Ah, great, just fine."

"I'm Marilyn Jones, Mr. Jefferson's assistant. If you need anything at all, just let me know."

"Thanks," then suddenly trying to make small talk: "You know my middle name is Jones" he replied lamely.

There was a hint of a smile. "Really, perhaps we are related," she replied crisply saying "we are" not "we're." He smiled wanly, tongue-tied without a good comeback.

As she led him across the large lobby toward the inner sanctum called the Executive Area, he gave her a quick look-over from behind. She was indeed fine, and could not be much older than him, if any older at all. She wore a dark blue tailored suit and a string of pearls.

Her legs, what he could see beneath the conservative suit, were slim and perfect. Her light brown hair was pulled back into a ponytail, revealing matching pearl earrings. Her face was bright and perfect, and she had on just the right amount of makeup. The appearance spoke of a strict dress code for women in the firm, few of whom were architects. It was after all, a man's profession.

A quick glance at her ring finger indicated single status. *"I wonder if you can date another employee at this place?"* he thought.

"Hey, could I get a glass of water? I mean, may I please have a glass of water? And I need to use the men's room."

"Ice?"

"Excuse me?"

"Would you like ice with the water?" she said, smiling broadly.

"Oh, just the water is fine…"

"And the rest room is down here just off to your right."

"Thank you, thanks!" and followed Marilyn to the men's. He entered a marble-walled stall, pulled down his trousers and put his head into his hands. After relieving himself, he went out to the long vanity and felt dampness under his armpits and a bead of sweat form slowly on his forehead. He ran his fingers through his thick hair, wishing he had brought a comb, and wiped his forehead with a cloth hand towel, provided in a basket next to mouthwash and hand lotion. It was all very first class. He took a swig of mouthwash to wet his parched mouth. Taking a deep breath, he came out and Marilyn was waiting for him.

"Better now?"

"Yes, much. Thanks for waiting."

Then after what seemed an interminable walk toward Mr. Jefferson's office, Connor regained his composure. They reached another, smaller reception area.

"Please have a seat, Mr. West. Mr. Jefferson is just finishing up a meeting, but he is looking forward to meeting you. I'll get you that water." She walked away a few steps and then turned back to Connor.

"Mr. West, a word of advice…relax, you're in like Flint." He processed Marilyn's remark referencing a current movie with James Coburn and was heartened by it.

"Maybe this will indeed be the day if you don't fuck it up," he thought. He sat down in a Wassily armchair, no less comfortable than the previous Mies version. Connor picked up a *Progressive Architecture* magazine from the side table and waited for his life to begin.

CHAPTER 2

He kicked the ground gently so his spit-polished Johnson & Murphy tas-
seled loafers wouldn't get dirty. Then he bent down and picked up a handful
of the dirt, not caring about his hands. He had to touch it, he had to feel it.
It was his now, these two-and-a-half acres. Oh, it was just a large rectangular
lot, overgrown with weeds, and two trees that had made it their home over
the last ten years during the time the property was caught up in a legal war
between the Chicago Canal and Bridge Company and the City of Chicago.
Two trees and a large shantytown of homeless people along the river.

The well-dressed man smiled. Yes, it was his now. Two years of
backroom politics; fishing trips and call girls for Big Jack Malone,
convincing him that a signature building was better than years of continuing litigation. Then the same treatment, but with bribes thrown
in, for the Board of CC&B. Finally, last year, the city dropped its lawsuit with the company. He was ready to buy the land for $2,000,000,
the amount promised by his friend on the Board. Then CC&B announced they would take sealed bids for the land.

Angered at their lack of loyalty, he had made a mental note to
even the score later on. But he was not dissuaded. The developer did
what he always did—he bullied and threatened all the other developers in town that this was his deal. All but one, Dan Drew, decided
it wasn't worth the effort or certain litigation to own this small parcel
of dirt right on the Chicago River by Lake Michigan and famed Lakeshore Drive. Prime property or not, for most it just wasn't worth
going up against Steelson Simpson.

Dan Drew was not a problem. Steel Simpson had once dated
Dottie, his private secretary, and was still on good terms with her, and
Dan knew nothing of their relationship. She filled out the bid form

and gave it to Dan who, checking that the price he told her was in fact the price she had written down, placed the bid in the plain brown envelope and instructed her to deliver it to the offices of the Chicago Canal and Bridge Company on West Washington Street. She complied, and on her way along the river stepped into a pay phone and called her former lover.

"You owe me big for this, Steel."

"What's the number, Dottie?" he replied, dispensing with small talk.

"I've decided I'll take the money over the Bahamas trip even though I hate Chicago winters."

"Fine—the number?"

"$2,500,000."

"Shit. That asshole. It's not worth that much."

"So, let him have it, you still owe me the $5,000."

"Your money will be in a locker at the train station, Box L-238."

"You gonna outbid him or not, sweetie?"

The consummation of their deal and the thought of her newfound money was warming her up. She might even be up for a romp in the bed for old time's sake, though he wasn't much of a lover. He never seemed to have his heart or his dick into it.

"I'll have to think about it."

"Think quick. The bid's due at 2:00 P.M. Gotta go, but we should have a drink. Ciao, sweetie."

Steel put the receiver down, harder than necessary. He looked at the geo-technical report sitting on his desk. He had received it this morning and had gone right to the executive summary. There was a little-known tributary of the Chicago River, an underground stream, complete with small caverns, flowing right through the center of the property. The information made him light-headed. He had no idea what the solution to this was, but suspected it would cost thousands, if not millions and probably affect whatever design was executed. Removing his Hickey Freeman suit coat from his shoulders, he got down to business. He slowly read the detailed report.

"Fuck it! This is my land," he thought. Some minor engineering problem was not stopping him now, not after suffering through those trips with that bore of a mayor, or the countless dinners with the good old boys on the board of CC&B. How they ever got where they were was a mystery. Some had grown up in Bridgeport, like the mayor, and were personal friends; some were aldermen; most self-made, hardened businessmen. But Simpson detested them anyway. They were not like him, though his father came from similar roots, and Steel had a generation's difference on them. He was born to wealth and privilege because of his father Lars' hard work.

Emigrating from Norway, Lars Simpson started as a ship's carpenter on the *RMS Olympic*, and it was only a twist of fate that he had not worked on her ill-fated sister ship, the *Titanic*. He had planned to come to America after upper school in 1913, but a depression in Oslo in 1911, and the untimely death of his father, made him advance his plans and come to America sooner. He planned to work and send money back to his mother and four siblings. The *Olympic* was brand new, and every bit as regal as her doomed sister ship. White Star Line was hiring anyone because the *Titanic* was following immediately the next year. A strapping young Norwegian with some carpentry skills, though just 16, was most acceptable to the company.

Arriving at Ellis Island in July, Lars found New York mean, insufferably hot and congested. On the *Olympic*, a coal stoker named Kevin West became a fast friend and even saved his life on the passage over. Lars told Kevin about a new city on a great sea called Michigan, a city called Chicago, which was smaller, but booming and full of promise. Lars Simpson was going to make his way to this new home, aching of homesickness but determined to succeed. West had an aunt in New York and passed on Simpson's suggestion, staying there and rooming in a corner of her small apartment. Young Kevin got a job in a boiler factory, a job he hated but that paid well enough to send back money to Ireland.

Lars Simpson quickly went to work as a carpenter framing houses, bungalows that housed the immigrants who were pouring in from Ireland, England, and Poland. Two years later, he went out on his own, establishing Simpson Construction Company in the up-and-coming Ravenswood neighborhood. Seven years later, prohibition started, and Simpson found he could make as much money running illegal booze to the suburbs as he could building homes. On the side, he made beer barrels.

Imbued with Scandinavian frugality, the side money was stored in sacks under his bed. Lars married a Norwegian girl and had two children: a son Steelson, named after his wife's maiden name, but later shortened to a more American "Steel"; and a beautiful but sickly daughter named Bridget, who died of pneumonia at age ten. They lived modestly in a two-bedroom apartment in Evanston. When the Great Depression hit, Simpson was ready, riding out the worst time in American history by continuing to make beer barrels. But he still loved to build, and with the onset of World War II, he did. He built factories and plants, warehouses and railroad terminals, airport hangars and apartment buildings. He became rich.

By the end of the war, he was worth millions. His remaining child, Steel, had been sent off to boarding school in Wisconsin by his disciplinarian and distant father. He then attended Northwestern University, where he secured a business degree and a fraternity paddle. He would inherit his father's great wealth and work ethic, and the personal detachment that many thought of as coldness. Some said it was because his father sent the shy and lonely boy off to boarding school. Some said that his sister's death affected him greatly and created a hardness that no one could crack. Others said that Steel Simpson was just plain mean.

Steel hunched over the bid form. He penned in a number: $3,000,000. There was no way the Board of CC&B would turn down a bid $500,000 over Drew's. He affixed his signature, walked out his office in the Wrigley Building and decided to walk the bid to Washington Street himself.

As he sifted the dirt and stone from one hand to the other, he began to wonder what he might make of this hard-won quadrant of God's earth. It was probably the best piece of dirt in all of Chicago, if not anywhere. It deserved a great building. He didn't have a design, but he already had a name: *Chicago World Tower.* It would be the tallest building in Chicago, if not the United States, and somewhere on its façade, facing the river in big bold letters, would be the name "Simpson."

Steel Simpson stood up and motioned to his driver, Lothar, who always maintained a respectful distance from the boss, especially when Steel wanted time to absorb, to digest, and to think.

"This is my land now. Get rid of that homeless scum."

"Now?"

"No, you idiot. Tonight, when no one is watching."

The alarm bell rang at 12:35 A.M. in Firehouse E-13 on Columbus Drive. Two fire trucks were dispatched to a vacant lot along the Chicago River just off Lakeshore Drive where a large brush fire was raging. The blaze was quickly extinguished. The veteran firefighters knew that this had been a homeless encampment for years.

The next day, from his aerie in the Wrigley Building, Steel Simpson looked across Michigan Avenue to his land, wisps of smoke still rising from the razed shantytown and smiled slightly.

"That's one way to evict a tenant."

CHAPTER 3

The alarm clock was ringing for the second time, signaling that he was a half-hour late for work. Bob Marlow rolled over and hit the clock, knocking it to the floor. His head pounded. *"Shit, what did I do?"*

Definition of insanity: repeating the same action over and over again, expecting a different result. Yet the result was always the same. He had gone three months without a drink, promising Francis and J. Vance he would stay sober, and was on the verge of a new record. Then after working late at NJ&M, he passed the Berghof, a landmark Chicago drinking and dining institution on his way to the "L."

He hated to admit it, but he loved bars. From the first time he snuck into Simon's on Clark Street, plying a fake ID that passed, he loved them: the brass rails, polished mahogany, the array of illuminated bottles on the back counter, sometimes three, four high, and the manly aromas of wool suits, smoke and cologne. The banter and bullshit, the card games in the back room, the billiards and darts. He knew he had found his real home on that day.

Robert James Marlow hadn't even thought about a drink. The little man on his shoulder wasn't even taunting him. "I'll have some dinner, that's it." Then right out of his mouth when the offer came in the form of "Whadda have?" was the answer.

"I'll have a draft." The words were out there before he could take them back. Then he tried. "Hey…"

"Yes, sir?" the white-jacketed bartender returned to Marlow's stool at the bar, just mildly annoyed.

"Never mind, a draft beer is fine." *"I'll only have two,"* he decided firmly.

It was actually six drafts of the Berghof's signature beer, full-bodied and smooth, served not too cold. There was dinner, but it was incidental to the party now at hand. Then the fun really began. The 800-pound booze gorilla had snuck in the door behind Marlow, and the date was on. Except the gorilla decided when the lovemaking was over. It was over after the beers and four bourbons and a Bulls' loss on the black and white TV that hung on the wall.

"Hey, my friend, we're closing. Time to go home." The bartender plaintively begged. Marlow complied and didn't even stagger out the door, such was his capacity for booze. Exiting the train at the Fullerton stop, he found his favorite corner bar open until 3:00 A.M. in his trendy but barely affordable neighborhood in Lincoln Park. Marlow had a couple more "pops," the bartender did not care, or want to know how much this familiar patron had consumed earlier.

After an elevator ride to the 21st floor, fumbling with his keys he entered the one-bedroom apartment, sparsely furnished and looking, he thought, rather contemporary with the items his wife had allowed him to take when she threw him out. He found the bottle of Evan Williams next to an aging bag of potato chips in the kitchen cabinet, and sitting on his bed, took a long, hard pull and passed out, the precious bourbon tittering on the edge of the nightstand and finally spilling onto the pillow.

It was 8:15 A.M. and he would be late for work. He would cab it instead of taking the "L." He would catch hell for sure, but he knew Francis Nolan wouldn't fire him. Marlow was like an adopted son to the senior Nolan, meeting expectations that his real son, Francis, Jr., never could. Plus, he was a full partner in the firm. He could only be dismissed for doing something illegal. Malfeasance was the term Nolan had used.

Bob Marlow was 19 when he started as a runner at Nolan, Jefferson and Shaw. He had come up from Bridgeport, Nolan's old neighborhood, and hung with a tough crowd, a street gang. He was on his way to doing five to ten at Statesville for a robbery he didn't want to be a part of, when his parish priest interceded. Monsignor Walsh asked the presiding judge, an old friend, to suspend the sentence.

Then he asked Francis Nolan to give the young delinquent a job. From the day he met Mr. Nolan, Marlow knew he couldn't let the man down.

After seven years going to school at Illinois Institute of Technology, and working for the firm whenever he could, he got his architecture degree. He moved up in the ranks, and upon John Shaw's retirement, made partner. Because Francis Nolan and the firm knew that at his best, Bob Marlow could put together a set of construction documents like no other—omplete, correct, and most of all, buildable. He caught discrepancies like a cat catches mice. Once he found a small dimensional error in a curtainwall detail. It would have cost the firm hundreds of thousands of dollars in a certain lawsuit when the finished building leaked like a sieve.

"So, this is how you pay back Mr. Nolan, you useless sack of shit," Marlow thought as hot water hit his face in the shower. Once out, he didn't bother to shave and got dressed.

He looked at his blood shot eyes in the mirror, applied Visine and sighed. Closing the door behind him, he headed down the elevator. Marlow went out into the bright daylight of the April morning, squinted, head pounding, and headed for the bodega down the street for some black coffee.

It was Day One again in his disintegrating life, a life over which he had little control. Except that he still loved the work at the firm, and he loved his two boys. If this year was as good financially as it promised to be, then there would be a large bonus. And maybe have a chance to set things right with his wife, Joan. He just had to get control of the drinking. How tough could that be? Walking down the street toward the grocery, he vowed to get it together. Again.

CHAPTER 4

"Connor West!" boomed J. Vance Jefferson. "So good to meet you at last! Come in, come in. I see you brought your portfolio. Excellent! I cannot wait to see it."

The office was larger than any Connor had ever seen. Three windows peered out over Grant Park and the deep green expanse of Lake Michigan. The walls were white, but the floors were wide, cherry wood planks and shined like teak floors on a yacht. The floor was covered with a thick oriental rug in an intricate mahogany and cream pattern. The desk was a massive slab of polished grey granite, supported by polished stainless-steel sawhorses. The desktop was totally uncluttered save for Connor's resumé in the center, and pens and pencils lined up in strict order. There was also a large crystal bowl filled with Tootsie Roll Pops, something that Connor thought interesting. There was a separate sitting area, furnished with couches and chairs that West thought looked comfortable. Finally, there was a round conference table with four armchairs. There was no drafting table. The only other nod to the contemporary was Ellsworth Kelly's *Green and White* painting over the couch. Connor assumed it was the real thing.

"Meet Francis Nolan, Sr. our founder. He has continued the legacy of Daniel Burnham and his firm. Can you believe that he started as an office boy for Mr. Burnham? And this is our senior associate in charge of design, Francis Nolan, Jr. I am also expecting Bob Marlow, who would be your immediate superior if we proffer an offer to you. He should be here shortly."

Connor walked over to the elder Nolan and shook hands. "It's a pleasure, sir. You have always been an idol of mine."

"Nice to meet you too, Connor. Did you hear that Vance: I'm an idol!" he said as he slowly stood up. Connor's face reddened and Nolan could see that he was embarrassed.

"Thank you, son, you are very kind. I suppose if you live long enough, you become someone's idol." He shot a glance at his son, who was oblivious to the conversation at hand.

Leaning slightly on an elegant, brass-capped walking stick, he stood almost six feet, and though somewhat portly, it was clear he once had a prize fighter's physique. He was well attired in a striped, deep blue Brooks Brothers suit from their 1818 premium line and sported a gold and red bow tie. There was a white, pressed handkerchief in his breast pocket. His hair was thinning, and Connor thought he looked like John Houseman from *The Paper Chase*. Everyone said that about "The Boss" as he was known around the office. The only thing giving away his common past was his decidedly Southside Chicago accent.

Junior was not tall, and in fact, was a bit slight, thin, and maybe 5'6", at most 5'7". His hair was red and straight, perfectly parted and he had green eyes, a true Irishman. He could have been Notre Dame's Leprechaun mascot.

Jefferson, by contrast was over six feet tall, maybe six three and had an imposing, aristocratic bearing—his grey hair long and combed back in one sweep. He had on horn-rimmed glasses, through which peered dark green eyes. Connor felt some relief that Vance's hair was as long as his.

"Vance, I really can't stay long. I have a marketing appointment in Oak Park."

Jefferson suspected that this was no sales call. Junior was only around because he was his father's son. He was ostensibly director of design, but that role was really filled by Gerhard Dietrich, a Bauhaus-trained German émigré. Francis Nolan, Sr., had hoped his son would go to one of the premier architecture schools in the country, like Yale. But school bored Frank, Jr., and all his father could do was to beseech his good friend Cardinal Meyer, to get Frank into Notre Dame, which he did.

And after six years, Francis D. Nolan, Jr. was a graduate architect. After three years, he passed his licensing exams with help from associates in the firm, who, with forged driver's licenses, took his tests for him. He idled away his days from eight to five producing vapid designs, few of which were ever used. At night, he pursued a young man's pleasures with his father's wealth—a cliff dweller apartment off Rush Street, endless parties, and lots of friends, most of whom were pretty boys. Vance Jefferson knew, as he knew all things related to NJ&M, that Francis was probably going to see his boyfriend, Ricardo, on the south side of town.

There was a soft knock on the door. Robert Marlow entered looking pretty much like he did when he left his apartment. Disheveled and wrinkled, eyes still bloodshot, in spite of several applications of Visine in the cab ride over; a faint aroma of bourbon entered the room with him.

"Oh, God!" mumbled Vance under his breath, and then composed himself. "Ah, Bob, we were just getting started. Connor, meet Robert Marlow, partner-in-charge of production. If you join our firm, he will advance your academic education into real-world knowledge. He will, I am sure, become one of your great mentors. Isn't that right, Bob?"

"You bet, Vance," replied Marlow trying hard to be a company man but thinking, *"What a crock. This kid doesn't know what's coming."* Then after nodding to the senior and junior Nolans, Marlow faced Connor Jones West. He did a double take and was struck by something unperceivable. The young man before him looked tough, but in a positive way. He was handsome, sure, even with what appeared to be a broken nose from a fight lost long ago. He had a bearing, worn tweed sport coat notwithstanding; a presence that said I'm going far in this world. Something inside him stirred. Somehow in this fresh face, the past of a young Robert Marlow came back to him.

"Good to meet you, Connor. I hope these three haven't grilled you too much?"

"Not at all actually, but I think I'm ready for whatever you might throw at me."

Vance chimed in. "Nonsense, this is merely a pleasant interview. So, let's look at that portfolio, as we've already studied your resumé. Impressive, I might add."

Francis Nolan, Jr., looked at his watch. Knowing he was useless to this whole affair; Jefferson created the excuse Junior was looking for.

"Frank, go on to that appointment and bag that elephant. Give my regrets to, to, well, to whoever it is you're meeting."

"I will, JV," he said as he quickly headed out of the office, using an abbreviation that J. Vance Jefferson hated. "JV" reminded him of Junior Varsity, a team he clearly was not a part of.

"Mr. West, these three are far better equipped to judge design than I am. Nice to meet you and good luck," the words barely making it out the room.

Connor West placed his portfolio on the conference table, confidently pushing two chairs to the side. He opened it with care, like he might have been opening the Dead Sea Scrolls. The projects began with his sophomore projects at New York's famed Pratt Institute of Technology, as Harvard only maintained a Graduate School of Design.

In his sophomore year, though his work was still raw, he showed his potential. A suburban park, a new car dealership; followed in his junior year with a summer home on Martha's Vineyard, housing for the elderly and an elementary school. In the fourth year he tackled the Yale Math Building national design competition held the year before.

Acing that, he decided in his thesis year at Harvard, to do a design for the Boston City Hall, another competition. This one with 256 entries and won by the little-known firm of Kallman, McKinnell and Knowles. The controversial design won both praise and ridicule, and Connor had visited the building many times. Its brutalism was popular in 1965, but it rightly offended many Bostonians' image of what a city hall should look like. The Boston City Hall was hard, covered in red brick and concrete, small windows and staircases everywhere.

Connor thought he had a better solution. His design was mirrored glass, reflecting the city around it; it was open and airy, and welcoming. While the design was not yet complete, Jefferson and Marlow were mesmerized by what they saw—maturity beyond years, sophistication, and elegance with strength.

West narrated the journey through his architectural designs with passion, and self-criticism, continually running his hair back as it fell over his eyes. "This one wasn't very good. I didn't like the way the exterior worked. Ah, this project...pretty good but I think I could have done the circulation a little better."

But his three potential employers weren't listening, just exchanging glances and nods over the unique and singularly creative work they were seeing. Finally, it was over.

"I'm sorry the Boston City Hall is not done. I have four more weeks."

The room was quiet. Finally, Jefferson spoke. "Most impressive, Mr. West, most impressive." He paused. "Connor, we are looking for people with talent, and with a fire in their belly. Someone with ambition who will work hard, and contribute to this firm. Frankly, we need new blood. We got along for years on city and government commissions, thanks to Mr. Nolan's efforts and friendships. But the private sector—office buildings, hotels, mixed-use complexes—that is the future. And we want to be a part of it." Marlow squinted, but had to admit Vance was actually right and he could still sell it.

"Connor, tell me, how did you become interested in architecture?"

"I used to see apartment floor plans in the Sunday *New York Times*. I was fascinated by their logic and geometry, not to mention the size of the apartments. I didn't live in anything like that. Then one day I was just walking around mid-town Manhattan and instead of looking down at the sidewalk, I looked up. I noticed the buildings. Some were solid with windows. Others, modern ones, were all glass. Still more were a combination. Then I realized there were infinite combinations. I went to the library, asked the librarian where the architecture books were, and took out volumes on Eero Saarinen, Paul Rudolph, and of course, Frank Lloyd Wright and Louis Sullivan."

"Very interesting. Where do you see yourself in ten years?"

"Partner, I hope."

Jefferson and Marlow laughed. Connor flushed.

"Perfect answer, Connor, perfect answer," Mr. Nolan was the first to comment. "It takes too damn long to get anywhere in this business, if you ask me!"

"Putting your seal on a set of documents is a huge responsibility. There's a lot to learn in this business," added Marlow, gaining his stride. Connor, impatient to succeed, did not like the sound of that, but certainly was not going to comment.

The room was quiet for a moment, then Vance continued: "Do you think you're ready to design a building that works, not just a piece of academic pie in the sky?"

"I am, sir. I realize school is, well, Fantasyland to an extent. But I decided to tackle real-life projects like the Yale Math Building and Boston City Hall so my designs could be compared to what was built."

"And they compare very well." Vance hesitated, and then asked a pointed question. "OK, Rauche and Dangerfield in New York, what did they offer you?"

Connor West was stunned. *How did they know?* "Sir, I don't think it's right for me to say."

"Well, I will tell you. A Harvard degree and $12,500 a year! See, we have done our homework too, just like your pending magna cum laude achievement will indicate that you did. They should be ashamed. How can anyone live on that in New York City?"

"How the…how did you know that?"

"It's not important. Like I said, we did our homework. Connor, we know you did not come from means."

"That's right, I didn't come from means. More like just plain mean," he said with an acidic edge.

"Indeed. Your father was a building engineer, right?"

"He was a janitor, not an engineer," he said with agitation, thinking again: *"How do they know this stuff?"*

"I think you do him a disservice, but nonetheless, that is one of the reasons you are here. No one gave you anything. You have worked for it. And we like that here at NJ&M. Take Bob here. He started as an office boy just like Mr. Nolan did. Anyway, let's give you the full tour. Maybe not the file room, but the grand tour. I think you'll be impressed. Later, Mr. Marlow will take you to lunch and let you know if there are any next steps."

Connor was expecting an offer right then and there. He could see they liked his work. His stomach tied into a knot; he thought he had somehow blown it. *"Maybe I should have cut my hair,"* he thought as he was led by Jefferson out the door and onto a tour he suddenly cared little about.

CHAPTER 5

The phone rang in Irving Montlick's office. He picked up the receiver and said nothing. Gloria, his secretary, spoke succinctly.

"Mr. Simpson on three."

Irving grinned and moaned at the same time. Steel Simpson was a pain in the ass but had made him rich. He filed lawsuits like a soldier handing out candy to refugees, and in doing so, most defendants chose to settle out of court for some "split the baby" settlement, and Irving Montlick got his 30% cut as if it were a victory.

He picked up the phone: "So, who are we suing today, Steel?"

"Up yours Irv. I haven't called you in what…two months? That's an eternity!"

"Indeed."

The firm of Montlick, Roth and Feldman was known as Chicago's pit bull law firm, the theme of their endless commercials on day-time TV. "Get a pit bull on your side!" the ads shouted, showing a dog biting the pant cuffs of an insurance company executive in fear of his life. It was very effective. The firm employed forty-five attorneys; they were all premier litigators. There was never any settling out of court until you were eyeball to eyeball with the judge, and then their opponents almost always blinked. The firm had worked for Simpson Development Partners, though there were no partners, only Steel Simpson, since the early sixties when they were a five-person firm, and before they began advertising and chasing insurance cases.

Flush with an inheritance from his father, who had keeled over from a massive heart attack in his office, Steel immediately left Simpson Construction and his uncle Josef, who he disliked, taking three-quarters of the working capital with him and starting his own venture.

At first, the new business struggled. He developed cheap warehouses on the far west and south side, cold, dark shells, complete with leaky roofs. Because he was new, the banks demanded equity as high as 70%; so his cash was quickly tied up with these properties. Then a recession hit, and they did not lease well. It wasn't long before he found someone to sue. He learned quickly that the only way to get his few tenants to pay their 90-day-in-arrears rent was to threaten eviction and litigation for non-payment. Irving Montlick was happy to take the work, as unpleasant as it was.

Finally, the market began to improve, and a German buyer came along and purchased all of his buildings. Simpson made a sweet upside. He took advantage of the upturn and built more warehouses and low-rise office parks. But he never got close to the Loop, Michigan Avenue or the Gold Coast, big sandboxes he yearned to play in. The new crop of properties rented well, and his net worth increased. He flipped them again, this time to a Dallas developer, and decided to look to the Lakefront for his next venture.

"Who pissed you off this time?" Irv asked with sarcasm in his voice.

"Chicago Canal and Bridge." The answer was succinct and definitive.

"Really, I thought you loved them. You just bought that primo piece of dirt along the river. Nice buy."

"It's shit. Got an underground river, which they never disclosed. I paid a lot more than I should have. I want a piece of the change back, maybe all of it if I can't unload it."

"*Caveat emptor*, my friend, buyer beware. Haven't you ever heard of that?" Montlick could already tell this case would not be easy or winnable.

"Listen, they never disclosed this. It was a key piece of information."

"Didn't you do your own due diligence? Like getting their soils report."

"Sure, I did but I didn't receive it until after the bids were due," Simpson said, lying through his teeth.

"What are we looking at?" Irving Montlick sighed. He knew that arguing with Steel Simpson was a waste of time and breath.

"One million dollars."

"Seriously? You're killing me Steel!"

"I'll settle for $500K, and that's the difference between my bid and that asshole Dan Drew's bid."

"Sounds like Dan knew a lot more about what it was really worth."

"What's that supposed to mean? Hey, I'm going to develop the greatest building Chicago has ever seen on that land. I'm going to call it Chicago World Tower."

"Got a name and all, huh? OK, I'll have to get creative on this one. I'll let you know when the paperwork is ready. But remember: CC&B is old and rich. They won't roll over like a lot of your victims, I mean tenants."

"Just do the paperwork. I'll handle those schmucks," Simpson said with bravado. He hung up the phone and started thinking about what the Chicago World Tower might be. Then the intercom buzzed.

"What is it, Ruth?" he spoke in an irritated voice to his third personal assistant that year.

"It's an Inspector O'Rourke from the Chicago Fire Department on line two. Do you want it?"

Steel Simpson slowly punched the number two on his phone. "Hello…" The bravado was suddenly gone.

CHAPTER 6

The offices of Nolan, Jefferson and Marlow were indeed imposing, if not because of the views of the lake and the top-notch art collection, but simply because of its size. The fourteenth floor was the executive floor, but the tour did not begin there. J. Vance Jefferson knew better than to start with the best. They rode a separately installed three-floor elevator down to the eleventh floor. This was where the engineering departments resided—the MEP Department, for mechanical, electrical and plumbing; and the Structural Department, composed of eight licensed engineers and twelve draftsmen, headed up by a Polish immigrant named Jerzy Stanizski. When he shook Connor's hand, Jerzy bowed, and was very pleasant and welcoming.

"Is a real pleasure to meet such a nice young man, a Harvard man, too! Please come and work here. We need bright people with future here!"

Vance interjected, "Jerzy, Mr. West is just interviewing with us. He doesn't have a position yet."

"Yes, but you can make it so. I can see he is very smart."

Connor's faced turned rose and they toured the area, Jerzy in tow.

"Jerzy and I worked together in England after the war. I was a GI who decided to stay for a while, and he had been freed from a Nazi POW camp. He was an officer in the Polish cavalry. That's why he survived. In fact, I used to be in charge of the structural department before Mr. Nolan made me the business partner."

Connor nodded without comment and looked around the room. Engineers were clad in graying white shirts and dull brown or black ties, and were from Poland or Germany, having escaped the Communists or the Nazis. They were happy to work long hours at modest pay. Since no building could stand without the proper steel or concrete design, taking into account lateral forces, wind shear and modulus of elasticity, the Structural Department had a prime location along Michigan Avenue and lakefront; it seemed to matter little to this group, who spent hours hunched over their desks with slide rules, frequently speaking in their native Polish or German tongues.

The MEP Department was in a much larger room occupying the west side, and looked into the rear façade of Carson Pirie Scott, Chicago's second largest department store, second only to Marshall Field. The room housed work-stations for over fifty engineers and draftsmen, a more varied group, including a few women. It was headed up by Harry Oliveri, a big man in his fifties, who was very friendly when introduced to Connor. Connor began to realize that all the department heads were in their fifties, a mental note he made for later consideration.

On shelves along the wall were housed all sorts of samples provided by vendors looking for their products to be "spec'd"—short for "specified" in the voluminous document issued with each set of plans, called the "Project Specifications." In this book each piece, part, or component of a building was "specified" by the architect or engineer in terms of the performance required, or more often than not, a product made by a specific manufacturer.

Connor was impressed with the size of it all. There was the hum of voices talking in hushed tones, phones ringing, and people at desks using slide rules with ease, unlike his ungainly and uncertain use of one in structures class. He was never sure he had the right answer. It was all getting a little overwhelming and depressing; he seemed to drift off, then realized he had followed Jefferson to the elevator lobby.

They rode to the 12th floor, home to the Architectural Department. The first stop was a vast room for over 100 employees that wrapped around to the south side, housing workstations comprised of drafting and rear reference tables, divided by aisles five feet wide. There wasn't any space between one drafting table for one employee and the reference table for another.

Along the windows were larger work-stations for job captains. These individuals were responsible for organizing and assembling the sets of drawings that were known as construction documents, sets of drawings that contained not only detailed plans of each floor, but exterior and interior elevations, wall sections, and thousands of details showing how to flash the roof to how to install a door sweep. It was not uncommon for a large, multi-story project to have over 200 sheets of drawings.

The corner offices were reserved for the project manager, usually an associate of the firm, responsible for the overall project, including the initial design. He was tasked at making it practical or "buildable," integrating the structural design and the mechanical, electrical and plumbing components. All these disciplines had to be incorporated into the project with no conflicts, a goal never fully achieved on any project.

Connor was introduced to a few of the employees. All were polite and encouraging. Connor noted how well dressed they were, each seemed to outdo the other with handsome checked shirts with spread collars and Rooster knit ties. Eyeglasses were wire rim or turtle shell with round lenses. One or two had bright red or yellow glasses. The hair styles were all over the place; there did not seem to be a grooming code.

They completed the 12th floor tour by passing through the east side, home to senior associate offices, and a large conference room, all with handsome views of the lake. Finally, they returned to the 14th floor. Nodding to superstition, the building did not have a 13th floor, as Daniel Burnham was very superstitious. On this floor, J. Vance Jefferson intended to set the hook as it were, showing off the main conference room with its 30-foot long table and high-backed chairs. At one end was an Alexander Lieberman print, at the other, three screens for the overhead projectors mounted above.

They walked past the same glass-walled executive offices that Connor had passed earlier. They passed the original destination of Jefferson's office and walked by Francis Nolan Sr.'s office. Connor saw that Mr. Nolan was in heavy conversation with Robert Marlow, who looked up and seemed a little embarrassed through a wan smile. Mr. Nolan, the father figure, was seated at his desk and looked like he was lecturing Marlow. Around the corner, they reached the end of the tour.

"I want to show you this in particular. It is our history museum, if you will." Vance Jefferson spread his hand out and Connor took the cue and began to walk through the dimly lit space illuminated by spotlights on drawings, models and artifacts. It was here—the reason that this firm was where he wanted to work. It was history, memorial, and homage. There were true blueprints, blue sheets with white lines initialed by DJB—Daniel J. Burnham—in the lower right-hand corner under "Checked By." There were the early great buildings and more modern ones designed by Francis Nolan. And photos of him with presidents, senators, and mayors. There were models of the great Chicago masterpieces designed by the firm, and maquettes of sculptures that would adorn the plazas created for those buildings.

"Wow," was all that Connor could muster.

"Wow, indeed! Connor, I'm sure you must be tired after all this. And I do have an appointment. I want you to take a breather, maybe walk around the Loop or go to the Art Institute. Bob Marlow will be seeing you back here for lunch at, I think, noon. Let's go back to my office and I'll get Marilyn to see you out." They returned on the same path, but this time Mr. Nolan's office was empty. Connor peered out the window as Jefferson rang up his assistant. She appeared quickly and without speaking.

"Connor, I have enjoyed meeting you and trust you will find today's lunch useful and rewarding. You have a bright future." The words were both encouraging and cryptic. Saying a lot but saying nothing at all.

"Thank you, sir, I appreciate all the time you spent with me and really hope, ah, I mean I really am impressed with this firm." He followed Marilyn out the door.

"How did it go?" she inquired.

"Who knows? I think they liked my portfolio."

"Oh, Mr. Jefferson loves keeping people twisting in the wind. I think it's some sort of power thing. After I interviewed, he didn't call me for a week, then finally invited me to dinner and offered me the job."

"I'm not sure I wanted to hear that."

Then she looked at Connor and gave him a sly smile. "Look, like I said, you are in like Flint. They did a lot of research on you, more than on others."

"Yeah, I know. Kind of creepy."

"Enjoy your lunch with Bob, I mean Mr. Marlow. He's good people. And I hope you like Bloody Mary's or Martinis. You'll be having several."

"Thanks, I hope I see you again."

"Yeah," then pausing and smiling just the right amount, "So do I, Connor."

The elevator door opened, and Connor entered, his mind swimming with perfume and pearls, architecture and history, big rooms and old associates, and an upcoming lunch. At that moment, he wished he were in his cubicle at Gund Hall working on his thesis.

CHAPTER 7

He sat in the conservatory, stirring a third cube of sugar into the freshly poured coffee. Benedetta, his Sicilian maid, left him to the newspaper, opened to the sports section. He let the patterned Ginori cup cool, as Benedetta always served the coffee piping hot.

"I love you, Cubs!" he exclaimed. Yesterday's win over the formidable Pirates, 3-1, powered by great pitching from Milt Pappas and a three-run homer by Billy Williams, had made him $1,200 richer. On this rare occasion, he had bet on the team to win. They were in first place, though it was very early in the season.

Carmine Messina studied the box score. He knew every player's batting average and their RBIs, and every pitcher's ERA. *"This is the year,"* he thought, even though José Cardenal had gone 0-3 last night. He put the paper down and scooped up his scrambled eggs with a piece of toast, taking a bite and then shoving a greasy piece of bacon into his mouth. He wiped his hands on a crisp white napkin. A silk bathrobe hung loosely around him, and his pajama top revealed a thick tuft of chest hair, salt and pepper, like the perfectly combed mane on his head. He turned the page with his manicured hands, adorned with a pinky ring on the right hand, and a large, gold signet ring with his initials, on the left.

Messina checked the line on the horses running at Arlington, wrote down some picks on a piece of paper, and closed that section. He was in a good mood. The take from the day before had been more than he expected. Off-track betting was up; the dice games were producing; all protection money had been collected save for a couple of businesses in Maywood, and the ladies were busy. He looked out to the rear yard of his expansive home in River Forest to the greenhouse. "I need to prune the camellias today," he reminded himself.

"Benedetta, sono finito," he called. Benedetta appeared and took the plate. "Grazie, signora," he said speaking kindly. She was dressed in a black maid's uniform with a simple white apron, not a frilly one but the kind you see on waiters in a restaurant. She spoke no English and Carmine wanted it that way. He had pulled a few strings at Immigration and brought her over from Sicily, claiming she was his cousin. In fact, she was the widow of one of his associates who had met an untimely end the previous year.

When Benedetta came to America, it was different than his return from the war, an ex-GI who had married in Palermo. After the fighting was over, he met a young girl waving at him in a victory parade; he was serving under General Patton. After hard-fought battles in Italy, he decided to return to Sicily. He had no thought for the future, and thinking entirely below the waist, he wedded this dark-haired beauty. Her name was Sofia. She was well experienced in bed. They were about to leave for Naples, where they would board a ship to the States, when she was raped and murdered by a rival Gypsy family. It was only then that he found out she was part of a family of crooks and thieves, a Roma, and married him only to get a free ride to the United States.

Carmine "Cookie" Messina arrived back in Cicero, Illinois, in 1946, with a useless army uniform and few prospects. At 24, he was a war hero. Having seen so much killing during the war, he had become immune to death and body bags. Too many of his friends had ended up that way, pinned down and slaughtered on the beaches of Italy. Before the war, he had wanted to become a doctor and save lives. Now, life was cheap. The sight of blood made him sick, something he never realized as a boy, but was clearly evident as a soldier.

At first, he hung around the Italian American Social Club, and through an uncle, found work as an apprentice concrete finisher. There was plenty of work and he was a quick learner. How hard could it be: pour out the "mud," as it was called. After the concrete was in its place, "strike it off"—level it out, just like icing a birthday cake. Finally, trowel it on your hands and knees to ensure that it was smooth and level. Then sweep it with a broom for a little roughness.

The days were long and hot and the work backbreaking. It didn't take Carmine Messina long to realize that this was not his life's ambition or purpose. Once again, the Social Club intervened. It was Friday night and Carmine, flush with his week's pay, was sitting at the bar, on his third beer. He knew about the back room in the place, past the arcade games and pool tables. The door was always closed and a misspelled sign on it said: "No Admittence." It was the older, well-dressed members who casually went through.

"Hey, Dominick, what's with the backroom? Got a card game goin' on?"

"None of your fuckin' business, kid!" was the immediate reply.

Ignoring Dominick, he got up and casually walked to the back, beer bottle in hand and entered the rear room.

"Hey, you can't go back there!" shouted the bartender, who knew his ass was now in trouble.

Carmine Messina didn't see anything particularly interesting when he entered. There was a card game going on as he assumed, with money, big money, on the table. But there was also a large desk, credenza and big chair. In it was seated a man Carmine had heard about and seen a few times, Paulie "The Waiter" Ricca, titular head of the "Outfit," as the Chicago mob was called.

Two bodyguards jumped Carmine, his beer bottle flying, and threw him to the ground despite of his strength from wheeling innumerable concrete carts called Georgia Buggy's. They were proceeding to kick him in the ribs; the card game suspended for the entertainment. Ricca got up from his chair and went over to his would-be assailant. Propped upright by the two goons, he looked him in the eye, Carmine coughing blood, but unbowed. Ricca took note of the muscular arms straining through Messina's concrete-stained Cubs tee shirt.

"Whattya doin' here, kid? This room's off limits to jamokes."

"I wanna be a part of whatever it is you do in here."

"The Waiter" looked him up and down. "What's your name, kid?"

"Carmine…Carmine Messina," he replied, spitting the words out through the blood and spit.

"You look like a working guy. I seen you here a couple of times. You mind your own business. That's good. I like that. Whadda you do? Lift iron?"

"I finish concrete."

"No shit. I own a concrete company! You ever heard of Cooky's Concrete?"

"You can't finish mud on the west side without knowing about it." Messina broke out into the jingle from the radio commercial, still catching his breath: "Looky, looky, looky here comes Cooky!"

The room broke out in laughter, but Ricca seemed not amused and Carmine could see that.

"But isn't that the jingle?" he asked quizzically. "One of the guys always sings it when the truck shows up."

Slowly Ricca's scowl turned to a grin. "Just messin' with ya, kid. Ya got guts. But don't quit your day job. Your singin' sucks!"

"I was hoping to get a different day job…"

And so, he did. Paulie "the Waiter" Ricca made him a bag man in Carmine's neighborhood of Cicero. It was not long before all the accounts in that part of Ricca's empire were 100% paid up. When Ricca retired at the end of 1947, Tony "the Bat" Accardo took over. He was at the poker table when Carmine made his entrance. He decided first thing to test Messina's loyalty. He had to earn his "bones."

A seriously delinquent gambler on the north side owed more than $50,000, with an interest rate, or "vig" for "vigorish," now upwards of 25% per week. No matter how much Brock Patterson, a down on his luck blue blood from the lakefront, could pay back, he always fell further behind. An example had to be made. So, Messina and a dim-witted "soldier" named Vinnie Raggulo, confronted Brock in a Lincoln

Park bar, got him into his car without protest, humored him to make him comfortable, and drove to the lake. Carmine Messina calmly put a .38 caliber into the man's mouth aiming upward into his brain and fired. He wiped the gun and placed it into Patterson's right hand.

He and Vinnie walked up the beach waiting for a car to pick them up. As Vinnie laughed and mouthed off about the guy's head being blown off, Messina reached in his back pocket for his six-inch blade, switched it open, and from behind, calmly slit Raggulo's throat. "No witnesses," he said. Then he walked to the shore of Lake Michigan and puked his guts out.

In 1957, Tony Accardo, in ill health, retired. No one questioned who would be the new Capo di Tutti Capi...Carmine Messina. That night on Lake Michigan had made him legendary and was followed soon after with three other assignments. He puked after all of them, and deep down, hated to see anymore killing. In addition, the payoffs to the police and coroner's office had to be doubled.

From the day Carmine Messina became the head of the Outfit, he determined that it would become a legit business. If possible, there would be no killing; there were no more soldiers, or consigliere, or capos. This was America after all. The organization merely provided services that the public at large wanted, but that the legal system had prohibited, just like they had with liquor in the 1920s. Everyone knew how that ended.

Under the legit business front of Cooky's Concrete Company, he set up offices from an undistinguished building on Milwaukee Avenue by Cicero Street, next to the Kennedy Expressway. You could pass it a million times and never see it. It was a square two-story building with a most useful basement. The concrete supply operation was on the first floor, run by his son Johnny, born illegitimate from a brief fling with a waitress he was infatuated with back in the late forties. The second floor ran the bookmaking: dice games and small casinos with poker and craps, prostitution, and numbers. All desired but harmless vices. Messina had his office there, in an interior space. He would have liked a window, but that was not wise. Anyway, he worked mostly from his mansion in River Forest.

The basement contained the accounting department and the drug business. It was accessed only from the yard in the back, heavily protected with an eight-foot fence topped with barbed wire, ostensibly because this was a bad neighborhood. There was 24-hour security at the gate. This is where the fleet of trucks parked every night along with huge piles of aggregate, sand and stone, tall mixing rigs, and a large washout basin. Regardless of Messina's aversion to violence, occasionally an example had to be made, and the bodies found their way to this deep sludge pit.

Contrary to the past when the Outfit's membership had to be all Italian, Messina hired reliable Germans on the Westside, Poles and Irish on the Southside, and even Asians. He had seen them die for America on the beaches of Italy too. Why shouldn't they have a part of this new American dream? In fact, his main bookkeeper was a Jap by the name of Kenny Ito, and one of his key associates was a German, by the name of Hans Dieter, who kept order in the Northwest Kraut neighborhoods, by the Dan Ryan freeway.

Cooky's Concrete Company grew partly because it made a better front for the other illegal activities, but also because, for Carmine Messina, it represented his roots, where he came from…a poor concrete finisher. He would never have to stoop down with a trowel again.

He moved from Cicero, now a poor excuse for a town occupied by an increasing number of lower-class whites, to River Forest. His Tudor manse had six bedrooms and four baths, an outdoor pool, conservatory, greenhouse and four-car garage with coach house above. It stood at the end of a quarter mile driveway and was surrounded by a brick and stone wall. It was his refuge and his paradise. And only he, Benedetta, the groundskeeper, and his driver Lucca, lived there.

Messina picked up the first section of the *Tribune* and glanced at the headlines: "Apollo 16 Launch Successful" was the banner headline. "To the Moon, Alice!" he laughed, mimicking Jackie Gleason.

An article on page four caught his attention: "Gang Violence Increases on the West Side." He scanned the article:

> *Recent gang activity on the West Side, most*
> *notably in Maywood and Forest Park, has*
> *police alarmed. Last night they found the*
> *body of a young black male in an alley.*
> *On his chest someone had carved the initials "LPC."*
> *A police spokesman said that*
> *they had no idea what the letters stood for.*
> *However, a local black gang has been on the rise*
> *of late, dealing drugs at school play-*
> *grounds, threatening shop owners for*
> *protection money, and running a prostitution ring.*
> *The slaying appeared to be an initiation*
> *ceremony that went awry.*

Carmine put down the paper and picked up the production sheets from the night before. He had scanned them too quickly. Maywood was indeed down 10-15% in all categories. While he was not a man of prejudice—one of his best friends in the Army had been Bo White, a black man from Atlanta whose head was blown off on the second day in Salerno—he did expect the blacks to maintain their second tier standing in the racial pecking order. He could not abide any competition on his turf, particularly Maywood, and certainly not from a bunch of Negro punks.

He kept turning the pages quickly; he had to get to his camellias. He set the first section aside and picked up the financial section, which included real estate. On the bottom of page two he noticed the small 18-point type headline: "Chicago Developer Has High Bid for Lakefront Land." He read the article. Then he put down the paper and called Cooky's Concrete.

"Let me speak to Johnny."

"Right away, Mr. Messina." Adele, the gal Friday, knew his voice all too well.

"Hey, Dad, what's up?"

"Johnny boy, haven't we been rolled over by contractors who worked on Steel Simpson's projects?"

"Is the Pope Catholic?"

CHAPTER 8

J. Vance Jefferson sat at his large granite desk and perused the morning *Chicago Tribune* during a break for lunch. Marilyn had brought him a Cobb salad from Johnny's Restaurant downstairs at the corner of Adams and Michigan. The place was always packed for lunch, and he detested wasting time waiting for a table. Besides, other than Francis, Sr., he really didn't like to dine or mingle with the employees.

Looking up from the newspaper, he stared out the windows at Lake Michigan and thought about the interview with Connor West that morning. He returned to the paper, biting his fingernails, a bad habit he had picked up whenever he was under stress. He was ashamed of how badly his nails looked and had recently started sucking on Tootsie Roll Pops to stop the habit. His salad eaten, he reached for his favorite flavor, raspberry, from the glass bowl on his desk. He pulled out the Finance and Real Estate Section immediately. Sports held little interest to him. An article on page two caught his attention:

Chicago developer Steel Simpson is apparently the successful bidder for a 2.5-acre tract of land owned by Chicago Canal and Bridge. The coveted parcel, located along the Chicago River at Lakeshore Drive, has been the focus of a six-year lawsuit between the city and CC&B. The lawsuit contended that the city had eminent domain over the land and wanted to use it to straighten out Lakeshore Drive and add a four-lane exit from the boulevard to

Lower Wacker Drive. Just last year the suit was dropped, and several months later, Canal and Bridge decided to accept sealed bids for the land. Though the company is disappointed that only two developers submitted bids, Simpson Development Partners and Drew Development Company, a spokesman for the CC&B, who is responsible for maintaining the retaining walls along the Chicago River and the key bridges across it, indicated that they were satisfied with the reported $3,000,000 bid from Simpson. It is not known what Simpson plans to do with this coveted tract. Recently, Simpson's company has moved from industrial developments and warehouses on the south and west side to the lakefront, building two apartment towers and a luxury hotel on Oak Street.

Jefferson looked up from the paper. *"We need this client,"* he thought, though he was not familiar with Steel Simpson. But he knew the property. It was the best piece of land in Chicago. It afforded views west down the Chicago River past the Michigan Avenue bridge where you could see the iconic Wrigley Building and Equitable Building with their large plazas, and the famed Chicago Tribune Tower, a neo-gothic wonder that was the winner of a famous 1922 design competition. To the south, the view was of the great open expanse of Grant Park and of Soldier Field. To the east were Navy Pier and the lake. To the north was a beautiful array of buildings along Lakeshore Drive. Though not easily accessed, that problem could be remedied by a boulevard connecting to Michigan Avenue. If Steel Simpson didn't know what to do with this prime piece of land, Jefferson could surely help him.

At that moment, Francis Nolan, Sr., walked in, leaning on his elegant cane.

"How do you think it went with young Mr. West? His work is certainly impressive." He reached for a crystal glass on the credenza and opened one of the doors below, pulling out a decanter filled with Scotch. He poured himself two fingers. He looked at Vance and smiled.

"My friend, it's Friday, and besides, I'm semi-retired. Enjoy your lollipop."

"Ah, Mr. West. We'll see. Have you seen that new movie *The Godfather*?"

"Hell, I don't go to the movies. I just go to White Sox games."

"I made him an offer he can't refuse. The mafia Don says that in the movie. 'I'll make him an offer he can't refuse.' As in take the offer or die." Vance chuckled. "Not the case here, but I think our Mr. West would be foolish to turn it down. After all, his mother works as a maid, his father is a building super, though West seems to have an issue there. He called him a janitor."

"I noticed, but I really did like the lad," Frank said sipping on the twelve-year-old whiskey.

"Harvard records indicate he owes over $25,000 in loans. But I think that he wants to be in Chicago. You also seem to be somewhat of an idol."

Francis Nolan waved his hand. "Nonsense. I'm no one's idol. I was the secretary to a true idol and got lucky."

"You built a great firm here, Francis. And together we'll make it greater."

"You, maybe. I just want to sail and go to ball games. Maybe take a trip to Europe with Kate. I'm sorry I didn't leave you a suitable heir."

"Frank, Jr., will sow his oats and eventually he'll get serious."

"Vance, he's a fag! Can you imagine how hard that is for his mother and me to stomach, Irish Catholics that we are?"

"Francis, it might surprise you that a lot of our employees are probably homosexual. And I think the new term they now use is 'gay'."

"Fine, but they aren't my kin. I don't care what they do at night as long as they can draw."

"You're getting all worked up. Have another Scotch. I have someone I want to ask you about."

Nolan gladly did as instructed, this time pouring three fingers, and sat down. "Who?"

"What do you know about a developer named Steel Simpson?" Vance knew that Nolan kept his ear pretty close to the ground because of his friendships with the mayor and multiple aldermen.

"What I know is not good. Why?"

Jefferson was not happy with the quick response and the immediate knowledge. "I just saw an article in the *Tribune*. He was high bidder on that prime piece of land at the lake."

"Yes, something didn't smell right about that one. One day Big Jack was suing the hell out of Canal and Bridge, and the next moment it's all forgotten. I asked him about it and he said that the City decided it wanted a building there instead of a road. But they never settled for even a dollar. Tommy Byrne, who's on the board of Canal and Bridge, told me they were ready to settle for up to $750,000 to get the eminent domain removed. But they didn't have to give up one thin dime. Somehow I suspect Simpson was behind it."

"What's so bad about that? The owner still gets $3,000,000 from Simpson and the mayor gets his building."

"The land is worth more—at least $5,000,000. And only two bidders? I heard this fella Simpson harassed every developer in town sayin' it was his deal. Personally, I think this guy has something on Big Jack too—he's no choir boy after all. You know how he likes the ladies. I also think Simpson paid off a few people at Canal and Bridge."

"But it was sealed bids…"

"Yeah, and Simpson showed up at Tommy Byrne's office when he heard that and said he had been betrayed. That he had been promised it would be quietly sold to his company for $2,000,000. Not sure we've heard the last of it…anyway, why are you interested?"

Jefferson looked out the window and said nothing.

Nolan looked at his partner and understood. "No, no, you're not going to get in bed with that bum! He's bad business, I tell ya! I haven't even told you about his trying to bribe Frank Kutka for a zoning change down by the museum for an apartment tower."

"But a commission to do a building on that land? It would put us on the map."

"We're already on the fuckin' map, Vance! You just said it! I built a great firm. Yes, I built it, and not by dealin' with crooks and shysters like Simpson!" Nolan's face was turning flush. "Vance, he builds shit. He's a Goddamn warehouse developer. He even bribed Tommy Keane to get the building inspectors to lay off of him on that fancy hotel he built on Oak Street. Construction-wise, it's crap. Oh yes, I know more than you think!"

"I'm not talking about being known in Chicago. I'm talking about nationally, internationally. That's the next big step, Francis." Jefferson began biting his nails, then stopped and reached for a Tootsie Roll Pop. He really wanted a glass of Scotch instead.

Francis Nolan stared down at his drink. "Look, when I'm gone, you and Marlow, if he's not dead from drinking, can decide what you want to do with this place. Just let Frank, Jr., share in the success. But for the love of God man, don't sell your soul to the devil to get there!"

"Francis, I'd never do anything to tarnish the reputation of the firm, you know that."

"Okay, if you wanna deal with Simpson, make sure you get a big commission, and a big retainer. And increase the errors and omission insurance. That prick loves to fuck architects and he'll sue you at the drop of a hat. Now I've had enough of all this. I'm going to the marina. Kate and I are going sailing tomorrow."

"Thanks, I'll keep your wise words in mind, as I always do."

Nolan put his drink down and ambled out the door, rubbing his left arm.

CHAPTER 9

With a little time to kill after the interview, Connor walked around the Loop and then up to and along the river, finally back to Michigan Avenue. He found the city of Chicago both dense and airy, from the tightness of downtown to the open canyon of the Chicago River. At Michigan Avenue, he turned south again toward the Railway Exchange Building.

"Yep, 'The City of the Big Shoulders' just as Carl Sandburg called it," he murmured as he headed toward his lunch appointment.

Returning to the 14th floor lobby, he asked for Mr. Marlow, and waited about 15 minutes.

"Sorry, I'm late. I was chatting with Mr. Jefferson. Let's go; we can walk to the restaurant." Bob Marlow smiled and seemed to be in a light-hearted mood, and even looked somewhat better than Connor's first impression earlier. He stood just under six feet and had a ruddy complexion, deep lines etched in his face, that made him look older than his forty-eight years. His brown hair was still dark but thinning. He had an open smile that put you at ease. Connor felt comfortable immediately and looked forward to the walk to the restaurant.

After leaving the building, they crossed Michigan Avenue and headed north to the Gibraltar Insurance Company Building, a 41-story high rise overlooking Grant Park. The building had been designed in the mid-fifties by Francis Nolan, and although it looked like an Eisenhower era monument, it was still clean in its lack of adornment and was somehow timeless. Marlow pointed out other buildings and sights—a one-man guided tour.

A brisk ride in an elevator, finished in brushed stainless steel and dark walnut paneling, took them up to the highest floor, home of Chicago's premier tourist restaurant, the Top of the Rock. From this vantage point, there was a commanding view of the park below that stretched to Soldier Field. To the left was the deep green and blue inland sea named Lake Michigan. Along the lakefront were a number of marinas. The white boats and their masts bobbed and swayed from the waves hitting against the marina bulkhead.

Upon exiting the elevators, Connor was immediately drawn to the floor to ceiling windows. Though he was no stranger to big cities, the lower elevation of the restaurant, not like the Empire State Building, afforded a more immediate connection to the ground below. It was a huge expanse of openness, not buildings, unusual for any city.

"Not bad, even at just 40 floors," Marlow commented.

"No, this is better. I like it. You are not so removed," replied West, turning his head to Bob Marlow, thinking, "*I could like this guy. He would be a good boss.*"

"Come on, let's get a table. I need a drink."

Though dated, the restaurant had white tablecloths and fine glassware, and crisp napkins stood at attention. It didn't resemble a tourist trap, but rather an exclusive men's club. Having made a reservation, the maître d' seated them in a round banquette of brown leather. Connor could face the man he hoped might be his future boss from one end, and Marlow could do whatever interrogation was required, at the other.

"Hello, I'm Michael, and I'll be your waiter today. Can I offer you a cocktail?"

There was no other option, no soda or beverage or water, although Michael's assistant was quietly pouring iced water into their glasses and placing a basket of warm rolls on the table.

Marlow gave Connor a glance and said: "I shouldn't but I really need a Bloody Mary. With Stoli but not spicy, and a couple of olives."

"Excellent. Sir?"

Connor looked at the waiter and asked for a beer without name, and once Michael had asked draft or bottle, gave Connor the list of bottle beers to which he replied: "I guess I'll try a Pabst Blue Ribbon."

"My personal favorite," Bob interjected. "Although here in the Midwest, we simply say: 'PBR'."

"OK, then, I'll have a PBR. With a cold glass."

"Certainly."

There was a moment of silence as Connor surveyed the room and Marlow loosened his tie.

"The tourists come at night but at lunch there is always a nice business crowd, and a lot of the patrons work in this building. Be careful, someone might want to sell you a life insurance policy."

"I don't think I can afford that right now," replied the young man.

"I understand. So, how do you think it went?"

"I'm not sure. Mr. Jefferson speaks somewhat cryptically and wished me good luck in my future endeavors. Not very reassuring."

Bob Marlow smiled. "Yes, he can be a jerk sometimes, playing with emotions like that. But I think he wants you to realize that if an offer is made, it is of value. And clearly the impact of those words made you realize that working for our firm is something you want to happen."

"Let's just say I would like to get an offer. No one likes to be turned down. Then I can decide the next step."

"Agreed, I understand. Anyway, Vance is a structural guy turned businessman, and he is a very good one. He has this firm on solid financial ground and doesn't really care about design trends. He understands we have to produce architecture that creates a stir in the marketplace, that keeps putting us on the map of being current, but he also understands that we need to keep the client happy and satisfy their needs."

Connor nodded, but didn't know how to reply. Being a young student, he was all about design and hadn't really worked with any clients, much less satisfied them.

Marlow continued. "Look, we all know, or at least I know that the design quality has been slipping a little at the firm in the past couple of years. Nowadays, it all seems to be glass boxes. I'll take this building over a Mies box any day. And that's why we're interviewing you."

Now Connor found his opening and summoned the courage to ask: "Can I ask you a question? How did you know I interviewed with Rauche and Dangerfield and how much they offered me?"

Michael returned with their drinks and Connor watched Bob Marlow take a deep swallow of the red liquid that seemed to have a nice vodka floater on top.

"Oh yeah, another JV flourish," replied Marlow using the hated nickname. He laughed. "Look, all big firms keep in touch. We go to the American Institute of Architects conventions. JV knows their CFO and ran into him at an AIA affair last week in New York and asked if he knew of any stars from Harvard. Your name came up. As for the salary, all the firms keep tabs on starting salaries for graduates. The profession is infamous for paying the lowest salaries to graduates with a professional degree, and a master's in architecture is certainly a professional degree. Look at what lawyers get out of law school, what engineers get. And doctors, once they're through with their residency make serious money. Once you're through with your so-called residency, your three-year internship, and get your license, you'll be at least $50,000 behind doctors."

"Thanks for the pep talk. My mom wanted me to be a lawyer. Too many words to deal with though. I guess I'm stuck with designing buildings…and I will be in debt."

"Sorry, I don't mean to get on a soapbox. But it's really criminal what most firms offer. They think that architecture is a passion, secondary to making a living. And frankly, there are too many firms vying for a limited amount of work. Salaries are tamped down by the low fees. Meanwhile at law firms…well, anyway, at our firm we are trying to change that, and in doing so get better talent. I guess that's as good an introduction as there is for this."

Marlow reached into his breast pocket and pulled out an unsealed envelope addressed to Connor Jones West. He handed it to Connor and then took another deep drink of his liquid salvation, and simultaneously nodded to the waiter to bring another.

Michael appeared and Marlow waved his hand over the table indicating a second round was desired. Michael looked at the barely drunk beer but made no comment. He headed back to the bar, the menus still lying unopened on the table.

Connor took the envelope with an unsteady hand and looked at it. "May I open it now?"

"I would hope so. We don't like to be kept waiting for a response. There are buildings to design after all!"

It was simply one sheet of paper. Bad omen. When a college rejects you it is a one-page letter. If they accept you, it is full of all kinds of forms to fill out. He opened it slowly.

Dear Mr. West,

It was a pleasure meeting you today and seeing examples of your fine work. Based on what we saw, your interview, and your excellent academic record I would like you offer you a position at Nolan, Jefferson and Marlow as a Junior Intern Designer beginning immediately after your graduation next month from Harvard at the starting annual salary of Twenty-Five Thousand Dollars ($25,000.00).

Connor put the letter down and picked up his beer. He took a long gulp and looked at Marlow.

"Damn..."

"What, you don't like the offer?" Marlow said, smiling slightly.

"No, it's fine. Really, yes, it's really great!"

"Consider it our way of saying that we would really like you with Nolan, Jefferson and yours truly."

Connor read on:

In addition to the above, the following benefits are included:

- *One-week paid vacation and one-week unpaid vacation. If the employee uses the unpaid week for purposes of education, such as study abroad, the company will compensate the employee for that week.*
- *Medical insurance fully paid by the company through Gibraltar Insurance.*
- *Paid holidays including: Thanksgiving, Christmas, New Year's Day, Memorial Day, July 4ᵗʰ and Labor Day.*
- *Annual discretionary bonus based on the firm's profitability.*

"No St. Patrick's Day off?" Connor joked.

"We have it off, but you don't get paid for it. What do you think?" Marlow looked at West intently.

"I think I'd be a fool not to say yes. I can probably pay off my loans now."

"So, I take it you accept?"

"I accept. And thank you! And I get paid to take Labor Day off?"

Marlow laughed. "Strange, isn't it? But great! Welcome aboard. Now let's eat."

They motioned Michael over to the table and Marlow ordered a New York strip steak and a loaded baked potato. Connor, head still swimming with the offer, thought that sounded great and ordered the same. Two steaks in two days. He was living large, and what a change from Ramen noodles or pizza day after day!

"OK, so who is Connor West anyway?" Marlow said taking another pull on his drink, feeling the effects and thinking that a celebratory bottle of cabernet would be nice. "You said a couple of things earlier that intrigue me. You called your dad a janitor when Vance described him as a building superintendent. Problem there…?"

"Let's just say I'm not real fond of my dad. I guess it was a dig. I mean, he did take care of my mom and me. He was never really happy with what he did. Always thought life gave him the short end of stick. And he was an alcoholic, too. Friday nights, or payday, were not fun times to be around him."

Marlow re-thought the bottle of wine. It would be tough, but it would have to be iced tea. "I see," he said.

"Anyway, after work he'd always head for the bar with his pay en-velope, and when he'd get home, a good bit of it would be spent. Mom would comment about not having enough money for food and then he'd start hitting her. When I was little, I just ran to my room and got under the bed. Later, when I was a teenager, I'd confront him, but he was a lot stronger and he'd throw me aside. I was kind of skinny and I was harassed a lot at school. Once I fought back and got my nose broken. So, I joined the wrestling team…"

"What high school did you go to? Was it in the city?" Marlow interrupted, thinking it would be good to give Connor a break from talking about his dysfunctional family.

"I was on scholarship to Regis High School. My mom was a maid for a wealthy family on the Eastside. There was no way they could af-ford the tuition. But my grades were good, and our parish priest put in a good word for me."

"And you joined the wrestling team…"

"I enjoyed it. Started working out, lifting weights, bulked up a little. I lettered in wrestling. One night my dad came home, and this time when he started in on my mom, I got him in an arm lock, threw him down and…let's just say I won the match. I told my dad if he ever touched her again, he'd be dead."

"So, did he stop?" Marlow was now intrigued.

"I told a brother at school. You know, a teacher, a Holy Cross brother. He was my guidance counselor. And he found an apartment for me and my mom, so we got out."

"Is your dad still alive?"

"Yeah, and he even came to my graduation from Pratt Institute. He told me he was sorry, but I could smell booze on his breath."

"It probably took a little liquid courage for him to come to your graduation and tell you he was sorry…" Marlow could easily put himself in Connor's fathers' shoes.

"Yeah, I guess you're right. I am probably too hard on him. I mean if I had to spend my life getting up doing something I hated… well, I just can't imagine…"

Michael and his assistant arrived with lunch. The steaks were sizzling, the baked potato was loaded, and there was also creamed spinach and a salad. It was a feast for Connor.

"Want another beer?" Marlow asked, always wanting drinking company.

"Sure, since we're celebrating."

Looking at Michael, "Another beer and I'll have a glass of cabernet—a good one."

CHAPTER 10

"Good afternoon, Mr. Simpson. This is Investigator John O'Rourke from the Chicago Fire Department, Forensics Unit. I hope you're doing well?"

"Fine, just fine. What can I help you with, Investigator?"

"I just have a few routine questions. This won't take a minute. I'm sure you are busy."

Simpson wanted to relax but couldn't. The man sounded like Columbo.

"Yes, so how can I help you? None of my buildings have been on fire that I know of," he said, trying to make a lame joke.

"No, but a piece of land you own has been."

"I don't own it, I mean I don't own any land," Simpson's sharp reply was perhaps too quick. "Just buildings."

"I apologize. You know what I'm referring to then…the land that you have under contract from Chicago Canal and Bridge, is that right?"

Simpson already had a good idea about the nature of the call. "Sorry, I have no idea what you're referring to. If you're talking about that land on the lake, I haven't decided to buy it yet. I was just the successful bidder." Simpson was trying hard to put up a good defense.

"Since you bid on it, it would seem that your intention is to buy it, am I not correct? And the bidding documents have a forfeiture clause of the $25,000 bid deposit if you are successful and do not purchase. And as you say, you were the high bidder. Must be nice to have that kind of money to throw away…"

Simpson realized that the investigator had done his homework. He had to be careful. "Okay, I'm probably going to buy it. What of it? It's a good piece of land." Simpson was beginning to be annoyed but tried to keep calm. He tried to remember the "routine questions" preface from O'Rourke.

"Did you visit the land lately?"

Steel knew that this was not a good time to lie. The man knew more than he let on. "Yes, I did visit it. After my bid was accepted, I wanted to see it up close. The soils report talks about an underground stream and I wanted to see if the ground was wet and soft."

"Was it?"

"Yes, and it will cost a fortune to build on. That's why I might decide otherwise. Look, I'm really busy…"

"I'm sorry. Let me get to the point. There was a fire there two nights ago. It destroyed a shanty town that had existed there for some time. It was home to over thirty people. They had built shacks, and obviously had a lot of, well…stuff. It went up very fast."

"I never noticed them." This time he lied and meant to.

"Interesting. There is only one way into the site off Lower Wacker Drive. The shacks were right there. In a clearing—didn't you notice them?"

"I was busy reviewing the contract for the land."

"You weren't driving?"

Simpson gulped. He was digging a hole he might not get out of. "No, my driver was. Now that you mention it, I do remember seeing some buildings of some sort…"

"I see. I'd like to talk to your driver. What is his name?"

"Lothar…Lothar Jensen. He doesn't speak much English."

"That's okay. The Fire Department employs all kinds of nationalities. Is that Swedish?"

"No, he's from Estonia. Look, I'm sorry about the fire and all, but why is this my issue? Talk to Chicago Canal and Bridge."

"Rest assured, I will. One other question, Mr. Simpson. Where were you last night?"

"I attended an alumni reception at Northwestern in Evanston."

"What time was that over?"

Simpson didn't say anything. This was the kind of question that could trip him up later.

"Mr. Simpson, are you there?"

"Sorry, my secretary interrupted me. I don't know. I went home to my house in Glencoe. Look, am I under investigation here?"

"Just a routine follow-up, sir. You don't remember what time you got home? And how did you get there? To the meeting and then home?"

Steel knew he had to lie now. He had driven by himself, but the question presented an opportunity to provide an alibi for Lothar. No one could disprove that Lothar drove him around all night. There was no way you could drive back to the Loop and set a fire.

"I got home around 11:30, I think. My driver, Lothar, took me. I hate driving on Sheridan Road during rush hour. That's what I pay him for: to drive me."

"Of course. I think that's all for now. Oh, did I mention that two of the residents of that village, if you will, were found burned beyond recognition? They had third degree burns over 75% of their bodies. We are still trying to identify them from their dental records. We also found a gasoline can."

Simpson took a deep breath, and a bead of sweat formed on his forehead. He loosened his tie. "I'm sorry to hear that. Truly, I am. I really didn't notice that homeless people were there. I just walked the land, saw those shacks and headed toward the lake. Anyway, why is it so unusual to find a gas can? Those people probably had it to start fires to keep warm."

"I agree. However, the can was new. And it wasn't close to the fire. Well, thanks for your time. Perhaps your secretary can tell me how to get in touch with Mr. Jensen?"

"She's at lunch. I'll have her get back to you with his contact information."

"That would be great. Have a nice weekend." O'Rourke gave Simpson his number and then the phone went dead.

CHAPTER 11

Steel Simpson put the phone down. His hand was shaking. *"Get it together. This is no big deal,"* he thought and then yelled for Ruth.

She was there in an instant. "Yes sir?"

"Where's Lothar?"

"I'm sorry, I don't know. Let me call him right away."

"Find him now!"

Ruth hurried out the door and back to her desk and began to dial.

Five minutes later she knocked on Simpson's door. "I'm sorry, sir, he isn't answering the phone down at the garage or at his office. I called the restaurant I know he likes. They said he did not come in today. I'll keep trying."

"Just great. Okay, keep trying."

Simpson had calmed his nerves a little by running through different scenarios. Lothar wasn't the sharpest tool in the shed by any means, but he had to know enough not to be seen. There was no way to connect the gas can to him if he hadn't been seen. That was the key. Anyway, the homeless had scattered and were probably all over the city by now. It wasn't as if the Fire Department has a list of the residents of the shantytown. No, these people were invisible. He relaxed some after running the logic through his mind.

"All right, let's move ahead," he thought. *"I have the best piece of land in Chicago. What is the greatest building Chicago has ever seen going to be?"*

From the left side of his desk he pulled a yellow legal pad. He began to scribble:

Office—how much?
Hotel—same flag as Oak St. Contact Roger at Four Seasons?

Others—Ritz, Hyatt (call Jay P.) Statler Hilton
Apartments or Condominiums???
Retail—too far from Michigan Ave—only support
Parking—how with underground river?
Equity—will need a lot!

Simpson got up from his desk and went to the window and looked past the Equitable Building to the land he was purchasing. On the west end was a blackened area, roughly six by six, away from the fire. He could make out a thin strip that was burnt grass as well, heading east toward the lake. It had to be about 60' to 75' in length, when it ended in another much larger black patch, all the vegetation gone. He scratched his head and wanted an explanation from Lothar.

Returning to his desk, Simpson poured a glass of water, and looked down at his notes. He began writing again:

Office—20 Flrs. = 400,000 SF
Hotel—250 rooms, plus meeting rooms 25 rooms per
floor = 10 Flrs.
Apartments or Condominiums???
On the lake should be Condos
At the top of the building
10 units / Flr. to 5 units per floor
Large size—most expensive on the lake
200 units
20 floors total
20+10+20 = 50 floors
Add lobby /retail = 2 floors
Meeting rooms = 1 floor
Add Health Club = 1 floor
54 Floors

NOT BIG ENOUGH!!!
Office - Go to 500,000 SF
25 floors or 59 stories
Add restaurant and observation deck—2 floors
61 Stories, OK!
Retail—too far from Michigan Ave - only support:
25,000 SF, including restaurants
Parking - how with underground river?
500K office = 85% usable = 425K / 1 car/1,000 = 425 cars
Hotel = 100 cars including valet
Condo = 1 car per DU = 200 cars
Guest and penthouse (say 10) parking = 60 cars
Total 785 cars, round to 800 OK x 300 SF car = 240,000 SF!!!
50,000 SF base = 5 floors of parking- now have 66 stories!
Maybe get to 70 stories. Good!
75 would be better!

Steel Simpson was beginning to realize that he was trying to skin a very big cat. But it had to be big. This building would make him world famous and rich to boot. The land was worth over three times what he had paid for it—at least $10,000,000. And what will the building cost? He continued to write:

Office: 500K x $50 SF = $25,000,000
Hotel: 250 Rooms x 300 SF = 75,000 SF x 1.15 circulation = 86,250 SF x $75 SF= $6,470,000 rounded
Meeting rooms: 25,000 SF x $100 SF = $2,500,000
Condos: 200 x 1,500 SF Ave. = 330,000 SF

*Say 350,000 SF including circulation and large pent-
houses
x $80 SF = $28,000,000
Retail Support: 100,000 SF x $50 SF = $5,000,000
Parking: 240,000 SF x $15 = $3,600,000*
Total: $66,070,000

The tallying continued and the number, when complete, staggered Simpson. His previous projects were small by comparison. The apartment towers were just $20,000,000 each. The hotel on Oak Street, with cost cutting, shoddy construction, and stiffing the general contractor, was just $10,000,000. He looked down at the sheet of paper: $66,070,000.

He slumped in his chair and let out a deep breath. With the land and design costs, other indirect costs, loan interest, he was looking at $100,000,000!

"I'm gonna need a lot of 'other people's money' to do this."

No one except the big insurance companies lent this kind of money, and with his limited track record, he was wasting his time with them. Even if he got lucky and the biggest bank in town, First Chicago Bank & Trust, was willing to lend him $73,000,000 to $75,000,000, he would need to find $23,000,000 to $25,000,000 in cold hard cash as equity. That was a lot of "OPM." He decided to call Taylor Wentworth at First Chicago, his cocky lender on the last two projects, to get his advice. This was a deal any bank would want because it was a home run. But he was still going to need at least a minimum of $20,000,000 with his own cash thrown in. He yelled at the door, "Dammit, Ruth, have you found Lothar?"

CHAPTER 12

Connor West and Bob Marlow walked out into the bright afternoon sun from their two-and-a-half-hour lunch. They were both high from the drinks and several glasses of wine. Connor could not remember a better meal in the last three years.

"Thanks so much for the terrific offer, Mr. Marlow. I humbly accept and thanks a lot for a really great lunch." Connor hoped he wasn't sounding too drunk.

"I think you better start calling me Bob. And you are very welcome. I think the weekend might start early. Geez, it's already 2:45 P.M. I better go back and tell Vance the good news and return a few calls. Connor, I'll see you at the end of May. Good luck these last couple of weeks. Marilyn will be in touch and send you all the forms, insurance and such to fill out. Have a safe flight back to Boston."

"Thank you. OK, great. Yes, I'll be seeing you soon." They shook hands and West headed up Michigan Avenue toward the Allerton. As he proceeded at a slow gait, trying to get his equilibrium back, Marlow's mention of Marilyn stuck in his brain. He had no time to waste.

He walked fast and arrived at his hotel in 30 minutes. In his room he sat down on the edge of the bed. Picking up the phone, Connor dialed his future employer.

"Nolan, Jefferson and Marlow," the pleasant voice answered.

"Marilyn Jones, please."

"My pleasure, sir." The phone rang immediately on the other end and Connor inhaled.

"Mr. Jefferson's office. This is Marilyn."

"Hi. This is Connor."

"Connor? I'm sorry…"

"Connor West. Connor Jones West…"

"Oh, yes. I'm so sorry. Yes, hello! Geez, well it's Friday. I guess I'm ready for the weekend. So how did it go? Are you a little drunk?"

"Maybe a little. Hey, I guess we're going to be co-workers."

"Really? That's fantastic! They made you an offer and you accepted?"

"Yes, and yes."

"Oh, I'm so happy for you. Chicago is such a great city; there is so much to do and so many great restaurants. You'll love it. Monday, I'll send you all the employment forms."

"About those restaurants…care to take me to one tonight? I'm buying."

"Oh, gee, I was supposed to go out with some girlfriends tonight…"

"I'm going back to Boston in the morning and I was hoping to be able to celebrate with someone," West spoke with an increasing sense of deflation.

Marilyn's mind was now in full throttle. *Dating an employee; standing up my girlfriends. God, he is so handsome! Isn't this why you came to work at this firm—to meet an architect? This is your chance…*

"Mr. West, let me make a call. You and I are on for tonight. I know a great spot near where I live. Say 7:00 P.M.? Here is the address…"

Connor took out his fountain pen and scribbled the address on a notepad by the phone, blowing on it so it wouldn't get smudged. "Okay, sounds great. I'll see you later. And I'm sorry but I'll pretty much be wearing the same clothes."

"Don't apologize. You looked great."

Connor West's heart was pounding. He hadn't had a date in over a year, neither possessing the time nor the money. He collapsed on his bed and in a matter of moments was in a deep sleep.

Bob Marlow ambled back to the Railway Exchange Building and rode an empty elevator up to the fourteenth floor. Nodding and smiling to all the secretaries, he headed for Vance Jefferson's office. Vance was on the phone but motioned Marlow in. He hoped he wouldn't appear too tipsy, as he had already caught hell earlier from Francis Nolan and had, for the umpteenth time, promised to quit the booze. Jefferson hung up the phone.

"Sooooo…?"

"So, we have a new employee. I mean was there any doubt? $25,000 a year! He'd be crazy not to accept. You probably could have had him for $20,000. But I'm glad you offered him twenty-five. He's a good kid. Reminds me of myself when I was younger."

Vance looked at Marlow and though he appeared to be a little tipsy, he had basically been closing a deal, after all…an important deal.

"Wonderful. We need talent like that. You and I are going to make this firm the largest in the U.S., and he is the first step."

Marlow heard the words with skepticism. Nolan's words from earlier that day were still resounding in his head: *"Watch out for Jefferson. I won't be around a lot longer and when I'm gone, he'll do anything to take over the firm. And for God's sake, Bob, whatever you do, please protect my son. I know he is, well, less than what I hoped, but he shouldn't be forced out. Make him a better architect. Vance certainly won't. And again, watch your back with him."*

"Vance, let's take baby steps. Connor is green, full of college idealism. He couldn't design a roof flashing detail if he wanted to."

"Yes, and that's where you come in. You will show him how it's done."

"He expects to be designing big projects day one with that title of junior designer. He wanted to know why 'intern' was in the title. I explained to him that all newly graduated architects were technically interns until they pass their licensing exams in three years."

"He'll be fine. Just keep him busy."

"Yeah, doing reflected ceiling plans. Another talent wasted in this big bureaucracy we call The Firm."

"Bob, I expect big things from this boy. Don't waste his talent on little shit. Anyway, he may get his shot sooner than later."

"How so?"

"Sorry, can't say now. But sit tight."

Marlow rolled his eyes. Palace intrigue! He couldn't stand it.

"Look, I've got calls to return. Have a good weekend. See you Monday." He got up and walked out the door, not waiting for a return salutation from Jefferson.

CHAPTER 13

Vance picked up the phone and dialed 0 for Marilyn. She answered quickly. "Marilyn, I need the number to call Steel Simpson, of, let's see..." Jefferson looked down on the opened page in the Financial Section. "Simpson Partners."

"Yes, sir, right away."

After a moment, "Mr. Jefferson, the number is 647-3800."

He dialed the number. Friday afternoon was usually a good time to make sales calls. People were in a good mood as the weekend was around the corner, and most of the week's business was concluded. Some executives might even be at their desks having a drink. Jefferson would have one when this important task was concluded, hopefully with success. He wasn't sure what kind of greeting he would get from Simpson, or if he would even take his call. But surely, he couldn't be as bad as Nolan had made him appear. Plus, this was Chicago. Everyone bribed aldermen. Even NJ&M did.

"Simpson Development Partners."

"Steel Simpson, please," Jefferson's voice was crisp and professional.

"May I tell him who is calling?" came the reply.

"This is Vance Jefferson with Nolan, Jefferson and Marlow, architects and engineers."

"One moment, please." This dance was repeated yet another time before an increasingly exasperated Jefferson finally hears the secretary's voice.

"Mr. Simpson's office. This is Ruth,"

"Really? Wonderful. Is Mr. Simpson available? This is J. Vance Jefferson of the architectural firm Nolan, Jefferson and Marlow. Perhaps you've heard of us?"

"I'm sorry, but no. I'm new here," Ruth replied. "What's your name again?"

"Jefferson. J. Vance Jefferson."

"Please wait. I'll see if he's in."

It was at this moment, one of many in his career, that Vance Jefferson decided why he hated marketing.

Ruth came back on the line. "I'm sorry, he's in a meeting. May I have him call you back?"

"Meeting my ass," Jefferson thought. *"Avoiding me; this will be a tough one."*

"Please, thank you. My number is 563-1200. And do tell him it's important."

"I surely will." Ruth hung up.

Simpson was indeed in a meeting. Lothar had surfaced after getting the Lincoln washed and shined. The mud on the tires and underbody had concerned him after his quick retreat from torching the shanty town. He was nothing if not thorough. He sat in a chair ramrod straight listening to his boss.

"Okay, you got it, dumb ass? You drove me to Northwestern last night. Then home. The time was 11:30. Remember that, 11:30 P.M. You stayed in the coach house. No one can say different except Reese, and I'll take care of her."

Simpson was referring to his North Shore bride of five years, Reese Anne Simpson.

Jensen glowered at his boss; he was anything but dumb. "Do not worry about me, boss. I dealt with KGB in Estonia. I leave no tracks."

Lothar despised authority, especially police in general and secret police in particular. As a young boy in Estonia in 1942, he watched as the KGB came to his house and rounded up his parents, never to be seen again. Lothar Jensen grew up with an aunt and spent his teenage years in the underground freedom movement. He knew how to cover his tracks. When he was eighteen, he stowed away on a freighter bound for Amsterdam, and from there made his way to Chicago. Its

Estonian community, small but close knit, took him in. He got a job as a limo driver, and he once drove Steel Simpson to a Bears game. Simpson was impressed by his 6'5" muscular frame and hired him as muscle to collect rents. From there, with Simpson's success and growing list of enemies, he graduated to full-time driver. He always carried. But in usual fashion, Simpson treated him like an indentured servant. Were it not for the large pay increase over what standard hacks made, he would have left Steel Simpson long ago.

"One other thing. The gas can. Where did you get it?"

"Boss, less you know the better. No way will police trace where I buy it."

"OK, right, but why was it dropped so far from the main fire?"

"I make trail of gas from shacks. Don't want bums to see me. Then I light gasoline like fuse. So far so good. Flame goes toward buildings. But leftover gas in can catches fire and explodes can. I burn hand but it is OK. I get out fast."

Simpson looked at Lothar's right hand. It was wrapped in a bandage across the palm. "Don't let the inspector see that." Simpson did not inquire as to whether it hurt, or if Lothar had seen a doctor.

"I won't. Only talk on phone." Jensen stared into space; he seemed unsure whether to talk more. Simpson was perceptive and picked up on Lothar's mood.

"Is there anything else?"

"Someone took a picture of me, I think."

"What?"

"I see flash. Maybe like a camera flashbulb go off."

CHAPTER 14

"Talk to me, Johnny."

Carmine Messina wanted to know how badly Simpson Development Partners had screwed him.

"Okay, three years ago, this clown Simpson was developing big warehouses in the Western suburbs. Like three hundred, four hundred thousand square feet. Billy Conlan was the general contractor. It's all flatwork poured in two, maybe three, pours. We gotta pour at night because it's like one concrete truck after the other going out on the Eisenhower when the traffic is nothing."

"Johnny, spare me the details. I know how this works after all. I used to finish concrete."

"Right, sorry. Afterwards the warehouse slab develops hairline cracks in it. Shit, its flatwork. It's always gonna get cracks. The specs say cracks no more than the thickness of a quarter are fine. Hell, they weren't more than the thickness of a red pubic hair. So, he stiffs Conlan for that, like a 25% reduction. And Conlan just passed along the pain to us."

"Anything else?"

John Messina began to wonder how all this was going to affect his future. He knew his dad hated to lose money. His dad had succeeded in making Cooky's Concrete one of the largest concrete suppliers in Chicago.

Carmine Messina decided that if Cooky's was going to be the front for the Outfit's many less than legal operations, it had to be legitimate. And if his son was the one to run it, he needed to know about business. But more than that, young John needed to learn about concrete. A good education was the key.

After graduating with honors from St. Patrick's High School, Johnny entered Illinois Institute of Technology and majored in Materials Engineering with a minor in Business. He immersed himself in school and graduated in three-and-a-half years. Considering that he handled a course load that included Strength of Materials, Statics, Metallurgy, Solid Mechanics, Structures, and numerous business classes, this was no small accomplishment.

Carmine Messina was extremely proud of his son's accomplishments and gave Johnny $10,000 in cash for his graduation. Then he sent him on a vacation to Italy and Sicily. In Sicily, he met distant relatives who spoke with pride about American uncles and cousins who had succeeded in the New World, and about the age-old blood feuds that were part of the history of Sicily, which became the DNA of the American Mafia. John returned, now understanding his heritage. It was then that Carmine offered his son a job.

"John, I want you to run and grow Cooky's concrete. It is strictly on the up and up." John Messina did know concrete; and he knew it was a changing business. For years, the strength of concrete never exceeded 5,000 pounds per square inch (PSI). But if concrete was going to be used in buildings that reached for the sky, taking the place of the ever more costly steel, it had to achieve greater strengths, and it had to achieve it faster than 28 days. Johnny was devouring industry periodicals and technical journals. He was determined that Cooky's Concrete, once nothing more than a funny jingle to contractors, would grow in its ability to be the provider of choice for stronger concrete, reaching strengths of 10,000 PSI.

"Yeah, there's more. Simpson developed an apartment tower on the Southside near the Museum of Science and Industry. You know that's a pretty untested neighborhood. He took a chance and fell flat. Then he took it out on the architect, contractor, everyone else. Stiffed us all."

"Why'd you even provide the mud after the warehouses?" Carmine said, making a point.

"No one knew it was Simpson. Fitzgerald was the GC and the client was 'Science and Industry Partners,' and a minority guy, a Pakistani, was the front man. But he was just in the deal for 10%, and Simpson owned 60%. So, when it went south, he stiffed Fitzgerald for the retainage, 10% of the entire contract, or $2,000,000 and Tommy Fitz spread the pain to all the subs, including us."

"So, bottom line, how much has this jerk-wad stolen from me?"

"I've got it right here. It's still on the accounts receivable. Let's see. About $2,350,000 and change. I'm very sorry, Pops."

Carmine whistled at the number. "This Simpson guy's gonna do something big at the lake, right by the river. He bought a piece of land there. Keep your ear to the ground. Read the papers."

"Always do, Dad! I'm the only marketer here."

"Good, see what develops. And we're gonna provide the mud for whatever it is he's gonna build there."

"Dad, why would we want to do that, after he's stiffed us?"

"Because Johnny, my boy, this time we're gonna fuck him up."

CHAPTER 15

Connor was late. He had overslept, but if he was lucky and a cab was waiting, he might get to Marilyn's on time. The piece of paper said 1357 Sandburg Terrace, Apartment 1210. He ripped it from the pad and put it in his tweed sport coat over a fresh, blue button-down shirt. He had put on a pair of denim jeans figuring this was going to be a casual date. Anyway, Marilyn had seen his nondescript khakis already.

The shower and shave were quick. Connor, experienced in squeezing maximum effort into minimum hours, bolted out the door of his hotel room, leaving clothes strewn everywhere.

In the lobby was a shoeshine machine provided free for guests and he quickly took advantage of it, then dashed out to the sidewalk to hail a passing cab. It was not necessary. A doorman blew his whistle and a yellow cab magically appeared from around the corner.

"1357 Sandburg Terrace."

The cabbie, a red-faced, heavy-set fellow flipped the meter up. "Ah, the Village, where everyone wants to live. Gotta date?"

"Yes, sir." Connor was not in the mood for small talk but wanted to be polite.

"They just finished the last building a year ago. Nine big buildings and a bunch of townhouses. It's beautiful, I tell ya, but they kicked out a lot of poor spics to build it. Do you know they get $175 a month for a one-bedroom apartment! I couldn't afford that."

West remembered the project, as he looked out the city that was going to be his soon. He had studied it in his Urban Planning course at Pratt. The ride west and then north took fifteen minutes and it was now 7:10 P.M. *"I'll be fashionably late,"* he thought. He paid the cabbie and gave him what he knew would be a good tip in New York.

"Thanks, son, and I hope you get lucky tonight," he said with a broad smile.

Connor did not respond but headed down the sidewalk to the distant high-rise building. He figured that Apartment 1210 meant the twelfth floor so it couldn't be a townhouse. Marilyn probably couldn't afford the rent for a stand-alone unit, which were clearly deluxe, and top-shelf housing in the Village.

He arrived at the building and finally saw the numbers 1357 to the side on a dark bronze plaque fixed into the ground. He had been looking above the door like a tenement apartment, just like the one where he had grown up in the Bronx. The lobby was large and handsome, only a few years old, and the furniture was again the standard Mies Barcelona chairs, and an eight-foot leather bench. There was a security guard behind a large marble-paneled desk that had several security monitors showing various locations around the building.

"Apartment 1210, please."

"Certainly, thank you." The guard had on a blue blazer, white shirt and tie. He was not dressed like a cop, but rather like a fraternity brother. The image was to emphasize the upscale nature of the property. By contrast, Connor's home in the Bronx had no doorman, just a phone and a heavy, locked door that opened with a loud buzzer activated by the tenant at points unknown in the building after you spoke into the intercom.

"Yes, you have guest. Okay, thank you."

The guard looked at Connor, giving him the once over in case there was a later need to remember this new visitor. "Elevator bank to the right. Have a good evening."

———

Marilyn was in a whirlwind. She was happy that Connor was late, as her roommate had monopolized the only bathroom of their two-bedroom apartment for a half hour. Both had arrived home at roughly the same time, but because Jane Sullivan had a date at 6:30 she got first dibs on the bathroom. The two had gotten together from a classified ad, neither being able to afford the $175 tab for a one-bedroom apartment. Jane was a nurse at Rush Presbyterian Hospital, and from the start she and Marilyn had hit it off.

The blouse was easy. She had just bought it last week at Marshall Field on State Street. It was a dark green print that honored her hair, now fixed straight and out of the confining ponytail. It was the pants that were the problem. Marilyn could not decide whether to go with tailored beige slacks or dress down in her favorite denim jeans. The restaurant, one of her favorite Italian ones off Rush Street, would be fine with either. But it was Connor she worried about. Connor West from New York. She wondered if his family were rich and lived in the city. Or, he could be from Boston, a Boston Brahmin, with a summer home along the Atlantic coast, maybe in Maine. She was not a gold digger, but a girl could dream.

"I'll go with the tailored slacks, dress up a little, but not too much," she thought. She put on a simple gold chain that matched the cross on her neck suspended by a shorter gold chain.

The doorbell rang. She was done just in time. Checking her overall look in the hall mirror, she went to the door.

"Hi, how are you, Mr. Architect?"

"Hello, just call me Mr. Intern," he smiled. Connor quickly perused the apartment, partly because he could tell volumes about a person by how they lived, and because he was interested, as an architect, in how this new version of urban living was configured. What impressed him the most was that unlike some of apartments of co-eds in Boston, this was pin spot clean, something he really liked.

"This is it: home sweet home," Marilyn said self-deprecatingly.

"I like it. Sure beats my dump apartment at Harvard."

Marilyn was surprised that a graduate student lived in a dump, particularly someone that she hoped came from money.

"Let me grab my coat. We can walk there."

As they walked, Connor was struck with how much Marilyn looked like Audrey Hepburn, with a touch of Sandra Dee thrown in. Freed from the office uniform, she had a carefree look—carefree, yet classy. He especially liked the tailored slacks that showed off her long legs.

"Thanks for breaking up your other plans to have dinner with me. The food at the Allerton isn't that good, and I hate to eat alone."

"Yes, you'll be my good deed for the week. Taking a poor student to dinner!" Sensing she might be taken seriously, she reached for Connor's hand and squeezed it and they proceeded out of the complex to Clark Avenue. The night was perfect, cool but lively. The couple headed south until they reached Rush Street. Trattoria Firenze was a busy place, but seven-thirty was still early, and a table was available near the window looking out onto Rush. The interior was a combination of red brick walls on two sides, and the others off-white stucco with paintings of the Florentine countryside. The tablecloths were the traditional red checked variety. In the background, the music was provided by Dean Martin singing "Volare." A waiter appeared immediately and filled their water glasses.

"Buona sera. How are you a doing tonight a? Ah, signorina, so good to see you again."

"Hello, Tony, this is my friend Connor."

"Perfetto. Buona sera, signore! Can I bring you some vino?"

Connor knew it was no time to stumble. "What do you recommend, Tony?"

"How about a nice Chianti? I know a perfecta one."

"Sounds fine. Thanks."

"Volare" ended and Dean went into "That's Amore." It was time for the date to really begin.

"I told you that you were in like Flint!"

"You never know. Some people hate long haired hippies these days."

"You look very distinguished. Mr. Jefferson gave me your offer to type up. I wish they paid secretaries like that. When he handed me the letter, he said that you were the most impressive recruit he's seen in a long while. He said your work was very forward and cutting edge."

"Really? Then I guess we should celebrate. And we can review the office policies."

"Like dating a fellow employee? It can be our secret. So, tell me all about Connor Jones West."

He did, and in spite of the reality that he was not from a wealthy family, Marilyn didn't care when he was finished. Connor had avoided the rougher edges of his life, his father's alcoholism and the family violence, and concentrated on living in New York, discovering architecture, being on the wrestling team and being a Catholic, although a lax one, and what it was like to attend Harvard. He was a good storyteller and it all took them through the initial bottle of Chianti.

"Hey, I'm sorry, I'm monopolizing the conversation. Tell me about you. How long have you worked at the firm?" Taking a cue from Marlow earlier in the day, he waved at Tony and gestured for another bottle of wine.

"One year this May. I went two years to Chicago Circle campus for business and stenography and really didn't care for it. I was ready to make some money and live in the city. Now, I kind of wish I had finished. I might start back this fall and get my degree. I really want to be a teacher."

The effects of the wine had relaxed Connor and he was genuinely enjoying himself. He didn't judge Marilyn's lack of college degree; in fact, she was just about perfect. And beautiful. The conversation continued and Marilyn told him about her stay-at-home mom, her father, an accountant who worked in Oakbrook, her two sisters and baby brother, and her strict Catholic parents and upbringing in Oak Park. It was all very normal and for Connor, that was fine. His life had been anything but.

After veal parmesan and spaghetti, they split tiramisu for dessert. Connor paid the bill with most of the cash that he had, and they walked out into the now very crowded sidewalks in the center of nightlife in Chicago.

"Come on, let's go to Butch McGuire's. It's a blast. And this time, I pay." Marilyn gripped his hand and they proceeded into the night.

Later, after giving Marilyn a kiss goodnight in front of her building, he walked back to the Allerton. Michigan Avenue was alive, and his head was spinning. That morning, he was waiting for his life to happen. Now it had been served up to him on a silver platter. He looked around and began to love his new city. He had a job that would pay him $25,000 a year, a king's ransom, and he had met someone extraordinary. Though he was on busy Michigan Avenue, he couldn't help but let out a yell, followed by a loud "Holy Shit!" Then he did a little jig.

CHAPTER 16

Steel Simpson wasn't going to talk to anybody on a late Friday afternoon, but Ruth's announcement that the firm of Nolan, Jefferson and Marlow had called, piqued his interest and his ego. *"Those shits wouldn't have given me the time of day two years ago, and now they're calling me. How things change,"* he thought.

"Ruth, I'll make the call. What's his name again?"

"I'm sorry, Steel, I forgot. Nelson Jefferson, I think. Here's the number."

Jefferson put down the receiver, smiling. Steel Simpson had just agreed to meet; had even suggested that they have dinner that night. Simpson thought a couple of martinis and a free meal would turn around his miserable day, plus he was taken with Jefferson's sales pitch: "We are Chicago's largest and most distinguished firm. We have all the right connections to get your job through zoning and permitting. We are being infused with new blood; you'll get cutting-edge design."

Simpson had responded, "I'm intrigued. I just happen to be free tonight. Is that too soon? Dinner maybe?"

"I'd be delighted," Jefferson replied, setting the hook that Simpson had placed into his own mouth. *"This might be easier than I thought,"* he mused. "Since you're in the Wrigley Building and I'm in the Railway Exchange how about The Blackhawk at 7:00 P.M.? That will give me time to put some materials together. And by the way, at some point I want to bring you by for a tour and meet Mr. Nolan, our founder."

Simpson wanted a martini sooner than that. He looked at his watch. 4:45 P.M. He wanted to complete his building program and bring a copy along. But he wasn't fond of The Blackhawk. It was old and dim but mostly he didn't want to go there because he had stiffed the waiter after a big party for twenty people with a paltry 5% tip.

"Mr. Jefferson, can I suggest Top of the Rock?"

"Mr. Simpson, it's Friday night. The Top will be full of tourists. Plus, I know Don Roth, the owner. I can always get a good table at the Blackhawk."

"He's probably right, the Top will be full, so I'll lose this opening round," Simpson thought. But he wanted a martini. He figured he could be at the Blackhawk by 6:30 P.M. And he needed to quickly establish the alpha position in this potential relationship.

"Mr. Jefferson, I have a finicky stomach. I don't like to eat so late. How about 6:30 P.M.?" Simpson was lying, but it was a white lie, although he was well versed in lies, white and otherwise.

Jefferson winced. "Sure, that would be fine. I'll get my marketing assistant going on things right now, but it might not be too complete."

"Don't worry about that. Your firm's reputation precedes you. I guess you heard I bought some land?"

"Land indeed. Very exciting. Congratulations to you. It is surely the best piece of land in Chicago."

"I think so. Look, I have some work to finish up, but I'll see you at 6:30 P.M."

Jefferson knew the owner like a brother, and although a Friday night, Don Roth always had a table for Mr. Nolan or Mr. Jefferson.

"Thanks Don, see you shortly. You're the best." Vance hung up the phone. He proceeded to assemble a folder of marketing materials along with the thirty-page, four-color brochure that had cost the firm a fortune. Then he went to the closet and picked up a hardcover autographed copy of *My Life in Architecture* by Francis D. Nolan, FAIA, a retrospective on his life's work. This coffee table book, full of color photos of Francis Senior's buildings, always impressed prospective clients.

Having assembled the bait, he poured himself a Scotch and dialed his wife. The phone call ended with a full understanding of the importance of the mission at hand, and he got up and walked to the window. Vance admired the view out his window saying under his breath: "Steel Simpson, you are my next client." He began to chew at his nails.

Vance Jefferson arrived early. He always wanted to be there and seated when his guest arrived. Don Roth had placed him in a booth in the rear, knowing Jefferson preferred a larger table, sometimes to roll out preliminary drawings for a client. The Blackhawk was a dark and heavy-set restaurant with tapestry walls, red carpet and brass chandeliers. Although Jefferson would have preferred something more contemporary, he had to admit he liked the men's club atmosphere of the place. He ordered a Glenlivet 12 with a splash of water and waited.

Five minutes later, Don was in pleasant conversation with Simpson when he arrived at the table. Though the two exchanged pleasantries, once out of earshot, Roth muttered "asshole" under his breath.

Although Steel Simpson was well attired, Vance didn't care for his purple shirt and matching purple paisley tie. The suit was definitely fine quality, but it had a sheen to it that suggested that this guy might be an undertaker. He was of medium build and his dark black hair was slicked back. In fact, the entire appearance was slick. No matter. Jefferson had courted all types of characters, and for the most part, Steel Simpson presented himself well, and his handshake was firm.

"Nice to meet you, Mr. Jefferson." Simpson turned his gaze to a waiter who was already at the table. "A Beefeater Martini, dry, up and in a cold glass. Olives, please." He sat down and studied J. Vance Jefferson.

"Please, call me Vance. So how has your day been?"

"Let's just say I'm looking forward to a martini and to hearing about your firm."

The martini was quick to arrive. Simpson raised it in a toast, "To my land and to your architecture."

"Let's put them together then," laughed Jefferson.

They each had three cocktails and then raised the menus. There was no question that the fare would be prime rib and the famous spinning salad bowl, plus loaded baked potatoes and fresh asparagus. During the meal, Simpson outlined his ambitious program and Vance went through his sales pitch. Toward the end of dinner, Vance went in for the kill.

"Steel, what I'm proposing, should you engage us, is unlike anything that any other architecture firm will offer you. I am proposing that I will stage a design competition in-house with three of our most talented teams of architects. You won't be served up just one take-it-or-leave it design, but you will be presented with three designs. Your only problem will be which one to choose, I'm so sure that they will be that good. And I won't charge you any more for the effort involved. Because I believe your unique property deserves a unique, world-class design, one that will put you on the map."

"And your firm, too, I assume," Steel said, knowing no one was in it for nothing.

"Certainly, but you know as well as I do that we are always a footnote at the bottom of the news article. You're the visionary, the one with the guts to break new ground. We'll get our kudos in the trade magazines, but you'll be Chicago's newest and best developer."

At his best, even with three large Glens and a bottle of the best French Burgundy on the wine list, no one could spin it like Vance Jefferson. And Steel Simpson's fragile ego was lapping it up.

"Chicago's newest and best developer." The words rang in his ears. And the three designs weren't bad either. When that was uttered, he immediately thought that he would just pay for one, but even that issue was removed by Jefferson. And there was no doubt that hiring Nolan,

Jefferson and Marlow gave instant credibility to this project, and he would need that in his upcoming pitches to the shylock bankers.

"Vance, it sounds great. Go ahead and make me a proposal for services and let's see if we can get together on this. I think we would be a great team."

Jefferson had hooked the big tuna. Now he just had to land him. "We will be a great team! Let's get some after dinner drinks and toast our new partnership."

Steel smiled thinking, *"Partnership, my ass. You'll work for me, mother-fucker. Just design me a great building!"*

CHAPTER 17

Bob Marlow was completing his last phone call. He had begun to come down from the high earlier in the day and his head was beginning to pound again. He swiveled around to a drafting table, one of two in his office. There was a third reference desk where older projects were stacked. Although he was a partner, his office did not front on Michigan Avenue like the other senior executive offices. He had to be close to the drafting hall and the over one hundred project managers, job captains, junior and senior designers, and finally, draftsmen, all of whom reported to him. The office was enclosed by glass from four feet up; it was pure business, no comfortable couch and seating area, only a four-seat conference table. His one nod to art was a reproduction of Edward Hopper's *Nighthawks*, a painting he always thought particularly apt because of all the late nights he spent at the office. Although his abuse of liquor was the ostensible reason he and his wife were separated, his long nights working, including weekends, were probably an equal factor.

He looked down at a set of shop drawings. The pounding was getting more severe, and Marlow poured the last cup of coffee from the pot he kept in his office, particularly for late nights. He had no stomach for this now. He looked at his watch. 5:10 P.M. *"Might as well head home,"* he thought, maybe even stop for a couple at Simon's and then buy a bottle of Evan Williams for home. That thought improved his mood.

The phone rang. "Seriously, Friday after five," he muttered.

"Hello, Marlow here."

"Ah, Bobby, glad I caught ya."

"Francis, you still here?" Marlow could always tell Mr. Nolan's unmistakable Southside Irish voice.

"Nah, I'm near home, at Muldoon's. Had a few at the office, so I'm taking after you!"

"That's not necessarily a good thing. My butt is still hurting from that ass chewing I got from you earlier about my drinking…"

"I love ya, boyo. I need ya. There's just more to life than booze."

Marlow thought, *"Yeah, what?"* He spoke: "I know, Francis. I won't let you down. I'll quit today; I promise."

"There are a lot a people promising to not let me down today, I tell ya. That's why I'm calling. Have you heard of a developer named Steel Simpson?"

Marlow ran the name over in his head, knowing he would come up blank. "No, I really don't follow the business in town that much. All the business I need is on my desk."

"The short of it is this. He's a scumbag that's making a name for himself. But he gets there by screwing people and doing under the table deals. And Vance wants the firm to get him as a client."

"Does he know all that about this guy?"

"He does now. I told him what I know about Simpson before I left today. I don't think I convinced him. You and I have got to speak to him again on Monday. This Simpson is bad business, I tell ya!" Nolan's voice rose as he went on.

"What's the project?"

"The man bought a solid piece of property along the river at Lakeshore. I don't know his plan, but Jack Malone told me he already had a name for it, Chicago World Tower; I'm guessing it'll be big."

Marlow's head was pounding more, and he wasn't sure he really cared. It seemed like all of NJ&M's clients were duplicitous in one way or the other. "Okay, Francis, sure, first thing. We'll corral Vance. Make him see your point. Now, go home. You sailing tomorrow?"

"Thanks. Yes, Kate and I are going out. I was supposed to go down to the marina this afternoon but, well… Look, this thing has me worried, Robert." Francis Nolan, Sr. never called Bob Marlow

"Robert" unless it was important. "Robert, remember what I told you earlier today. I wouldn't trust Vance Jefferson."

Marlow said goodbye and hung up the phone gently. He got up, put on his coat, turned off the lights and headed for the "L." With luck, he would be sipping on his first Bourbon and Ginger in thirty minutes.

CHAPTER 18

The April morning was the reason Chicagoans put up with their interminable winters. The day's temperature was already in the low 60s and the bold wind of the day before had receded to a pleasant breeze from the West, perfect for sailing. The sky was a strong blue and there were no hints of clouds. Pulling the 1968 Chevy Impala out of the driveway, the backseat full of the necessary provisions for the day, Francis and Kathleen Mary Nolan headed for the Grant Park Marina. Kathleen, Kate as everyone called her, married Frank right after he came home from World War I. They were high school sweethearts at Tilden High School, and lived with Kate's parents, the Kelly's, until they could afford a place of their own.

Kate had packed a lunch basket with the fixings for sandwiches and homemade soup that she could warm on the small stove on the boat. Francis packed a cooler of Meister Brau beer, Cokes, and a bottle of Scotch for the end of the day. This was their routine most weekends for years, spring, summer and fall except for Saturday White Sox games, weddings or baptisms.

As the Dolphin 24 made its way past the breakers into the chop of the open water, old memories flooded Frank's mind. He couldn't believe it had been thirteen years earlier that his wife had presented him with the boat as a present for his 60th birthday. Now Kate came up from the galley and without words, they hoisted the sails; she handled the smaller jib, and he the mainsail, which got larger and heavier every year. Kate finished her easy task and came aft and helped Frank complete his work. Then they sailed north and east toward a point off Oak Street Beach, and if they made good time, they would sail farther, to a point east of Montrose Wilson Beach just north of Wrigley Field. As they worked the sails, Nolan thought of his son Francis, and his sexual orientation.

"Penny for your thoughts? And we're steering off course." Kate's words brought him back to the present.

"You know, I think I'll call Francis tonight."

"Oh, why? What has he done this time?"

"Nothing, I just think I need to tell him that I love him, no matter what he is."

Kate frowned, but said nothing, and went down to the galley to prepare lunch.

Having decided on making some sort of peace with his son, his thoughts turned to the unpleasant discussion of the day before with Vance. N J&M had their pick of clients: the city of Chicago, the state of Illinois, Gibraltar Insurance, and other corporate citizens that paid well, on time, and were professional in their dealings. Courting free-wheeling developers without a decent track record or financial deep pockets was risky, and Steel Simpson was the riskiest of all. The man was scum. He didn't know why Big Jack Malone had rolled over on the Chicago Bridge and Canal deal, but it smelled to high heaven. Simpson probably had photos of Jack with three hookers, that was how low the guy was. *"Stop it, Frank, you're obsessing,"* he thought, a habit he had had since boyhood. *"You're ruining a perfectly beautiful day."*

"Ah, fuck you, Vance and the horse you rode in on!" he muttered. He and Bob Marlow would set things right on Monday. He turned his attention back to the sailing tasks at hand.

Frank prepared to come about as they had reached the midpoint of their voyage. This was the toughest job of the day, but once complete, he could relax, head the boat into the wind and let the sails go limp as they ate lunch. After that, Kate would take the tiller and sail them back to the marina while he downed several Meister Brau's, enjoying the day.

As he pushed the tiller to port, Frank felt the numbness in his arm again. *"Probably been steering too tight,"* he thought. The boat quickly came about. Frank released the lines on the mainsail, then as the boat turned, pulled in the lines on the opposite side. There was a lot of hissing as the ropes flew through the blocks and pulleys, the sail flapped noisily in the wind, and the boom swung from one side of the boat to the other, moaning and clanking. The sails filled quickly with new air.

The first jolt of pain was like a thousand volts of electricity searing through Francis Nolan's heart. He lurched forward as if he had been hit from behind by a wrecking ball, his mouth open and gasping for breath. He took several deep breaths and thought: *"Steady, boyo, steady."* His hand went limp and it let go of the tiller.

The second round was like being pummeled on the chest by Joe Frasier. The pain spread from his heart to his chest in tormenting bursts. Francis leaned forward fighting for air. He slowly slid off the cockpit cushions and reached with his good arm for the support of the tiller. But he was on his knees now, straining to remain upright. By the time the third wave hit, Francis Daniel Nolan Sr. was already dead. His upper body was hunched over the tiller; his head hung down; saliva dripped from his mouth. The boat swung around from the weight placed on the tiller and the sails emptied, the bow of the boat hitting the waves hard.

"Frank, what are you doing? Have you forgotten how to sail?" Kate came up from the cabin below balancing a tray of soup and sandwiches, mayonnaise and mustard.

"Francis! Oh, my God! Help! Help! Frank!" The tray crashed to the deck.

He could hear the phone ringing.

Bob Marlow was pulling his keys from his jogging pants and quickly opened the door, making a dash for the phone. After last night, it was once again Day One in a hopeful life of sobriety. The run through Lincoln Park, to the Zoo and then east to the beach, and south to the residence of the cardinal archbishop on North Avenue, then back to his apartment, had rid his body of many, though not all, of last night's toxins. If you're going on the wagon, might as well have a last fling.

"Hello, Bob Marlow."

The words were brief but hit every bit as hard as the heart attack had hit Francis Nolan. Vance Jefferson was consoling, but sometimes you cannot be consoled. The death of a good friend is pure anguish, coursing a deeper sadness through you than can ever be imagined. Maybe not as bad as losing a child, but damn close. Francis Nolan was, after all, Bob Marlow's surrogate father, friend, and certainly his mentor. He slowly hung up the phone and immediately looked toward the kitchen at the bottle of Evan William's. It was half full. "*It won't be enough*," he thought. But it was a start.

CHAPTER 19

The funeral had been a grand affair. Our Lady of Perpetual Hope Catholic Church in Bridgeport was packed to the rafters.

Francis Nolan, Jr. handled the sympathies of all of the well-wishers as best he could but he was devastated. His mother came up to Francis, not looking at him.

"It's a beautiful thing, Frank, seein' all these people honor your father. He was a great, kind man. I'll miss him terribly. It was too soon." Kate Nolan looked down and stirred her cup of tea. She had just added some Jameson to it to steady herself.

"Mother, I won't disappoint him. I know I've been lazy and uninterested, but I promise, I'm going to change. I'm going to make him proud of me."

"You mean you're going to quit sleepin' with boys? Knowin' that you're a queer, a homo, that's…well, I'm sorry, but I think that's what killed him. Truly I do. Stop that and he'll be proud. And so will I. It's a grave sin after all!" her voice rising in muted anger. Frank looked at his mother and then just shook his head. He slowly walked away, headed for the bar. A beer wouldn't be strong enough. He walked up to Bob Marlow. Marlow looked up and spoke.

"Frank, I'm sorry about your dad. He was a father to me as well. Look, I know we have had our differences in the past, but you're important to this firm and we, Vance and I, we need you."

"It's fine. Dad did love you like a son, sometimes more than he loved me. The name on the door is now my name, and I'm going to step up. I have a lot of encouragement from other people. I guess it's time I got a coffee pot in my office and stayed late too."

"Just keep it all in balance. And one more thing. Vance wants to, shall we say, broaden our client base. I don't know what that means at this point, but it will be up to you and me to keep him in check. Your dad admired Vance for how he handled the business affairs of the firm, but I was never sure he totally trusted him."

"Are you suggesting some sort of alliance, you and I?"

"No, what I'm suggesting that as a partner, your job is now a lot more than just designing buildings."

"Like I did much of that," Nolan noted with sarcasm.

"Your time will come, and soon, but you and I have to preserve the legacy of your dad by making sure we keep our good name. Sometimes I think all Vance wants to do is make money. That's fine, but we create fine architecture too. And maybe there's a price to pay for doing that."

"Got it." Frank saw the bartender. He took a deep breath, then said, "A beer, please."

CHAPTER 20

May 2, 1973

Dear Mr. Architect (AKA Sweet Connor),

It has only been a week since you left Chicago and I am missing you so much! Thanks for staying an extra day. I had so much fun riding bikes along the lake and going to the Cubs game. Dinner at that little Chinese restaurant was great too. I wish I could handle chopsticks like you do!

I have some very bad news to tell you. Mr. Nolan had a massive heart attack on his sailboat last Saturday and died. The funeral was beautiful. I know how much you admired him, and I hope you won't change your mind about moving to Chicago. There are still a lot of great people here like Mr. Jefferson and Bob Marlow. And ME!

I have started to search the listings in the newspapers for an apartment for you and think I have found two possibilities. They are just a little north of me in Irving Park. Both are one bedroom—one in a six flat and the other in a high rise on the 22nd floor! Can't wait for you to come and see them. I'm also looking in the ads for used furniture. Can I help you decorate your apartment?

Well, I have to get back to work. I'm working on a proposal for a huge project called Chicago World Tower for a

new developer. The project includes office, a hotel, and con-
dominiums. The fee is immense (Sorry can't tell you the
amount.)

Miss you bunches,
Marilyn

Connor West read and re-read the letter many times. He was sick of working on his thesis, and it provided the only relief from the endless drafting that he was now deep into in order to graduate. It was sad to learn about Mr. Nolan, but he realized that the only time he probably would have seen the man again would have been at the Christmas Party. The city, the money, the design opportunities and the general feeling that everyone conveyed of wanting him were the prevalent reasons he had accepted the job.

He put the letter down, thinking about Marilyn, excited at her memory. Though exhausted from only three hours of sleep every night, either laying his head down on a pillow on his drafting table or curling up in a ball in the corner of his work carrel, he returned to the task at hand. The design effort was long complete. Now he had to single-handedly draw every elevation, building section, and as best he could manage, a rudimentary rendering or two. Fortunately, he had finished the plans. On top of that there was the model of the building made of illustration board and balsa wood, with surrounding buildings—again now complete—all fifteen of them created from pressboard. He had three more days to go.

Connor was in the first class to occupy the newly completed Gund Hall, home of the graduate school of design. The GSD had a distinguished pedigree going back to 1909, when urban planning was taught at Harvard. Landscape design was added in 1913 by none other than Fredrick Law Olmstead, designer of Central Park. In 1937, international architect, Walter Gropius, became dean of the department of architecture and since that time, the professors and alumni of the GSD read like a "Who's Who" in American Architecture.

He looked over the vast room that was the design studio. It had five levels, called "trays" by the students, all under a vast sky lit roof. The upper class or second year students occupied the two upper trays, although this made little sense in terms of seniority as you had to climb three or four flights of stairs to get to these upper reaches.

From his top tray perch, Connor saw only four other second year students. Among them were Richard Auburn Tomlinson and Silvio Marchetti, two of his best friends. Both were smoking cigarettes at Silvio's drafting table. Connor returned to his drafting. Then he heard it.

The drumbeat was slow but increasing in tempo. Ta dum, ta dum, ta dum dum, ta dum dum dum. The beat grew faster and louder. He looked down again and Silvio, or "Pisgetti" as he was nicknamed, looked up at Connor with drumsticks in his hand and wore a great, big Italian grin. He was unfairly handsome with black, wavy hair and a tanned Latin face. He had attended university in Rome and learned classical architecture. He was rich, but you wouldn't know it. He was a true Italian and loved to have fun. Harvard had accepted him in its ongoing effort to create a "fruit salad" of individuals from all walks of life and different nationalities.

"Rat" by contrast was as American as you could get. He traced his ancestry back to the Mayflower and was from Greenwich, Connecticut. He had gone to undergraduate school at Yale, and his father occupied a seat on the New York Stock Exchange. Getting into Harvard was no big deal, but he was not destined to be a great designer. He produced workable but uninspired work. Someday, he would be the Vance Jefferson of a big New York firm.

The drumbeat, emanating from a pair of five-inch sticks with wooden balls at their ends meant only one thing. These so-called musical instruments had come from a topless bar named Jato's and were given out to the customers to tap on the bar to encourage the dancers to strip.

Connor yelled down to Pisgetti: "No, no! No way can I go to-night. I have way too much to do!"

"Come on, Sullivan," replied Rat. "Sullivan" was Connor's nick-name, referring to Louis Sullivan, America's first and best-known ar-chitect, meaning that everyone in his class knew West was destined for great things. "I'm driving; we'll have just one."

"Of course, we'll have just one," Connor thought. By the time they got there, already half past midnight, there would be time for only one. Besides he only had money for one if Rat loaned him twenty-five cents so he could afford the $1.25 for a beer. Properly nursed, you could see all three dancers do their sets with just one.

"Hey, don't a worry! You gonna graduate anyway. You know they gonna lova your design!" By this time Pisgetti and Rat were up at Connor's workspace and were grabbing his coat and dragging him away from his work. Resistance was futile, and well, he was pretty horny thinking about Marilyn. Maybe seeing some fake tits would help relieve him.

When he got back at 3 A.M. to his apartment, his drunk and tired body demanded sleep. The thesis could wait, and if he didn't finish, so what? He got to the door of his garret, painted umpteen times in dark green and found a message taped above the lock.

"Call your Mom. It's Urgent, SM." The initials were those of the owner of the large house and the garage that he lived above.

CHAPTER 21

Connor reached King's County Hospital around six in the morning, managing to avoid most of the daily rush hour traffic. When he talked on the phone with his mother, her voice was flat, matter-of-fact. He didn't ask if she had reconciled with his father or whether she was coming to the hospital.

The room was on the 7th floor, a double, which by this hospital's standards, qualified it as a suite. His father lay motionless with tubes in his arms, taped monitors on his chest and arm, and a large mask over his mouth. His color was the same as the graying and thread-bare sheet below him, ashen. He drew the curtain between the adjacent resident, an old black woman, so he could have a modicum of privacy with his father. His mother was not there but it didn't matter. He knew this would kill the day, and he'd be further from finishing his thesis than ever.

"Hi, Dad." Connor took his father's hand and squeezed it.

Kevin West slowly opened his eyes, and seeing Connor, they began to glisten. He instinctively tried to pull away from his son's grip, and then decided otherwise. It was good to feel his son's strong presence.

"You came to see me, boy..."

"How you feeling? Ma called me last night, but I was at the studio working late on my thesis. She said you started coughing up blood at the bar. The bartender called an ambulance, but you were unconscious when they arrived. You need to quit drinking that rotgut booze, Dad."

"Yeah, I guess you're right," was all the elder West could muster, pulling off his breathing mask. Then the coughing began in earnest and his whole body shuddered from the wave of hacks, doubling him over on the bed. He began spitting blood. Connor put the mask back on and the coughs subsided. Kevin West lay exhausted. Years of smoke from both cigarettes and furnaces had taken their toll. Connor reached for a cup of water and lifting the mask, gave it to his dad. When he attempted to place the mask back over the mouth, his father stopped him.

"Tell me about what is happening with you." He laid the mask close so that he could feel the clean fresh air and he breathed it in.

"I got a great job after I graduate in Chicago. $25,000 a year to start."

His father looked at the ceiling and into the past. He tried to whistle in amazement but couldn't. There was nothing but dry air. "I went to Chicago once to get a job." He began coughing again and Connor tried to quiet him. But his father persisted. "I knew a guy on the ship coming over. He went there and I heard he had made it." The coughing began again.

"It doesn't matter, Dad. Don't talk." But Kevin West seemed determined to tell the story.

"It was the depression. I had no job in New York. I took the last money we had and took the train there. I knew this man would give me a job—he had a construction company. It was my last chance. But when I went to see him...him all decked out in his fancy clothes, he said he didn't know me and had no work." This time the coughing began again in great spasms, and blood sprayed out his mouth. Connor grabbed his father's arms and forced him down onto the bed, wiped his face and placed the mask over his mouth yet again. The coughing slowly died.

"It's all in the past, Dad. It's not important. You rest. We're going to get you better."

His father turned his head and looked him in the eyes; once more he removed the breathing apparatus. "Son, I'm proud of you. Damn proud. I'm sorry about the way I treated you and your mom and all the booze." Tears welled up in his eyes; the life was going out of him. He took a deep breath and spoke again. "Lars Sim...that son of a bitch didn't give me a job and I saved his life on that ship..." Then Kevin James West took one last breath and passed into the next world. Monitors around the bed started beeping. Connor turned to look for the nurse. He saw his mother standing there.

"He was never the same when he came back from Chicago. It was like the optimism was gone. He worked hard before the stock market fell; but he was out of work for a year. I told him it was a crazy idea, but he was sure this man in Chicago would hire him. After that, well, you know after that. Anyway, my love, it is good to see you." Margaret West, old and tired, but still regal in her blue cloth coat and pillbox hat, looked down at her only son.

Connor got up from the chair turned and hugged his mother and kissed her on the cheek. "How are you, Ma?"

"Relieved, I guess—for him and for me."

CHAPTER 22

Bradley Wentworth's office was located on the 31st floor of the First Chicago Bank and Trust Tower, in the heart of the Loop. The base of the forty-story building flared out at the street and tourists loved to stand at the columns and look up. The optical illusion made you believe that the top curved out ominously above you. Steel Simpson walked briskly past the huge Marc Chagall mural in the plaza. He looked at his watch; 12:45 P.M. Perfect; you never kept your money source waiting. It was, in fact, no small feat that First Chicago even did business with him, a relatively new and inexperienced developer. Simpson's first loans for his warehouses had been done with small banks in Oak Park and Schaumberg. But their success caught the eye of a young and aggressive banker named Bradley Logan Wentworth.

Wentworth seemed to possess all the right attributes for a banker. He looked like James Dean, had all the social graces, and played rugby on weekends along the lake, which gained him a handsome scar on his chin. His father ran a small bank in Evanston. Steel Simpson was a few years older, and they had met at an alumni function. Simpson was Bradley Wentworth's golden boy, having hit several home runs in a row with loans from First Chicago, garnering Wentworth a "senior" status to add to his vice president's title. Wentworth, however, never considered Steel Simpson his equal on the social ladder.

Wentworth greeted Simpson at his office door, the developer escorted by Wentworth's private secretary. "Steel, good to see you. Have a seat. To what do I owe the pleasure? Can I get you a soft drink?" For reasons that he could not put his finger on, Wentworth was always circumspect of Steel Simpson. You always wanted to count the fingers on your hand after shaking hands with him.

Wentworth's office was typical of his status. Though not a corner office, its views to the east, including Michigan Avenue and the lake, were impressive. It was large enough for a large traditional desk, three guest chairs of black leather, and, off to the side, a conference table for six. Above a credenza was an original landscape oil painting by the 19th century American artist, Seth Eastman.

"Just water is fine. I haven't seen you since your promotion. Congratulations. Nice digs."

"Thanks, and in no small part due to you."

Simpson was pleased to hear this. He might have an ally for his project.

"I read about you scoring on the lakefront property. Nice. What are you going to build there, another hotel? I'm not sure that's the best location. Too far off Boul Mich…"

Steel shook his head and said nothing.

"Condominiums maybe? Markets kind of getting saturated since they built Lake Point Tower," referring to the stunning 70-story undulating form near Navy Pier. Steel shook his head again. *Fucking bankers; they'd shit on a birthday cake. Always finding the one reason not to do a deal. A hotel or condominium on my property would be a home run,"* he thought. *"What I'm going to do will be a grand slam."* He kept his composure. He needed First Chicago in this deal.

"Come on, man, tell me. I'd love to be a part of it. Hell, you know us bankers, always looking at the downside. But that's how I keep you in business and out of trouble. It's not office, is it? No, not office. You don't know office, plus it's too far from the Loop."

A sly smile broke out across Steel's face. Time to cast his line into the water. "All of the above, my friend. All of the above. Office, hotel, condominium, retail, health club, rooftop park. A true city within a city! They are calling it a mixed-use complex, but that term hardly does it justice. Imagine working in a building and taking an elevator to go home? Having a meeting in the office component, and then staying in a suite at the hotel? Living on the lake, and dining in the finest restaurant on the top floor. Or having your groceries delivered to you from the market on the plaza level?"

Bradley Wentworth was stunned. He had to give it to Steel Simpson. The man thought big. He whistled under his breath.

"What did you pay for that land again? Three million?"

"Two and a half when I get done with Chicago Canal and Bridge."

"How so?" Wentworth was skeptical.

"Not important. And I don't need your money to buy it either. I'm paying cash. But I will need a few bucks to build Chicago World Tower."

"Hmm, I like the name. And how much we talking about?"

"I'm still fine tuning the program and the numbers, but roughly one million square feet and a hundred million dollars. I'll take the check now. Oh, and it will be the tallest building in Chicago."

Wentworth got out of his chair and stood against the window. He loved the height and seeing all the tiny, antlike people on the ground. He lived in rarified air. This deal could either keep him there or get him a teller's position in Skokie. He reached for the intercom.

"Evelyn, bring us two Cokes with ice." It was too early to drink, but suddenly this meeting was going to take some time.

"I don't know, Steel, aren't you biting off more than you can chew? I mean you're doing great with apartments and hotels." Wentworth thought to himself: *"This guy is such a fucking cowboy."*

"For God's sake, Brad, to do any less on this parcel of land would be criminal."

"How much office?" As much as he hated to admit it, Wentworth was being drawn in.

"500,000 SF."

"You're kidding me—out on the lake? Hotel rooms?"

"250 rooms, but I think we can go 300."

"Condos?"

"200 units, 20 top floors. Only 5 units per floor at the top."

"My friend, you have a set of brass balls...I'll tell you that! Retail?"

"Support only, I figure 50,000 SF. And another fifty for the health club. It will even have a pool and racquet ball courts."

"Who's your architect?"

"Nolan, Jefferson and Marlow. We have a handshake deal. The schematic design will be done in June," Simpson said, lying. He hadn't even negotiated the fee.

"Really. Lots of turmoil over there with the death of the boss."

"Yeah, unfortunate, but I never met him. Just dealing with Vance Jefferson. He runs the place anyway."

Wentworth was back in his chair, his feet propped up on a lower open drawer. "I'm surprised they are venturing into the private sector. They've done pretty well with contracts for the city and state, not to mention the big corporations."

"Vance says it's time to expand. This project will get them lots of press. He's practically jerking off over it." As soon as he said the words, he knew he might offend the proper Wentworth.

"I'm sure he is. They aren't cheap, you know." The comment had not seemed to bother Brad.

"Only a few firms could handle this size of project, and I like that they have all disciplines in-house. Better coordination that way. So, let's get back to money. How much are you gonna lend me?"

"Whoa, not so fast. Okay, you have piqued my interest. But one hundred million dollars! Where are you securing the equity?"

"How much equity do I need to secure? Then I'll secure it."

"Thirty, forty million…"

"You're killing me. Give me seventy-five and I'll get the twenty-five in equity."

"I can't do seventy-five. It's way above our loans to one borrower. I'll have to get participation. Your problem is the equity, and it's going to be at least thirty."

"I was hoping you'd have some ideas." Simpson had to reveal that he needed help here. He had no clue where to find a money source for thirty million or more dollars.

"You can forget the big insurance companies. You haven't been in business that long. Hell, I shouldn't be doing business with you! And to be honest, your reputation isn't the most, shall we say, sterling. You might want to call off Irving Montlick once in a while."

"Hey, this is a tough business."

"Well, how you do business is not my first concern. Anyway, I was reading the *New York Times* today. Do you know we import more oil now than we produce? The USA has more cars than any country in the world and our consumption is going through the roof. And do you know where we're buying that oil from?"

"I don't know. Mexico?"

"Not even close. A little sandbox of a country in the Middle East called Saudi Arabia. You know *Arabian Nights*. Sheiks, flowing robes, Bedouins."

"Really?" Simpson immediately recalled seeing an old classmate at the Alumni meeting a week earlier. An old classmate who was a wiz in economics—Ali Zyiad Sharif. He was now head of the Saudi consulate in Chicago. Simpson used to beg him for his class notes in international economics, a subject that held little interest to him. "The Saudi's have oil?"

"Billions of gallons of it! Where have you been anyway? Where's that newspaper?" Wentworth moved around the papers on his desk. "Here it is. Their per capita income is higher than the US. They are sitting on one quarter of the world's oil reserves. Their monarchy controls the country, and they're up to their eyeballs in oil money. There's your equity, my friend."

"I knew a guy at Northwestern..."

"Okay, start there. I'll also make some calls. Look, I've got to run. Another meeting. But good to see you. Keep me apprised; you have my interest. But not our money. Yet."

Simpson walked out the door. He couldn't wait to get back to the office and call his new best friend, Ali Zyiad Sharif.

CHAPTER 23

"Mr. Jensen, you understand that you are here on your own accord, correct?" Sergeant Mike Grabowski, Inspector John O'Rourke's number one man, was trying hard to be professional, but for a street cop turned arson investigator, on the beat for fifteen years, niceties did not come easy.

"You told me you wanted talk to me. So, I say sure. But why fingerprint and photograph me?"

"Standard procedure. It's really to protect you. Would you like an interpreter? How about a Coke?"

"No. I speak English pretty good. Like what you just said is total bullshit. Not thirsty either."

"Well, I see you do. Your boss Mr. Simpson said you didn't understand much English."

"He never ask me to talk. How should he know?"

"I see. Well then, is your name Lothar Jensen?"

"Yes. Lothar Hans."

"Are you an American Citizen?"

"No, I have green card. Will become someday; soon, I hope."

"Your cooperation today may help speed that process along, if you understand what I am saying."

"Police OK, it is KGB I hate," though in truth he hated anyone who wore a badge and was some kind of police.

Grabowski weighed in slowly. If he could get Jensen to roll over on his boss in one meeting, it might mean a promotion for him. "Where were you the night of April 26?"

"I don't know."

"Let me help. That was a Thursday. During the day, you drove Mr. Simpson to the property he had bought at the lake. Does that help?"

"I drive him everywhere. I am his driver. But yes, I remember going to lake property. I could not figure how to get to at first."

"But you figured it out. You took him there?"

"Yes. I know Chicago. Is only one way in off Lower Wacker. Very hidden drive. Do not know why he buys property you can't get to but is not my business."

"Did you see an encampment of shacks there?"

"I notice. Remind me a lot of many villages in Estonia. So what?"

"How long were you there?"

"I don't know, thirty, maybe forty-five minutes. Mr. Simpson said he wanted to see land."

"Did he notice the shacks and tents?"

"He always reading papers in car. I don't know; don't ask him. He pay well but he not very friendly to me."

Grabowski saw an opening. He could tell there was no love lost between Lothar and his boss.

"What did you do that night?"

Jensen knew this was the reason he was being questioned by the police. He remembered his marching orders from Simpson.

"Most nights, I drive him to condo on lake."

"But on that particular Thursday night…"

"Oh, remember now. He has meeting or party at Northwestern College. I took him there, then home."

"What time did you get there and what time did you leave?"

Lothar stuck to the script and Grabowski was getting frustrated. He wasn't making any headway. He took a different tack and decided to get tougher.

"Mr. Jensen, we found a gas can at the site, some distance away from the fire. We've photographed and fingerprinted you, and we're going to check the can for your prints, and then we'll trace the purchase of the can back to you. So, you had better cooperate. Or that green card will be torn up and you can deal with the KGB. I'm sure they're still looking for you."

Lothar Jensen wasn't scared of Grabowski. He had been inter-
rogated by tougher KGB agents and had been beaten by them as well.
And he wasn't worried. He had handled the gas can with latex gloves
and paid a teenage boy twenty dollars to go into the Ace Hardware
Store and buy it for him. He knew he had a face no one could forget.

"I do not know anything about a gas can. I take Mr. Simpson to
college and then take him home. I sleep in coach house above garage,"
he said raising his hand and running it through his hair. Grabowski
noticed the bandage around Jensen's hand.

CHAPTER 24

Billy Flanagan was cold. The wind whistled through Lower Wacker Drive like the wind tunnel it was, open on one side to the Chicago River. No matter how he covered himself with the blankets he had salvaged from his old home in the vacant field by the lake, he could not escape the biting wind assaulting his hands and face. "God damn, son of a bitch, I want my home!"

Flanagan had it made back in the old shantytown. He had dragged enough construction refuse from neighboring building sites to create a two-room shack. One room functioned as his living room, where he had an old, overstuffed chair and kerosene lantern, and there was a small table where he ate the food he found in local restaurant trash cans. His favorite was Billy Goat's Tavern; he could always find some tossed hamburger patties. The other room contained his bed—an old twin mattress, but pretty upscale by any homeless person's assessment. He had been there three years, ever since he had been released from the county hospital as a harmless schizophrenic. He heard voices in his head, and imagined he was Irish royalty waiting for his army to return him to the throne of Ireland as its rightful king. And he had the Celtic medallion around his neck to prove it—a Kodak Starflash camera. It was his most prized possession. As a teenager, he had taken an interest in photography. It was a Christmas present from his aunt with whom he lived. Even then, he was already starting to hear the voices of ancient Irish knights telling him to reclaim his crown.

Billy wedged himself deeper between a concrete barrier along the drive and the masonry wall of a basement. He placed one blanket above his head to block the wind. But it didn't really help. And then there were the automobiles screaming by at thirty-five to forty miles an hour. The cars added to the wind, and their exhaust fumes made this a particularly unhealthy environment for any long period of time. Now he had to move all the time, too; the police rousted him from one day to the next. He had heard the area around Soldier Field was pretty nice, if he could only find it.

Flanagan yearned for the open air of the large field nearby. He also missed his two friends, Mouse and Pat who were burned in the fire and would no longer be with him. The fire had changed that. He had barely gotten away from the flames in time.

"Gotta get warm, sum bitch. But I caught you…I caught you." He held tightly onto the talisman around his neck and looked down at it. It was precious, for in it he had captured the person who set his home on fire. He could never get out of the Brownie box as long as Billy kept the camera close. He had even been willing to lose one of the last things that he owned to capture the bad man. He had used up his last flashbulb. Now he had the man inside, the tall ugly man with the gas can. Billy Flanagan huddled lower into his lodgings and finally slept.

O'Rourke finished his hot pastrami sandwich and slaw, and went downstairs, and climbed into his black Crown Victoria sedan to make the 20-minute trip to the lakefront. The vehicle fit him well. He was over six feet tall, with thinning black hair, turned white at the sideburns and ears. While he had developed a policeman's paunch after twenty years of duty, he was still imposing and strong muscled.

He neared the parcel of land and he realized there was no direct route to the site from Michigan Avenue. He finally found a poorly maintained roadway, full of potholes and cracks that went up and then opened onto a vast field where it just stopped. O'Rourke parked on the pavement. He did not want to drive over any tire tracks. He exited the car and walked the remaining fifty feet into the bright sun of a spring afternoon in Chicago. Standing now on Steel Simpson's land, he could understand why the property was so coveted. It was huge for any parcel in the city, but it was also on the river and next to bustling Lakeshore Drive. He could almost understand the greed that coveted such land. But murdering two helpless people?

As he began to walk, he was disappointed. Fire trucks, arson units, and other police cars had created a spaghetti of tire tracks. There would be no way to find those of a Lincoln Continental. Anyway, the police drove Fords, and all used the same Goodyear tires as Lincolns. O'Rourke continued toward the fire, or more precisely the start of the fire. There was a patch of burnt grass and earth about six feet in diameter. This was where the gas can had been found and where it had exploded. There was nothing else, not a matchstick, a cigarette butt; nothing. He walked slowly, deliberately, from there directly along the thin line that was the liquid fuse toward the shantytown. It was no longer than one hundred feet, far enough to get away from what had to be a sudden explosion of flames, but not so long as to make a quick getaway impossible.

He turned and continued his slow march to the site of the homeless village. It was surrounded by yellow police tape (arson was always a joint exercise between Police and Fire, a protocol he disliked but had grown to accept as Fire took the lead). The remnants of the encampment were there, though no longer smoldering. Charred pieces of 2x4's; roofing shingles; a burnt-out chair with nothing left but a scorched hardwood frame; an old mattress and box springs. Frustration was growing tight in his shoulders and neck. He shook his head. This was a crime where it would be hard to even locate the victims. They had scattered like cockroaches after the fire.

John O'Rourke began to think that he might have his first crime that could not be solved. He turned and walked back toward his car. He was now about three to four feet away from the black line that had been the fuse that ignited the fire. His boot touched something. At first, he thought it was just a rock, but he instinctively looked down and then bent over. From deep in the lime green weeds he pulled out a spent flashbulb. He rolled the bulb in his hands. It was fairly new, the base silver, with clean metal posts.

"Well, I'll be damned!"

CHAPTER 25

The Consulate of the Kingdom of Saudi Arabia was located in a perfectly maintained, three-story brownstone, one of several on tree-lined East Scott Street just west of Lakeshore Drive.

Simpson was surprised at how cordial his old classmate was on the phone, and even more pleased at the invitation to lunch. He didn't realize, that as the Chief Diplomat of his country to the City of Chicago, Ali Zyiad Sharif Al Saud had little to do with his time except throw lavish receptions in the evening and fill his days with tennis and bicycling along the lake. Such was the life of the son of a prince in the Saudi royal family.

The needy developer walked up the steps to the imposing pair of mahogany doors, filled with ornate cut glass. To the right, above a large doorbell, was a polished brass plaque with a palm tree and a pair of crossed swords etched upon it, and the words:

Consulate
Kingdom of Saudi Arabia

Simpson rang the doorbell. Almost instantly, he saw a servant approach in a white thobe and matching keffiyeh, the traditional headdress of Saudi men. He opened the door and spoke:

"Mr. Simpson, please come in. The Consul is expecting you."

"Thank you." Steel was impressed with the greeting. He checked his watch to be sure he hadn't arrived late. No, it was 12:02 P.M.

"This way, please."

The foyer ran the length of the first floor and was decorated with ornate, gold leaf furniture and chairs, all a little excessive, but what

Simpson expected. Above a large reception table was a large portrait of King Faisal in his ceremonial robes complete with a short sword in a bejeweled scabbard. Flanking it were small palm trees, which seemed out of place in Chicago, but Steel remembered that he was not in Chicago anymore. This building was, in fact, solemn territory of a strange country that he knew little about. Except that it was rich and getting richer every day. At the end of the gallery was a wall of glass and beyond that an open, multi-level courtyard full of ornamental trees, manicured shrubs and large beds of spring flowers. On the first level was a round table, set with a white linen tablecloth and fine English bone china. Ali Zyiad Sharif was reading the *Financial Times* but got up as soon as he saw his approaching guest.

"Steel, so good to see you." Sharif was wearing a dark blue suit, white dress shirt with spread collar and a conservative dark blue Brioni tie with small white dots. In his breast pocket was a perfectly pressed four-square. He, like his servant, was wearing a white keffiyeh.

"Ali, I'm impressed. All this for me? The one who always borrowed your economics notes..."

"You still owe me for that, but you've done pretty well for yourself, I think, in spite of knowing next to nothing about international economics. I had Karim set the table out here today. It's so rare to have a nice spring day in Chicago. I hope it's okay."

"Perfect, just perfect. I was just hoping you might afford me fifteen minutes. So, I really appreciate the lunch invitation."

"I have an entertainment budget. If I don't use it, I get chastised. Oh, and please excuse my garb," pointing to his headdress. "I'm required to wear it on any official business here in the Consulate. Sit, please."

The two sat down and exchanged pleasantries, mostly reminiscing about their college days at Northwestern. Water glasses were filled and the first course, a hearts of romaine salad with tomatoes, was served.

"Steel, I must apologize that there is no wine. You know our Muslim religion forbids drinking alcohol."

"I think I remember you shot-gunning a few beers at some of our frat parties," Steel joked, and also trying to get the upper hand. "Why do you think I lent you my notes? To bribe you into keeping quiet!"

As the main course was served, lamb kabobs with dark rice, the conversation turned to Nixon and Watergate; the Cubs chances that year; and oil in Saudi Arabia. Then there was the inevitable silence followed by Ali Zyiad getting to the point.

"OK, so let's get down to business. Why after several years, are you trying to re-connect? What can I do for you?"

"You're right, Ali, and I apologize for not staying in touch. I guess it just happens after college. We graduate and start a career. I certainly did, to the exclusion of a lot of other things."

"Like friends. Anyway, other than borrowing my notes, I'm not sure how much of a friend you wanted me to be."

Simpson looked down and was getting uncomfortable. "Ali, I apol…"

Sharif's eyes narrowed and his pleasant demeanor suddenly turned sour. "Steel, I understand how it worked then. But don't patronize me now. Just tell me what you want from me."

Steel Simpson knew that his host could see through his hypocrisy. He never really liked this dark-skinned foreigner with a strange name, but he needed to pass the class in International Economics. He decided he might as well swing for the fences.

"I need money—a lot of money. I'm looking for someone to put up the equity for what will be the greatest building Chicago has ever seen. On the lake. Chicago World Tower. Mixed-use: hotel, office, residential, retail. Even a health club. And a fabulous restaurant on the seventy-fifth floor. I thought you might know a few of your countrymen who might be interested in such an opportunity."

"Ah, I suspected so. I read about the land purchase in the papers. OK, you have my attention. Go on." Ali took a bite of the dessert, chocolate cake.

"I have a commitment for the debt financing from First Chicago Bank and Trust. Brad Wentworth, my banker, suggested I talk to you. And Nolan, Jefferson and Marlow are designing the building as we speak." Simpson was lying through his teeth and knew it, but this is how you made it happen. By pretending it already had happened. Anyway, he was unlikely to be caught in the lies. No one ever checked.

"What kind of equity, as you refer to it, are we talking about? And what kind of return will I get?"

"Twenty-five, thirty million…cash on cash return of 6.5%. Twenty percent ownership in the deal."

Sharif's eyes widened. "Really? How much is this project going to cost?"

"One hundred to one-hundred-twenty-five million." Simpson let the numbers hang in the courtyard's fragrant air.

"The hotel down the street," referring to Steel's last project on Oak Street. "What did it cost? Total all in?"

"Ten million. What's your point?" He could see where this was headed.

"Ten million to ten times that. Big jump for anyone, wouldn't you say?"

"It's just another zero. The process is the same, and I know more than anyone about the process."

"Does the process include suing people?"

"I know how to get the most out of my contractors, and sometimes they don't perform." Simpson did not like where the conversation was going.

"Steel, from what I hear, what you know is how to screw people. Yes, your reputation precedes you."

The meeting was heading south and Simpson was getting tired of kowtowing to this raghead. "I'm sorry to have taken up your time, Ali. I can see you only know about oil, not buildings."

"Look, maybe how you do business is not such a bad thing. And I am in no position to judge each situation, so calm down. And please listen."

Simpson looked down at the chocolate cake and took a large bite, washed down with coffee. He was trying to relax.

"Steel. I'm going to Europe next month. New York to Paris on the Concorde, then on to Monaco on my family's plane. My father, the Crown Prince, will be attending the International Economic Conference there. He also wants to discuss our real estate investments. Come with me. I'll tell you all I know about buildings on the trip over. You might be surprised."

Steel Simpson did all he could to keep a straight face. "Well, okay. Yeah, sure, I'd love to come."

Sharif stood up. The meeting was over; he put out his hand. "And don't worry, we'll discuss the money you need too. And I suspect it will be more like forty million. But us 'ragheads' make that in a week or so. Or do you prefer the term 'dune coon'?"

"I never called anyone that!" Steel was turning flush.

"No worries. I'm not offended. But I believe I overheard you at one of our frat parties. I was rather amused actually."

Ali Zyiad Sharif walked Steel Simpson to the front door and opened it. "I'll call you with the arrangements."

"Thanks, Ali. This will be a great project. Thank you, and I'm sorry..."

"I'm sure you are. And Steel, I seriously doubt twenty percent participation will cut it."

CHAPTER 26

The shades were pulled down low over the windows at 2017 Warren Avenue in Maywood. Streams of late afternoon light tried to invade the premises through slits on the sides of the windows, highlighting the pall of smoke from countless doobies. The darkened living room was illuminated by one lamp and a 25-inch TV, broadcasting *Dark Shadows*. It was mid-May, and the room was hot because the window air conditioner was broken. The walls were a dirty, yellow-cream adorned with posters of Malcolm X and Muhammad Ali.

Latrice, or "Tiger," Gibson held court from a large easy chair covered in a heavy, tapestry fabric. His feet were propped up on a coffee table in the center of the room, covered with overfull ashtrays, *Ebony* and *Jet* magazines, a mirror, a rolled Benjamin, and a heavy cardboard case of Schlitz Malt Liquor, in the kind of reusable box they sell only to bars. Several empties stood like soldiers on the table. There were also fat envelopes and stacks of money. Several members of the Lucifer Player's Club sat on a green, velvet sofa yelling at vampire Barnabas Collins to bite yet another girl on the Gothic TV show that was a staple of their afternoon highs.

Gibson sucked in the last of some premium weed held, fast by a roach clip. His eyes were dark and dull, which made him look all the more dangerous. A do-rag swaddled his hair covered with straightener, an acid that burned his scalp but achieved the desired effect— the straight hair of a white man. He wore a wife beater tee shirt that exposed the large Greek letter "Omega" branded onto his arm during the initiation ceremony for Omega Psi Phi at the Chicago Circle campus. Tiger Gibson had attended the school for two years, where he excelled in accounting. However, he had a bad temper and it flared one afternoon in the Student Union. An untoward word from the member of a rival white fraternity caused Gibson to take umbrage at the remark and proceed to beat the offender to within an inch of his life. He left him bloodied and unconscious in the campus dining hall. A four-week suspension followed, but when he was reported being back on campus, accosting a black coed and bitch-slapping her, he was officially expelled.

But it was all good. In those two years, he had learned all he needed to about business, compound interest rates and cooking the books. He went back home to Maywood and started paying attention to his surroundings. First, he noticed that the demographics of his hometown were changing. More and more blacks were moving into the small and aging row houses in the town of 27,000 residents. White flight had begun, and he knew that within a few years, Maywood would be all black. But today the shopkeepers, white and black, still paid homage and protection to the Outfit. The Italians controlled the town, his town, and he had determined that this had to change. He knew about the two brothels; from rear alleys he saw the dice games and the young boys running numbers and off-track bets. He saw junkies coming out of basements with their eyes rolling and bulging. On Fridays, collection day, he watched large muscular goons enter the small bottegas, dry cleaners, and restaurants and walk out with suit pockets fattened with protection money.

He would start small. Remain inconspicuous. Play the black shop-keepers off against the whites. Offer better protection at lower costs. Staff a whorehouse he owned with younger, better looking bitches. Drugs were different. That was a hard nut to crack; the Outfit con-trolled it tightly. He'd figure that out in time. Within three years, La-trice Gibson was taking in over $100,000 a year and had a reliable crew of fifteen "players." They liked to call themselves "Lucifer's Players" and then added "Club" to the name, like it was something social. Tiger didn't like the name but let it roll. His own moniker had been firmly established when he bit into the face of an underperforming crew member who dared talk back to him. And his long finger-nails, that for some strange reason he never cut, had ripped into the back of the same unfortunate individual. When he got off of the delinquent crew member, Gibson's face was covered in blood and his hands were dripping red. No one dared cross Gibson again and his moniker "Tiger" was born.

"Where's Tiny? Where's Maurice?"

"I don't know, man. Still collectin', I be guessin'," muttered Artemus, one of his lieutenants seated on the couch along with Jerome and Biggy. Artemus was the senior of the three, the enforcer.

"Those boys should have been back an hour ago. Go see where they are."

"Soon as I finish my Malt, Tiger."

"I said now, mother fucker. We need to finish counting the week's take. I have plans for tonight." Unlike the others in his posse, Gibson did not talk ghetto. He preferred the King's English. It reinforced his position as being smarter than everyone else. It was a by-product of his mother's training, who worked as a maid cleaning condos for the upper crust on Lakeshore Drive.

Artemus shook his head, slowly got up, said nothing, and headed for the door. He looked outside to make sure there were no nosy neighbors checking the house. He hoped he might see the errant bag boys coming up the street. He was in luck. Rounding the corner were Tiny and Maurice. Artemus went back inside.

"They be comin' now, boss."

"Man, Tiger gonna ice us. Last three customers stiffed our asses." Maurice could sense the worry in Tiny's voice.

"Chill man, we cool. We be Tiger's best collectors. But I tole you we didn't need to play pool at lunch. 'Fore we know it, was two o'clock. Time we get to ol' man Vincenzo's, he already give his protection to the Outfit."

"Yeah, you right. Bad idea. But we was just five minute late. You see those dagos walk out of the bodega laughing?" Tiny was slowing as they approached the house.

"Straight up, we ain't laughin' now, are we?" Maurice stopped at the front steps. "Let's get this over wit."

Latrice didn't look up when the two miscreants entered. He had finished his joint and was commencing the weekly ritual of counting the week's take. He leaned forward and took a long pull on a fresh Schlitz Bull.

"You boys are late. It's not cool to be late. I hope you have a good excuse. Best one would be you collected from everyone."

Tiny spoke first. "Boss, we got a little bad news. By the time we got to Vincenzo's bodega, he had paid up to the Outfit. Then Carl at the barbershop wouldn't pay. He say he don't need to pay. Only thing he need to worry about is a nigga gang holding him up."

"Anything else?" Gibson continued in a flat voice counting the money on the table. Now it was Maurice's turn.

"Yeah, old man Lucca at the Esso gas station tole us he didn't have it. Bad week. Said he'd make it up next week."

"Who won the pool game? Must have been Tiny. He's a pretty good player."

"We sorry, boss. You know we be good collectors for you. We do right by you next week. Promise." Tiny's voice was cracking, realizing that their lies were getting them into deeper shit.

"Artemus, what am I going to do with these two?" For the first time Tiger, looked up and over to his associate on the couch.

"You want me to take care of it, boss, I do it." Artemus pulled out his Glock from behind the back cushion and cradled it. "Or you could let 'em sit in the hole a while. Get their heads on straight."

Gibson stood up. He glared at Tiny and Maurice with his dead eyes. They took a step back in certain fear. They knew one missed collection could be forgiven…but not three. Artemus stood up as well and pointed the Glock at the two. Tiny clasped his hands as if in prayer. Gibson said nothing. It was better than talk.

"Mr. Gibson, please," Maurice stammered. "We'll, we'll get, get, the money next, next week I promise." Tiny standing next to him, tears streaming down his cheek, a yellow puddle had formed by his shoe. Gibson's cold stare turned slowly into a smile. "I guess I'm getting soft. But seeing as how I have a date tonight to see Smokey Robinson with my lady, I'm in a good mood. Next week, get to those accounts before the guineas and collect. Or you'll be pissing in your pants down in the hole for a week. Are we clear?"

"Yes, boss. Yes, boss. Sure thing." The two grabbed the last two malt liquors and began to leave the room.

Gibson shook his head and smiled. "Put the Bulls down. Along with whatever you did manage to collect. Now get the fuck out of my sight."

CHAPTER 27

"Are you out of your mind?" Steel Simpson was apoplectic.

"Steel, calm down. Enjoy your lunch. Eat while I explain." Vance Jefferson spoke in his most reassuring voice, hoping it would do a little to assuage Simpson's growing anger. The two sat in Nolan, Jefferson and Marlow's private dining room, located on the northeast corner of the executive floor, adjacent to the main conference room. It afforded stunning views of Grant Park and the lake. Both the conference room and dining room were served by a common kitchen. An elderly black man in white coat served the two executives in a discreet fashion.

The dining room was large enough to handle twelve people at three tables, but for this meeting, two of the tables had been removed making it a more intimate setting. The remaining table was placed by the large windows, which were framed by simple white linen drapes. On the far side was a large sideboard with an arrangement of fresh gladiolas that partially obstructed an original Frederic Remington painting.

Simpson looked at the perfectly prepared club sandwich cut into four triangles, with a generous scoop of German potato salad in the center. The white-jacketed black man then poured iced tea into a cut crystal glass.

"Thank you, Baxter," Jefferson said as soon as his Cobb salad was placed before him, followed by ice water. As quietly as he had entered, Baxter left through a swinging side door with a porthole.

"Steel, an 8% fee is totally justified for this project. You have a very complicated building."

"Vance, that is eight million dollars, for Christ's sake. On my last project, the entire fee was less than seven hundred thousand."

"Yes, and what was the total project cost? Ten million or so, am I right? So that works out to 7%. And it was a single use. A twenty-story hotel. This is a monumental project with five uses in 75 stories!"

Simpson looked down at his sandwich. It was already one o'clock and he was famished. But eating now would display weakness, giving Jefferson the upper hand. He had wanted the meeting at his office so he could stand over Jefferson as he was seated before Simpson's desk, and Simpson could dress him down for the outrageous proposal. But Jefferson had insisted on the meeting being held at NJ&M so he could give Steel Simpson the grand tour. It had taken most of an hour, and Simpson had been truly impressed, as were most potential clients. The size and depth of the firm were undeniable. And just as it had impressed young Connor West, the museum had blown Simpson away. Not only did he know that this was the only firm that could execute his multi-function project, but it was the only one that had the stature to help him acquire the equity and the debt financing that he needed. So, all he could do was posture and hope for a better result. And in addition, if he was to have any chance of securing the equity from the Saudi royal family, he desperately needed a design to show Crown Prince Zaidan in four weeks.

He looked down at the lightly toasted bread and the turkey, bacon and cheddar cheese with fresh green lettuce and red tomato. He picked up the first triangle and almost inhaled it.

Seeing that Simpson could not talk, Jefferson seized the opportunity. "Steel, I'm not trying to screw you, I promise. I knew that when you received the proposal two days ago, you would be upset. That's why I wanted to discuss it in person. What we have here is five separate buildings in one huge envelope. A hotel, an office building, a condominium, a health club, and a shopping center. And yes, did I mention a parking garage? We are just finishing the Grant Park underground garage. Look out there. You see the last of the construction fences? The city of Chicago paid us two-and-a-half million for that project, and it is only three parking levels underground."

With the remains of his first wedge of club sandwich still in his mouth, Simpson muttered: "I know what's in my building. And my parking will be above ground." The weak response was all he could muster.

"Correct!" Jefferson was now on a roll and kept talking as Simpson lifted a large forkful of potato salad. "And why does it have to be above ground? Because you have a river under your site! Fortunately, I have the best structural engineers in the country to devise a solution to that small impediment. But that will take research, calculations, and time. And a unique solution! That is why the fee is eight percent."

Simpson was on the ropes, but he had to punch back. "Vance, it is still eight million dollars. There has to be some economy of scale here. It is still one building. And the uses are not all that different. This is not my first rodeo, Vance. I know how these buildings work." Simpson paused, looking out the window while starting the second wedge of sandwich. The German potato salad was so good he thought it must have come directly from the Berghof.

"Alright, I'm probably crazy but I'll pay you six percent."

Vance Jefferson's jaw dropped. He looked incredulous. "Mr. Simpson, that won't work. I can't do that. I won't do that. I have to make some profit."

"Maybe you need to draw faster...but that's all I'll pay." Simpson was bluffing; he knew he needed a deal. He could feel his armpits getting moist. He did his best to stare at Jefferson, although he wanted another quarter of the sandwich. His appetite was still raging.

Jefferson shook his head. "Okay, okay, because this project will be mutually beneficial to both of us. If I can get compensated up front for the design charette—the three schemes, say $250,000—I agree to a seven-and-a-half percent fee."

"Seven percent. That's my bottom offer." Simpson picked up another triangle of sandwich and shoved it in his mouth as if to say: "I'll eat your lunch, Jefferson."

"And the design fee of $250,000?"

"Sure, whatever…no, $200,000." Everything was a negotiation. The words were barely recognizable as he chewed on his sandwich.

"I must be losing it, but okay I'll find a way to make it work. Do we have a deal?" Jefferson put out his hand and Steel, wiping mayonnaise off his, took it and shook it lamely.

"By the way, I need to see the designs in three weeks. I need to show them to my equity partner in Monaco."

Jefferson was taken aback both by the time frame and the fact that Simpson was indicating that he already had an equity partner.

"Steel, we need at least two months. Again, please understand how complex this building is. For example, the elevator design is a project in itself. Every component needs its own dedicated set of elevators. It just goes on and on."

"Look, that's why I'm hiring you guys, to figure this stuff out. Okay, four weeks or the deal is off. I've got to have it by then."

"Mr. Nolan warned me about you pirate…uh, I mean, private developers. Okay." He took out his pocket planner and looked at the calendar. How about June 12ᵗʰ? Does that work for you?"

"I'll make it work. I leave for Europe on the 15ᵗʰ. On the Concorde."

"Traveling in style, I see. Need a presenter?"

"I think I can handle it, but thanks for offering. Just draw up the contract. I'll have my lawyers review it and if we don't get it executed by the twelfth, we'll just do a Letter of Intent for the design portion and I'll send you a check for the three schemes."

"I'll have three teams working day and night, not to mention the model shop and renderings." Jefferson knew that the contract negotiations would be long and arduous. He needed the first payment as a sign of good faith.

After Vance walked Simpson to the elevators and repeated his pleasure at the handshake deal they had just made, he made his way back to his offices, passing by Marilyn's desk. She was waiting in anticipation.

"How did it go? Did you bag the elephant?" she said smiling broadly.

"Indeed, I did!" Vance smiled back, wanting his assistant in every way.

"Eight percent?" Marilyn was prying, but wanted to know.

"Seven. But I was ready to go to six. Plus, some up-front bucks. I'll need to talk to Marjorie Fleet. It's time to increase our errors and omissions insurance. And I'll need to set up lunch with our banker, Asa Morton. But I'll get the contract done first. Yes, yes, that was a pretty successful lunch." He was already counting the profit he estimated at two million dollars.

"Congratulations, Mr. Jefferson. As Mr. Nolan always said, you're the best negotiator he knew." She got out her Rolodex to find their insurance agent and banker.

"Oh, and get in touch with Connor West. We need him to start ASAP!"

"Yes, sir!" Marilyn's heart skipped a beat. "Mr. Jefferson, one other thing. Bob Marlow and Francis Nolan want to see you tomorrow morning."

Jefferson frowned. "Fine, get them on my calendar at nine."

CHAPTER 28

Connor West was staring down at his father's mortal remains, having a one-sided conversation.

"Once again, you've screwed up my life. I was all set to graduate and you decided to die on me. Your timing has always been impeccable. Like when you arrived an hour and a half late for my high school graduation, even though I was the Valedictorian. And of course, you were drunk."

Kevin West lay in the cheap, light blue metal casket lined with cream-colored artificial silk fabric. Intertwined in his bony grey hands was his rosary, unsaid for countless years. Above the body, resting on the lid of the casket was a wood crucifix provided by the funeral home as a part of the funeral services. He was dressed in a new white shirt that his mother had hurriedly bought at Sears. She couldn't afford a new suit, so she had the only one he had owned, dry cleaned. It still carried the scent of liquor, poverty and a life unfulfilled.

Connor looked intently at his father. Why did anyone ever have an open casket? His father's face bore little resemblance to the man he knew, even the man he had seen two days ago in the hospital. The pallor was not white, or grey. It was a faded, pale brown. The cheeks were sunken and lips badly colored from lipstick applied by the embalmer. The skin was dry and almost cracking. The only redeeming part of the whole picture was the bright blue tie he wore, a Christmas gift two years ago from Connor. He didn't know what to buy; it certainly wouldn't be a bottle of Cutty Sark. Connor told his dad that it was for church on Sunday, though he knew he went only infrequently.

"Fuck all of it…" Connor muttered. He turned around and walked away, tears streaming down his face. He went back to the rear of the funeral parlor and sat next to his mother, Margaret West. He took her hand in his and hugged her. She took out her handkerchief and dried his eyes.

"You look tired Ma. How are you doing?"

"I'm fine. I just didn't know so many people would show up. It's quite exhausting really, lying about what a great fellow your dad was."

"They were all your friends, not his, and they meant well I'm sure."

"I know. Listen, you need to get back to school and finish up. I want you to leave tomorrow after the Mass and burial."

"I'm not leaving you now, Ma."

"Nonsense! I'll not hear of it. You have an excellent job offer in Chicago and I'll be just fine. I've lived alone for the last five years, remember?"

"But I need to take care of you. Maybe I'll work in New York."

"We'll not discuss it now. You go back to school and finish. I want my son to get a degree, a master's degree from Harvard!"

The burial the next day took place in a light spring rain attended by only seven people. Afterwards, Connor West, dutiful son, headed back to Harvard. He couldn't wait to get the damned thesis finished and had no idea what kind of jury would critique it. He had lost a week and now his classmates had graduated and moved on. Because of his father's death, he had missed saying goodbye to Rat and Pisgetti. The architecture building would be as quiet as a tomb. He wanted to be in Chicago, be with Marilyn and work for NJ&M. West's head pounded with resentment and anger as he drove on into what had become a hard rain.

West got back to his garret apartment around dinner time. He was hungry, but knew there was little food in the icebox, and what there was, was spoiled after his long absence. He looked over to his phone and the answering machine light was blinking. Getting a phone with a tape recorder was a small luxury he afforded himself because of the long hours he spent in the architecture building. If his mother called because she had been beaten by his father he wanted, needed, to know immediately. There were six messages. He pressed the play button.

"Connor, this is Marilyn. Please pick up. It's important. Why haven't you answered or called back? I'm worried sick. Anyway, like I said before, this isn't about us, if you want to stop seeing me, fine, but it's about your job. Mr. Jefferson wants you to start right away. But we haven't heard from you. He doesn't know what to do. So please, please call back. Okay?"

Connor called the number. "You've reached Nolan, Jefferson and Marlow. Our offices hours are…"

Connor slammed the phone down and looked again at the business card. "Direct Number: 563-1210." He dialed the number and the rotary slowly did its job.

"This is Vance Jefferson. I'm sorry I can't take your call right now. Please feel free to leave a message or contact my executive assistant Marilyn Jones at 563-1215. Thanks, and have a fine day."

By now sweat was running down Connor's forehead; his hands were clammy. His heart was pounding. He dialed Marilyn's direct number. It rang and rang and rang.

"Marilyn Jones."

"Thank God, Marilyn! This is Connor."

"Connor, I was so worried. Where are you?"

"Cambridge. I just got back to my apartment. My father died. I was in New York."

Marilyn was stunned by the news. It took a moment for her to process the information. "Oh, Connor, I'm so sorry. If I had known I wouldn't have left all those messages."

"Do I still have a job?"

"Oh, Connor, of course you do. Mr. Jefferson was as anxious as I was. He needs you for a big project we just got. How soon can you get here?"

"I don't know. Another two weeks? I have got to finish my thesis. My Dad dying totally screwed up everything. God, I hate the man!

He's fucked up, I'm sorry, messed up everything I ever wanted. Can Jefferson wait two weeks?"

"No, Connor. He needs you now."

"I see. It might not work out then. I need a job, but I need a degree first. Maybe I'll just go back to New York. My Mom needs me."

"Connor, please don't go to New York."

"Look, I gotta go. I mean, not to New York. I better get to the studio. Maybe I can get a thesis project done overnight. Anyway, I can't sleep the way I feel right now. I'll talk to you later."

"Connor, Connor…don't hang up."

"We'll talk tomorrow. Bye, Marilyn." He put the phone down without waiting for a response. Suddenly a job on Seventh Avenue was looking like his future.

"Sullivan, Sullivan. Wake up!"

Connor's head was on the drafting table; he was in a deep sleep. He stirred from the rough shaking. It was Pisgetti. Slowly Connor's eyes focused on his friend.

"Silvio? What are you doing here? Didn't you graduate?"

"Sure, I graduate, but it's not like we live in New Hampshire. My parents come over here from Italy. We stay awhile. Gonna see Washington and Mount Vernon. Just came to the building to get my stuff."

"Oh, yeah, I see. Congratulations. Maybe I'll graduate by September."

"Listen, the dean, he look a for you yesterday. He wants to talk to you."

"About what?'

"How should I know? He just a want a to find you. I mean badly. He says if we see you to tell you to come to his office. Capisce?"

"Yeah, I capisce. Probably to hand me my 'Incomplete'."

"Just see him. Now go home and get soma sleep. You look terrible. Oh, and this is for you."

Silvio Marchetti took a bottle of Italian Brunello wine from behind his back and handed it to Connor.

"My parents brought wine for all the graduates. Drink some of it before you go to bed."

"OK, thanks. But I'm not a graduate…"

CHAPTER 29

"Bob, Francis, come on in. I was just getting ready for another red-letter day in the profession of architecture. Francis, are you settled into your new office digs? And Bob, good job on the CDs for the Chicago Convention Center expansion. First rate."

The two visitors settled into Jefferson's sofa, one on each end. Vance pulled up a chair from the conference table.

"So, what's on your mind, gentlemen?"

Bob spoke first. "Well, quite simply, the future of the firm now that Mr. Nolan has passed."

Francis chimed in. "Yes sir, I mean Vance. Dad was always passionate about architecture and design. We hope, I mean, we need to keep it that way." Awkward as he sounded, Marlow was impressed by Francis' new assertiveness.

"And why would I think any differently?" Vance looked directly at the younger Nolan, as if in a staring contest. "I have run this firm with your dad for over twenty years; that has always been the cornerstone of our existence. It's in our blood. And Bob, the future of the firm has never been brighter."

"I'm not so sure, Vance. Why the private sector? City and state contracts and corporate work are our forte."

"Oh, I see, you talked to Frank Sr. about my wanting to go into private sector work." Jefferson was not surprised. In fact, he suspected that this was the reason for the meeting.

"Yes, he talked to me about it. Especially about a new potential client."

"Someone named Simpson. A new developer," Francis interjected, determined to stay in the conversation.

"Boys, boys, relax. I have great news. I just met with Steel Simpson at lunch yesterday. We just bagged a seven-million-dollar contract. Talk about a bright future indeed!"

The number dropped like a rock on them. Marlow looked at Francis with a look that said: *"I'd better take it from here."*

"Ok, yes, that's a pretty good commission by any metric. How much is he paying upfront?"

"$200,000.00. And we start immediately."

"Start immediately on what?"

"A project that will redefine this firm. Simpson has acquired that tract of land along Lakeshore Drive and the river. You know it. It's been vacant for years."

Bob and Francis nodded, exchanging glances.

"Why was it vacant so long?"

"It was caught up in a frivolous lawsuit between the city and Chicago Canal and Bridge."

"It is a pretty nice location for…well, anything." Francis was getting his sea legs and Marlow continued to be impressed.

"And anything and everything is what Mr. Simpson wants to build. A seventy-five-story mixed-use development. A city within a city gentlemen. Office, hotel, condominiums, retail, a health club. Restaurant at the top."

Marlow smiled wanly. *"JV is really pouring it on,"* he thought. Yes, Jefferson was into full "sell" mode.

"Bob, Francis, this is a one-hundred-million-dollar project. It will be the tallest building in Chicago. He's calling it Chicago World Tower. And here is the best part: we're going to have a competition in-house to develop three designs. Simpson picks the one he likes best. That's how I sold him on NJ&M. He loved the idea."

"Wait…" Marlow squeezed the single word in. "We're going to produce three designs for $200,000? We spend that on one design!"

"Sure, we'll take a hit on the front end, but the back end is huge. Almost a two-million-dollar profit. And there will be no compromise on design. Steel Simpson will have three outstanding ones to choose from."

"Vance, look at it the other way around. Out of every dollar we make, only twenty-five cents are profit. We complete CD's and that accounts for over half the fee, and then don't get paid, we're underwater by almost three million dollars. We don't have near that in reserves in the bank. You'll be borrowing money all over town to cover salaries and expenses. And Francis Sr. said this guy Simpson is a shyster. No, he said 'scumbag.' We're taking a big risk. We know that a corporate client or the city is going to pay. Where's he getting his money anyway?"

"He's going to Monaco in four weeks, that's all I know. Look, Simpson is not some new kid on the block. He has apartments and hotels: that new one on Oak Street, the Royalton, and tons of warehouses on the west side. I'm sure he'll get the money. Our risk is just a couple hundred thousand. We practically piss that much away on the Christmas party."

Marlow looked at the young Nolan. He needed an ally. "Francis, your dad knew everything about what goes on in this city, and he said this guy, Steel Simpson, didn't pass his sniff test. I'm against it."

"Bobby, listen to me. I know the business and how to deal with scumbags. But I have to tell you after my meetings with him, he's a pretty straight shooter. Tough, okay, but he listens to reason. Senior told me to increase our E&O insurance, and I'm doing that. I'm also increasing our lines of credit at First National to cover any late payments. And you know as well as I that until he pays us, we don't release any sealed drawings for construction," referring to the seal of the architect stamped on the top of every sheet of construction documents, giving the architect responsibility for the design. "And you're the guy that stamps them, so you have me and Simpson by the balls. Okay?"

Francis' head was spinning with the discussion about E&O insurance, lines of credit, and late payments. He was trying to keep up, but he just wanted to design, and the project in front of them was pretty tempting.

"JV, tell us about this competition. What do you have in mind?"

"Right, Junior, ah, Francis, as I said three teams. Each headed by a senior partner to organize and run the team. Delegate assignments, check progress, act as an in-house critic. Immediately under him is the head designer. Team one is headed by yours truly and you, Francis, are the head designer."

Francis Nolan's eyes brightened. This could be his big chance at last.

Jefferson, continued, animated by his scheme. "Dick Schiffels will head team two and Gerhard Dietrich will be the lead designer."

Marlow was shaking his head. "No, don't put me in charge of a team. I'm really busy."

"Bob, you will head up team three with Connor West."

"Are you out of your mind? The kid just graduated. You can't put that kind of pressure on him. Plus, there are three or four other junior designers who will be pissed as hell because they didn't get to lead a team."

"Robert, everyone who is not currently active in a project will be on a team, I can assure you. You're worried about our $200,000 budget. In three weeks with overtime, working his ass off, West will cost us about $2,500 with benefits. Hell, I may make money on this competition!"

"Vance, he is wet behind the ears. His head is in the clouds. Probably the first thing he wants to do in Chicago is find a flat and get laid. I know I would…"

Jefferson turned to the young Nolan: "Francis, if you had stayed at the interview, you would have seen the work of this youngster. He's advanced beyond his years." The comment directed to him was meant to pander to the mediocre head of design, but it only worried him.

"I don't know, Vance. I think Bob is right here. It may be too soon to let this kid West head a team."

"Jefferson, I won't have it! Connor West will be hated by every architect in this company who sweated years to get where they are."

"I have no intention of letting Mr. Simpson pick Connor's design anyway, whatever it may be. I'll see to it that he picks Francis'. His name is on the door, and this will signal the true passing of the torch from father to son."

Marlow couldn't believe what he was hearing. A Francis Jr. design was guaranteed to redefine the firm as mediocre and predictable.

"As I said, I'm against it. All of it. Simpson, the competition, Connor West being taken advantage of. At least let me put Leo in as head designer and Connor under him," referring to Leo Skoroshod, their Russian émigré, who did solid work. Connor could learn under his tutelage.

Jefferson's patience was running out. He was senior partner and this meeting was going to establish it.

"Okay, fine. Have West work under him, but I want the kid designing. I'm telling you this is the best opportunity to come to us in a long time. And as senior partner I'm going for it."

"Hold on there, JV," knowing the nickname would piss Jefferson off. "There are three of us senior partners now, and that means going forward we vote. Majority wins. I vote no. You vote yes; Francis, what do you say?" Marlow looked to Nolan with pleading eyes thinking, *"Do the right thing, boy."* The room was silent. Even Jefferson had finally stopped selling.

"Bob, I loved my dad, but his ways were the old ways. He even told me that he was sick of sucking up to aldermen and the mayor for city jobs. They always had their hand out. Surely this Simpson fellow can't be any worse. I trust Vance to protect our interests. And it is a great project. And I get to design it. So, I say yes, let's turn this big ship in a different direction."

Marlow slowly got up. He had won on two out of three points. That wasn't bad. Jefferson would be held in check. And he wasn't stamping any documents until the firm got paid. And what did he expect when Jefferson said that he'd be sure Junior's design won? The boy probably creamed in his pants hearing that.

"Okay, that's it. But I'd like to know how the errors and omissions numbers work out, and about our line of credit. In the meantime, I'll quit thinking about my Christmas bonus. We'll need it to pay salaries." Marlow walked out the door thinking that today would be a good day for his friend Evan Williams.

CHAPTER 30

The dean's offices along with the faculty offices were located in the in-fill space below the cascading trays of design studios that were bathed in daylight from the many skylights. By contrast, the Graduate School of Design professors' and administrators' offices were rather dark, and looked out to a courtyard that was more concrete than trees and plants.

Connor gingerly opened the oak and glass door and entered a large reception area with some fairly comfortable Knoll chairs. He sat down just as the dean walked in.

"Ah, Mr. West, the prodigal son has returned!" Dean Kilbridge extended his large hand and shook Connor's vigorously. "Very unfortunate timing about your father's passing. Just before graduation. A shame, a real shame. Come on back." The dean was wearing a summery seersucker sport coat, dark blue slacks and a blue polka dot bow tie. Always representing. An unlit pipe was held loosely from his mouth. If he had a boater hat, it would have completed the ensemble perfectly.

"Sit down, sit down. Goodness, you look tired, boy."

"I worked on my thesis all night, until I fell asleep, and I have a lot on my mind. Look, I'm sorry my thesis isn't done. I lost time interviewing for a job in Chicago, and then my Dad died. And thanks for the extension. I can really use it. Except…"

"Except what?" He knew what his young charge was going to say.

"Except, if I take the two-week extension, I'll lose the job offer I got in Chicago. They want me there immediately."

"Connor, you know the requirements for a master's degree are quite clear. The Curriculum Vitae states exactly what needs to be presented for the design portion of your thesis. It includes completed drawings and a model. You have neither."

"I know, I know. I could put off Nolan Jefferson and Marlow for a few days, work this weekend, but by the time I pack and get to Chicago, it will be a week or more."

"What's so special about this offer in Chicago? I'd imagined you'd go to New York and hitch your star to a firm there. Of which there are many."

Connor's temper flared.

"$25,000 a year salary, that's what's so special! And I'm sick of New York City. I'm sick of living in a tenement. I fucking hate New York! It has nothing but bad memories for me. And I'm sick of people giving me advice who think they know me." His voice continued to rise and all the hurt and anger were now coming out in his state of exhaustion. "I'm not going to New York. Forget it. Fuck this place. Fuck architecture!"

From the reception area the secretary turned her head.

"Connor, please calm down," Kilbridge raised his hand, then slowly lowered it.

Connor hung his head. A job in Newark, New Jersey wouldn't be so bad after this disastrous meeting. He slowly raised his head and found that the dean was smiling.

"Sullivan, I wouldn't turn down twenty-five grand a year either! And Vance Jefferson was terribly impressed with your work. Yes, he called me. We're old friends, you know. Used to work together at one of the big New York firms too. Frankly, I hated it. I couldn't wait to get back to New Hampshire. Anyway, he told me about a terrific project they want you to work on. I'm envious really. So that brings us to the unfinished thesis. What do you have left to do?"

Connor tried to regain his composure, wanting to apologize.

"Two elevations, a section and the main model. The surrounding buildings are done. Look, I'm sorry I lost my temper..."

The dean ignored the last remark. "You know the distinguished jury we assembled this year was really looking forward to seeing a different Boston City Hall design than the brutal piece of crap that was built."

Connor was taken aback. Usually college professors were very deferential toward their fellow colleagues in the profession.

"Well, sir, it isn't that bad. Maybe it's a little...complex. Hard."

"Hard indeed. Anyway, so after all the presentations were done and the whole class had passed, three of the jury was staying overnight because they are from out of town."

"Yes…"

"And since it was too early for cocktails, I asked them to come up to the rarefied air of Tray Five and check out your Boston City Hall design. There was plenty to look at, lots of preliminary drawings, no final model, though the earlier mass model sufficed. They were impressed. Very impressed."

"Thank you. But it's still not done."

"Connor, great buildings are really never done. They just have to be built, flaws and all. And doing great architecture takes time. More time than a mere semester. We here at the Graduate School have guided you all we can. Hell, you've even taught us a little about design."

Connor's heart was racing. He liked where this might be going but he held back. He did not, could not, take any more disappointment.

"Connor, I polled this mini-jury. I told them of the requirements for graduation. They all agreed you had met them hand over fist. Congratulations!"

Dean Kilbridge reached back to his credenza and fixed his hands on a leather-bound folder with the Harvard crest embossed on it. He turned around and stood. Connor did as well, not knowing why, but because his dean had.

"Connor Jones West, as the Dean of Harvard University's Graduate School of Design, I award you the degree of Master of Architecture, *Magna Cum Laude*. Now get your ass to Chicago and never look back. And make us proud!" He handed the prized degree to Connor. Tears were streaming down the young man's face. He shook the dean's hand and turned to leave. In the reception area, the staff and faculty were applauding and cheering.

PART TWO

THE DESIGN
MAY 1973

CHAPTER 31

Bob Marlow looked out to the vast drafting room from his office, steaming coffee mug in hand. Unlike usual Mondays, there seemed to be a sense of excitement in the air—a new optimism. Perhaps he had been wrong about the new project. It had definitely given the firm a renewed energy. There was no denying that this seventy-five-story building was the largest commission the firm had landed in a long time. In addition, it was a new type of building, a mixed-use project, heretofore only discussed in trade journals and talked about by visionaries like Buckminster Fuller.

"A city within a city," Marlow muttered. "Catchy and challenging. Three weeks to design it. Well, good luck…" He looked down at the detailed program that had been handed out to the three design teams. Vance had drawn it up in the face of Steel Simpson's unwillingness, or more likely, inability to develop one. Once again, the architect was doing the client's work without remuneration. Simpson had endorsed and praised the effort, silently worrying that indeed he had bitten off more than he could chew. The document was over twenty pages long.

Each team had twelve to fifteen professionals assigned to it, from the principal-in-charge down to intern draftsmen. Each team was given a model-making crew and rendering artist from that in-house department. Jefferson would eventually augment those people with independent contract labor during the final week of the "charette," as time-based design competitions were known as in the profession. The volume of work to be accomplished in such a short period of time demanded it.

The presentations were scheduled for June 12th. That allowed 25 business days, or more importantly, 33 non-stop workdays including weekends and holidays, to complete the effort. One thing was certain; no one would be grilling out this Memorial Day weekend. From his vantage point in the center of the activity, he saw desks being rearranged for the teams and temporary partitions set up defining those areas. Structural engineers and mechanical engineers had moved into the room from the eleventh floor to be with their assigned teams. Old rolls of drawings and specifications were being tossed into trash dollies. The soft, vinyl tops and parallel bars of the large drafting tables were being cleaned with Bab-O cleanser for the effort to come.

"Well, we were long overdue for a cleanup. This place was starting to become a dump," Marlow thought to himself. He took a final gulp on his coffee; and felt pretty clear headed on this Monday. He'd worked out at the gym, jogged, and stayed off the sauce over the weekend. There was a knock on the glass of his open door.

"Mr. Marlow…"

"Connor, you made it. Come on in. Here, sit down." Bob made space in one of his conference chairs by tossing several specification books into a trash bin right outside his office. It was a nod from Jefferson that Marlow's office could use a little cleanup too. "How was the trip? When did you get here?"

"On Saturday. I graduated last Tuesday."

"Wow. Your mother and dad must have been proud seeing you in that cap and gown. I know mine were. They expected me to get my GED in prison." He shook his head and laughed.

"Actually, the dean gave it to me in his office. I missed the ceremony by a week. My dad died just before graduation. I never finished my thesis."

"Really? I'm so sorry." Marlow hoped this new employee had a permanent diploma. "You don't need to go back and finish the thesis, do you? Any family business to take care of?"

"No, not at all. Mr. Jefferson called Dean Kilbridge. They knew each other. He kind of greased the skids for me. Anyway, the school decided I had done enough work to show my competence. And my dad owned nothing, so I'm all yours."

"Wow. Okay. Can I get you a coffee? I was just pouring some myself. And when you're working, feel free to come in here and use the pot. The vending machine stuff sucks."

"Yes, that would be great. I like coffee in the morning. What's all the activity?"

Marlow found a clean Chicago Cubs mug and poured a cup. Connor added an ample amount of creamer and several sugars, and Marlow shook his head. *"Kids,"* he thought, *"always trying to make cappuccino."*

"Yes, we have a lot to tell you about. But first, where are you staying? I have a couch in my apartment…"

"Thanks, but I'm staying with a cousin up around Sandburg Village." In fact, he was sleeping on Marilyn's sofa. But conscious of their relationship, and the office policy, he acted like he hardly knew her when she pointed him in the direction of Bob Marlow's office.

"That's convenient. I hope your cousin is okay with a house guest for three weeks. We're going to keep you pretty busy. You won't have time to go apartment hunting."

"I'm sure sh…he'll be fine with it. By the way, where do I sit?"

"Oh yes, your assigned space. See that open area over there, where they're rearranging those tables? Between the two large screens. That larger area, with a desk and three drafting tables. That's where you'll work. Pick any drafting table."

"Seriously? Don't I belong on a lower floor?"

"No, you're with team number three, the team I head up. You're one of my three assistant designers."

"Me? A designer? Really? For what?"

"Yes really. Seems like Mr. Jefferson was pretty impressed with your stuff, as I was. We need talent and he has assigned you to work on one of three teams for this project. We're doing an in-house competition." Marlow tossed the program in Connor's lap.

Connor looked at the title page: "Chicago World Tower, A Vertically Integrated Mixed-Use Development." He read it again. He didn't even know what it meant. Connor's head was swimming. "Sir, excuse me, but I just graduated. I thought I'd be doing roof details or something like that. I'm a designer right away? But…"

"Look, just treat this like a design charette. You'll work under a great guy, Leo Skoroshod. He's the lead designer. Anyway, they're not going to pick our design. In fact, Mr. Jefferson is going to steer the client toward another team's solution. But it will be good practice for you. And fun. You'll be working with about ten, eleven people. As one of Leo's assistants, and with such a big building, they'll be lots to do. But we have to be done June 12th."

West stared into the vast drafting room. He felt a rumbling in his stomach; his mouth was dry. "Wow, okay then!"

"Just keep your head down and do what Leo wants. Connor listen, you remind me of myself when I was young. You're talented. You just lack confidence in your abilities. But they're there. This will give you a chance to bring them to the forefront. And remember, I'll have your back. Look, when these thirty-three days are done and the presentations are complete, I'll give you a long weekend to find an apartment and get settled."

"Thank you, sir," Connor responded taking a deep breath, "I appreciate that."

"No 'sirs' around here; just call me Bob. Oh, and one other thing. You ought to know that no one has a bigger ego than an architect. The two other designers working with you—they've worked for the firm oh, about two, three years now. Dan Caudy and Will Taubert. They're good, they're competent and they're ambitious."

"Yes and…" West sensed there was more.

"They would rightfully be very upset if they had to work on an equal footing with someone who just graduated. I told them you had three years' experience in New York working for Philip Johnson. So just go along with this little…fabrication. It will make for a calmer team dynamic."

Connor felt a knot in his stomach. His architectural career was starting out with a bang. First, he would be way over his head with this design, which looked daunting as he flipped through the program. And now he had to live a lie. Two, in fact, his work background and his new girlfriend. He finished his coffee, stood up, and headed to his new office.

"I guess I'd better get to work reading this."

"Wait up," Bob said catching up to Connor. "Let me introduce you around and help you get supplies. I've called a Team Meeting at 2 P.M. to discuss Chicago World Tower; and I'm buying lunch today."

"Thanks, but if you don't mind, I'd like to skip the lunch. Can I see you at the meeting?"

"Fine. Rain-check then."

The two o'clock meeting took place in an enclosed conference room on the twelfth floor, called ironically "The Sullivan Room." On its walls were old photos of the great Chicago buildings designed by Louis Sullivan, the first American architect to eschew the Classical and Beaux Arts styles in favor of "New" American architecture. The conference table was old but perfectly maintained in a rich, red mahogany. The chairs were a nod to the contemporary, designed by a trend-setting furniture manufacturer from Zeeland, Michigan, by the name of Herman Miller.

Team Three consisted of twelve individuals. There were welcomes all around for the new face, some genuine, others like Taubert, reserved and standoffish. West held his head high and decided that the best way to start his first day at Nolan Jefferson and Marlow was to adopt what Robert Tomlinson once told him: "Fake it 'till you make it, Sullivan."

"I see Mr. Jefferson took my advice. He hires you. Good. Very good." Jerzy Stanizski had put his hand on Connor's shoulder and squeezed slightly. Connor turned and the head of the structural department was smiling.

"Mister...ah, Mister..."

"Just call me Jerzy. Welcome to firm. I know very well you will design great buildings here!"

"I hope to. It's pretty daunting, this project…"

"Follow Leo. Even though he is Russian Communist, he help you. Very good designer."

"I am not Communist. You should go back to Poland, my friend. They need you there to design structure for Soviet style buildings!" Leo Skoroshod had come up to the two with his hand open. "Welcome to American sweat shop. I am Leo."

Connor shook Leo's hand and it was like a vise, the grip lasting for five full seconds, followed by a bear hug.

"We make a good team, I know. I should like to see your portfolio. Jefferson has told me it is impressive. I would have like to been there at interview, but instead, you got little Francis."

"Actually, he left for a marketing meeting." Connor was maintaining his composure but barely.

Leo shot a look at Jerzy. "Yes, marketing meeting, I am sure. But he is lead designer on Team One. We must out-design him. So, tell me…"

"Gentlemen, please sit, let's get this show started." Bob Marlow had entered the room and taken immediate command, avoiding small talk with anyone to avoid the appearance of having a favorite. In no particular order, Team Three sat down.

"Once again, Vance Jefferson has not only pulled a rabbit out of the hat, but a very big rabbit. And instead of NJM creating one design, we have to do three. Fair enough. However, this team gets to do one, and I can assure you it will be the best one!" There was a chorus of cheers and "damn right" along with hands pounding on the table. Once again, Marlow had to admit to himself that this in-house design charette might be a good morale booster for the firm in the wake of Mr. Nolan's death, and so many dull civic projects. Even he was getting tired of parking garages and vast boxes called convention centers.

"I want to introduce everyone to Connor West who joins us today by way of New York and will be one of the designers on this project.

He comes to us with a great resumé, a Harvard diploma, and I hope you'll all afford him the utmost courtesy and assistance." Marlow directed his gaze to Taubert, who glared back; he had kept the introduction vague so no one would quiz his new charge too much. The message was: "He's here. Deal with it."

The meeting began with an in-depth review of the program, specifically the site and the sub-surface conditions. It was established that the structure of the building was paramount, as it had to address a substantial underground stream beneath the property. The next issue was the range of uses, stacked one on top of the other, all with a different bay spacing: that is, the distance from support column to support column. In order to make it work, some uses would have to adapt to less than ideal column spacing. Lastly was the sheer size of the project and the workload required to design it within 33 days. Marlow's budget was one-third of the total fee less profit margin or $60,000. In order to stretch the funds, he told half the crew to go back to their regular projects for a week and a half. He only needed designers and structural on the project now.

As Team Three left the conference room, full of enthusiasm and excitement, Will Taubert bumped up against Connor West.

"So how many seventy-five story buildings have you designed, Harvard boy?"

CHAPTER 32

Connor turned the key to Marilyn's apartment door. It was 8:30 P.M. and his first day was finally over. He wanted a cold beer, maybe two.

Marilyn heard the door open and rushed to greet him. She was wearing a Chicago Bears' jersey and cutoff jean shorts. She hugged him and gave him a kiss, and then she slapped him hard on his ass. Jane, her roommate, was reading in the living room and tried to ignore the encounter.

"That's for pretending you didn't know me today, Mr. Big Shot Designer!"

"Ouch, that hurt!" Connor responded smiling. "Hey, I just don't want you to get in trouble by dating a fellow employee. Believe me, if I could have, I'd have kissed you!"

"I bet you would have. And then your tenure at Nolan, Jefferson and Marlow would have been pretty short-lived. Well, maybe not, you're going to be busy."

While Marilyn's job had little to do with the design competition, Vance Jefferson was one of the three principals in the firm and she knew a lot about everything. In return for her lowly salary of $8,500 a year, she kept regular hours from eight to five; for more than forty hours per week, she was paid time and a half, an extra cost NJ&M preferred not to incur. Jane by contrast had attended Loyola University School of Nursing and was a registered nurse. Her job at Rush Presbyterian Hospital on the maternity floors paid $15,000 a year, shockingly low for having spent four years in a tough curriculum and two years as an intern. But such was the fate of educated women in 1973.

"Yeah, I've got a shit...I mean a boatload of work to do. The program for the project I'm assigned to is unbelievable." Connor slung off his backpack and threw it down on the couch, immediately following it in feigned exhaustion. He pulled off his new, dark red Rooster tie from his new, white button-down Oxford shirt. New dark blue khaki pants and a pair of new Thom McAn loafers finished the post-grad look.

"Mr. Jefferson calls it a mixed-use complex. I did the proposal on it. The fee is enormous. I worked on the contract today. He wants it to be ironclad. It's all very exciting. I don't think I've seen morale so high around the office. There was even an article today in the *Sun-Times* about the project and our getting the commission. Mr. Jefferson was taking congratulatory calls all day."

"Good for him. But I'm beat…and hungry."

"I saved you some dinner. I made a chicken casserole."

Jane put her book down and joined in the conversation with the new roommate. She did like Connor, though not necessarily enough for him to stay with them for any length of time. "It's really pretty good, Connor. I've been giving Marilyn lessons and she learns fast. She'll make a good wife someday." Marilyn shot an "asshole" glance at Jane, who smiled broadly. Connor pretended to ignore the remark, but he had heard it loud and clear.

"Right now, Ramen noodles would be great. I'm starved." He got off the couch and sat down at the second-hand Danish modern dining table. He was about to ask if there was any beer, though he knew there was from his early morning reconnaissance of the fridge. Marilyn placed a cold Pabst Blue Ribbon in front of him.

"A PBR! Such service! I could get used to this." Now Jane shot an *"I hope not"* look to Marilyn.

"My pleasure, Mr. Intern Designer. I'm warming up the food. I didn't expect you so late."

"Sorry, I should have called. I had to read the program, and then there were meetings, forms to complete, and I was taken around and introduced to everyone. I'm one of the three assistant designers on our team."

Jane looked up from her book again." Sounds pretty cool for someone right out of college. After I graduated, I was changing bed pans for three months."

"I know. I don't understand it. I've never done a hotel or an office building, or any other of the building's components for that matter." He took a long pull on his beer and remembered when he left this morning that there were only two left. He hoped that Jane had not drunk the other one.

"He picked you because you are very talented, Connor. I told you what he said. He had never seen such design maturity in a young man. Plus, there's a whole team, right? You have help, don't you?"

"That's another thing. Bob Marlow inflated my resumé telling the two designers with me that I had three years' experience already. I'm living a lie! Anyway, a lot of good it did. This guy, Will Taubert, already has a big chip on his shoulder. He asked me how many seventy-five-story buildings I've designed."

"And what did you tell him?"

"I said four or five, I'd lost count, and he walked away. The other designer, Caudy, laughed. I don't think he cares that I'm new. I thought I smelled some weed on him. So, I've got an asshole and a pothead working with me. And we have 33 days to pull a rabbit out of our collective ass!"

Jane interjected, becoming more interested in the conversation. "You should try to pull a baby out of that ass sometime, Connor."

"Jane! That's gross!" laughed Marilyn. She placed her casserole in front of Connor, complete with peas, carrots and a salad. She went back to the refrigerator and got the last beer.

"I'll go out after dinner and get some more beer. Oh, and look what I pulled off the bulletin board in the lobby: "Studio Apartment—furnished, six-month sublease available, 1350 Sandburg Village, Unit 1010, call LP5-6944. That's the 10th floor, right?"

"That building is just up the street from this one," Jane remarked.

He looked at Marilyn and Jane. "What do you think the rent would be?"

"Well, we pay almost $300—$295 to be exact for two bedrooms and Molly, a friend of ours, has a one bedroom, and it's on the third floor. I think she pays $165. And the higher the floor, the higher the rent. Ours should really be $320 but I kind of sweet-talked the rental agent," said Marilyn.

"She means she dated the rental agent for a month after we got the apartment."

"Jane, shut your mouth! Connor, I don't know, maybe $175?" She was thinking that this could be the perfect arrangement for them. "You can afford that, you make…well, you can afford $175?"

"Give me the phone, please." There was an edge to his voice. He was really unhappy that Marilyn knew so much about his hiring at NJ&M, particularly his salary. Marilyn got the phone off the end table; it had a twenty-foot cord so it could reach to either bedroom. He dialed the number; it rang just two times.

"Hi, hello. I'm inquiring about your ad on the bulletin board about the six-month sublease." Connor listened intently. "Right, well, I just moved to Chicago. I'm an architect working at Nolan, Jefferson and Marlow. Can I ask how much is the rent?" Again, the other party prattled on, and Connor seemed to be deflated.

"Would you accept less? I promise I'll take good care of the place." Pause. "I see." Pause.

Marilyn was hanging on every word of the one-sided conversation and by his tone and look on Connor's face, she was seeing this apartment wasn't going to be an option.

"OK, can I come by and see it tonight? I know it's late, but I really need a place." Long pause. "OK, great. Yeah, I'll see you shortly. Bye." West put the receiver down. He looked up at the two girls.

"He wants $185 because it's furnished. But he said he might reduce it if he feels I'll take good care of the place. I better get over there and see it. It's already 10 P.M. Look, don't wait up for me. I might take a walk around the neighborhood to get some more beer and clear my head. It's just a lot to deal with."

He came back to the apartment around midnight. Connor needed sleep. He looked over to the couch and then Marilyn's door. He paused. He went through the bedroom door and stripped to his boxers and slid under the covers. He put his arms around Marilyn. She woke and squeezed his hand. He whispered. "$165 a month and he'll pay the electric. I can move in this Saturday."

Marilyn turned and kissed him. "You're my golden boy."

"Nice view, too."

"Hush. Get some sleep."

CHAPTER 33

Once Connor West had read and re-read the building program document, committing much of it to memory, he and the rest of the team were at a standstill waiting on Leo to come up with some great vision about what form Chicago World Tower should take. The program was just facts. There was no concept, no grand idea of what the project in its physical form might take. For this, they waited on Leo, who seated in a corner work area, puffed on his pipe and looked at the walls and ceiling for some great inspiration that would blind him in a brilliant ray of light from on high. West decided to stop waiting and come up with his own ideas, but foot after foot of bumwad tracing paper lying on the floor proved that he was no more successful than his supervisor.

As the week wound to a close, West just wanted to get to Saturday and move into his subleased apartment. He couldn't believe his good fortune. While the studio apartment was small, it was actually larger than his garret apartment in Cambridge, and it was new and modern, and it had an awesome view of the North Shore, looking over Lincoln Park and the lake beyond. And best of all, he was around the corner from Marilyn. He hoped she might sleep over on Saturday, and he even planned to buy a bottle of champagne to toast his new digs.

"How it is coming along, Mr. Connor?" West turned and knew it was Jerzy Stanizski by his distinctive accent.

"It's a little slow. We are all still waiting for Leo to come up with the grand design," nodding his head toward Leo, who looked like he was now in a deep trance.

"Ah, Leo. Good designer, but, well, not the fastest. I am surprised they pick him for such a charette. I think he dreams too much of Mother Russia!"

"I'm not doing much better. Look at the floor," pointing to the reams of bumwad at his feet.

"It is beautiful day. We should take a walk outside."

"Walk, but I can't do that..." Connor never assumed he could just leave his desk during work hours.

"Why not? You big shot designer. You do what you want. You think they are going to fire you? They need you, especially once Leo gets his big concept."

"All right then. And where are we going?"

"To learn about structure."

Out of the building Jerzy hailed a cab and told the driver to go to the marina. The day was picture perfect, a deep azure sky with light puffs of clouds. The temperature was in the high seventies. Connor momentarily thought that he would have enjoyed an outdoor job better.

Soon the two were strolling along the esplanade by hundreds of boats gently bobbing in the water. Their masts, some as many as two or even three on the larger yachts, were great cantilevers into the sky, soaring thirty to almost fifty feet high.

"Someone once told me sailboat is a perfect structure. Turn around and look at buildings in the city. They are just boring framework of many columns and beams. But sailboat has but one column, the mast they call it. From the mast hang the sails that make the boat go through water. It is simple. And this great mast is anchored inside boat to what is called a tabernacle. Interesting term. Then there are only slim ropes or wires from hull to top keeping it secure. Is really amazing, and has worked for hundreds of years."

"I guess I never thought of structures in that way. I only considered structure in the framework of buildings. I never really enjoyed structures class..."

"Oh no, Jones, look at seagull flying there. Its body and wings are perfect structure, too. The trees over there are structural perfection. Just like sailboat. One trunk, one mast, with branches or sails coming off of it. Have you ever been to Barcelona?"

"Yes, while I backpacked through Europe."

"Did you see Gaudi's cathedral?" referring to La Sagrada Familia.

"I did. That's right! He made all the columns look like trees and the tree canopy was the roof."

"Yes! As I say, everything in life is structure."

"And what kind of structure do you plan for Chicago World Tower, especially with the underground conditions, the water?"

"First, we wait on Leo. But water is not a problem. Everyone thinks it is when water is on land. But I know very well that when you build a bridge, you must build it over water, through water. And I think there are many bridges in the world, right?"

"True. I never thought of that. I read the geo-technical report and just assumed we had to deal with it; either build around it or move it."

"We may do either, but I think we must make the land do what we want it to do. We are architect, right? Anyway, we should get back. Yes, sailboat. A perfect structure. And I have secret…what I just tell you was not my thought. Mr. Nolan told me that. I had never thought of it before. But now you learned what I learned from him."

As they headed back to the offices, this time on foot, Connor's mind suddenly began to race. At the entrance to the Santa Fe Building, he turned to Jerzy.

"Tell Marlow or whoever inquires about where I am that I went to the library."

"Library? Fine, but why?"

"Just tell them if anyone wants to know."

Connor walked north up Michigan Avenue. The main branch of the Chicago Library was just two blocks away. He walked briskly with a sense of excitement, as if on a scavenger hunt looking for treasure. He walked through the door into a massive two-story lobby where there was a round desk about twenty feet in diameter. There were several matronly looking ladies, hair up in buns, wearing the most modest dresses conceivable.

"Excuse me, where can I find books on sailing ships?

When Jerzy returned to the twelfth floor, he saw that Leo was in an animated conversation with Vance Jefferson.

"Skoroshod, you mean to tell me that a whole week has gone by and you have done nothing. Nothing other than blowing smoke rings?" Jefferson was quite upset.

"I have ideas in head. Will put on paper soon," but it was unconvincing. In fact, Leo had nothing.

"Leo, I hired you. I gave you a chance. And now you have an opportunity to be the designer of Chicago's tallest building. Quit doing whatever it is you're not doing, and fucking get me a design! We have three weeks left and one of those has to be for asses and elbows drafting it. I promised the client three designs. Understand?"

"Yes, boss. I am very sorry. I just have many troubles on my mind."

"You'll have more if I don't see something Tuesday morning." Jefferson turned and headed toward Bob Marlow's office. Maybe he needed to kick a little ass there as well.

"Connor? Earth to Connor?"

West was staring out the window of Maison Michele looking into space. He looked at Marilyn. "I'm sorry. Where were we?"

"Is everything OK? You're not yourself tonight. Can we order now?" Marilyn was perplexed. Her boyfriend was becoming an enigma.

"Sure. I'm sorry. It's not you. I think I have an idea for the project, but I'm not the lead designer, and I'm tired of waiting for Leo to come up with something. I think that after I sign the sublease tomorrow, I'll go to the office. Until I do, I won't know if my idea works. Then tomorrow night, I was hoping you'd come to my place and we'll order Chinese and celebrate my new home with some champagne."

Marilyn grabbed Connor's hand and smiled broadly. "Oh, I can't wait to see it. Is it nicely furnished?"

"A lot nicer than I could have done. I'd have concrete blocks and two by twelve's for shelving!"

"Tell me about the design idea you have."

"No."

"No! Why not?"

"Because I'm an architect. I'll draw it for you." Connor smiled and reached for his newly purchased Mont Blanc pen. All designers at NJ&M carried them as a badge of distinction and as an indication that they were, indeed, designers. It had cost him over thirty dollars but was worth it. He reached for a large paper napkin and unfolded it. And he began to sketch. Marilyn looked on silently in awe. Poor or not, she was falling in love with this handsome and talented young designer.

CHAPTER 34

Irving Montlick slid the document across his desk to Steel Simpson. It read: "Demand for Relief and Summary Judgment."

"Just give me the Cliff Notes," Steel Simpson said to his lawyer, annoyed that his attorney expected him to read this legal jargon.

"We go to court and ask a judge, based on your contention that you were denied pertinent information on the land, that you deserve relief in the amount of $500,000. If he agrees, it is so."

"I wanted one million."

"Yeah, and pigs can fly. You'll be lucky to get half that."

"When can you submit it? When can I get my relief and then close on the land?"

"That's the problem. First of all, there is the matter of your contention that you were not given the information on the underground conditions, the river, as you refer to it. You were given the information at the time the offering was made available. CC&B have a signed record of you picking all the documents up. Second, I reviewed the soils report, and the offering. Both speak to the sub-surface conditions, referring to the water as a series of underground tributaries that are part of the Lake Michigan aquifer, creating an unusual amount of groundwater and subsequent soil instability."

"So? What else?"

"Then there is the language in the bid documents about pending legal actions against Chicago Canal & Bridge. If there are any pending, current or past legal actions by an Offeree, that's you, against the Offeror, that's CC&B, then the Offeree is barred from bidding on the land. Since you still have not closed on the land as of yet, if you were to submit this motion to the court, you would be creating a pending legal action against CC&B, and your bid would automatically become null and void."

"But I have the high bid by a half million."

"That's right, and if you want the land, it needs to stay that way and no lawsuit. And when I talked to Tommy Byrne, he said he really hoped you'd sue them because then they could get every developer in town to bid on the land. Byrne figured the bids would exceed five, maybe six million dollars this time."

"They can't do that."

"They can and they will. He said the board was mighty pissed about your arm twisting everybody in town, telling them it was your deal, and threatening legal action. That's restraint of trade and maybe blackmail in their eyes and he told me the Board thought long and hard about suing you over it. It was only those 'enjoyable sails on the lake' that had him and others vote against such an action."

"You see, I knew it would help me get the land." Simpson said slumping in his chair. "And I've got pictures of Byrne with a Negro hooker."

"Well, you can burn them."

"Those rich bastards."

"Steel, I'm not a magician, or a miracle worker. I'll do your dirty work because it pays well, but I don't appreciate my clients lying to me. You had the Offering in your hands, because you couldn't make the offer without it. You had the soils report. You had a survey of the land. If you had spent any time there you couldn't miss the streams of water seeping through the concrete abutment by the river. I'm a lawyer, not a developer, and I saw the water."

"You checked out the property for this suit?"

"I do my homework, which is more than you did. And what about the burnt out remains of the shanty town that was there? If you had anything to do with that, find another lawyer. I'm not a criminal defense attorney whose clients commit arson."

"I had nothing to do with that. It was just a coincidence. The bums there must have started it themselves."

"That's not what Inspector O'Rourke seems to think." Montlick looked Simpson directly in the eye, but Simpson was brushing lint off his sport coat.

"Now, if we're done here, I can arrange the closing on this land for $3,000,000 cash to take place in two weeks, or per Tommy Byrne, CC&B will declare your offer null and void and proceed to re-bid it."

Steel Simpson slowly got up out of the chair and turned toward the door. "Fine. Do it and fuck them…"

Montlick smiled. His fee for the closing would be $50,000.

"See you at the closing, Steel."

Simpson cabbed it back to his office. Sitting down at his desk, he loosened his gold paisley tie, staring into space, when Ruth buzzed him.

"Mr. Simpson, the mayor is on the phone for you."

Simpson thought: *"Good, maybe Big Jack can help me with the price of the land."*

"Mr. Mayor, Jack, to what do I owe the pleasure? Say, we need to have lunch this week. I'm having a little trouble with Chicago Canal & Bridge on the land price."

"Steel, I don't know what you're talking about. Your three million bid was a binding offer and it's a steal. And I'm not doing any more than I've done already. If it wasn't for me withdrawing the City's lawsuit, you'd have nothing but your dick in your hand."

"I know, Jack, and I appreciate that but…."

"But nothing. Listen to me, Simpson. I understand there is supposed to be a closing in two weeks. If you're smart, close and you'll own the land, and our business will be concluded. So, who is your lawyer anyway?"

"Irving Montlick. Why"

"Fine, he's going to get a call from Belmont Real Estate Sales. They represent the buyer, that's you, on the transaction. They made the deal happen. Their fee is a typical 10% on a land sale. I think if I'm doing the math right, that's three hundred thousand bucks."

"What are you talking about? There were no real estate agents involved. It was a sealed bid!" Simpson's temper was rising.

"Yeah, but they counseled you on the proper amount to bid; hell, they even told you the land would be for sale. So, they get a ten percent fee."

"I don't even know who they are."

"You will at closing."

"Oh, I see. Yeah, I see. Look, maybe you deserve fifty grand for your fucking greasing the skids. But not three hundred k…"

"Me? Steel, I get nothing. I'm happy to have helped. The commission goes to Belmont Real Estate. What happens after that, I've not a clue."

"You miserable S-O-B!"

"Be careful, Steel. You're talking to the mayor of Chicago. One call and they'll be a shanty town back on that property and another eminent domain suit brought by the City. Now I'm hanging up before I get pissed. But we should sail sometime. Goodbye." Jack Malone hung up the phone.

"But Jack, Mr. Mayor. Look…" Simpson realized the phone was dead. Now he needed to borrow $3,300,000. The hill he had to climb was getting steeper by the hour.

Steel Simpson's favorite restaurant for lunch was Johnny Lattner's Steakhouse because it exuded old Chicago class with white tablecloths and black jacketed waiters, but mostly because it was an elevator ride away from his offices in the Wrigley Building, and only a short walk along the river to Marina City where it was located. Tiered seating, and large picture windows gave everyone good views of the river and its many tour boats. He entered the restaurant, nodding toward his banker Brad Wentworth, who had already arrived

"Brad, you beat me. Good to see you." Simpson hated being the last to arrive but slid into the opposite side of the black leather banquette. A waiter quickly appeared.

"Welcome. May I get you a cocktail?"

"Sure. Brad, what are you having?"

"Iced tea, the drink of bankers."

"Beefeater martini, please, up and cold. Olives." He didn't need to make an impression on Wentworth. He had already borrowed a fortune from him.

"Right away, sir." The waiter headed toward the bar.

"Didn't we just see each other a week or two ago, Steel? My interest is piqued. Another deal?" Brad Wentworth was fishing. And if he couldn't drink, he was ready to eat. While he did business with Steel Simpson, he personally did not like spending time with him. He couldn't put his finger on why. It was just a personal distaste, like drinking cheap Scotch.

"Brad, thanks so much for meeting with me on short notice. I hope you like this place. It's one of my favorites; Johnny and I are good friends."

"I'm sure…"

"Brad, I want to talk with you about getting in on the ground floor of Chicago World Tower."

"I thought I was already in on the ground floor. We've already met and discussed this."

"But I mean being first in line to do the whole deal by way of financing the land."

"I thought you told me you had that covered?"

"I do. I do. But I need to stay liquid and not tie up all my cash now."

"Didn't you say the land was two point five million? That's not a lot of liquid. If you don't have that, you shouldn't be doing a one-hundred-dred-million-dollar project."

"Brad, Brad, of course I have it, but I'm meeting with the Saudis in three weeks and want to present a strong balance sheet to them. Cash is everything to those people."

"Really? Who are you meeting with?"

"None other than Prince Zaidan bin Al Saud in Monaco," said Steel, full of himself.

"Damn! You mean your friend, that classmate from Northwestern?"

"Exactly. His son, and thanks for the tip. And I'm buying lunch."

"You were buying lunch anyway. Let's order. I'm busy. I mean, I'm hungry."

The waiter returned with Simpson's martini and Wentworth ordered fish. *"Typical"* thought the developer, *"ordering fish at a steak restaurant."* He went with a NY strip steak rare and a side of fries.

"You want to finance two-and-a-half-million dollars, is that right? The land is certainly worth that and more, but you need to have skin in the game." Wentworth was skeptical but tried to keep an open mind. If Steel could come up with some strong at-risk equity, he didn't want to lose the construction loan over refusing a chump change land loan.

"Actually, it's now three-and-a-half million. But that includes the preliminary architectural services." Simpson hated to throw out a new, higher number, but Simpson needed what he needed and would eat crow to get it.

"How did it increase by a million?"

"I thought I might get Chicago Canal and Bridge to reduce the cost, but they were adamant that it was going to be $3,000,000. Then there are brokerage fees, closing costs, the design services...."

"Steel, I can't finance design costs on a land deal. All the other stuff maybe, but you know we don't like to do land deals; it will muck up things when you want the big money." Wentworth was going into "back out of the deal" mode.

"Brad, this is going to be the biggest deal of your career. It's a home run, I tell you."

"Look, you got to come out of pocket on the land. Like I said, have some skin in the game. I don't want to own that land or your house in Glencoe."

"OK, I'll handle the fees for NJ&M, but I really need to get this land deal done. CC&B wants to close in two weeks."

"Steel, the best I can do is a letter for the prince expressing our strong interest in doing the debt financing, no commitments you understand, if that will help."

"Sure, that's great. But you've got to do the land loan, too."

"Steel, going to committee on such a small deal will raise all kinds of red flags in our shop. If it's not approved, your chances, our chances, of getting fifty to seventy-five million in debt will be out the window."

"Brad, I need this loan," Simpson said, sounding desperate.

"OK, let me make a call to my dad at First National in Evanston. It's the right size loan for them and in a year, if you have the equity, I'll, I mean First Chicago, will take him out with the construction loan."

"Brad, you are my man with the money."

"My dad's a tough nut, so I'm not promising anything. And it's not going to be one over prime. More like two-and-a-half plus one-and-a-half on the commitment fee. Can you stomach that?"

Simpson was not happy with such terms; that was a lot of baggage. "*Shylock bankers,*" he thought. But he smiled meekly and said, "Brad, work your magic. It sounds like a reasonable deal to me."

Wentworth, worn down from the discussion, relented and ordered a rye and ginger ale.

Brad Wentworth sat down at his desk and wished he had ordered a filet mignon, or whatever was the most expensive item on the menu. Though he had drunk two rye and gingers, his head was clear. He dialed his father's number.

"Hey, Dad, I think I just got you a cherry loan with some big fees attached."

He listened for a minute, nodding his head.

"Yeah, $3,300,000, one-year term, two-and-a-half over prime. Just remember I get half a point on the commitment fee."

He listened for a minute.

"No, not First Chicago. Me. I get the half point." He listened for the response.

"Yeah, now we're on the same page. I'll see you Saturday night."

"Ass-wipe developers," he muttered once he hung up the phone.

CHAPTER 35

Connor was annoyed. He stood on the balcony of his efficiency apartment, looking forward to seeing Marilyn later that evening; they would drink some champagne and toast his new digs. But he really wanted the day off to go shopping for items he wanted for the apartment. Or maybe, head to the grocery store to stock the empty pantry, or run in Lincoln Park. Enjoy his new life in Chicago. Have that Saturday off. No, that wasn't going to happen. His annoyance grew. The intern architect had an idea for a building in his head, and everything was secondary to that. He needed to get the idea down on paper. Not in a notebook with small sketches, but onto large sheets of yellow tracing paper. He had to know if his idea worked. It was like a bad itch you couldn't reach. He knew that the Santa Fe Building was almost as busy on any Saturday as any other day of the week. It was common for people to come in and work, at least a half day. He decided to head to Michigan Avenue immediately, so he could leave by three.

And Marilyn now occupied hours of his thoughts. She was a distraction at this point in his life, a life that was becoming a lot more complicated and stressful than grad school ever was. He threw the books he had borrowed from the public library in his backpack, made sure he had his Mont Blanc pen, and went to the closet to put on a clean shirt. Damn! He still had everything at Marilyn's, packed in three suitcases. He'd call her from the office and arrange to meet her first at three-thirty to move his stuff. It was going to be a busy day.

It was ten-thirty when he sat down at his drafting table in the drafting hall known as the architecture studio. Today it seemed more immense than usual because he was the only one there.

He took out his Mont Blanc pen and opened the book on Man-O-Wars to the page he had dog-eared. He looked at the sails on the main mast. He wrote down on the onion skin paper:

Mainsail = Office
Topsail = Hotel
Top Gallant = Condominium

Then he opened the program and studied the daunting requirements. While Jefferson had the condominiums at the top, he believed that their floors needed to be larger than those of the hotel. He hesitated. He didn't want to change the program from the outset. Then he decided it didn't make any difference. His design would just be his own pipe dream. He put the hotel component at the top.

West sketched a rudimentary diagram: the concept was simple. The building would be like a mast with sails. While most boats at the marina used triangular sails like jibs, old three-masted ships used square or rectangular sails as well. His research at the library was heartening. He found out that, as far back as 1679, sailing vessels had plied the waters of the Great Lakes. He found a lithograph of a three-masted ship docked alongside Navy Pier in the 1800s.

Since this great building would be on the lake, it was a fitting concept; each section would represent a different size sail hanging onto a mast in ascending order. The shape would mimic sails full of air. The building would be an ellipse, the exterior walls convex, bowing out at the center in a gentle curve to the ends of the structure. The short ends of the building, east and west would be slightly concave mimicking the way sails looked in a full wind. Each component of the building, each ellipse, would be smaller than the one beneath it. A wedding cake in a way, but one that mimicked the great sails of old barkentines. The mast of the ship would be the main central core containing the elevators and mechanical rooms. As Connor got more excited about the idea, his grand concept, he scribbled again:

> *The Keel:* *2 levels, delivery, storage, mechanical and service related.*
>
> *The Hull:* *the platform for the building—include 5 levels parking; then 2 levels—great lobbies for each function; the health club; the hotel ballroom and meeting rooms; support retail and restaurants; main entry—7 levels total, maybe 8.*
>
> *Mainsail:* *Office—25 floors, largest size—25,000 SF / floor rented area*
>
> *Topsail:* *Condominium—20 floors plus 1 lobby, say 17,500 SF / floor*
>
> *Top Gallant:* *Hotel—15 floors plus 1 lobby and restaurant / workout / 13,000 SF*
>
> *Crow's Nest:* *Round element. Revolving restaurant and observation deck—2 floors*

> *Total: 71 / 72 floors (will somehow get to 75)*

From this basic division of building components, he could begin to organize the many spaces of the program into a seventy-plus story tower. It was surprisingly easy, having done this through six years of architectural school, both at Pratt and Harvard…second nature, really. Connor decided to start at the top with the hotel. But he had never designed a hotel. He got up and headed for the firm's library located on the fourteenth floor. He hadn't been there before. Jefferson hadn't included it on the tour except in reference as they passed by.

West slowly got the organization of the room down: it was not alphabetical, but historical and by building type. In a far corner he found several books on hotels, but most showcased the behemoths like the Waldorf Astoria in New York. After searching he found a smaller book called *"The New Way to Sleep—Hotels and Motels of the Sixties."*

Connor quickly flipped through the pages. He finally found what he was looking for, a layout of the New York Hilton. Its plan was a simple long rectangle, a single corridor with twenty rooms on each side. In the center was a lobby containing six elevators. Each room contained about 350 square feet. Connor closed the book, clutched it under his arm and went back to the twelfth floor. Sketching freehand on onion skin he began to draw ten modules on each side, 15 feet wide: a total of 150 feet in length. Since his floor would be deeper at the center, he placed the lobby off the corridor with three elevators on one side. He continued drawing and when one sheet got too busy with ideas and conflicting layouts it was ripped off, crumpled and tossed onto the floor, or used it as the basis for his next effort. He would start again, continuing sketching, adding suites; a service elevator; stairs at the end of each hallway for required exiting; alcoves for ice machines; linen closets for daily housekeeping located behind the elevators to mask their noise from guest rooms. By now his reference book was set to the side and unused. He had become a hotel designer in an afternoon.

And on it went. He was tiring now and looked up at the clock on the far wall - 5:15 P.M.!

"Shit! I'm screwed," he said out loud. Not only had it taken him a whole day to just work out one component of this project, and it was still rough, but he had used up the whole day. He ran over to a phone located on one of the columns and dialed Marilyn.

"Hi there."

"Marilyn?"

"Connor, are you OK?" Marilyn answered the phone and seemed not too upset.

"I'm sorry. I got totally caught up in the design for the hotel part of the project. I'm leaving right now. I'll be there at six."

"Why don't I just meet you at the apartment? I've been there all day. Jane and I moved all your stuff. I also did a little decorating and bought you a few things."

"But how did you get in? You don't have a key."

"Remember, I used to date the leasing agent. He told security it was OK to let me in. When I didn't hear from you by 3:30, I assumed you were deep in whatever it is you architects do when you design. And I had no way to get a hold of you, and well...just know that there is cold beer in your fridge and a bottle of champagne as well."

"You're the best! I don't deserve you."

"That's right. You don't. Now get going. I miss you."

Sunday afternoon, Connor stared at the blank sheet of onion skin. He was having trouble concentrating on the tasks at hand. He could not stop thinking about the previous night. Having quickly consumed the bottle of bubbly, Connor went to the package store near the building while Marilyn called in Chinese to be delivered. He bought another bottle, this time Moet, the good stuff, and several bottles of Liebfraumilch wine, and more beer. By the time he returned, Marilyn had the table set on the balcony, and in a short time the food arrived.

Later that evening Marilyn took Connor's hand and led him to the bed. "Nights in White Satin" played low in the background.

Nights in White Satin never reaching an end
Letters I've written never meaning to send...
Cause I love you
Yes, I love you
Oh, how I love you...

And for the first time they made love. Slowly at first, perhaps a little awkward, but with laughter and tenderness, so sweet and deeply felt, finally with excited and lustful passion.

"Do you feel like you just committed a mortal sin?" a spent Connor asked.

"How could that be any sin at all?" Marilyn responded, holding him tightly and caressing his face.

The phone rang in a distant office, shaking him from his dreamy reverie. *"Get to work,"* he thought, wondering if tonight might end in the same result. Anyway, his head hurt from all the booze of the night before, and he had to get a floor of condominiums designed. He got up and went to Bob Marlow's office where he had made a pot of strong coffee. He poured another cup. Returning to his desk he looked again at the book on famous Chicago apartment buildings. He was just trying to get the idea of what a high-rise apartment might need to be like. His own past experience in the public housing of New York was not a great guide. But he had to accept that the layout of what he had grown up in, along with wealthier friends' apartments, larger and smaller, were utilitarian, functional, and surprisingly well designed. They did not have any wasted space, and this made sense to him, no matter what the cost of these palaces in the sky might eventually be.

The program called for each typical floor to have four studios; four one-bedroom units; a single one-bedroom with den; five two-bedrooms; and two three-bedroom units. This would be the case for seventeen of the floors. Then there would be one concierge floor of just ten large units, capped by eight, two-story penthouse units. In addition, a lobby level needed to be designed with an owner's clubroom for parties; two meeting rooms; management offices and a workout center. The program also called for a swimming pool. West's head ached; the coffee pot was dry. He went and got a Coke from the vending machine in the break room and again questioned why he was here working on a Sunday. More to the point, why wasn't Leo? If they were going to have a design, they needed it on Tuesday. Connor labored on.

He arranged his apartments to fit into this great sail form, and he found that they worked very well. The studio units would be lined up two on each side in the deepest part of the footprint of the floor. Next to them on either side the one-bedrooms would be placed, then the two-bedroom units, and finally at the corners, the three-bedrooms. There, the depth of the building was shallow, which allowed a living / dining area with spectacular views to fit perfectly. After about a dozen attempts and refinements, he thought he had the design down. Then he remembered the trash chute. How would he accommodate that? And it needed to send the trash past the office floors!

"Maybe Leo will have an idea," he thought. He laid the final rough plan off to the side. The office tower waited. He had to get that done before heading to Marilyn's. Jane was cooking roast beef with potatoes and carrots and he was bringing red wine. *"Just what I need, more booze,"* he thought as he powered on.

The office portion seemed fairly straightforward. He had to calculate the area of the lowest ellipse so that it contained 25,000 SF of actual office space, but in doing so, he was expanding the office from 500,000 SF to 625,000 SF, a huge increase, but one necessary to make his form work properly. It could be adjusted later, maybe drop back to 20 floors. Twenty floors of office would match the program of 500,000 SF, but then the building would only be 68 floors and the first "sail" would be too short and too fat. After a while he thought he had a reasonable plan.

West placed each individual component on the drafting table. Then he realized that the structural grid for the office could not correspond in any way to what he had laid out for the condominiums and the hotel above it.

"Shit!" His head hurt.

It was obvious that the office had to govern as it was below the two other functions, but only to a point. The column spacing was more flexible, but it had to work for office systems furniture. Every design decision was impacting another previous decision. And whatever the solution, every plan would probably have to be re-drawn. He was drained. He turned off the drafting lamp, put on his coat and headed to the door. "Fuck it!"

As Connor walked outside into the warm spring air, he saw smiling people coming out of the Art Institute, bicycle riders maneuvering around pedestrians, lovers strolling hand in hand along the wide sidewalks. "God, I fucking hate architecture!" He headed for the subway.

CHAPTER 36

It was about 7:30 A.M. on Monday morning, Memorial Day, when Connor, his head a dense fog, walked into the immense drafting hall. Still no Leo.

"We're doomed. No design and mine isn't working." At least his head didn't hurt; he had only two glasses of wine and went home to his studio and slept alone, a deep sleep. Marilyn was disappointed; she asked Connor to take the day off. But somehow, she understood; this design was a chance for Connor to prove himself to the firm.

By 9:00 A.M. there were a handful of people in the room, working in their assigned team spaces trying to ignore the other designs. Connor had hung his sketches and elevations on a large tack wall by his team's work area, and as others passed, they stopped, some nodding approval, others thinking that Leo had worked all weekend. Connor, however, was growing increasingly frustrated. No bay spacing, no module seemed to work; he was getting wrapped around the axle. At this rate, he would have nothing but pipe dreams on Tuesday morning. Then, by chance, he looked toward the main lobby. Leo was coming in to work.

"Mr. West, what is this? Who has done all this? Taubert, Caudy?"

"No. I, I did this…"

"You? You did this?" He walked over to the tack wall and looked at the elevation. There was a large podium drawn and from it a towering building of three ellipses, each smaller than the succeeding one. At the top was a small circle. It was a rough sketch, but beautiful in what it conveyed.

"Explain to me, this concept."

Connor did, just as if he were before a jury in school. The walk by the marina with Jerzy; his idea; the research at the library; the concept of sails and the mast; how he had changed some of the program to make sense with his design; how it was coming together and then seemed to be falling apart. His growing frustration.

"West, is very sound concept; is very strong concept. If concept is strong, it cannot be diminished. You just need a little help. You were not so good in structures, yes?"

"Let's just say it wasn't my favorite class."

"Good, let us begin. Fortunately, I have done structures for many hotels, a few apartments, and of course, many office buildings. And while all are very different, some things are the same. You were correct in doing hotel first. While it seems that in this case tail wags the dog, it is the smallest floor plate and easiest to design because there have to be walls between each room, and that gives opportunity for column. So, hotel has each room thirteen-feet wide with a four-inch wall. Why? You start with bed, right? You have bed on one wall with headboard: that is seven feet. Space in front of bed three-feet-six inches and two people can pass each other. No fights. Then add a dresser, two-feet-six inches. Total equals thirteen feet. Perfect. Module is thirteen feet four inches, which includes dividing wall."

"I was at fourteen or fifteen. Design from the furniture out. I never thought of that." Connor was enjoying the lecture. Leo reminded him of a few of his better professors at Harvard.

"As they say, close but no cigar. Anyway, you rookie; you do fourteen feet, you waste eight inches. Eight inches costs money when building costs $100 a square foot."

"That's true," replied West.

"Now, Connor boy, what is good module for apartment? I tell you. Same as hotel, because most apartments are bedrooms. If you want small bedroom, you add closet. Two-feet-six inches in depth including wall, leaves a nice ten-foot-six bedroom. Also, thirteen feet fine for master bedroom. For living dining room take thirteen feet and double it. Twenty-six feet. Very nice space, very large. Can include living, dining and even maybe kitchen can be part of that space, if necessary. Does not matter.

"So, the ideal module for all three buildings is multiples of thirteen-feet-four inches." Connor might be a rookie, but he was quick to pick up the dictates of real architecture.

"Yes, and that leave office. How many modules is office?"

"Three?"

"Exactly! 40 feet. Is ideal span for concrete with twenty-four-inch-deep beams. Works for new system furniture as well."

The master and apprentice continued on. Both were drawing on the same sheets of paper as they developed the three components again, this time around the forty-foot module.

"What about the other dimension, the interior columns?"

"Ah, the other dimension. Have you laid out parking deck? Whole building must sit on it. A column in the way of where you drive car can be very big problem."

"No, I haven't even gotten to the base."

"Tell me ideal parking bay?"

Connor remembered that he had just been drawing the parking trays underneath the Boston City Hall weeks earlier. "Ideally, double-loaded with two cars and a drive aisle are 60 to 64 feet. The other way, to get three cars between columns you need at least 27 feet clear and then the width of the column, so what—30 feet?"

"Good. We have 40 feet so four cars fit in spaces nine-and-a-half-feet wide. But 60 or 64 feet too long of a span for building above. What is depth of parking space?"

"Twenty feet. Eighteen if things are tight."

"So, as long as column is not beyond 20 feet from outside, we are good. We put first interior column at 12 feet. Most big shot offices are 12 feet wide, anyway."

"Leaving the space between interior columns at 36 feet," Connor was doing the addition in his head.

"Which is good, but 38 feet would be better."

So, it went, the back and forth, the push and pull. But the three-sail concept stayed solid, and it adapted to the changes that Leo and Connor had made.

"Now that parking is figured out, time for you to design the hardest part, the base. All three buildings come together onto one big square. You college boy, figure it out. I will keep working on tower. There are refinements I think to be made. Check back with me in two hours, and we go have lunch."

At his drafting table, invigorated with new enthusiasm and by a new teacher, the apprentice labored over the base. West designed three individual lobbies, each two stories in height, each with its own porte-cochere and access to parking. Using the 40-foot-wide by 12 / 38 foot-long-grid, he laid out tray after tray of parking, and then divided it with walls and ramps for dedicated areas for each component. He needed 800 cars, and his head started to spin with each count. He was short about 75 cars but forged on. The ballroom and meeting room of the hotel along with pre-function areas and large banks of restrooms were next. He located these above the main entry facing south. He reserved the north side, the side facing the river with the best views for the restaurants with support retail, and the health club. He even worked out a rooftop running track for the club, where the joggers could enjoy the view of the river. In all, when complete, the base comprised a total of 10 floors, one more than he had planned on but the parking now exceeded the requirements by 75 cars; he reviewed the program and checked off each required component. He had gotten it all in: the jigsaw puzzle was complete and it seemed to work. He looked at the clock. Leo sauntered over. They had been working four hours straight. He was drained. He looked up at Leo who was standing at his table.

"I am hungry. Let's go eat. I look at this when I come back."

"Leo, did you figure out where to put the pool for the condos?"

"There is pool?"

"Yes, and I couldn't figure out where to locate it. It needs to be outside."

"That is a problem…"

"Your problem. I figured all mine out," West said smiling.

Leo was impressed with the apprentice's growing swagger. "Okay, we do this when we get back. I look at base; fix your mistakes. You look again at tower and get us a pool and a mast."

"Deal. But good luck finding any mistakes," Connor smiled and jabbed Leo in the ribs.

CHAPTER 37

Connor and Leo stayed until 2:00 A.M. Tuesday, working over the evolving and improving design. Connor had called Marilyn and told her not to expect him for dinner. She hung up the phone frustrated, and wished she were dating a teacher.

But it took until midnight for the pool solution to come.

"Leo, I got it!"

Skoroshod sauntered over and looked down at a blank piece of paper. "What? Where is solution?"

West took his pen and slowly drew three ellipses. On one side, all the exterior walls met and aligned at the center. On the other, there was a widened space from the lower, wider ellipse to the smaller ellipse above. In that area, Connor drew a kidney shaped form—the condominium pool. On the other side, where the three ellipses met at the center of their shapes, he drew a circle, along with small circles.

"Voila, the pool! And this circle is the core, at least the elevator core. And these are outside elevators—the apartment elevators and the hotel elevators. Oh, and of course, the observation tower elevators. The office elevators will all be inside the core."

The form, the concept, was complete. Three sails supported by a strong mast of elevators: that mimicked sailors climbing the mast. Each building component set back just like real sails as they diminished in size. Open terraces at the condominium level and the hotel level. All set upon a massive hull or base that, with Leo's experience, had now been improved in ways big and small, but with Connor's basic design intact.

Leo put his arm around Connor. "You have a great design here. It is competition winner."

"But you'll come up with a better idea? This was just my, my student adventure."

"West, this is the design for our team. We do not have time for my design. Anyway, I do not have any idea; at least nothing this good. And time has run out. This is our team solution. Let's go home. I must write letter to my wife in Russia. Is more important to me now than design of building."

"Bob Marlow said they were going to pick Mr. Nolan's design anyway. So, I guess it will be folly in the end. But it was fun. Although my girlfriend is pissed at me working so much."

"She marry architect, she better expect it. So, go home to her."

"No, I think I just want my bed. See you tomorrow."

"Yes, then the dull work begins. Lots of refinements to do. Then presentation. But this is a very good start. I see you tomorrow."

As Connor walked out the building into the cool of the early morning, he thought about the fact that his design would be one of the three used in the competition. He realized then this was why he had become an architect. He smiled as he headed for the subway.

CHAPTER 38

Maurice and Tiny got up early on Friday. They knew what was in store for them if they didn't collect from all their customers this week. They would be in the Hole, a crude cell in the basement of the house on Warren Avenue. Formerly the coal storage area, the space had been enclosed with steel bars and a metal door. It was dark, dirty and damp, and any guest was chained to the walls with handcuffs that made eating or drinking difficult. After a week in the Hole no one disobeyed Tiger Gibson.

Maurice carried a pair of brass knuckles on his hand in case he needed to persuade one of their clientele that paying the protection money was the best way to be protected. From them. Tiny carried a bag of nails tucked into the back of his jeans, worn low to show off his tighty whiteys. They started with the easy customers, black owners who appreciated that they now tithed to a black man, not an Italian mobster. Miss Rene, a fifty-year-old ex-hooker owned a hair styling salon. She hoped to get young Maurice in the back of her shop someday and show him what kind of cougar she was. Next was Ernie's Auto Repair, where the boys hoped to score a hot car some-day. The way Ernie looked at it, the money that went out to Tiger Gibson was the same as the money Tiger paid them to repair and modify the boosted cars that came in every month. He kept all the legit money for himself.

The shoeshine stand was easy, but only yielded about $50. DuP-ree's Florist was easy. Jermaine DuPree was a queer and was scared to death of both the Outfit and the Player's Club. Whoever showed up first, got ten percent of his take, though business was bad lately. Not enough people were dying.

And so it went, up the proverbial ladder from easiest marks to the last businesses where pride, ethnicity, or anger over having to pay anything to anyone made collecting a challenge.

Carl Johnson was a proud black man, who after driving a bus for the Chicago Transit Authority for twenty years, went to hair-styling school and learned to be a barber. He took his life's savings, and watching the influx of blacks in Maywood, opened a small barber shop with his friend. Don Smith had cut hair all his life and was happy to partner with a black man who had some money to open a shop. The store had a barber pole outside and in large classical letters on the windows, announced "Carl & Don's Barber Shop," giving a nod to his friend for all the years he had stood on his feet cutting the hair of white executives in the Loop. The modest shop had three chairs that Carl bought used but in good condition. The store smelled of Pinaud Talcum Powder, Clubman Aftershave, and Fantasia Frizz Straightening Gel. In one corner was a brand new thirty-one-inch color TV, a small luxury, tuned to either the Cubs or White Sox.

There was a worn, but comfortable sofa and six additional chairs. Carl never had that many people waiting, but the shop had become a gathering place for the men in the neighborhood, old, unemployed, or retired, and the banter and smack talk were always lively.

Inside a closet in the rear, a broom and baseball bat were at the ready, and there was a shelf stocked with Four Roses whiskey, Inver House scotch, Remy Martin cognac and Mogen David red wine, otherwise known as "Mad Dog 20/20," containing 18% alcohol. There was a jar by the booze for monetary offerings to keep the bar stocked.

As to protection, reluctantly, Carl had decided that discretion was the better part of valor and had worked out a deal with the Outfit's neighborhood collectors, Gino and Eddie, to give them complimentary haircuts and shaves every Friday in return for a reasonable three percent off the net, for as Gino called it, an insurance payment. It had worked out well, and the only time Carl and Don were robbed it turned out to be a very bad day for the punks who had broken in and stolen the booze and the booze money from his shop.

Maurice and Tiny walked into Carl and Don's. There was one person in Don's chair, one seated on the couch and Carl was in the back taking a leak.

"Look what the cat dragged in. Two niggas. Sit down boys. Relax. Carl be right out to give you a shampoo and cut." Being sixty and having survived Omaha Beach, Don didn't take shit from anyone.

"Man, we don't want no haircut. You know what we here for." Maurice was not too quick on picking up Don's sarcasm.

"Yeah, where Carl at? We here to collect." Tiny, the so-called brains of the outfit, took over.

"Hey Carl, some people be here to see you. Best you bring a broom."

Carl understood the implication of "bring a broom" and he came out with his Louisville Slugger, the engraved Mickey Mantle model. It was his prized possession, having played minor league ball in his youth for the Atlanta Crackers.

"Hello fellas. Now, you'll get nothing here. You know who I pay insurance to. So just turn around and go on down the street. Unless you really do need a haircut." Carl looked at Maurice's wild Afro and shook his head. "Man, you need a cut. You look like a scared punk!"

"This is Player's Club turf now, and you'll pay us what you pay to the dagos, plus five percent."

"And I said get the fuck outta here." Maurice made a move toward Carl and that's all it took. Carl swung for the fences and hit Maurice right in the chest. He dropped like a ground ball, screaming, "Shit, you hit me, you fuck!" Tiny recoiled and took a step back, out of range of the bat.

"And I'll hit you again, you don't leave now. Or maybe I'll just call my friends."

Tiny grabbed Maurice who was still bent over in pain and dragged him out. "You ain't seen the end of us, nigga!"

After the two had stumbled down the sidewalk out of view, Don spoke.

"Carl, maybe you need to get a gun. Or maybe better, start paying them a little."

"Shit. I ain't paying those losers. We barely make it as it is. They just punks."

"Yeah but they'll be back."

"Fine. Me and Mickey here be waiting on their sorry asses."

The two amateur thugs went down to the corner and Maurice caught his breath. "I'm gonna kill that muthafucka!"

"You ain't killin' no one, dude," said Tiny. "Tiger said no killin' anyone. Bring down the police on the whole gang. Plus, how you gonna collect from a dead man? Look, let's get the rest of the collections, but maybe not be so nice. We come back later and deal with the barber."

"I'm down. But I'm gonna teach him manners later." Maurice was now recovered. "Where we go next?"

"Let's hit the gas station."

This time Maurice and Tiny went right into Lucca's Esso Full-Service Gas Station and Car Repair and went behind the counter to the register. They opened it and pulled out all the cash. Lucca saw them enter but was filling up Mrs. Romano's '65 Ford Fairlane. He didn't want to stop fueling the car but knew immediately what they were up to. He let go of the gas pump handle and hurried into the store. Maurice was waiting for him. His brass knuckled fist came down hard on Lucca's back and he staggered. Tiny then swung his bag of nails like David against Goliath and hit Lucca in the chin cutting him as more than a few nails had escaped the confines of the bag. The old man slumped to the floor blood flowing, and then Maurice kicked him violently in the stomach.

"That's for not paying the Player's Club last week."

"Yeah, see you next Friday, you wop." Tiny had to have the last word.

But Maurice had the last act of violence. He went back outside to the waiting Fairlane and removed the gas hose. He kicked over the bucket containing soapy water to clean windshields and filled it halfway with gasoline. Then he returned to the small dirty office and poured the gasoline on Lucca. He took out a match and lit it. Lucca screamed.

"No! No please! I pay from a now on!"

Tiny recognized that the situation was close to getting out of control. Maurice would kill someone someday in the not too distant future.

"Maurice, let's bolt. He gets the fuckin' idea. Remember, no killin'!"

Maurice put out the match. The two left for the last collection—Vincenzo's. Having success with their methods at Lucca's, Vincenzo was treated in the same manner. The two punks entered the mini-mart and grabbed a couple of Yoo Hoo's and proceeded to the cash register. The Italian was ready for them with a billy club, but Maurice managed the first hit with his knuckles right to the man's forehead, grabbing the upraised arm holding the crude weapon. Tiny scored a direct hit with his nail bag to Vincenzo's family jewels and it was over. The old man was in a fetal position on the floor mumbling in Italian. Cash drawer emptied, they took a six pack of Budweiser and several bags of chips.

The small park two blocks away was a good place to drink the beer and celebrate their day's take. Latrice Gibson would be happy with his two lieutenants. But first Maurice had some unfinished business. Having shot-gunned four of the beers that got him higher than a kite, Maurice was full of himself, and was worked up into a hard rage.

An hour later, Carl Johnson lay bleeding on the ground outside his barber shop. The front door glass had been shattered, and finding no money in the cash register, the broken body was searched, and they found an envelope containing two hundred dollars.

"Man, I hope you didn't kill him. You went pretty bad ass on him." Tiny was worried.

"He be fine. Let's get to the house and report to the boss. We collected $1,875 bucks today. Gibson be given us some Martell for this."

Carmine Messina took out his Cubs jacket and laid it on his bed. He was wearing a pair of starched blue jeans, a Le Coq Sportif polo shirt and Gucci loafers without socks. The Cubs were playing the hated New York Mets and the game began at one o'clock. He had two prized season tickets behind home plate in the third row, a gift from a grateful alderman. On these days, he afforded himself the luxury of two Meister Brau beers, brought to him by the longtime usher Samuel Thomas, a black man who knew that his patron was important and dangerous. But he tipped very well. For every $1.50 beer, Samuel received $5.00 and a "Keep the change." Samuel also brought Messina hot dogs with sauerkraut, and occasionally a cup of ice cream with a wooden spoon.

He was putting on his silk Cubs jacket when Benedetta came into the room and picked up the phone, lifting the receiver from the base and extending it toward him. She said nothing but "Importante, Don."

"Mr. Carmine, sorry to call you on a Friday. It's Gino. I've got some bad news."

Messina listened for several minutes without interruption or comment. Then he spoke. "Is Mr. Johnson going to live? What about Lucca? And Vincenzo?" Pause. "Good. We'll take care of that gang of jiggaboos. But for now, do nothing. Understand?"

"Yes, sir. And you want me to visit them next week and give them a pass compliments of well…our organization. Right?"

"Right, and send flowers to the hospital and give Mrs. Johnson two hundred dollars. Give the same to Lucca and Vincenzo. And give them passes for four weeks."

"Got it. Enjoy the game."

"After what you just told me? Anyway, thanks. Now go home and see your family."

Carmine put the phone back in the cradle. Maybe he'd have three beers today and two hot dogs. At least his son, Johnny, was going to the game with him.

The Cubs lost 5-4 in extra innings. Carmine Messina had had better days.

CHAPTER 39

On Tuesday morning, after the long Memorial Day weekend, Bob Marlow strode into the offices proud that he had managed to stay sober over the extended break. It was his turn to have the boys and he had rented a cabin on Lake Geneva in Wisconsin; they had fished, swam, water-skied and cooked out steaks over an open fire. Even after Austin and Ben had gone to bed early, exhausted from the day's activities, he had managed to drink nothing but tonic. Never mind that tonic was all he had brought. He knew that his wife would quiz the boys about their father's drinking, and he didn't need to give her any more ammunition in a probable divorce fight.

As he turned the corner and walked to the long wall that was the east side of the large drafting hall, he saw that large sheets of paper were taped to it. He stopped in front of the collage. The drawings— plans, sections and elevations were of a building, an amazing building. He studied each individual illustration. He looked around the vast room. There were only a few early arrivals, but no one had an answer to his question, "Who did this?"

Marlow went to his office and turned on the lights. He fixed coffee, and while he was waiting for it to brew, he was drawn back to the wall. The more he studied the unknown effort, the more he was taken by the design. If Leo had done this, it was his best effort ever. It could only be Leo. It did not have the boredom of a Francis Jr. design, or the Miesian rigidity and order of a Gerhard Dietrich effort. Yet, it wasn't really Leo either. He walked around the room querying anyone who was there. They knew nothing. In spite of the deadline on the competition, no one had wanted to give up their one precious extra day off. Marlow went back to his office, poured a steaming cup of java, and waited for others to arrive to solve this mystery. The phone rang.

"Bob Marlow."

"Good morning, boss. This Leo. I am sick. I do not come in today. Maybe tomorrow."

"Leo, did you work this weekend? The design on the wall. It's terrific!"

"I work, yes. But only yesterday."

"What did you pull, an all nighter? Sure, sleep in. Come in to-morrow. I mean it's fantastic! I'll get the team working on the details."

"No, boss. Is not my design, is Connor West's design. He very bright kid. I help him only yesterday, but he works on it from Saturday on. He designs it all."

Bob Marlow took the phone away from his ear and looked at it. He could not believe what he was hearing. Then, not wanting to lose Leo, he quickly spoke into the mouthpiece again.

"Leo, you still there? Listen, are you serious? Connor designed this?"

"Yes, boss. You must use for competition effort. I am sick. Not sure when I come back in office. Connor will finish." The phone went dead.

In Leo's absence, Bob Marlow put Connor in charge of refining the design. Marlow would organize the presentation. Once it was known that it was West's concept and his design, even Taubert had to give his grudging approval, if not outright respect to West. The team rallied around him and he quietly distributed assignments. Caudy would work on refining the condominium layouts; Taubert, the hotel. He would work on the complex base. The project managers would assist with building systems and code compliance. The only uncertainty was the structure. The core of the building came down squarely onto the stream bed below the site. If there was not a structural solution to this, the design was garbage. By noon West was at Jerzy's desk. Stanizski was working his slide rule with the geo-technical report open to the individual soil borings—sections through the earth indicating the various layers of sand, earth and rock and their depths. If rock could not be found within a reasonable distance of the surface, there would never be a seventy-five-story building on the site.

"Jones, Jones, you make my life very difficult with the design. I took you to look at boats, not design one!"

"You told me the architecture comes first and the land should do what the architecture wants it to do. I was only learning from you."

"I know very well what I told you. Leave me. Come back to-morrow. I am waiting for additional soil borings I ordered because of your design. Then maybe I have solution, or maybe not."

Connor walked back to his desk with a knot in his stomach. If Jerzy could not design the building around a great mast, a great core at the center, then the design was doomed. He fidgeted around and then Marilyn came by with the mail cart. It was the highlight of his day, although he couldn't care less for the mail he received. Invitations to join the AIA Associates Group—young unregistered architects; brochures on various building systems; seminars he had little interest in, such as building intercom systems. He chatted with Marilyn, smiling at her as he took the few offerings and glanced at them. Then he saw a postcard. It said: "Greetings from Key West, Florida" in large block letters with illustrations of beaches and palm trees in the letters. He quickly turned it over.

Hey Sullivan,

How's Chicago? Working hard or hardly working? I decided that architecture could wait and I moved down here and bought a charter fishing boat. The weather is great and the tips are good. The babes are not so bad either. Screw architecture for a while. Come to Key West and see me!

Best,
Rat

"Damn, son of a bitch! He's soaking up the sun and I'm working my ass off and probably getting fired when my grand idea doesn't work," West figured. He took the postcard and pinned it to the tack board in front of his desk. "Something to dream about, I guess." He got up and headed for Marlow's office.

"How's my chief designer?" Marlow reached over to the coffee pot and poured Connor a cup in the Cubs mug that had become his, in a new morning ritual that Connor looked forward to. He looked upon Bob Marlow as a friend and mentor, plus a guy that wouldn't bullshit you.

"We're fucked, pardon my French, if Jerzy can't support the center core smack dab in the center of the stream."

"I suppose your inspiration could have been a volleyball net since you were on the lake. The columns are at the end in that idea."

"Funny. We were at the marina, not in the park."

"Relax, Jerzy can design the structure for anything. He once designed a ramp that went over the barbed wire fence at the POW camp he was in during the war. They hid the ramp under their bunkhouse, and when they brought it out at night, they opened it in four separate sections and it was fully supported by the single top strand of barbed wire."

"Did he escape?"

"Yes, but the next day he was recaptured. Then they tried a tunnel. He designed the structure for that too."

"Amazing to have lived such a life!"

"Yeah, a column in a stream bed is pretty much a walk in the park for him."

"What are the other designs looking like? I've been too busy to go around and check them out."

"Gerhard didn't read the program very well. He has three buildings, the office tower, and the condominium and then the hotel all arranged very nicely on a larger, slimmer podium, all looking very Mies

Van der Rohe. Nice, but the big-ego developer wants a phallic symbol taller than any other. So, your design is safe."

"And Francis?"

"I have to say it is probably his best effort. And it turns out to be 80 stories tall, which may score points. But it is all the same from bottom to top. Deep punched square windows in a granite façade. Office windows, six by six; hotel windows, six by six; condo windows, yep, six by six. What it lacks in imagination, it makes up for in symmetry for sure. I guess he only had one idea and used it for all three elements. You know, if 1960 ever came back, it would be damn good. But really, what do I know? I just get paid to make sure the building won't leak."

"Do you think this client, whoever he is, will select it?"

"It will be the most economical to build because of the repetitive nature of it. I really don't know a lot about the guy, but word has it he's a bit unscrupulous. Doesn't pay his bills, screws contractors, sues people. But Jefferson has been warned. One thing for sure, your little creation will be the most expensive to build, curved walls, outside elevators, and that revolving restaurant."

"You don't like it, do you?"

"I love it because this business has not worn you down. It is still, and don't take this the wrong way, a college project. It isn't constrained by lots of 'don'ts'."

"I guess I'll take that as a compliment."

"Connor, in the end, the great designers, the great architects don't give a damn about the client. It is their building; the client just pays for it. They aren't afraid to let it all hang out there. Most times, clients, especially the ones with big egos, love it. When you labored over this design, you weren't thinking: 'I wonder if the client will like this or like that.' You were thinking, 'Hell yes, this is right, this is what I think it should be.' Never lose that feeling."

The coffee mug was empty and there was work to do. Connor got up from the chair and headed for the door. "Thanks for the pep talk."

"Anytime, West, anytime."

_____

It was almost six o'clock on Thursday. Connor stared at the postcard from Rat, worn down from the week of non-stop work. Palm trees, white sand, blue water. "*So much packed onto a three-by-six-inch piece of cardstock,*" he thought. "*Fuck me. What am I doing here?*" West ran his fingers through his long dark brown hair and rubbed his eyes. When he opened them, he was still looking at the same scene. "Tomlinson, you got it right. Key West. I could design houses down there. Sure looks like a nice place…" Connor got up from the drafting table where he had labored all day trying to resolve issues at the main building lobby; it was too small for the program requirements. He needed to fit ten pounds of shit into a five-pound bag.

The three designers had been given a phone at the singular desk assigned to them, a rare perk for young employees. He dialed Marilyn's extension.

"Mr. Jefferson's office."

"Marilyn Jones' desk," Connor noted with sarcasm.

"Yes, it is. And who might this be? I used to know a designer in the firm but I think he quit."

"You're reading my mind. Yes, it's me, your overworked head-hurting boyfriend…"

"I hope no one can hear you…"

"Right now, I really don't care. Would you care to leave this sweat-shop early and have a walk along the lake and then dinner?"

"I don't see how I could refuse that offer. I'll meet you in the lobby in ten minutes. The building lobby that is."

"Got it. I'll wear a disguise. Look for someone that keeps normal business hours." West hung up the phone headed for the executive restroom. He needed some mouthwash.

Marilyn was waiting in the building lobby, her back to the elevators, staring into one of the shops that opened onto it, hoping she wouldn't be noticed. In the reflection of the shop window, she saw Connor exit an elevator. Her heart pounded as if she had just met him. Though his deep brown eyes were bloodshot, he was more handsome now. He looked more mature, more of a man, not a boy. She could almost see the mantle of responsibility on his shoulders. Connor noticed Marilyn immediately. In a dark green suit and the ever-necessary pearls, she was so beautiful.

"Damn girl, you are fine." He walked up to her, took her in his arms and kissed her long and hard. She pushed him away and smiled.

"Not here Romeo, later!"

That night in his apartment, as the weather turned foul and a driving rain beat against the sliding glass doors of Connor's studio apartment, they made love again and again, until exhaustion brought on a deep sleep.

CHAPTER 40

By any standard, the house in Glencoe was impressive. Though there was no fence, a high hedgerow protected the property and the house was well back from the road. Grabowski noted that the drive was not paved in concrete or asphalt but consisted of small brown gravel pebbles confined by granite curbing. He whistled slowly.

"Must be a bitch to shovel in the winter," he mused to himself. *"I bet Mr. Simpson doesn't worry about that."*

The black sedan with grey cloth seats and cheap hubcaps maneuvered slowly up the drive to the front of the residence. As Grabowski rounded the curve, he could see glimpses of Lake Michigan beyond the backyard. The house was a large Tudor manse with stucco and diagonal wood beams above a brick base and with large stones interspersed here and there. It looked like Shakespeare might have lived there. At the far end of the house he saw that it even had a round turret element.

He parked the car in the drive, not caring if anyone could get by him. The drive continued back around to the street, but just beyond the house it curved rightward and he could make out the garage with a second-story and three dormers—the coach house.

"So far Lothar is telling the truth. There is a coach house." He strode up to the pair of front doors, which were imposing slabs of wood supported by three large hinges for each door. There were small windows, but they were covered with iron grills as if the place were a speakeasy. Off to the right was a doorbell, but there were also large hammer door knockers on each door. Grabowski, mimicking an old horror movie, slowly pulled back one of the knockers and pounded it against the door several times. After a minute he heard footsteps. The door opened.

"Hey, asshole, there's a doorbell. This isn't Transylvania." Grabowski was surprised. In front of him was a woman dressed in tennis whites, blond hair pulled back into a ponytail. She was short, perhaps five-three at most, with ample breasts straining against a tucked-in blouse and strong, tanned legs below her short tennis skirt. She had on makeup but needed little; she was naturally attractive.

"I'm sorry, I didn't notice. I just saw the knockers." Grabowski realized at once that the remark could be taken another way, so he continued without pause. "I'm Sergeant Grabowski, City of Chicago Arson Investigations. And you are…not the maid."

"No shit. Maid? What planet do you live on?"

"I just thought, this lovely house, Glencoe, the lake?"

"I am the maid most days, except once a week when a cleaning service comes. What is your name again, and what do you want?"

"Grabowski, Sergeant. Are you Mrs. Simpson?"

"Gee, you're quick. I'm Reese Simpson. Yeah, I live here as in owner. I suppose you want to come in, and why are you here?"

"Yes. I would. I do have a number of questions to ask, so if you don't mind, perhaps we could sit down?"

"I suppose you'll expect the butler to serve us tea, too? Believe it or not, we live a lot like you do down in Chicago. We just have grass to mow."

"Thank you, this won't take long." Grabowski took off his hat and entered a large foyer. Through the glass doors beyond a large staircase he could see the lake. *They ought to have a maid and a butler,* he thought.

"So how did it go with the lady of the house? Any luck?" John O'Rourke was fixing a cup of coffee and saw Grabowski come in and slouch down at his grey steel desk. He pounced.

"And good afternoon to you too, Inspector. Can I take my coat off?"

"Sure, and talk to me while you're doing it. We need some good news on this case."

"Well, you won't get it from me. But let me tell you, Mrs. Simpson is some little firecracker! She might be only five-two, five-three, but I wouldn't want to meet her in an alley late at night."

"Oh, how so?"

"Let's say she don't take shit from anyone. Has a lot of attitude. Anyway, Lurch's story checks out. Yeah, she called him Lurch. Hates the guy; gives her the creepy crawlies. Said he even made a pass at her once. But she said she remembered that evening because it was the only time in a couple of months that her beloved husband slept there. Said he works so hard that he almost always stays at the condo on Walton Street. She stays there too just so she can see him, but sadly it interferes with her tennis league."

"I did some checking on Reese Anne Simpson, formerly Reese Anne Benfield. Very wealthy Kenilworth family. Father has a seat on the Chicago Board of Trade, but the family money comes from cattle and slaughterhouses on the old Southside. Seems the family wasn't too happy about the only daughter marrying the son of an immigrant, even though the father, Lars was wealthy, too. I found an old society column on microfiche from the *Tribune* from four years ago, when they got married. It seems that the old man, Preston Benfield, cut off Reese when she married Steel."

"They must have money. That house is right on the lake. And it's huge."

"Right. So, while you were sipping tea or martinis with Mrs. Simpson, I was pouring over Steel Simpson's finances, at least those I could get a hold of through public records. Everything is closely held. He's like most developers, leveraged to the max. That house has a mortgage on it would choke a cow. Or is it a horse? Anyway, the monthlies are almost more than you and I make in a year."

"Yeah, Ms. Simpson seemed a little annoyed about the big lifestyle without the trappings that come with it. She noticed dust on the coffee table and started bitching about the once-a-week cleaning crew. Talked about what a half-ass job they did."

"Is that all you discussed, the travails of getting good staff? Wasn't there anything that didn't add up in what she said?"

"I haven't had a chance to check my notes against our interviews with Mr. Simpson or Jensen. Let's see. She said it was a Thursday night. Said she always goes to bed at 10:30 sharp. Then she heard a car drive up. It worried her. Mrs. Simpson said she was not expecting Steel that night. She says when he drove into the garage, she knew it must have been him. They have separate bedrooms. Can you imagine that when you have that hot of a wife, and that he stuck his head into her room and said goodnight. When she got up the next morning, he was already gone."

"10:30 P.M. huh? Didn't Simpson say they got to the house at 11:30 P.M.?"

"Give me a few minutes and I'll check."

"Did she say that she saw Jensen that night? You said he gave her the willies."

"That was when I was asking in general about Lurch, Lothar being her husband's driver. You know she never said she saw him. In fact, she really never included him in the conversation about that night. It was just Steel this, Steel that. Steel works so hard. And why was I even asking about that night? And so on."

"How about the drive from Glencoe to the piece of land? Could Jensen have gotten there in time to set the fire?"

"I'm doing that drive tonight. But it might be possible. It only took me an hour in mid-day traffic to get back here. However, there's some construction going on along Sheridan Road. Didn't affect me; it seems like they are just doing it at night. I'll check with the DOT; it's a state road. See what is going on."

"You do that, because something isn't adding up."

CHAPTER 41

Connor and Marilyn took the bus together to work on Friday. It was only when they arrived at the Santa Fe Building that they separated, Marilyn taking the elevator to the fourteenth floor, and moments later Connor went to the twelfth floor but not before the two had exchanged several deep kisses in an alcove off the lobby. He whistled softly to himself and decided once again to bypass the most direct route to his office and take the long way around. He glanced through the senior offices to the views of the lake. He stopped in the conference room, which afforded the best views to soak it in. "I love this town," he quietly intoned.

"Ah West, there you are. I was just by your work area to see you." Vance Jefferson was in the doorway, attired in a neatly pressed khaki suit with green and blue rep tie. His thick graying hair was enhanced by the round tortoise shell glasses balanced atop.

"Good morning, sir. I was just looking out at the lake. It's beautiful this morning. I like to come this way to see it first thing, with the sun rising over it. Beats the view of the back wall of Carson Pirie Scott."

"You don't care for your workspace?"

"Oh, no, Mr. Jefferson. They're a lot better than I imagined they would be. And I enjoy working with Taubert and Caudy. They're good guys."

"Good, Bob Marlow tells me you've been quite a big help to Leo and his terrific design for the competition."

"Ah, thank you. But his design?"

"Yes. Leo is one of our best, and that concept of sails and a mast; very imaginative. Bob tells me you're doing a great job helping refine things. Keep it up: you'll make associate before long. Oh, have you seen Leo today?"

"Ah, well, no sir, like I said, I just got here. We sure need him. He's been gone all week. We only have a week left. I'm in a little over…"

Jefferson interrupted before Connor could finish; he wasn't really paying attention. "I'll talk to Bob about Leo. Now get to it. Like you said, you only have a week left."

"Thank you, sir," Connor slipped by Vance Jefferson through the conference room door.

"Oh, one other thing, Mr. West. You do know that dating other employees is against company policy?"

West's face flushed. "Yes, sir, sure I do."

"OK. Good. Have a productive day. Win the competition."

"Good morning, Marilyn. Why you certainly look lovely today. There's a glow about you." Vance Jefferson did not wait for a reply, and strode into his office, taking off his coat and sitting down at his large granite slab of a desk, opening the morning edition of the *Chicago Tribune*. Marilyn followed soon thereafter with a steaming cup of black coffee, her face also flushed from the compliment, but under her makeup, it was hard to tell. She laid the coffee on the desk; no coaster was required on the granite. She was at the back of the desk alongside Jefferson. It was indiscernible at first; Marilyn thought she was brushing up against the credenza. Then she felt it again. A hand was on her buttocks moving slowly up and down against her skirt, squeezing slowly. She stiffened; the breath went out from her. Slowly she moved away, around to the front of the desk. She stared at Jefferson who had a sly smile on his face.

"What's on my calendar today, young lady?"

"You have lunch with Asa Morton from First National."

"Oh yes, that's right. Wonderful. Make a reservation for 12:15 P.M. Let him know. That reminds me. Call Marjorie Fleet at Fidelity and Guarantee. Set up a call with her at 3:30 P.M. Need to increase our E&O."

"Yes, sir. Anything else?"

"Yes. Why don't you stick around at five? We can go over the plans for the summer picnic in July."

Marilyn's head was spinning. Her boss was making a move on her; this was unchartered territory.

"Ah, I'd love to but I'm a meeting a friend for an, a, an early dinner."

"I see. No worries. We can do the logistics on the picnic another time. Get Asa on the phone and remind him of our lunch. Close the door on your way out."

Marilyn shut the door behind her, perhaps with too much force. She shook her head. "Asshole," she intoned under her breath.

Marilyn set up the lunch with the executive vice president of First National Bank of Chicago at the Drake Hotel's premier restaurant, the Palm Court. As its name implied, eight large palm trees and an expanse of windows looked out to Oak Street Beach and Lake Michigan.

The lobby of the Drake was impressive, three stories high, three imposing chandeliers, and rich tapestries on the wall imported from France. The Palm Court was up a flight of grand stairs in the center of the lobby.

"Vance, good to see you. How is everything at Nolan and Jefferson?" Asa Morton reached out for Vance Jefferson's hand. He always omitted Marlow as he considered the newest partner an interloper in an old and established firm. In addition, he used to be close friends with the late T. Robert Shaw, one of the original founding partners. Shaw was the business partner back then and Jefferson headed up production for the firm. Francis Nolan, Sr., was, of course, the singular design thrust of the organization begun by Daniel Burnham.

"Great, Asa. Just great." Vance Jefferson shook the tall, lanky Morton's hand mightily. He took Morton's arm and they walked up the staircase to the restaurant. No words were necessary for the maitre d'. He recognized the two men and nodded, taking them to a table by a window. Greeting them by name, he slid out the large comfortable chairs so the two executives could sit and discuss business.

Asa Morton did not look like a banker, but like an aged basketball player for the Chicago Bulls. His hair was grey and thinning, his eyes were sharp and he needed no glasses. A boney face stood atop his six-six frame, towering over the solid 6'2" Jefferson. He had only worked at First National, working his way up from a teller in the 1940s to head of the Commercial Business Department. Back in the mid-fifties, Morton and First National took a flier on Francis Nolan who had taken over as Director of Burnham and Shaw. Architecture firms were not exactly looked upon as lucrative clients.

"Did you read about our new commission? It's a dandy. Going to be the biggest building Chicago has ever seen. And it gets us out from under all those dull city contracts."

"I did read about it in the *Tribune*. Yes, I guess congratulations are in order."

"You guess? Our fee is seven million dollars. That's over half of our total commissions last year!"

"Sorry, you know us bankers. We hate to see any change in the status quo, or in your case, risk. Those city contracts may be dull but they pay like clockwork, and Francis had a pretty good relationship with Jack Malone. No other firm would get those high fees."

A white-jacketed waiter came over and took their order for drinks: two Gibsons up and very cold. Vance preferred a real martini or scotch but knew that Morton, who with his position and success at First could have as many drinks as he liked at lunch, was a Gibson man. Jefferson always thought the pearl onion's flavor overwhelmed the gin.

"Francis is gone, God rest his soul, and times they are a changing. We haven't gotten a big assignment from Jack or his building department in a while. Last job we did was an interior renovation of a floor in City Hall. We can't keep the lights on with that kind of work."

"Certainly. I realize that if a company, any company, even an architectural firm doesn't adapt to the times, they will soon go downhill. So, did you check out Steel Simpson? You know his reputation is not the best."

"And that's why we're having lunch. Certainly, I checked him out. And I've had a number of meetings with him. He's tough; he a developer for God's sake. There's nothing wrong with being ambitious and playing a little hardball. I'm not going to be pushover."

Morton sipped his drink with eyes closed. He could tell this would be a three-drink lunch. He set his stemmed glass down gently and spoke in a monotone voice.

"Simpson banks at Chicago Bank & Trust. I know young Brad Wentworth over there. He handles the Simpson account. Brad's a sharp young man. I even tried to hire him away, but he's on the fast track. Anyway, he speaks well of Simpson. But it seems disingenuous; I can't tell if he trusts the man or doesn't want me stealing his main client."

"Well, there you are. Wentworth speaks well of him. From a banker, that's quite a compliment. Look I expect that I'm going to have to browbeat this guy to get paid every step of the way. I'm even sticking my neck out now. We're in the middle of schematic design that's due in a week and I did give him a deal on that fee."

"A million dollars, I hope?" Asa smiled and took another inhale of the cold cloud in front of him; it began to have its salutary effect.

Jefferson was not amused. "You're not serious? These developers never have money at the beginning of a project. Most of the time they want us to do it for free so we get in on the ground floor, but we'll never agree to that."

"That's a good thing! I'd be reviewing your balance sheet if that were the case." Morton looked out the window at the people sunning on the beach.

"Look, we are doing the design for $200,000 and its payable when we present on June 12. And I'll remind Simpson of that on June 11. The following week, with our design in hand, he is off to Europe to secure his equity financing from some Saudi sheik that has lots of oil money."

"That they do, Vance. Our oil fields in Texas and Oklahoma are playing out and it won't be long before the Middle East will dictate the price of oil. And demand for cars in this country is through the roof. Do you know they predict that by 1980, 50% of families in the U.S. will have not one, but two cars?"

"I'll still have one car and I'll be taking the commuter train to work. At least then I can have a drink on the way home."

"I'll drink to that." Asa motioned to the waiter for another round. "Let's get to the point. I assume our pleasant lunch has something to do with the big commission and a developer who hates to pay anyone? In spite of what Wentworth told me, I've heard more than a few stories about Mr. Simpson. Maybe they're just grousing because he has had a lot of quick success, but I don't think so."

Jefferson's interest was piqued. He didn't want to hear anything bad about his new client, though he had already heard plenty, but he did love street gossip.

"Asa, we go way back. You can tell me."

"Alright. A general contractor, Fitzgerald and Son, you know them, banks with First. Had for years when the old man, Brendan was starting out, and came to me for a loan to buy construction equipment and a truck. Anyway, they were the contractor on Simpson's apartment project, a dog location on the Southside by the museum. It didn't rent worth a damn, so Simpson stiffed them by not paying the retainage."

"I heard a Pakistani by the name of Patel was behind that project."

"He was just the suit in the front. It was Simpson's deal from the get-go. Simpson was the majority partner. Fitzgerald had to write off almost a million dollars after spreading the pain to his subs. It's all tied up in court now, another Simpson trick. Anyway, we had to reduce Fitzgerald's line of credit. I'd hate to have to reduce yours after Simpson gives you a haircut."

"Asa, that's why I am seeing you. With a seven-million-dollar contract, we'll need a bigger line of credit to make payroll if Simpson is slow pay."

"Not if, my friend, but when."

"Maybe so, but this project will require around seventy to one hundred professionals working on it for six months. That's a lot of overhead, and I have to make payroll. You can't expect a developer to pay like clockwork. He needs to get draws from his bank and his equity partner. But in the end, I know we will get paid."

"What's your profit margin on this deal?"

"Between one million seven fifty and two."

"Solid. But Vance, you're an architectural firm. You'll be lucky to clear one and a half. You guys never can manage your designers."

"Fine. I'll take one and a half any day of the week!" Jefferson was becoming agitated. *"Fucking bankers. They only want to lend you money when you don't need it."* He took a large sip of his drink, and decided that he really detested Gibsons.

"Vance, I had an idea about what this lunch was going to be about. I knew you weren't going to make a big deposit. I looked over your file. You have a great track record. You've only drawn on your five-hundred-thousand line three times in ten years. Impressive. Considering that I've warned you about Simpson, I think I can take and additional request of five hundred thousand more to committee."

Vance winced. "I was hoping for an increase to two million…"

"In your dreams! If you get stiffed for two million and can't pay it back, Nolan and Jefferson are history."

"I'm not going to get stiffed. I'll stop production if we don't get paid."

"Look, I'm hungry. Let's order and let me think about it; I'll call you on Tuesday. Okay?"

The two executives ordered the veal medallions and another round of drinks. Jefferson ordered a martini with an olive.

It was three o'clock by the time Vance Jefferson returned to the four-teenth floor. His head hurt and he was not looking forward to the phone call with Marjorie Fleet. She was ten times tougher than Asa Morton. He walked past Marilyn's desk. She looked hard at her boss. He acted like he didn't notice.

"Mr. Jefferson, Bob Marlow wants to see you. He says it's urgent."

"I'll call him."

"I'm sorry, sir. He said when you came back to see him in his office."

"Fine. Call Marjorie Fleet. Tell her I got tied up and would like to call her tomorrow." Jefferson headed to the elevators out of earshot.

"Why can't you have lunch with her, Mr. Asshole?" Marilyn muttered when her boss was around the corner. She knew. Women who had made it in a man's world were still considered second class. They did not get taken to lunch even if they had power over you. They just got a phone call.

CHAPTER 42

"Hello Bob. What's so urgent that I have to come to your office?"

Bob Marlow looked up from the set of construction documents that he was reviewing. The floor surrounding his office was a buzz of activity as the three teams continued to refine and hone their designs.

"Leo hasn't been in since Monday. He called and left a message for me on Tuesday, but since then nothing. Said he was sick."

"Have you called him?"

"Three times today. No answer and no answering machine. I think we need to go over to his house and check."

"You go. I've got a lot to do. Anyway, why do we need him? You told me that West is filling in fine in his absence."

"That's not the point. Something's wrong. Leo hasn't been himself lately."

"He did mention to me about two weeks ago that he had many troubles on his mind. And on Wednesday, I got a call from Immigration about his employment here. Said he had applied for an extension on his green card. I handled it. OK, let's go then. You have his address?"

"Right here. 3481 Damen Avenue. I think they call that neighborhood the Ukrainian Village."

"Fine. Let's cab it over there."

The bungalow at 3481 Damen was drab and rundown. Its exterior was asphalt wall shingles that tried to look like brick. The trim was light brown, but in some places appeared to have been painted over in grey. There were seven uneven steps up to a small front porch. Several of the handrail balusters were missing. There was a rusting screen door with ripped mesh at two corners. Bob Marlow opened it and knocked on a front door that had been painted too many times. This time the color was purple.

"What a dump, Leo," Vance blurted out. "I mean, you're a senior designer in the firm."

"With what we pay him, are you surprised?" Marlow retorted.

"Hell, he makes two times more than what he would in the Soviet Union."

"Exactly…my point." Marlow knocked again harder. He tried the doorbell but it didn't work. The door was locked as well. He looked at Jefferson with an expression of, "What now?"

"We're here. Let's go around to the back. Maybe there's a back door that's open."

The two men went back down the steps and around to the side of the house. Opening a chain link gate that grated hard on the sidewalk, they made their way down the narrow walkway to a small but tidy backyard. There was a flower and vegetable garden. Several tomato plants were already in the ground and doing well in the new spring warmth. The old cellar door had been replaced with a piece of painted plywood, so they walked up to the back door. This time they didn't knock, they just tried the handle. The door was unlocked.

Marlow was very familiar with this type of house; it was built all over Chicago and was just like the one he grew up in. The two would-be sleuths entered into a dingy yellow kitchen that had a Formica table in the center surrounded by four metal chairs with shiny yellow vinyl seats and backs. The sink was full of dishes; an old refrigerator chugged away in a corner. There was a large white stove. The burner pans were wrapped in aluminum foil that had not been replaced in ages. There was a foul odor, but it did not seem to come from the room. Jefferson took in the unkempt nature of the house; he would have a discussion with Leo about it since he was Leo's sponsor for his green card. The two walked down the hallway to the stair hall; on the right the staircase ascended to the second floor then wrapped around the front where the railing and hallway became an overlook to the first floor.

Marlow recoiled. Stepping back, he almost knocked Jefferson over. Leo was hanging by a sheet tied to the railing, his body lifeless and face ashen grey. His feet dangled a few feet above the floor, his feet bloated and red. It was clear he had been dead several days. Then the heavy stench of death overtook both men and they gagged. Marlow reached for a handkerchief and Jefferson retched at the entry to the dining room. Marlow went to the front door, flipped the dead bolt and opened it, a wave of cool air dissipating the reeking air of the hallway. He went back to Jefferson who was now upright, vomit on the floor. He glanced at the table in the dining room. Strewn among several days of mail there was an opened letter on some type of official stationery, a handwritten letter in a foreign language and another short note. He ignored them and motioned to Jefferson to follow him up the stairs. Once at the bed sheet, Marlow pulled it up with all the strength he could muster so Jefferson could untie it from the railing. Then they gently lowered the rigid body of their dead employee and friend to the floor.

It was eight o'clock when Marlow returned to the office; Jefferson went straight to the Damen Avenue elevated station and the ride home to Evanston. The lights were still on in the architecture studio and Marlow noticed Connor West was still at his drafting table. He slowly walked over to it, not knowing how to break the news to his young charge.

"Pretty late to be working, isn't it?"

"Yeah, I was just about to leave. I was making some changes to the base of the building. What are you doing back here?"

"Come to my office."

Connor looked at his boss with a questioning expression. He tidied up his desk, turned off the drafting light, got up and followed

Marlow. Bob was already getting two glasses and a bottle of Evan Williams out from his desk drawer. He sat down at his desk and pulled the cork from the bottle and poured two generous measures into the glasses. He slid one over to Connor who was now seated and still staring at Marlow.

"What is it?"

"When Leo did not show up again today and after I called his house three times, I was worried. Vance Jefferson and I went over there. There's no good or easy was to say this, but we found him. Leo took his own life."

Connor looked at Marlow with shock and disbelief. He looked down at the glass in front of him and with his hand trembling took a drink. "What? Killed himself? Why?"

"I don't know. We called the police and they questioned us pretty hard, but it was obvious he was dead for several days. Finally, the guy from the medical examiner's office confirmed that and we were free to leave. I needed to check on a few things, so I came back here."

Connor took another swallow; he was turning pale. "Mr. Marlow, Bob, I can't do this project on my own anymore. I'm in way over my head. Leo could have solved what I've been working on the last six hours in one hour. And now he's gone."

"It might be a comfort to you to know that he left a note. In it he said to tell you to keep going. He said you have great talent."

"But why would he kill himself? He could design rings around me."

"There was a letter from the State Department. He had made an application for a visa for his wife to come to the U.S. It was denied. They called her a 'political undesirable.' They also were denying an extension on his green card status. He was going to have to go back to Russia."

"I assumed he was an American citizen."

"He wanted to be, but only if his wife were here."

"There was another letter, but it was written in Russian so the police called for an officer who speaks and reads the language. It's a Russian neighborhood so it didn't take too long. I do know this. He left his wife in Russia where she was a professor of political science at the University of Moscow. He thought if he were here, it would be easier for her to join him. He had told me that because of her views on Communism, she was constantly being watched and harassed by the KGB. So, he was trying to get her a visa. Then when she got here, she simply would not go back, asking for political asylum. I guess that effort failed."

"What did that other letter say?"

"It was from his wife, Ludmilla. The KGB had arrested her and the letter was written from the jail in Moscow. She got it smuggled out by a guard she bribed. The letter told her husband that she had been convicted of crimes against the state and was being sent to a labor camp—where she did not know—but it was certainly a long way east of Moscow. She told Leo that she didn't know when she would return, if ever."

"Holy shit." West finished the last of his bourbon and reached for the bottle. Marlow slid it toward him and then refilled his own glass.

"I guess the news was too much for him. He also told me that he had once spent three years in Siberia as a young man for re-education. He already knew what she was going to experience. Fucking Commies."

West lowered his head and put his hands on his forehead. It was starting to ache. "The real world is a hell of a lot tougher than school. First you lied to everyone about my background; the design is fucked if the structure won't work; my co-worker kills himself, and I can't tell anyone I've got a girlfriend because she works for the firm!"

"I know it's a lot to deal with. In Leo's sui-...in his note, he said that he felt confident that you could handle the refinements to the design of the 'Tower,' as he called it. He said the project was in good hands—your hands. It is after all, your design. But to help you I'm going to put Jerzy in charge of the project as lead designer as we finish. It's all structure now anyway, and he really cares for you. He'll help you get it done. As far as the girlfriend is concerned, you're not the first guy to date a secretary in this place."

"You know?"

"I've got eyes. She lights up every time she comes back here with drawings; even takes the indirect way past your work area. Marilyn is a great girl. She just has to watch out for Jefferson."

"What do you mean?"

"It's no secret he has gone through several assistants. It's a plum job, and he only hires great-looking women, but after a year or so, they just resign without reason. One lasted a while, but then left because she was pregnant. I'm pretty sure the firm paid for her to go to a lay convent in Wisconsin where you have the baby and then they put it up for adoption."

"Oh God. Any more bad news?"

"Sorry. I'm sure Marilyn can handle herself better than the others. But she's been here a year or so, so…however, I wouldn't confront him. If Jefferson finds out about you two, it's your job."

Connor got up and slowly went to the door, but then turned around.

"One more thing. Why'd you tell Mr. Jefferson that Leo designed the building?"

"What? I never told him that. Haven't really spoken with him all week until today. And that was about Leo's absence. He must have assumed he designed it after Leo told me about the ass-chewing he got. I'll talk to him and let him know you're the genius behind it."

"No, don't say anything. With Leo gone, just leave it be for now."

"Whatever you say. Anyway, you know you did it. That's really all that matters."

West left for the main lobby with Jefferson's admonition from the morning running in his brain.

CHAPTER 43

On Monday morning all three teams assembled in the largest space available, the main conference room on the 14th floor. Connor went to it by way of Marilyn's desk, but she was not there. Vance Jefferson informed everyone of Leo's untimely death. Funeral arrangements were pending and everyone would be informed as to the time and place. He asked them to work hard and finish their designs in his memory.

In spite of the Russian intrigue, Connor somehow felt partially guilty for Leo's death. It could not have been easy to deal with a design done by a green kid. He put the thought out of his mind and went over to Jerzy so they could walk down to the 11th floor; maybe take the stairs for a little exercise. Connor had worked all weekend, the only relief being a late bike ride then dinner Saturday with Marilyn; he did not tell her about what he knew of Jefferson's reputation because he didn't want to ruin the day. On Sunday she went to her parents. He could not shake the feeling that something seemed off with her.

"Ah, Jones, so sad, so unfortunate about Leo. I understand he took own life. Such a waste. I thought of doing so several times during war but couldn't do it. Plus, it would be easy way out for Nazis."

"I can't tell you how much I learned and how I enjoyed working with him for just that one day. He could have been a great mentor to me. Can I tell you something?"

"Please, Jones, you tell me."

"I feel like some of it is my fault. He comes in on Monday ready to get to his design, and here I've already done one. Me, a kid right out of college. It must have upset him. I'm sure it added to his depression."

"Stop such thoughts. He told me Tuesday that he loved your design. He called it 'diamond in the rough.' He was happy to polish it with you that day."

"You talked with him on Tuesday?"

"Yes, but not unusual. We good friends coming from old country and many troubles. I ask what he was sick from and he said nothing. He said he was trying to get his wife to United States. He told me he would come to work on Wednesday to help make your design better."

"Then why would he take his own life?"

"I do not know. Maybe it was letter from State Department. He would have to return to that Communist shithole. Marlow told me about letter. I know he would want us to do best job possible on your diamond. So, I have received additional soils report. Let's us go to my desk and discuss."

The two arrived at the 11th floor, where Stanizski's permanent office was located. Entering his office, Connor thought it smelled of mothballs, dust and ammonia. There were no personal pictures of family. Neither the drafting table nor the desk faced the view to the lake through the two large windows. *"What a waste,"* Connor thought, *"I'd have the drafting table turned so I could see that view every day."*

"Quit looking out window. This is much more important. I get additional soils report yesterday. Mr. Jefferson upset I ordered it. Cost $4,000. He says we on tight budget. But I could not know if your big scheme works otherwise. Is very interesting what it tells us."

"What does it say? We're screwed, aren't we?"

"On contrary, is very interesting. Did you know Chicago is basically built upon a swamp?"

"Great. I knew I should have gone to New York where there's bedrock..."

"Do you not see big, tall buildings here? We figure out how to build around swamp."

"But what about all the water under the site?"

"That is expensive part, but doable. We divert it around major core in big pipes. Run pipes between central caissons and ends of building where there is bearing and rock. Deposit water into river."

"So, my design concept will work."

"Since you are Irish, you are very lucky boy. Yes, I can make it work. With a few conditions."

"Sure, whatever. Wait, what conditions?"

"I think you will be okay with them. First, ends of building need to be bearing walls. And I like idea that they should be concave in shape. It will make for stronger walls."

"But I need the ends to have windows though. The views to the east and west are important."

"Not to worry. We can make punched openings in the solid wall for windows."

"Anything else?" West was getting an adrenaline rush, knowing his design would work.

"Central core of building too small. Jones, it not able to resist wind loads, which at end of Chicago River are big trouble. The buildings on both sides of river create wind tunnel beginning from where the river splits and heads east to building. At the lake they will rush out and create havoc for structure."

"Shit." Once again, the wind had literally gone out of Connor's sails.

"I have solution though. All these elevators on exterior of core are big problem. First, their shape will catch wind and make core more unstable. Second, the weather will be constantly affecting them."

"Like water and leaks?"

"To start. But cables and rails and electrical equipment around cab will be constantly wet and then rust. Many days elevators will be out of service for repairs. Then you have angry customers and client."

"So, what do you suggest?

"Relax, Jones. We will design outer structural core, concrete frame with beams extending from solid part of core out to it. Outer core clad in clear glass curtain wall, so you can still see elevators going up and down building. But protected from elements. And outer core stabilizes inner core. Plus, I think it has better proportions. I'm not just engineer you know. I care about looks of your 'sailboat.'"

"I like it. Yes, I think that will be great."

"I work on this today. Make sure it works. Then time to send design to model shop and do presentation drawings. Only five days left."

"OK, great. Let me get back to the 12th floor and check on Taubert and Caudy. I'll tell them the good news."

"One other thing. Like I said, I'm not only engineer. I have crazy idea, but you must approve, Mr. Big Shot Designer."

"Sure, what?" West felt like he had found a new mentor.

"I think the restaurant and observation floor at top are too literal."

"Literal? What do you mean?"

"I know you want it to look like a crow's nest, which is too literal. Round shape is not subtle. I think I have better idea. And it rotates."

Jerzy pulled out his sketchpad and opened it. He had already drawn the core and outer core. Connor looked on it in amazement. Jerzy had been way ahead of him. He turned the page. There was a drawing of a small ellipse on top of the building. In another drawing it was rotated thirty degrees, and in another a full ninety degrees to the main structure. When fully rotated the ends of the ellipse hung over the façade of the building by fifty feet.

"The first floor is observation deck: upper level restaurant. When ellipse rotates, visitors to the observation deck look straight down all seventy-five stories. Floor will be glass. Heavy glass, but clear glass. People look down in amazement standing in space!"

"That's fantastic!"

CHAPTER 44

Marilyn arrived back from her parents' home in Oak Park around seven. Jane was cleaning up the kitchen after making herself some leftovers.

"Hey, how's it going? How was the visit with the Ps?"

"Oh, just fine. They worry about me all the time down here in the big, bad city."

"Have you told them about Connor yet?"

"I just told them that I'm seeing a guy, nothing special. If I told them how it really was, my mother would be sending out wedding invitations!"

"Yeah, I know how that goes. They don't want us to date, but then can't wait to plan a wedding."

"Jane, I've got a bit of a problem. Can we talk?"

"Sure. What...is it? Connor?"

"No everything's fine with him, except he works so much I hardly ever see him."

"You see him every day at work though…"

"Employees are not allowed to date other employees. I can only say 'Hi' to him and then we need to sneak around in the stairwell of the building."

"Wow, that's pretty 1950s, I must say."

"I think that's when they made the rule and it never got changed."

"Does your boss know?"

"I don't think so, but it's Mr. Jefferson I want to talk about. The other day he said I was looking lovely, but he kind of creeped me out."

"Sounds like a nice compliment to me."

"Then…" Marilyn paused. This was like going to confession, though she had done nothing wrong.

"Then what?"

"When I brought him his coffee and I was setting the cup down on the desk, he put his hand on my butt."

"You sure you didn't imagine that? Like maybe he was reaching for something."

"No, I set the cup down next to him. I was standing on his side of the desk. That's something I won't do again. And then I thought it was the credenza I was backing into. But it was his hand. He was running it all over, squeezing my ass. Then he wanted to know if I'd stay late to go over the summer picnic plans. I made an excuse but I don't think he bought it. Seriously, I think Jefferson is coming onto me."

"I'm not surprised really. You are pretty good looking...and he is a man after all."

"You know, after I first started, dear Mr. Nolan said something to me I never understood."

"Oh, what did he say?"

"He said, 'Stay on your toes around Mr. Jefferson and always keep it to business.' I just thought he meant that Mr. Jefferson was all business and didn't care for small talk. I should have known. I mean after he took me to dinner and gave me the job, he wanted to go to a bar and have a nightcap. I'm beginning to think he's a jerk. He has lunch with his buddy banker but only wants to talk on the phone with our insurance person. Why? Because she's a woman."

"Marilyn, you're getting all worked up over nothing. Do you know how often I get hit on by the doctors at the hospital? One even asked me to go out with him during surgery. And he's married, for goodness sake. Everyone in the O.R. heard him, and he didn't care."

"Men, they're such pigs!"

"Including Connor?"

"No, not Connor. But you know what I mean. These old guys, hitting on us!"

"I can tell you lots of stories, roommate. That same doctor cornered me in the supply closet and grabbed my boobs, trying to kiss me. Saying 'Come on, Sweet Baby Jane, we can have some real fun together.'"

"Oh God! Really."

"Don't you remember what happened when you were in college? That professor hitting on you? And he was what sixty?"

"Sure, but that's college. Professors always hit on co-eds."

"They're all the same; all the same."

"What should I do? I mean what did you do with the doctor?"

"I went to dinner with him."

"You went to dinner, after he groped you?"

"Yes, and then drinks, and then dinner again. But I never went to bed with him. He tried, and I just said 'No!' Finally, he got tired of the pursuit and he started bothering someone else."

"Really?"

"That's right. Look you can't complain to anyone about him. He's as high as it gets there, and anyway, no one would listen. So, you have to play his game. Go have dinner with him and discuss the picnic. Let him have a grope or feel your thigh. It's a small price to pay for a great job. Just don't go to bed with him. I assure you he'll lose interest."

"But then he'll find a way to fire me and hire someone else."

"Look, how many women work there?"

"Maybe twenty or twenty-five."

"He'll move on. Let them deal with him. Don't take any shit from him in the office. You play him, not the other way around."

"OK, I guess so…"

CHAPTER 45

On Monday, June 11, one day before the presentation, J. Vance Jefferson was in a foul mood. The hours spent on the design competition had been accounted for through Friday of the prior week. Even allowing for the slow start by Team Three, all the members of that team had still charged the project for their time. Project 1973-88 had accrued $313,850 in billable hours against a $200,000 initial fee. Additionally, almost everyone had worked over the past weekend, and it would no doubt be asses and elbows until late tonight. Architects like to use that term because those were the only anatomical parts of a body you might see from the back of a drafting room. Today, walking through the immense architecture studio, that term was more apt than ever. Then he thought of the additional model-making team he hired, several freelancers to add to his own staff of five. He rubbed his temples. This whole boondoggle would cost the firm over $400,000 and on June 13, two of the designs would be thrown into the trash dumpster in the alley. Two hundred thousand dollars never to be recouped!

Adding to the fact that the biggest project undertaken by Nolan, Jefferson and Marlow was already underwater, Asa Morton had called and told him that First National could only increase the firm's line of credit by $500,000. Though it had not gone to Committee, Morton had polled most of the members and everyone was concerned about NJ&M's new client. Not that they really knew anything about him, but because the project was so large for such a novice developer. First National had not become Chicago's largest bank by taking flyers. Let First Chicago Bank and Trust stick their neck out.

He returned to his office, stopping by the 11ᵗʰ floor first to check in on the Model Shop. He could not help but be impressed. Though he almost got high on the aroma of glue and paint, the models were almost done and were stunning. He looked first at Gerhard Dietrich's three buildings set on a huge park-like pedestal; it was as good as anything Mies Van der Rohe had ever imagined. Each building had perfect proportions and they were masterfully arranged on the podium. Unfortunately, and though he personally preferred this design, he knew Steel Simpson would disregard it. He wanted a tower, not another Sandburg Village.

Francis Nolan's design was not at all elegant, but an exercise in Brutalism, a current trend in European and American design that featured strong forms, deep recessed windows, and interior elements expressed on the outside of the building. From the base—a massive colonnade of columns, the building rose eighty stories. It featured punched windows that were now four-foot-wide by seven feet high, giving emphasis to the vertical nature of the tower. Its proportions were good, but Jefferson knew that the small footprint of the hotel, situated in the middle of the tower, was governing the size of the office floors below. Those floors would be too small to be practical. Finally dividing each element was an interstitial floor for mechanical and other systems, and it too was a colonnade of columns. It was if Francis had stacked one Greek temple on top of the other. He shook his head.

Finally, there was Connor's design. At first, he did not believe Bob Marlow when he told him that it was West's effort. No green kid out of school could come up with anything so imaginative, despite his impressive portfolio. But Marlow insisted, and though Leo had had a big hand in making the floors work and the building function, the concept was Connor's. He had to take some comfort that in hiring Connor West, he deemed Leo Skoroshod was no longer essential to the firm. In fact, he told the people from Immigration that Leo was going to be let go. Once the design competition was done, he was going to give him his pink slip and one-week severance pay. He had no intention of using whatever design Leo came up with anyway. Leo's suicide had solved one problem but created another. He knew that if he were Steel Simpson, he would pick Connor's design, and what would that say about the firm's design depth? He rubbed his temples some more; he was getting light-headed from all the fumes, only exacerbating his headache. He returned to the 14th floor and his office sanctuary. He sat down and began to chew on his fingernails, then reached for a Tootsie Roll Pop to take the place of his bad habit.

The intercom buzzed. "What is it, Marilyn!"

"Sorry sir, but Marjorie Fleet is calling. It's three o'clock."

"Damn," Jefferson muttered. He didn't want to talk with her now but had already rescheduled her call once. "Fine, put her through. And get me two Anacin."

"Yes sir. Right away."

"Marjorie, how are you?"

"I'm fine, Vance, fine. I understand that you want to talk with me. How can I help?"

"First, let me apologize. I would have liked to discuss this matter over lunch, but things have been really crazy around here. We have a new commission. It's called Chicago World Tower. In fact, our presentation to the developer of three schemes is tomorrow."

"Yes, I read about it. Congratulations. A nice commission, I'm sure." Jefferson could hear the cold, all business, no nonsense tone, but today she sounded more curt than usual.

"Yes, I'm sure you're very busy as well. Let me get to the point. The cost of this project is probably going to be seventy million dollars. While I have every confidence in our firm's abilities to manage the technical aspect of such a huge project, things inevitably can be missed, though I have my best people on it, I assure you. And additionally, well, mistakes do happen...."

"Vance, you are one of our largest clients, certainly our largest in Chicago. We've already extended what, $2,000,000 in Errors & Omissions? Any contract you write, should state that amount as the maximum exposure your firm is willing to risk. If that is not satisfactory to the client, I suggest you look for better clients."

Jefferson bit into his Tootsie Roll Pop; he wanted to get to the best part of the candy.

"Marjorie, we are talking about a project where the structure will be worth millions of dollars. The curtainwall contract could be as much as five million. It is logarithmically bigger than any project we have done. I'm going to need more than that."

"If it's any consolation, underwriting is reviewing all our coverage limits. They know that buildings are getting taller and more expensive. But it's all about risk, our risk. You can make the mistake, but we pay for it."

"Yes, and we pay a pretty penny for that coverage too. It's over ten percent of our annual budget."

"I know. So, what are you thinking?"

"$5,000,000." There was no sound at the other end.

"Let me warn you up-front, that much coverage won't be cheap."

"Fine, whatever. And what about lowering our out-of-pocket deductible?"

"Vance, when its $100,000 out of your hide you pay a lot more attention; $25,000, maybe not so much.

"No one in the firm thinks about those things. They are just trying to do the best job possible."

"I'm sure. I'll get the numbers, the cost together. Five in coverage and what, $50,000 deductible?"

"Sounds perfect."

"Look, anything else?" Marjorie Fleet had anticipated the call. Her company had already tangled on bogus claims with Steel Simpson through two other clients.

"Sorry Marjorie, but just one more question: What if the client's claim is without merit? It's bogus, and he hasn't paid us our fees to boot?"

"The claim will be reviewed by us and an independent third party to determine whether or not your client has a valid claim. But until he pays you what is rightly owed for your services that have been performed in good faith, then we would not consider his claim. In other words, he can sue you all he likes, but we will demand that he makes payment to you for your services first. A court may disagree, but we'll not be coming out of pocket for the claim. Believe me, we have recent experience here."

"That's good to know. I'm relieved. Get back to me on lowering the deductible then. I'll look forward to hearing from you."

"Nice chatting, Vance. And you owe me a lunch." She hung up the phone.

Marilyn noticed that the call was over. She got up, knocked on Vance's door and walked in.

"Ah, the Anacin." His head was pounding. "Get me Steel Simpson on the phone."

"Certainly." As Marilyn walked out, he took note of her shapely ass. When the presentation was over, he and Marilyn were going to discuss the picnic—over dinner if not in a hotel room.

"Steel, I was just calling to tell you we are very excited about the presentation tomorrow. I think you'll be impressed."

"I'm sure I will be. What time is it again?" Steel Simpson knew exactly what time he was to be at the offices of NJ&M. He couldn't wait to see what his project would look like, and three choices to boot. But he was trying to sound casual, even mildly disinterested, like he had a lot of other projects under way and this was just another.

"Eleven A.M. Didn't Marilyn call?"

"I'm sure she talked to Ruth. Oh yeah, here it is on my calendar. Are you going to have lunch? I really did enjoy that club sandwich and the terrific potato salad."

Jefferson couldn't believe it. His new client was more interested in lunch than the design for the biggest project he had ever undertaken. He took the wrapper off another Tootsie Roll Pop.

"Certainly. I'll make sure we have that for you. Steel, I just wanted to remind you that per our agreement, payment is due tomorrow for this first phase of the work."

"What agreement? I signed a Memorandum of Understanding after our dinner. It didn't say when the design fee was due."

Jefferson's headache was not going away in spite of the two pain relievers he had taken.

"The contract I sent you. It's very clear. Payment is due on completion of the services rendered. I sent the contract two weeks ago."

"Oh yes, that. Yes, I have it here on my desk. It's a pretty lengthy document." Steel had indeed received it but wasn't going to read all the legal mumbo jumbo until after he had seen the designs. Then, if he liked any of them, he would get Irving Montlick to look at the contract. "Sorry, I've been too busy to look at it. You want a check for $200,000 tomorrow?"

"As stated in the agreement, yes. If it's any consolation, we've spent far more than that on this competition. But I'm fine with it. I didn't expect to make anything on this initial phase. I, we, just want to get you a great building."

"OK, fine. Let me see what I can do. I'll see you tomorrow." He hung up on Jefferson. Simpson knew he didn't have that much in the company account. The closing for the land was not until Friday and First National Bank in Evanston would only fund closing costs; there were no funds for predevelopment or design. "Ruth, get me the checkbook for the Oak Street Hotel project." Simpson always yelled at Ruth through the office door kept slightly open so he could do so.

Ruth rushed into his office. "What do you want?"

"The checkbook for the Oak Street Hotel project."

"But that account is closed."

"I know."

Marilyn was tidying her desk, preparing to leave. She had arranged for fresh flowers for the main conference room; lunches ordered for all the participants, and had the large three section conference table separated—one section for what Jefferson said would be four meeting participants, each place with a notepad and pen. She wondered why there weren't six chairs. Another section would be off to the side for box lunches, iced tea and fresh baked cookies. The last table would have sets of prints of each scheme. This arrangement allowed for generous space for the three models and the numerous presentation boards. She was checking the catering order and felt two hands on her shoulders.

"Miss Jones, you are very tense." Vance Jefferson was giving her a shoulder massage. She jolted upward.

"Mr. Jefferson, what are you doing? You startled me."

He removed his hands from her shoulders.

"You seem so tense lately, my dear. I hope all the pressure of this competition isn't bothering you."

Thinking about not seeing Connor for over a whole week, she replied. "In a way sir, in a way. But tomorrow is the big day."

"Indeed. It will be behind us. So, we need to get some other business done. How about we discuss the company picnic afterwards?"

"Certainly. I'll be right here as always."

Jefferson once again put his hands-on Marilyn's shoulders and now moved his hand to the back of her soft, smooth neck. She stiffened again. "No, we should discuss it over dinner. My treat. You deserve a night out after all the commotion of the last four weeks."

Marilyn remembered Jane's advice. Though it went against every instinct she had or felt, she replied, thinking: *"Fine, let's get this over with."*

"Thank you. That will be nice. I'll…I'll wear something dressier tomorrow."

"Do that, because we're going to someplace nice. It will be fun."

Marilyn slowly got up from her desk chair and got her handbag out of her bottom desk drawer. "Well, thank you, I really should be going now."

She headed for the lobby and once in the elevator she fought for breath, and tears began to run down her face. "Jerk off!"

CHAPTER 46

Connor put down his Koh-I-Noor drafting pen. The last drawing was done. And it was only 7 P.M. He walked around Team Three's space. Everyone was still there, but the mood seemed relaxed. As he looked about, he could see that everybody was finished or was close to finishing. Taubert came up to him.

"Well, Superman, I think we're pretty much done here. Caudy is just about complete with the last elevation, and I sent the draftsmen home. There is nothing more to do. We should celebrate."

"Yeah, good idea. We should. Any place in mind? The Berghof?"

"No, I have a better idea. I just happen to have a new membership to The Playboy Club." Taubert took out his gold Club Key from of his pocket and waved it at Connor.

"You're joking, right?"

"Nope, bought it last month. Cost me $100 but let me tell you it is worth it. The Bunnies are soooo hot! I'll get us in, but you have to pay the guest fee of $10."

Connor had read all about the Playboy Club. He never thought he would get to go because it was a private club. Jato's topless bar was more in his price range.

"Sounds great. After these last few weeks, I could use some fun."

Taubert polled the team. Caudy was in; so was Muktar and they caught young Tweedy, a draftsman on the project as he was leaving. No arm-twisting there, he was a go for sure. From his office Bob Marlow could see the smiling gathering of five members from Team Three. He got up and walked over to their space. It was strewn with bumwad, overfull wastepaper baskets and in-progress blueprints. It was a mess.

"Well, is it finished, Buonarroti?" referring to the Pope's constant question to the famous painter about the ceiling of the Sistine Chapel.

Connor replied: "Yes sir, Bob, as finished as I think it can be. Taubert's taking us as his guests to the Playboy Club. How about coming along?"

Marlow hesitated but only for a moment. The offer was tempting, and it did involve drinking. After a difficult late afternoon meeting with Jefferson, he knew he could use several drinks.

"I really shouldn't."

"Come on. We all need a celebration. We finished before midnight."

"Okay, sounds like a capital idea. Taubert do an expense report and charge the guest fees to marketing. The firm is picking this up. Let me get my coat. We can take cabs there."

Then West remembered. He had told Marilyn they would go out tonight when the work was finished. He went back to his desk and dialed her extension. No answer. Well, he would call her from the Club.

The cabs arrived at 116 East Walton in short order. The entrance was immediately recognized by an outer enclosure of steel and multi-colored Plexiglas panels illuminated from within. Above it, three Playboy flags hung off the building. Though it was early evening, the partiers found the club packed. After Taubert showed his key to the Welcome Bunny, he presented his new American Express card to pay for his guests and they made their way to the Playmate Bar. West was amazed. The Playmate waitresses were all gorgeous, decked out in white collars and bow ties, tight fitting satin outfits that accentuated their breasts, white bunny tails, fish net stockings, and the signature rabbit ears on their perfectly coiffed hair. On the wall behind the bar were back lit photos of many of the centerfolds he recognized from his days at Pratt and Harvard. There were probably over fifty naked women smiling at him.

"Some of these babes were actually Playmates in the magazine" Caudy yelled in Connor's ear above the din. Connor was instantly missing Marilyn. He was getting aroused by all the beautiful flesh. Although the bar was large, with seats for at least twenty-five people, it was standing room only. The place was dark but elegantly appointed with real teak paneling, accented with red, blue and yellow spotlights. Off to the side of the bar was a small stage where a group called The Lighter Side trio was playing. The big acts like Bobby Short, and even the likes of Ella Fitzgerald were booked into The Club Room. There was also The Dining Room known for its excellent Porterhouse steaks, and for the high rollers, The Living Room was on the upper floor. Here you could sit and party with the playmates. If you were lucky, they'd sit in your lap and feed you your drink.

"I need to make a call. Get me a Seagram's and ginger. I'll pay you back." Caudy nodded and tried to get the attention of Crys-Tail, a buxom, blond-haired playmate. Once he made contact, he couldn't believe how friendly she was. It was part of the magic of the place. The girls were more than just waitresses; they were "Bunnies," feeding your fantasies. She would return with the drinks, a big smile and a tab for three dollars.

West suspected he would find the pay phones by the restrooms and he was right. The noise and music from the bar area invaded the hallway, and he picked up the phone and deposited a quarter, then dialed Marilyn's apartment.

"Hello."

"Marilyn?"

"No, this is Jane. Connor?"

"Yeah, it's me. Can I talk to Marilyn?"

"Let me get her. She's been expecting you to come by."

After a moment, Marilyn came on the line. She had put herself back together after another pep talk from Jane and a large glass of Cabernet.

"Connor, where are you? I've been waiting for you."

"Sorry, that's why I'm calling. I can't make it. Some of the guys from the office wanted me to go out and celebrate finishing the presentation. I tried to get you at the office, but you were gone."

"Connor, I can hardly hear you. Where are you?"

"I'm, I'm at the Playboy Club. Taubert got us in. Bob Marlow's here too." West was trying his best to put an "officially sanctioned" office function on the night's adventure by adding Marlow's name.

"The Playboy Club? But we had a date…I haven't seen you in over week because of that damn project and you're drinking at the Playboy Club! It just figures Marlow and that playboy Taubert would drag you there!" Marilyn was taking out her anger with her boss on her boyfriend.

Connor was feeling the suffocation of a new relationship. "Look. I'm sorry, okay? And it's not a damn project. It's what I do. It's my job! I haven't gone out with these guys since I started here. I couldn't say no!"

Tears were welling up in Marilyn's eyes for the second time that day. "But I need you. We had a date!"

"Marilyn, I'll have plenty of time to be with you after tomorrow. I'll spend all of it with you."

"Right, well guess what? I'll be working. So, enjoy the cute little bunnies and screw you!" She slammed the phone down and began sobbing. Jane overheard the one-sided conversation and was there to offer Marilyn another glass of wine.

"I'm not married to you! Screw you back!" Connor muttered. He headed back to the bar. He hoped Caudy had his drink. He found him quickly holding the Seagram's and ginger. He took it and downed about half the glass.

"I guess that call went well. Girlfriend?" Caudy said to console Connor. From day one, they got along well and he had liked West immediately.

"Just the normal girlfriend problems."

"Women, can't live with them, can't drop them off at the curb when you're done with 'em."

"Yeah." Connor was taking another pull on his drink when Bob Marlow walked up.

"I see you're ready for another drink…" Marlow loved having drinking buddies, even if they were employees. Marlow got the attention of Bunny Tiffanie and ordered two double Evans on the rocks.

"What's wrong? You look down. Sorry the hard work is all done?"

"No, girlfriend problems."

"It's an occupational hazard. Let me guess. She expected to see you tonight?"

"How did you know?"

"I'm older and I've been through it. That's why I live by myself now."

Tiffanie returned with the drinks and a big smile, brushing Connor's hand as she gave him the liquid redemption. Connor smiled right back and for a brief moment, wished Tiffanie were his girlfriend. No bitching, just a smile and a drink. Bob paid her with a ten-dollar bill and told her to keep the change, ensuring she would stop back frequently to service their every need.

"To a job well done. I think Team Three has a fantastic design, thanks to you." Marlow clinked Connor's glass.

West took another deep pull and felt the alcohol doing its job; his anger was ebbing. "I better watch myself, there's a big presentation tomorrow."

"Glad you brought that up. Before you saw me tonight, I was meeting with Jefferson. He said he only wants Francis and me in the presentation. Something about not wanting to overwhelm or outgun the client."

"Sorry. I didn't hear you right; it's loud in here. Did you say I wouldn't be in the presentation?"

"That's right. No need. I'll present for us, Jefferson for Gerhard and Francis for his own effort. Look at it this way. You can party all you want tonight. You deserve it. And you can take the next three days off. Look for an apartment. I'm sure your cousin is tired of his house guest."

West took another swig of the Evan Williams. It was pretty strong on the rocks without the ginger ale. He didn't know what to say. He was disappointed, but quickly realized that Bob Marlow, a partner in the firm could present his idea as well as he could, and with more import. Plus, he just got three days off. He stared at the Centerfolds on the wall and smiled. "Well, I guess I'll just get blasted then!"

Tiffanie returned, and Connor ordered another double, as he stared right at her bunny tits.

CHAPTER 47

Vance Jefferson arrived at his office at 8:30 A.M. sharp and after being handed a cup of coffee from Marilyn, they headed to the main conference room.

"My, you look lovely today, my dear."

Marilyn was dressed in a dark red cocktail dress that was sleeveless but that closed high around the neck, somewhat oriental in style. A simple gold chain, not pearls, was the adornment hanging down to her taut breasts. She had on light hose and black satin pumps. She could fit in to any gala for the Chicago Symphony.

"You said we were going to a nice restaurant. I hope it's not Johnny's Luncheonette."

"Ha. No, not Johnny's." Vance was wearing a dark grey Glen Plaid suit complete with vest, white shirt with cufflinks, rep tie and a Rolex. She noticed his wedding ring and thought: *A lot that ring signifies for you, jerk.* She had to admit that for a middle-aged man he was quite handsome, especially his longish graying hair combed back and topped with the ever-present tortoise shell glasses. She imagined that the other jerk in her life, Connor, might look the same way in middle age.

When they got to the room the different teams had already arranged the drawings and models around the room. The projects faced the conference table where the client, Simpson and the partners would sit. The first project was Francis, Jr.'s, then Gerhard's, and finally Connor's. Jefferson started rearranging the order. He put Connor's first, left Gerhard's in the middle and then put Francis' effort on the right side. She could not make sense why, but in spite of their argument the night before, hoped it was because his design was the best. She decided it really didn't matter; she would be at her desk anyway and would only return at noon to check on the lunches. Marilyn admired the fresh spray of flowers on the side table. It was enormous and had cost the firm $150. It contained gladiolas, red roses, snapdragons with artistic palm fronds and wood branches. It was too early for the box lunches, but she had arranged for a platter of donuts and hot coffee even though the meeting was to begin at 11 A.M. "Hostess with the mostest!" she murmured under her breath.

At 10:45 A.M. Bob Marlow walked in. His head hurt, but he knew he could get through a five-to-ten-minute dissertation of Connor's design.

"Vance, I don't understand the order. Wait, now I get it. Junior's is last because that's the one we're pushing on Simpson. And I'll be first."

"Not quite. I've decided to present all three. I'm already doing Gerhard's, and Francis isn't a very, shall we say, persuasive presenter. I think I better do his part as well. So, then it doesn't make any sense for me to present two and you to do Leo's…I mean Connor's. I think I can handle it."

Marlow was by now getting a cup of black coffee and perusing the donuts. He was looking for a Boston Cream, his favorite. With his head pounding, Marlow shrugged; he was in no mood to disagree. There were no Boston Creams, so he settled for a jelly-filled.

"Fine, any way you want to handle it, Vance." He walked around and looked for the first time at all three finished designs. One could disagree with the architecture, the concepts and design, but they were all solid pieces of work. And the presentations were beautiful. The models were finished to a level you see in sales centers. The rendering team had produced two for each scheme, evoking the character and life this great project would bring to the city of Chicago.

Francis Nolan, Jr., ambled into the large space just before 11 A.M., and Jefferson immediately walked him back out of the conference room. Marlow thought it strange but got up to refill his coffee. He also looked for another donut and then decided his waistline didn't need it. Jefferson and Nolan returned and Junior looked confused and out of sorts.

11:00 A.M. 11:10 A.M. 11:15 A.M. No Simpson. Jefferson was annoyed by 11:20 and his blood was beginning to percolate. He thought, *"That fucking scumbag. He could at least be on time. We did all of this for him!"*

Finally, at 11:25 A.M. Marilyn escorted Steel Simpson, premier Chicago developer, into the room. All three partners stood up to shake his hand.

"Guys, so sorry to be a little late. I had an urgent call from my likely equity partner. Can't ignore the money now, can we?" But there had been no such call. Simpson was late because he wanted to be late, show the architect who was the main player in this deal. After Jefferson made introductions, Simpson went right to the donuts, picked one with colored sprinkles and took a bottle of water. Then he sat down, taking a big bite out of the free food. Finally, he looked around the room.

"Wow, Vance, you have outdone yourself." He scanned the three presentations, especially the models. The one on the left, the tower with three ellipses and a round core on one side was the most intriguing.

"I told you we would!" Jefferson went into his dog-and-pony-show mode. "Well, let's get started. We have lunch coming at noon. Hopefully I can show you all three schemes by then."

"Fine, but I have a hard stop at 12:30. Another appointment I'm afraid." Another lie, but Simpson wanted to control the agenda. Jefferson simmered, thinking, *"Three weeks of work on one of the most complex projects ever and he has just over one hour for it. What a dickhead!"* His dislike for this new client was growing by the minute.

"No problem. Let me start in reverse order if you don't mind. I also thought that I would present all schemes, so you're not swayed by one presenter over another."

"Good idea. Proceed."

Out of the corner of his eye, Bob Marlow was sizing up Steel Simpson. He could see that Jefferson was annoyed with the man's late arrival and limited time for what had to be an important meeting. Simpson had on a dark blue pin stripe suit, but the pin stripes were not subtle. He resembled a gangster. His hair was black, but with all the pomade on it, slicked back, it looked like a helmet. Except for a too loud and too bright red tie, Bob thought he was just another suit. He decided to reserve final judgment until after the festivities were all done. Marlow began to wish he had gotten another donut, but the strong coffee had helped his head.

Jefferson walked over to Francis's eighty story tower. *"Why is he starting with the one he wants to sell Simpson on? You save that for last,"* Marlow wondered.

"This effort was done by Leo Skoroshod, one of our best senior designers. Unfortunately, Leo passed away last week in the midst of the presentation work. I thought of calling you, Steel, and asking for an extension for today, but we forged on in his memory."

Bob Marlow could not believe what he was hearing. He looked at Francis Jr., who had his head down and was drawing cartoons on his pad of paper. He continued to stare at Francis to get his attention, but it was unsuccessful. He turned his gaze to Vance, who met his stare for a moment and kept on talking.

"You wanted a tower and this one is 80 stories. The base is all parking, and then the first floor of the tower has distinct elevators going to each element. First, 40 stories of office with very nice floor plates of 13,000 square feet. We thought that your market here would be small executive and private firms, not big corporations who would want to be downtown in the Loop. The middle section..."

"13,000 square feet won't work. It's too small." Simpson was bringing a quick negative tone to the scheme right away.

"A detail, I'm sure. But I think when you do market studies, you'll see that I'm correct." Jefferson would not let the comment go unanswered.

"Whatever." Simpson's reply was dismissive, thinking, *"Fucking architects always think they know more about development than the developer."*

"As I was saying, the next component is the hotel at 20 stories and at the top, 20 stories of condominiums."

"No restaurant or observation deck at the top?"

"No, we didn't want to take up more space for two dedicated elevators. And Leo thought that these functions over time would become less popular."

Simpson shook his head and thought, *"Now the designer's a developer!"* He said nothing but looked at his watch.

Jefferson continued. "The windows are all very generous in size, four by seven, and fit all three components."

Simpson glanced at his watch again. "Let's keep moving."

Marlow got up, poured another cup of coffee and reached for a blueberry donut, making a mental note to tell Marilyn about Boston Creams.

"Certainly. The next effort was done by Gerhard Dietrich, another of our very talented designers. He has obviously departed somewhat from the program, thinking that a grouping of three differently sized elegant buildings on a park like podium would work best. It might be called Chicago Center. We did some research and there are other properties around your site that could be acquired and developed. Eventually it might be called Chicago World Center."

"I don't pay you…sorry, I thought the program was clear—a tower."

"Yes, but it's always good to have options…choices."

"So, for my $200,000 I get only two schemes in reality, not three. What about the last one?"

Jefferson was getting flustered. The man had no tact whatsoever. Marlow shook his head. He still had enough booze left in him that he didn't care what he would say.

"Mr. Simpson. I don't know you, though I do know of your reputation. I've watched over 40 professionals work on these schemes over the last four weeks. Frankly, and I told Vance this, you only deserved one for $200,000. So, if you don't like the design, fine, but please do us the courtesy of appreciating the fact that we've invested our best talents on these schemes and we're taking a big hit on this phase." Marlow took a drink of his coffee.

Vance glared at Marlow. "Bob, its fine. Let's move on."

Simpson realized he had pushed too hard. He knew at times he could be a real prick. "Bob, Mr. Marlow, I really appreciate all that has been done here, and this middle scheme is attractive and well-proportioned. I might develop it somewhere else in the future. But my investors expect to see a tower, that's all I meant by the comment. I mean no offense. I am really interested in the last scheme. I think you've saved the best for last, right Vance?"

"Certainly. This last scheme was designed by Francis Nolan here. He is of course our most senior and talented designer and this design illustrates why our firm has and always will be at the forefront of the architectural profession."

Marlow almost spit out the last of the donut in his mouth. He could not believe that Vance was giving all the credit for the design to their mediocre partner. How was he going to explain this to Connor who had just been thrown under the bus by the senior partner?

Jefferson proceeded to describe Connor's design in detail. He even pointed out that the condominiums and hotel had been switched location wise, and Simpson agreed that was a great idea. After all, once the condos were sold, he did not own them. But the hotel…over time he could easily sell a hotel that started on the 60th floor of a building at a premium price. Simpson got up, looked at the renderings and studied the model intently. He even understood the metaphor of the building as a sailing ship on the lake. Then Jefferson flipped a small toggle switch on the side of the wood base. Slowly the small ellipse topping the building started to rotate.

"We thought it would be fun if the restaurant on the top floor rotated. But the floor below is the observation deck, and we thought it would be really nifty if the observation floor was glass." By now the ellipse had rotated a full 90 degrees to the main structure and extended well out over it. "Visitors will be treated not only to exceptional views of the whole of Chicagoland and the lake but can look straight down 75 floors to the ground below."

"I love it. This is the one!" Simpson beamed.

At 12:15 P.M., knowing that the meeting had started late, Marilyn entered through the kitchen door with a cart containing five white boxes, a bowl of salad, and the plate of warm chocolate chip cookies. There were also pitchers of iced tea and water. Simpson was walking around the model with Jefferson and Francis who had been motioned over by Vance.

"This is just a fabulous design, Francis! No wonder you are the chief design guy. I really look forward to working directly with you on this project. We'll start right after I get back from Europe. Maybe we can have dinner first to discuss ah, refinements."

"Sure, Mr. Simpson, I mean, Steel. That would be great…"

Marilyn overheard the conversation; she was confused. They were standing over Connor's design, but Simpson was congratulating Francis.

"Francis, how did you get the idea to change the location of the hotel with the condos? That was spot on, and you know I've been thinking about that, too. It makes much better sense." It was fortunate that Simpson's question was rhetorical as Francis had no reply anyway. His own design was exactly per the program.

"Steel, Francis is kind of quiet and all, but he is a great designer and this scheme shows that. I mean the concept of sails and a mast, and the outside elevators. Like sailors climbing up the mast. Great idea, Francis."

Marilyn put the lunch on the table and quickly left the room. In the kitchen she poured a glass of water and gasped as she drank it. She had to tell Connor.

Simpson looked at his watch. "Damn, look at the time. Gentlemen, I'm sorry but I have to go. He pointed to the box lunches. "Can I take a..."

"Certainly. By all means." What else could Jefferson say?

"It does have that great German potato salad, right?"

"Of course. But Steel, ah, do you have a check for me?"

Simpson picked up a box lunch and stuffed three cookies in his pocket. He wished they had cans of Coke.

"Oh yeah, here it is in my pocket." He produced a white envelope and handed it to Jefferson. Then Simpson was out the door with a quick, "See you later," his free lunch in hand.

CHAPTER 48

"Just what the hell are you doing, Vance!?"

"What do you mean?" Jefferson replied, trying to act perplexed at the question, then biting into his ham on rye.

"You know fucking well what I mean. Giving Francis credit for someone else's design. Connor's design. That's just plain wrong! He busted his ass working on it."

"And Francis did likewise on his design. Unfortunately, it happened to be lacking in many respects and was not what the client wanted. And what the client wants, deserves, is for the head of design in this firm to have produced the project he wanted. That gives him confidence in our abilities from the top down, and we validate young Francis as the heir to his father's design reputation."

"But Connor came up with the concept. You can't steal it from him. He needs to be recognized. It's unethical, Vance!"

Jefferson paused from his lunch. "The way I look at it, the design does not belong to Connor West but to Nolan, yours truly, and Marlow. It was produced by the firm and the firm paid for it. The firm owns it, not West. And I assure you, young West's star is rising fast in this firm. You told me he came up with the idea, fine, though I have my doubts…"

"Come on, everyone knows it is his. It was there on the wall Tuesday morning."

"Yes, and Leo worked on it with him on Monday, and maybe over the whole weekend. And Jerzy really gave him the idea. He told me so."

"What? That's bullshit! All Jerzy did was to verify it could work structurally."

"Look, we have a client that is pleased with what we produced. Isn't that all that matters? The design, God willing, will be built; we'll make a ton of money, and Connor, if you handle him properly, will go far in this firm. He'll eventually have many designs attributed to him. After all Leo is gone, and someday Junior will sell his interest to you and me and move to some place where all the queers hang out."

"You got it all figured out, don't you? Francis Nolan told me not to trust you."

"Oh, he did? Well, his time is past. All that Chicago cronyism and doing business with his pal the mayor and the governor. This project will have every developer in America calling us."

"If they're anything like Simpson, I might sell you my interest too!" Marlow left the room, leaving behind his box lunch. He had lost his appetite.

"Wha...allo, yeah?"

"Connor are you OK?"

Connor shook his head and tried to focus on the phone. It was fuzzy. "Marilyn? Yeah, I'm OK. I was sleeping."

"At 1:00 P.M.?"

"It's 1:00 P.M.?"

"Yes, it is."

"I'm fine. I guess I got a little drunk last night. Good to hear your voice. Look, I know we had a date, but it couldn't be helped. I'm sorry. I don't want to fight." He was sitting up in bed now, and the call from his girlfriend was almost better than a Bloody Mary.

"No, I'm sorry. You have every right to go out with your friends and have a good time. I just had a really bad day yesterday and wanted to see you. Listen, I have to tell you something; I don't have much time."

"What? Is something wrong?"

"Well yes, but it's not me. I just overheard the end of the presentation with Mr. Simpson, the developer. Mr. Jefferson gave Mr. Nolan, Francis Junior, credit for your building design!"

West shook his head and rubbed his eyes. The bright afternoon sun was flooding into his studio. He squinted, and his head felt like it was full of sawdust. "What? Jefferson did what?" He had heard Marilyn's words, but he wanted confirmation.

"He told that developer that Francis was the one who came up with your design. It is so wrong. I'm so sorry."

"OK, let me get this straight. Jefferson told, what's the guy's name, that Junior was the designer of my building?"

"Simpson. His name is Steel Simpson. He's the one who's going to build Chicago World Tower. Yes, he told him that Francis designed it."

West was finally starting to comprehend Marilyn's message. "That son of a bitch gave Junior credit for my design. Shit!"

"Look. I just wanted you to know. I think you should discuss it with Mr. Marlow. I think he was just as surprised as I was."

"Yeah, hey I'm off for a couple of days. I want to see you tonight. Let's go out. I miss you so much…"

"Connor. I can't. I have an appointment."

"An appointment? What kind of an appointment?"

"Sorry, I can't say. We can go out tomorrow. Maybe I'll even take a day off. The weather is supposed to be nice and we can bike ride."

"I told you where I was last night. Why can't you tell me where you're going?"

"I just can't. I've got to go. I'll call you first thing tomorrow. And don't be hungover. We'll have a fun day. I'd love to show you the Lincoln Park Zoo. I love you." She hung up the phone and headed back to the conference room to clean up.

Vance Jefferson returned to his office. He was unsettled, but glad he did what he had done. It was the best move for the firm. Screw that self-righteous alcoholic Marlow. He opened the envelope from Simpson. He smiled. $200,000 made out to the firm, and correctly spelled. As he was getting up to take the check to the company's accountant, Norman Weese, he glanced at the check again. "Oak Street Hotel Development Partners Corp."

"Odd." Jefferson stared at the issuing entity on the top left-hand corner of the check. The signature was clearly Simpson's. He shrugged and headed for the accountant's office. "Developers, always moving money around," he mused to himself.

"What are you doing here? I gave you a couple of days off. You look like dog shit that got run over by a lawnmower."

Connor sat down in the guest chair of Bob Marlow's office. The coffee pot was empty but that was not what he wanted; he hoped Marlow might take out the Evan Williams. At this moment he needed some liquid courage.

"I quit!"

"What the hell you talking about? You can't quit. You just finished designing an outstanding building."

"You mean Francis' outstanding building?!"

Marlow instantly knew what West's trip to the office was all about. But how did he know so quickly? Then he remembered Marilyn setting out the lunches.

"OK, now just hold on. I knew nothing about this. I think it sucks too!"

"Bob, it's my design! How can he give Francis credit for it? What kind of a company is this? That's totally unethical. So, fine, I quit! Let Francis complete it and completely fuck it up."

"Like I said, hold on. You're exhausted from the last two weeks and I'm sure a little hung over after last night. Here. You're off today, so be my guest." Marlow reached in his drawer for the bottle of Evan W. He poured Connor a double shot and decided the best strategy was to change the subject. "Hey, that was a lot of fun last night. Those Playmates are certainly pretty hot. If I were only 25 years younger. I kind of envy you."

"Why? I keep getting shit on! Leo dies, someone else is handed my design on a silver platter, and, and…"

"And what? Sounds like a pity party to me. Poor kid from New York graduates from Harvard, gets big bucks from the top Chicago architectural firm, and now his first design is gonna be built. Excuse me, but where's my hanky…"

West took another sip of his bourbon. It was truly welcome. He was mellowing. "I'm sorry, you're right…to a point. But I busted my ass on that scheme, and I get no credit. The developer thinks Junior did it and his scheme was a piece of crap."

"If it helps, Simpson picked your design before he even knew who did it. He was staring at it from the minute he walked in the door."

"So why not give me credit?"

"As Jefferson says, and to a point I have to agree with him, it's not your design, it's the firm's design. You're an employee of this company, so we basically own you, and by extension, anything you design."

"Fine, but how about thank you, a little recognition?

"Haven't I paid you that compliment several times? And everyone on the team looks up to you. Even Taubert. Hell, he bought you two Tequila shots last night! And Jefferson did make a valid point. How would it look if the best design we presented was done by a green kid right out of school, not by the head of design? It wouldn't reflect very well on the firm, would it?"

The bourbon was mellowing the young architect. "I guess not. I can understand that."

"Connor, as I told you before, you remind me of me long ago. You have a great future here. Your first design is going to be built! Francis will tire before long of this business. He just wants to spend his inheritance. He has no passion for architecture. But you do! Why else would you have come into this tomb on a beautiful Saturday and start designing, when you could have been doing whatever you kids do on the weekend? Because it's in your blood. It's what you do.

Listen, in five years you'll be a full partner, maybe the firm will be Jefferson, Marlow and West."

Connor slumped back in his chair. Without waiting for an invitation, he poured himself another drink. "OK, as I've said before, thanks for the pep talk. I'll take back my resignation…for now. But there better not be any more monkey business. You and I, Taubert, Caudy, we're going to finish this building."

"Absolutely. Whatever you say. Now go find an apartment."

"I've had one for two weeks—a sublease in Sandberg Village. It's on the 10ᵗʰ floor. View of Lincoln Park."

"Very nice. I'll expect to get an invite for dinner. Now get out of here."

Connor left not feeling totally placated, but much better than when he walked in. Marlow put the booze away and went back to checking shop drawings. The phone rang.

"Marlow."

"Bob, this is Vance. Just heard from Simpson. We need to get the model down to the shipping department along with the presentation boards. It's going to Monaco."

"Which design?"

"Very funny. Your boy's design. I mean Francis' design."

"I'll get right on it."

"And one other thing. On Monday, Connor reports for work to Francis. He'll work under him. That way Junior can't fuck up Connor's design too badly."

CHAPTER 49

"Jane, I'm nervous. I don't think I can go through with this." Marilyn was talking to Jane on the phone. It was 6:00 P.M. and she had just come back from the women's restroom on the 14th floor, where she applied fresh makeup, and dark red lipstick to match her Mandarin cocktail dress.

"You'll be fine. Take the Valium I gave you. It will calm you down. Just remember, you're in charge. He just wants to be seen with eye candy on his arm. He's living a fantasy; his wife is probably at home in sweatpants and curlers getting ready to order pizza. Oh, and order a cocktail, not white wine. Like a daiquiri or a whiskey sour. He'll be impressed."

"I don't want to impress him!" She hung up.

At that moment Vance Jefferson walked out of his office. He looked ready for the evening as well. Marilyn could smell some recently applied English Leather cologne. She put the Valium in her mouth and finished the water in the glass on her desk, looked up at J. Vance Jefferson and smiled. She hoped it wasn't too forced.

"Marilyn, you are radiant. I love that red dress. Am I paying you too much?"

"Seriously sir, too much? I can barely afford my apartment, and I have a roommate."

"We may need to rectify that. And you'll have to tell me all about a…"

"Jane. She's a nurse at Rush Presbyterian Hospital. She's great."

"Wonderful. Let's get going. I have a car waiting for us. I hope you like French food?"

"It's my favorite!" Marilyn actually liked Italian better, but it was time to play the game.

The black Cadillac pulled up to a long, covered canopy that led up to the front door of 660 North Rush Street. On either side on fabric panels were the words "Chez Paul." Chicago's most famous French restaurant beckoned. Housed in the former mansion of Robert Hall McCormick, it was a Chicago landmark, both for the building and the food. Marilyn was vaguely familiar with the place; she had booked a few lunches for Jefferson with important clients, and knew it was very expensive from his expense reports. She was a little excited and nervous at the same time. The driver opened the door and they exited, Jefferson taking Marilyn's arm.

"Bonjour, Monsieur Jefferson, how are you?" The owner Bill Contos, son of Paul Contos who opened Chez Paul in 1945, greeted the handsome couple.

"Fine Bill, just fine."

"Mademoiselle, enchanted." Contos bent down and kissed Marilyn's hand. "Come, your usual table is ready." Taking two large leatherbound menus and a book that was the wine list, Bill led them to the Louis Room, the restaurant's most elegant and romantic space, complemented with an ornate fireplace. Its marble mantel had been given to Robert McCormick by King Victor Emmanuel III of Italy. Each table in the room was set with white tablecloths and the finest china and crystal. There was a vase of fresh flowers. Contos pulled out a cream-colored armchair for Marilyn and then with a flourish, took the napkin from the table, shook it gently and placed it on her lap. The Valium was beginning to have its intended effect, and Marilyn started to relax. She had never been to a place like this. It was magical.

"Would you care to start off with a cocktail?"

"Yes, we would. Marilyn?" Jefferson was interested in what his date might order, probably a glass of white wine.

"I'll have a Cosmopolitan." Jane wasn't the only one who knew cocktails. "I like it pink, please. Plenty of cranberry juice. Absolut Vodka."

"Excellent!"

"Yes, excellent." Jefferson was impressed. He had underestimated his secretary. "I'll have a Tanqueray martini, dry, up, with olives. Thank you, Bill."

"Very fine. Your waiter this evening is Roger. Enjoy the evening."

"Oh, I believe we will," Vance smiled at Marilyn, who was smiling back. "Now tell me all about your roommate, and then we can talk about the picnic."

"It's me. Buzz me up." Reese Anne Simpson was annoyed that she didn't even have a key to her own condominium on Walton Street. The building, containing only two units on each of its 10 floors, was too small to have a doorman. Hearing the buzzer, she opened the imposing door and entered a small but elegant elevator lobby. She pressed the call button and the door of one of the two elevator cabs opened. She pressed nine. Steel Simpson was waiting at the door when she exited, wearing a dark blue bathrobe and matching silk slippers with the initial "SS" on the tops.

"Why don't I have a key to this fucking bachelor pad, Steel?"

"And hello to you, too. Maybe if you stayed here more often, you might have one." Simpson was surprised to see his wife; she rarely visited their home in the city.

"We live in Glencoe, remember? The house with no maid."

"I don't have a maid either. Just the same once a week cleaning service you have."

He walked over to a polished sideboard in the living room. There were crystal decanters of Scotch, bourbon and gin, and an ice bucket. He filled a Baccarat glass with ice and poured Reese a generous glass of gin.

"But you have Lurch."

"Lothar. The name is Lothar. So what? And to what do I owe this visit, and are we staying the night?"

Reese took the glass and stroked her husband's hand. With his slicked back hair and dark blue bathrobe, he was handsome in a nasty sort of way. She was horny and the thought of spending the night intrigued her. If only he were a better lover. The five-minute wonder, she called him.

Reese wasn't much for pleasantries. "What the fuck is the Arson Investigation Unit doing coming to visit me?"

"Oh shit, I forgot to talk to you about that. Damn! What did you tell them?"

"The truth. What was I supposed to tell them? They wanted to know about your brief sleepover last April."

"Did they ask you what time I got there?"

"As a matter of fact, they did. I looked at the clock. It was 10:30 P.M., and I had just gone to bed. And what the hell were you doing up in Glencoe at 10:30 P.M.?"

"Never mind that. 10:30 P.M. Fuck! I told them 11:30 P.M."

"You haven't told me why they're interested in you."

"There was a fire."

"In one of your warehouses? I thought that cop Grabowski told me it was at the lake. You don't own anything down there except that piece of shit land."

"Look, if he calls back, tell him you made a mistake. It was 11:30 P.M., okay?"

"Well. I guess I could tell him I stayed up to watch Johnny Carson. I do like it when he has Don Rickles on."

"Imagine that…"

"And when am I going to get a full-time maid? Everyone on the lake has one."

"Maybe if your old man hadn't cut you off when we got married…"

"I'm beginning to see why," Reese Simpson acidly replied.

"Screw you. When I get Chicago World Tower done, you'll be able to afford all the maids you want. Now, I'm tired and I'm going to bed. You coming?"

"Yes, master. You gonna tie me up again?"

CHAPTER 50

The arrangements didn't work out as planned. Since there were no more seats available on the Concorde flight that Ali Sharif was on, Steel Simpson flew from Chicago to JFK on Northwest Saturday morning, and then booked a first-class flight to Paris aboard TWA on a Lockheed L-1011. While he had wanted to fly the Concorde in spite of its astronomical cost, the L-1011 was as new and much more spacious. In fact, this was the first time Steel Simpson had ever flown across the ocean.

As he enjoyed a glass of champagne, he was glad that he was not traveling with Ali. The man was a smug ass. Simpson reached for a notepad from his briefcase. He reviewed the trip logistics. He would connect at Orly Airport by Air France to Monte Carlo, principality of Monaco. If Jefferson had done his job, the model and presentation boards, along with three sets of schematic drawings, would be waiting at the Ritz Hotel across the street from Monte Carlo's world-famous casino. If he could get the equity from Ali's dad, Prince Zaidan bin Al Saud, he might try his luck at the casino, even though this whole venture was costing him a fortune—rooms at the Ritz were $125 a night. Renting a conference room large enough for the prince and all of his entourage was costing $3,600 without food. It was a good thing the camel jockeys didn't drink.

Once he arrived in Monaco, he hoped there would be time for a nap to offset the jet lag and the booze. He needed to be sharp. He would cab it to the marina where the yacht *Flying Carpet* was docked. This was scheduled at 6:00 P.M., but Ali told him to be late as it was customary in Saudi culture. He said there would be much small talk before dinner and not to be annoyed at the many personal questions that would be asked. He further cautioned that this evening was purely a "getting to know you, getting to know all about you" affair. There was to be no discussion of his project. He was not to show the soles of his shoes. He needed to eat with his right hand, even though he was left-handed. Do not discuss sex; try every dish prepared at the table. The Prince will say yes to most things, but do not misconstrue that to mean he agrees; he is just being agreeable. Presenting a business card is not necessary but a firm, long handshake is.

The presentation was set for the following day at 11:00 A.M. at the hotel. There would be a break at noon for prayer, when the Saudi's went to another room that he had to book and get on their knees on little rugs and pray. Then the Ritz was serving lunch to the dozen people in the entourage, another $600.

He reviewed the final design statistics written on his pad. He was getting hard just thinking about his great building and he was sure the sheiks would be blown away with the design.

Lunch arrived before he could order a real drink. He grabbed a stewardess by the arm. "Hey, can I get a martini here?"

"Certainly, sir, certainly," replied Cindy, pulling her arm away. She returned to the galley where Elizabeth, another stewardess, was putting hot rolls in a basket.

"The guy in 4B is a jerk. Why don't you drop a hot roll on his lap?"

"Will do, girlfriend."

At 4:00 P.M., Simpson's journey was done. He was a little drunk and a lot tired. Maybe he should have traveled with Ali; he obviously knew his way around Europe. He collapsed on his soft hotel bed. Immediately, there was a knock on the door. He got up, stumbled over and opened it. It was his luggage followed by a waiter with a cart. It contained a bottle of Stolichnaya vodka, two crystal glasses, a bucket of ice, and a plate of crackers with a small dish of caviar.

"I didn't order caviar."

"Compliments of the house, monsieur. Welcome to the Ritz." The bellboy handed Simpson the bill. He looked at it and realized he didn't know how much 438 Francs were in American dollars. He signed it and gave the baggage boy a dollar. The young man looked down at it and said: "Merci," in a disdainful way and left.

After a half hour nap, a cold shower and taking two aspirin with a good pour of Stoli, Steel Simpson was ready for his big date. He dressed conservatively, another tip from Ali—black suit and dark blue tie. He went down to the lobby and though ornate, aged and heavy, it suited the developer. It was impressive by every standard. Much more regal than the cold, modern design that Royalton had incorporated into his hotel in Chicago.

Outside, the doorman hailed a cab, which fortunately, was black. Simpson wondered if he should have ordered a car for a more impressive entrance, but decided it would cost too much. Maybe in the dim light no one would notice that he was not in a limousine.

He read from the note that he penned in the room. Ali told him not to bring a briefcase for this introductory meeting. "Port Hercule, Chicane Quay, Berth 14."

"Oui, monsieur. Monsieur, s'il vous plait, I can only take you to the quay. You must walk to Berth 14."

"Fine, OK." Simpson was pleased he had not rented a limo. No one would have seen it anyway.

Simpson exited the cab at the entrance to the dock. There was a small booth with an official wearing a captain's cap and a locked gate with chain link fence extending four feet in either direction, beyond the wooden planks of the dock. He assumed that he had to check in, and after announcing who he was visiting and presenting his passport, the door clicked open and the needy developer was in Candyland.

Ahead of him were yachts the likes of which he had never seen on Lake Michigan. Each one seemed to be larger than the next, an exercise in nautical one-upmanship; whoever had the biggest yacht won. As he walked toward the *Flying Carpet*, he fantasized about owning one of these floating mansions one day and having a crew to care for it. Finally, he arrived at Berth 14, and the *Flying Carpet* looked distinctively larger than the rest. It had to be at least 150 feet long, two decks high above the promenade deck, and from looking at the portholes, two more decks below it. The ship was painted gloss black and white and had a traditional smokestack, painted in green with a gold band, the colors of the Saudi flag. At the ramp were two dark-skinned, heavy-set men, dressed in black suits. Simpson announced himself and produced his passport once again. The larger of the two men asked him to raise his arms and he was patted down. But his arrival, now 6:20 P.M., had been anticipated.

As soon as he crossed the gangplank, Ali Sharif came out from the main lounge in traditional Saudi robes and a red and white keffiyeh, signifying that he was a member of the royal family.

"Steel, you made it! I was worried."

"Nothing to it. I've been to Orly a couple of times. Good to see you." He shook Ali's hand and as instructed, made sure it was firm and lasted at least 15 seconds. Ali ushered Simpson into the main lounge, larger than his living room on Walton Street. It was laid out with four large leather sofas around a coffee table. There were banquettes on either side. The walls were a rich walnut in a high lacquer finish, adorned with nautical paintings. At one side was a bar with four stools and a full array of the finest booze. Simpson was taken aback. *"I thought these rag-heads didn't drink?"* he thought, confused.

"Please, Steel, this way. Let me make the introductions." Sharif led Simpson past the couches to an open area where a half dozen men were talking. All of them were attired in the finest silk robes, red and white headdress with headbands consisting of two gold ropes. Two wore black shoes, but the rest wore simple leather sandals.

"Father, may I present my good friend, Mr. Steel Simpson, from Chicago. Mr. Steel, my esteemed father, His Excellency Prince Zaidan bin Abdullah Al Saud." The Crown Prince of Saudi Arabia turned and looked through Simpson with deep piercing eyes, as if he could read his soul. He was tall and thin, probably five feet eleven, with a narrow, tanned face and perfectly trimmed goatee. His thobe was deep blue silk trimmed in gold. He bowed slightly and then held out his hand. Simpson took it and shook it perhaps too much and too hard.

"Mr. Steel, I am honored to meet you. My son tells me you were classmates at university. I am sure you contributed to his fully matriculating and receiving his diploma." The Crown Prince spoke in precise clipped tones, a result of his English boarding school and Cambridge education.

"Your Excellency, the pleasure is mine. I am honored to be in your company. I assure you though that it was I that benefited from your son's friendship. I would never have passed International Economics had it not been for Ali's class notes."

"It would appear then, that you both benefited. I understand you are very successful in Chicago."

"Hardly sir, just a working stiff, as we say in America."

"Come sit down. I am curious to know all about you. Would you care for a drink? We have, as you can see, a full bar."

Steel was not sure how to answer. Ali had not given him any tips on what to do when offered a drink. He would have killed for a martini at that moment; his stomach was in knots. He had never been in the presence of royalty. Yeah, a drink was the ticket.

"Thank you. I'll have, have a… an orange juice please. With ice." The waiter standing by nodded

Ali spoke: "I'll have a Coke. Father?"

"I will join Mr. Steel. Orange juice would be very refreshing. Tell me Mr. Steel, are you married?" The personal questions had begun.

"To a wonderful woman, Reese Anne."

"Is she from Chicago, too? Who is her father?"

"Yes, Excellency, from Chicago. Her father is Walter Banfield. He has a seat on the Chicago Board of Trade. He's the best father-in-law one could ask for. They're an old Chicago family."

"Impressive. And what does he do to warrant such an esteemed position? I am very familiar with that board."

"They are in the—a—food processing business. Cattle, cows…" Simpson thought that saying his for-shit father-in-law was in the slaughterhouse business would be unseemly.

"I see. Most interesting. Tell me, Mr. Steel, do you have children? I myself have 21, with four wives, however. Ali, though, is my most precious son. I have indulged him more than the others. Some day he shall succeed me."

"No, Excellency, not yet. We are, well, I guess very busy. Some-day though…"

"Pity. Children are a blessing from Allah. And they will take care of you in your old age. Assure me that someday you will have many."

"I'll have to ask my wife about that."

"So, tell me where in Chicago do you live?"

The interrogation continued right through dinner. Simpson was seated between the crown prince and Abdul Bin Salman, a minor interior minister who spoke only broken English. Platters of lamb, chicken, rice, vegetables and traditional Saudi dishes like kabsa, quzi, mandi, and markouk bread were served. Simpson took small portions from each plate, and except for the grilled chicken and the lamb, he detested all of it. He wanted to throw up. Dessert, however, was vanilla ice cream with kleeja, a type of cookie. Strong coffee followed.

It was now 10:00 P.M. Jet lag was overcoming Simpson in spite of the all-too-brief nap. His head pounded from the never-ending conversation; he hated chit chat. He wanted to discuss his project and oil money, but he knew if he breathed any word on those two topics, that his hopes of making either a reality were non-existent. The crown prince stood up from the table.

"My new friend, Mr. Steel, I am sure you must be very tired from your travels today. My apologies for being so inconsiderate and thank you for indulging me in our most enjoyable conversation. I am afraid it is a custom of my country."

"Not at all, your Excellency. The pleasure is mine and I have enjoyed our talk and the delicious food. You are very kind to extend such hospitality." Exhausted or not, Simpson could sling it. "I look forward to our further discussions tomorrow. I am very excited to show you the design for... I mean to our meeting tomorrow."

"Ah, yes. Again, I must apologize. I am afraid I must cancel our meeting. I have to meet with the Minister of the Exchequer of Great Britain, what you would call the Secretary of the Treasury. It cannot be helped. As I told you this is the first time my country has been invited to this International Conference and I must take every opportunity...Well, nevertheless, we must reschedule."

Simpson's posture told the story. He deflated like a balloon. This was the worse news possible. Plus, he would never get back the cost of the two rooms, the lunch, the set-up, all of it. "Uh, well, I understand Prince," forgetting that "Excellency" was the correct title. "But I'm only here until the 19th."

"Perhaps you can extend your visit until the 20th? I was hoping you might show us your project here on the boat on the 19th. We can rearrange furniture. We have easels. At 1:00 P.M.? We will have the afternoon. I promise my full attention."

"OK, I think I can do that. Certainly."

"Excellent then. We can even discuss the financing if the project holds interest for my family. I'll let Ali show you out. Good night, Mr. Simpson." With that he turned and left through the right passageway that led to his bed chambers.

Simpson followed Ali out to the rear deck, where his host paused. "Good job, Steel. I believe my father is impressed. Sorry about the sudden change of plans. Another Saudi tradition. I'm afraid you are just not as important as the Minister of the Exchequer. This is the first time we have been invited to this conference to sit at the table with the big boys, former colony that we are. But then we discovered oil. Now everyone likes us."

"Well, I'll do whatever it takes. I know both of you will be impressed with the design. But one question. Was that a test about the offer of a drink?"

"Indeed, it was. And you passed it with flying colors. It would have been taken as a great offense if you had a cocktail in the presence of my father. Now, if he had insisted that you have a drink that would be different."

"Then why it is even on board the yacht? Isn't it Saudi territory after all?"

"No, the yacht belongs to a Swiss corporation set up by the family, so it is technically Swiss soil. We use it to entertain Europeans and Americans. These days you can't get deals done without the necessary liquid oil, and I don't mean the black kind. I'll see you Tuesday. Go home and have a stiff drink and a good night's sleep. And by way of apology, I'll send a driver by at 11 A.M. with a car to take you sightseeing. He speaks excellent English. He'll show you all the sights, and in the afternoon, will take you to Eze, across the border in France. It's a beautiful little town."

The glass was empty. Simpson reached into the ice bucket for the last few pieces of ice. He poured the Stoli into the glass, swirled his finger in it to cool the clear liquid and took a deep pull. "Sand gophers!"

CHAPTER 51

The seating in the main lounge of the *Flying Carpet* had been re-arranged so all of the couches were on one side of the room, and Steel Simpson's design for Chicago World Tower was on the other, displayed on easels, with the model in the center on the coffee table. The wait in the morning had been interminable. But now Steel was standing in front of his audience, the crown prince, Ali Zyiad, and three other family members, who had not been present two days earlier. The prince was smiling and gently applauding.

"Very impressive, Mr. Simpson. Very dynamic. A truly exciting design."

"Thank you, your Excellency."

"We must do away with the formalities. From now on you must call me Zaidan. And I will call you Steel. Bring Mr. Simpson a drink. After that excellent presentation he deserves one. Please have a cocktail, Steel."

"Thank you, your...I mean, Zaidan. A beer would be nice..." The attendant nodded.

"Excellent, bring us three. Ali and I shall join you. Is Heineken all right?"

Once again, Simpson was stunned and looked it. He knew Ali drank from the many frat parties at Northwestern, but the crown prince? Plus, the new informality. He might be gambling in the casino yet.

"Are you shocked, Steel? I went to Cambridge, you know. We were fond of our pints. And anyway, we are technically in Switzerland now. So, let's talk financing. I know that Ali has briefed you on our real estate investments. They are admittedly conservative, but that has been done on purpose. We are new to this arena and we hate to lose money, as well as you, I think."

"That's correct. Fortunately, all my properties have been big suc-cesses." Simpson caught himself. It would not be good to be caught in a lie. He knew Ali had done his homework. "Well, almost all of them. The apartment tower I did on the Southside of the city by the Museum of Science and Industry will be fine eventually. It's just ahead of its time."

"Indeed. What is the saying you Americans like to use: 'Don't try to be a pioneer; you'll be killed by the Indians!'" The gathering laughed; Simpson had never heard that expression before, but man-aged a weak smile.

"Uh, exactly."

"As I was saying, our investments are conservative; older well-rented buildings that achieve four to six percent return. Hardly ex-citing. And with so many people driving cars now, demand for our high-grade oil is increasing by the day. We, shall we say, have consid-erable financial assets that need to be invested. And there are not enough small properties. We require a large project."

"I have one right here, Prince! Pardon me, Zaidan." Simpson re-strained himself. He didn't have the equity yet.

"You do indeed. You do indeed. What amount of equity are you looking for, and what ownership in this lovely project will we receive for our investment?"

"*Finally, we are cutting to the chase,*" Simpson thought. The court-ing was over and he was ready to get on with it; he would throw out his best offer.

"I need 25 to 30 million. For that you get 20% ownership. Inter-est at 1.5% over prime during the construction period; it accrues, of course. Then after completion interest drops to 1% over prime. You'll get half the proceeds from the sales of the condominiums. I estimate that at three to four million dollars profit. Then you'll get interest on the balance outstanding at one over prime, which should be around seven percent. Next, I'll sell the hotel to the operator, I'm thinking Four Seasons, and you get 25% of the upside profit on that. I'll take you out after four or five years with my share of the profits from the office and everything else."

Ali Sharif couldn't wait to open his mouth. "That's a bullshit deal Steel, and you know it!"

Zaidan bin Al Saud raised his hand and smiled. "Forgive my son for his language. I knew I should have sent him to University in England. A very interesting proposition, Steel. But as Ali said, and I paraphrase, not very realistic."

"It's a great deal. A fair deal."

"For you perhaps. Just so you know, Ali, upon my urging, discussed this project with your banker. What is his name?" He looked to Ali.

"Wentworth. Brad Wentworth."

Simpson was surprised. "You spoke with Brad?"

"Oh, Steel, we did more than that. We deposited $10,000,000 in first Chicago. So now we and Mr. Wentworth are, shall we say, very good friends…" Simpson was speechless. He could only shake his head; he was being zoomed by the Arabs.

"He said that he was indeed interested in your project, but that it was so big, and you are so, how shall I put this so it will not offend, so modest in assets and experience, that he would require 40 million dollars in equity. It is a large sum to be sure, but our initial ten million is already in his bank and would become 25% of the total equity should we reach agreement."

"OK, fine then, tell me your offer."

"It is not an offer yet, but hypothetically, we could provide $40,000,000 in equity, which we know will be second to the bank's loan position. In return we will receive interest on that money as it is drawn down in amounts proportional to the bank's funding at 2% over the prime rate set by the Bank of England, not the Federal Reserve in your country."

"Go on." Steel's blood pressure was rising. He knew that the Bank of England's interest rates were higher than those in the U. S.

"For our equity, we receive a 45% stake in the property. We get 75% of the sales proceeds from the condominiums, and 50% of the proceeds from the sale of the hotel. You pay only the interest on our loan until the balance of the property is sold, but if you desire, you can pay down the principal from your yearly profits to reduce the equity loan amount."

"First Chicago Bank won't agree to those terms. They're outrageous."

"Oh, but they have, Mr. Simpson, they already have."

Simpson was stunned. He thought: *"Zoomed again!"* These goat herders were smarter than he realized. "I won't do it!"

"I am sorry to hear you say that. I guess we'll just work with Harry Helmsley."

"Or Trammel Crow," Ali added.

Simpson started to head for the glass door that led to the rear outside deck, then thought: *"This is the best deal you're going to get, maybe the only deal."* He turned and looked directly at the prince.

"40% for your 40 million dollars equity."

Zaidan looked at his son who thought a moment and then nodded. "Done, with one caveat."

"What?" Simpson was ready to leave the lounge one more time.

"Ali will be a paid consultant to the project providing financial oversight of our money. The fee is $200,000 per year, for what we hope will only be a two-year construction project."

Simpson thought a moment and remembered the $200,000 he owed to the architect.

"Fine, but to get the ball rolling with further design, and as a sign of good faith, I need immediate funding of $200,000 into my account. $400,000 total. I've already paid for the land and the schematic design." The lie hung in the air, but no one was going to question it.

"My friend, I think that will be acceptable. I'll have our attorney begin the paperwork." The prince rose and the two men now shook hands and the prince kissed Simpson on both cheeks. Simpson pulled back, and then remembering Ali's tutorial, realized this was an indication of their new partnership. He returned the gesture.

"I have to go to Rome tomorrow. My new flight arrangements have me leaving from Leonardo daVinci on the 22nd. First flight I could get. Can you wire me the paperwork at the Grand Hotel the day before?"

"Steel, I will see that it is so. I think we should toast with champagne." And they did.

That night Steel Simpson won 3,800 francs at the craps table. Though he had no idea how much that was, it had been a very good day.

J. Vance Jefferson was humming in his office, something he rarely did. Things were going swimmingly at Nolan, Jefferson & Marlow. In addition to Chicago World Tower, the firm had picked up two new contracts, one from the city for a parking deck on the Southside over the CTA lines, called a Kiss N' Ride; and a new private client named McDonald's Corporation for a new building out in Oakbrook, a newer southwest suburb booming with growth. Thoughts of Marilyn kept floating into his mind as well. At first, he thought she would be difficult to conquer. But after their dinner at Chez Paul's several nights earlier, when she allowed his hand to roam freely on her leg and thigh, even allowing a brief brush on the inside where he thought he felt her silk panties, he knew it was just a matter of time before he bedded her. He had even informed accounting to increase her pay by $100 a month. Later in the day they were going to walk over to Grant Park and check out the area by a ball field for the summer picnic.

The phone buzzed. "Hey, Vance, this is Norman."

"Good morning, Norm. Did you get that retainer from the City for the new Southside job?"

"Yes sir. I did, but that's not why I buzzed you."

"Oh, well?"

"The check from Steel Simpson bounced. I mean like a thousand feet. The check was from a closed account. No money in it at all."

"That son of a bitch!"

John O'Rourke was sitting at his desk staring at the flashbulb. Grabowski had reported on his late-night drive from Glencoe to the land by the lake. With the construction and lane closures on Sheridan Road it had taken him an hour and a half, arriving at the lake at 1:00 A.M., twenty-five minutes after the fire at the shanty town was called in. Even if Lothar had experienced lighter traffic, there did not seem to be anyway for him to set the fire and it to be called in by 12:35 A.M. By the time the fire trucks arrived, the place was mostly burned to the ground. The only thing that did not check out was the time Simpson said he got home—11:30 P.M., and the time his wife said she saw the car drive up—10:30 P.M. He'd have Grabowski circle back on that one. Then he felt a hand on his shoulder. His boss, Chief Jack O'Halloran, was at his desk.

"How's the lake fire investigation going, John?"

"Not as well as I'd like. We have a conflict in alibis and can't connect Simpson to the fire yet. But we will." O'Rourke's tone of voice gave away his growing uncertainty as he looked at the spent flashbulb.

"That's why I stopped by to see you. It's time to close it down and put it in the dead files. We have limited resources and money, and I can't have you waste any more time on a dead-end street."

"It's not dead end. I'll find something."

"John, it was a shanty town inhabited by bums and crazies. They have no political base. No advocate. But the new owner does, and his alderman called me. I'm getting a lot of pressure. I'm ending it. Shut it down."

O'Halloran patted O'Rourke on the back one more time and as he walked away said: "Let's grab a beer one night." Then he was out of the room.

"Signore Simpson, una telegramma for you." The clerk at the front desk of The Grand Hotel in Rome, trained to recognize all American guests, noticed the well-dressed developer as he approached the counter.

"Really. Great. Hey, can I send a telegram from here?"

"Certamente, signore."

He handed the clerk a piece of hotel stationery. The handwritten note was addressed to Brad Wentworth, First Chicago Bank & Trust, 671 East Madison St., Chicago:

> *Brad,*
>
> *Have secured $40 M in equity.*
> *Ready to proceed with financing immediately.*
> *Will contact upon return.*
>
> *Regards,*
> *Steel*

The clerk took the note. "Subito. Grazie."

"Oh, and I'm checking out in one hour. Bring my luggage down to the lobby." There was no subtlety to his voice; it was a command to an underling.

"Si signore. Pronto."

Simpson walked out the door into the bright warm June morning. He opened the telegram.

> *Steel,*
>
> *Talked to Fire Investigator.*
> *Good news.*
> *They have dropped your case.*
>
> *Reese*

Steel Simpson smiled. He decided to check out the Spanish Steps, only two blocks away. In his hand was a large envelope with a red seal stamped with crossed swords: the commitment letter from the prince. He would read it over a cappuccino at a sidewalk café. Everything was coming together.

PART III

THE DOCUMENTS
NOVEMBER 1973

CHAPTER 52

Steel Simpson stared in disbelief at the last handwritten number on Page 26 of the estimate. Josef Simpson fidgeted in his chair. He knew this was bad news, very bad news.

"$78,536,480! No. This can't be! Did you check the figures, Uncle?"

"Three times, Steel. Twice by my chief estimator, and once myself. Look, everyone is busy right now, plus a lot of subs didn't want to bid."

"Why not? This is the biggest project in Chicago."

"Your reputation in this town isn't the best." What Josef Simpson, president of Simpson Construction Co. really wanted to say was, *"Because you've screwed almost every trade in the city one way or the other over the last 10 years, including me, and it's payback time."* But he continued in a calm voice: "It's a preliminary price. They were just design development drawings," he said, referring to the plans on which he based the price for the construction of Chicago World Tower.

Josef had to admit it. He was surprised, no stunned, when he received the call from his nephew, Steel. He said he wanted to negotiate the contract for the construction of Chicago World Tower with his uncle. "Let bygones be bygones," he said. That would be hard. Steel had promised his father, Lars, that he would leave his inheritance of two million dollars in the construction company as working capital. Promised on his father's deathbed! Josef had taken over the construction operation and needed the money to remain in the company as liquidity upon which the firm's bonding capacity was based. The more ready cash in the bank, the greater the bonding capacity, and the more projects a general contractor could build in a year.

But shortly after his father died, Steel took his two million dollars inheritance and started Simpson Development Partners, leaving his uncle high and dry. Though Josef had received $250,000 from Lars, and the company had other liquid assets of roughly the same amount, the total left in the bank set the company back substantially. It had taken him 10 years to build up the company's liquidity to $1,000,000. During that time he took a meager salary, and never a bonus. He lived in a small house in Evanston. Meanwhile, Steel bought a mansion in Glencoe on Lake Michigan.

Josef looked at Steel as he went over the pages of the estimate and thought to himself: *"You little shit. I should have told you to go fuck yourself when you called. But I didn't. The promise of securing such a large project and waiving any bond requirement because 'We're family after all' caught my interest. Or perhaps it was my greed? No, it was a chance to get even. You can look for days but you'll never find the four million bucks I have hidden through all the line items. And that's on top of the 4% fee of nearly five million more. Yeah, that's a lot more than the two million you took out of my company. So, fuck you."* But Josef Simpson said nothing, waiting for his nephew to speak.

"The bank and my equity partner won't go for this. My loan is $60 million and the equity is $40 million. This is $12 million over budget."

"I can do math, Steel. I know what the budget is. But it's garbage in and garbage out. Your prima donna architect and his underling, Nolan, just kept telling me to price the job as shown. I suggested a lot of different alternatives, cheaper alternatives, and I always got shot down."

"Well, we're gonna have a come to Jesus meeting with Mr. Jefferson, I can promise you that."

"Let's hope that helps. Look here's a list of cheaper alternatives. But truth be told, this is just a very expensive design. The curved walls, the circular core with those fancy elevators. Plus, the land is shit."

"Don't you think I didn't know that?"

"I mean, it's a very creative structural solution for sure. There are four large pipes diverting water through the site and eight 72" diameter caissons supporting the central core and another six caissons 60" in size supporting the outer concrete bearing walls, three on either side. I've never seen anything like it and I've been doing this a long time. It's a lot of concrete. At least the concrete price was good. In fact, surprisingly low."

"What would you do to the design then?"

"Hell, I'm no architect, but I tell you, you can't do anything about the ground conditions. You have those no matter what goes above it, but why do the walls have to curve? The curtain-wall price is twice what I expected.

"All right, I'll get back to you."

"I think you should have stuck with warehouses."

"Thanks, and fuck you very much." Steel Simpson took the estimate, put it in his briefcase and walked out the door.

On his way to Glencoe, as it was too late to return to his office in the Wrigley Building, Simpson couldn't wait to call J. Vance Jefferson and give him a royal ass-chewing for blowing the $66 million dollar budget. Then he reversed that thought. No, not Jefferson. Instead he would call Francis Nolan. Anyway, Jefferson would only respond that World Tower / Al Saud Development Corp. was over 60 days past due on their oldest invoice. Nolan, Jefferson & Marlow was already owed $1,500,000 for the design development phase of the project. So what? When he borrowed the money from Ali Sharif, the interest meter started running. Simpson was putting off paying the increasing mountain of invoices on his desk, paying as few professionals as possible, and there were many besides the architect, to keep the wheels greased and the project slowly moving ahead.

"Yeah, I'll call Francis. He's scared of his own shadow. I'll intimidate him and he'll change the design without Jefferson even knowing." The

Mercedes headed up Sheridan Road toward Glencoe. He hoped his wife would be out with her girlfriends. He would enjoy the house without her and the attitude.

CHAPTER 53

J. Vance Jefferson was furious. He had just drawn down the last of $500,000 of his firm's line of credit to make payroll. From the beginning he had been stiffed by his new client. First, the bounced check for $200,000.

"I'm so sorry, Vance, my secretary handed me the wrong check book. We have another one for that project that has over a million dollars in it."

"Yeah, bullshit, Simpson! I'm not that dumb," was all he could think at the time. And every invoice since then, August, September and October, all unpaid and a half million each. There was always some lame excuse, so many he couldn't recall them all. "If bullshit were money Simpson, you'd be a multi-millionaire!"

He picked up the phone to buzz Marilyn to call Simpson. *"Marilyn, Marilyn,"* he thought. She was a puzzlement. He had taken her to dinner at The Pump Room in the Ambassador East, even tipping the maître d' extra to sit in Booth One. Then there was Jacques. The tab there was so high he heard about it from Norman Weese. And even though he didn't like to go to lunch, he had taken Marilyn to The Walnut Room in Marshall Fields, just a block away on State Street, and then bought her a new dress. But still she had not gone to bed with him. He was getting annoyed and hornier by the week.

"Marilyn..."

"Yes, Vance?" He insisted that she now call him by his first name.

"Get me Steel Simpson."

She dialed the number that she now knew by heart.

"Hi, Ruth. Marilyn. Is Mr. Simpson in? Mr. Jefferson would like to speak to him."

"Sorry, hon, he's already gone for the day..."

"He won't like that. Have him call Vance tomorrow OK? Thanks. Bye."

She buzzed Jefferson back. "Vance, he's gone for the day. He'll call in the morning."

"Like hell he will. Hey, are we on for Friday? There's a new restaurant I think you'll like."

"Vance, look, I appreciate the nice dinners, the new clothes, the three raises, but wouldn't you rather go home to your wife on Friday and well, relax with her. My boyfriend is getting suspicious…"

"But we need to discuss the Christmas party. We need to decide where to have it."

Marilyn hesitated, but gave in. "Fine. Friday it is."

"Great, thanks."

Marilyn called Jane at work, something she rarely did, but needed to. After they paged her roommate at Rush Presbyterian Hospital, she waited several minutes, and hoped that Jane would answer before Jefferson came out of his office to give her another back rub.

"This is Jane."

"Jane, Marilyn. He's done it again. Asked me to dinner. I feel so used and dirty!"

"Have you slept with him yet?"

"Of course not, but I know he wants to take me to a hotel after these dinners. You said he'd lose interest. But he hasn't and I don't know what to do!"

"If you haven't slept with him, you're not a whore, and you've increased your salary by over $3,000 a year; so that's not so bad."

"I feel ashamed to take it."

"Don't. You deserve it for taking his shit."

"But allowing him to feel me up. I feel like such a slut."

"Okay, this time lay it all out for him. Tell him you're done and you're ready to quit. I promise he won't want a new secretary, and he'll move onto someone else around there."

"Francis, this is Steel Simpson." He let the salutation hang in the air. He rarely called Francis. Connor West seemed to know so much more about the Chicago World Tower project than Francis Nolan. Strange.

"Listen, I need to discuss the project with you. We have some, shall we say, challenges…"

"Sure, is the morning okay? It's like 5:00 P.M. and I was just leaving. Is Mr. Jefferson going to be there? I really think he should be there."

"No, you're head of design and this concerns you."

"Okay, if you insist. I can be there by 8:30."

"That will work. Goodnight then."

Francis Nolan was puzzled. Why did the client want to meet with him, alone?

"Norman, on that one fucking check we got from Simpson, what was the entity it was drawn on?"

"Entity?"

"You know the name of the corporation Simpson set up to do the project."

"Oh, that. Let me pull the canceled checks. Just a minute." There was a pause during which time Jefferson reached for a Tootsie Roll Pop—this one orange. "Here it is. Chicago World Tower / Simpson, Al Saud Partners, Ltd."

"Spell that word at the end?"

"A-L space, S-A-U-D. What is that anyway, a name?"

"I think so, but I want you to find out."

"How?"

"I don't know. Go to the library. Call that big shot Wentworth at First Chicago. It's their check. I want to know who Simpson is in bed with. I'm tired of rattling his cage. His money partner won't like that Simpson isn't paying anyone."

"Got it. First thing in the morning." Weese hung up.

CHAPTER 54

Connor's relationship with Marilyn intensified. As much as he didn't want to be, he had to admit he was in love with her. She was spending most weekends at his studio apartment and his sublease had been extended for three more months. He was annoyed that Marilyn wouldn't tell him about those nights she was out. At first, he suspected another guy was in the picture, but then figured that it just could not be. She was just too affectionate around him; though she did seem more distant than usual at times and was easily startled when he touched her, pulling away—then realizing what she had done, moving close to him. It was all very strange. Women!

"How's my favorite girl tonight?"

"Connor, I can't talk. Vance, I mean Mr. Jefferson is still here. I already think he knows about us." She spoke in a hushed tone looking toward Jefferson's door. Through the glass she could see he was immersed in some paperwork.

"He's given you three raises. I don't think you need to worry. He even gave me a raise after he transferred me from Bob to Francis. I think we're safe. I'm leaving, meet me down in the lobby in five?"

"Sure, OK. I'm so glad you're finally keeping decent office hours."

"Junior ignores me and I'm kind of coasting right now until we find out what the cost of Chicago Tower will be."

"When do you expect the price?"

"Maybe tomorrow. I'm a little nervous. I was told by Bob and Jerzy that it would be an expensive building."

At that moment, Jefferson buzzed Marilyn. "Gotta go. See you in a minute. Yes, Vance…"

Brad Wentworth had not lied to Jefferson when he and Steel Simpson met with him in early July. When he received Simpson's telegram from Rome, he had decided to finance the project. He first assumed that the Saudis had passed on the deal, and that his best developer-client had managed to get a deal with some wealthy Italian, probably in the fashion industry. But it was indeed the House of Saud that was going to financially back the project.

Wentworth scanned the Memorandum of Understanding that Steel had brought back with him against the final Articles of Incorporation establishing Chicago World Tower—Simpson / Al Saud Partners, Ltd., which had been delivered earlier that day. Along with this all-important document was an Initial Operating Agreement with Four Seasons Hotels to manage and operate the Four Seasons Sky Hotel. In addition, Simpson had pulled other rabbits out of his magic hat—letters of intent to lease 358,000 SF of his 800,000 SF office component; a Memorandum of Understanding with Healthy Life Fitness Centers to operate the state-of-the-art health club; and finally, four letters from potential restaurateurs to open food venues. With all this ammunition, Brad Wentworth was ready to go to loan committee for $60,000,000 in debt financing. Approval of the loan was the last step before Simpson would release NJ&M to produce the final construction documents. The developer owned the land, thanks to the loan from Wentworth's father, but Steel had "stepped to the line" too, by funding over $500,000.00 in development costs: schematic and design development fees for the architect; further geo-technical studies; civil engineering; market studies; and a glossy four-color brochure to entice hotel operators, tenants, and Chicago's upper crust to purchase a "Skyhouse" condominium.

"If this isn't a home run, I don't know what will be." Brad could almost hear the buzz on the street about Chicago's tallest building all the way

up to the 31st floor of the First Chicago Bank Building. His reverie was interrupted by the buzz on the intercom. "What is it, Evelyn?"

"It's a Norman Weese from the architectural firm of Marlow, Nolan and Jeffers. I think that's what he said." Wentworth understood the fractured name and pushed the lighted button.

"Brad Wentworth."

"Mr. Wentworth. This is Norman Weese. Thanks for taking my call. I'm the head of the accounting department at Nolan, Jefferson…"

"Yes, I know. How can I help you?"

"I was calling to inquire if you might be able to tell me, who, well, on the Chicago World Tower checks, ah, who is, or what is 'Al Saud?'"

"That's Mr. Simpson's development partner."

"Is it a company, or a person?"

"Why do you ask? I'm not sure I should disclose that information." Wentworth remembered that he had advised Simpson not to put the name of his money partner on the check. The less anyone knew about the financial structure the better. But Simpson had insisted, saying it was a requirement of Ali Sharif, his new development manager and partner.

"We need to know here at Nolan, Jefferson and Marlow. We are investing substantial hours in this project and need to know who's paying us."

"What does it matter as long as you're getting paid?"

"That's the problem, Mr. Wentworth."

"What's the problem?" Wentworth was chafing at the call but was curious.

"We haven't been paid for the last three months. There is $1,500,000, plus over $50,000 in reimbursable expenses that is over 60 days past due. We just got a good check last month for the $200,000 for the schematic design."

First Chicago's senior vice president remembered the day he got the call from auditing to tell him that a $200,000 check had been presented by NJ&M drawn on a closed account. The phone call that followed with Steel was not pleasant. He told Steel that the act was felony fraud, Simpson putting all the blame on his forlorn secretary,

Ruth. After apologizing up and down, Wentworth let it go. But that was back in June. If he had heard the accountant correctly, the architect had just gotten paid in October.

"I see. I'm sorry to hear that, and I will discuss this with Mr. Simpson."

"We want to call this 'Al Saud' entity too. My boss, Mr. Jefferson, doesn't believe they know that Mr. Simpson isn't paying anyone."

"What do you mean not paying anyone?"

"I've been calling around to the other consultants: Chicago Consultants, the geo-technical firm. To the civil engineer, that's Hillner and Anderson, and others. No one's been paid."

"Mr. Weese, I'm terribly sorry to hear that. This is most disturbing. I assure you I will bring this up with the equity partner."

"I guess that will have to do. And while you're at it, send over a check for a million and a half."

"I assure you, Mr. Weese, that it will be forthcoming very soon. Goodbye."

Wentworth went to the window and looked down at the ants below. He suddenly wished he were one of them. "Go ahead, Simpson, shit on your birthday cake! Why in hell I'm in bed with you, I don't know…" he muttered aloud.

CHAPTER 55

"Francis, good to see you. Come this way to my office." Steel Simpson was trying to be as friendly and cordial as possible to put the young partner of NJ&M as ease. He needed him to be compliant.

Francis Nolan, Jr., followed Simpson into his large corner office that had two large windows looking out to Michigan Avenue and two looking down onto the Chicago River. The desk was nothing special, something that came from an office furniture wholesaler. There was a large black high-back desk chair and a credenza. He sat down in one of two dark red leather guest chairs. Off to the side was an easel with a rendering of Chicago World Tower. Ruth came in with a carafe of coffee and two cups.

"Coffee?" Simpson began pouring a cup for himself.

"Sure. Two sugars." Francis looked over to the rendering and Steel caught his glance.

"You did a bang-up job on that design, Frank. I can call you Frank, right?"

"Sure, that's fine. Thank you, but I really don't deserve all the credit. We, I, well there was a team…"

"I'm sure, but it was your concept. That's what Vance told me anyway."

"Look, how can I help you? And I really think Vance should be involved here," Francis said.

"Nonsense. You're the partner-in-charge of design correct?"

"Well, yes, but he is in charge of the business."

"This involves design. We have a problem. Your design is twelve million over my budget. And we need to do something about that."

Nolan fidgeted in his seat, his hand slightly shaking as he picked up the coffee cup. "Well, I'm sorry to hear about that; I'm not surprised though…."

"Not surprised?"

"No, of the three schemes, I knew it was the most expensive."

"I guess great design costs money. Look, let's get to the point. It's not your design, is it?"

"Ah, well, a, it is, yes…"

"Really? Whenever I asked questions at meetings, it was that young kid Connor that had the answers. You never said anything. You appeared to be bored. At the presentation, your face flushed in embarrassment when Vance gave you credit. Don't bullshit me, Frank, Connor West designed the building."

"OK, so what? It's the firm's design."

"Look. I don't give rat's ass who designed it, but you're the one that's going to make the changes I need to get the twelve million out of it."

"I can't do that. You accepted the design. Changing it now means everything done to date is trash."

"I'm sure the newspapers would be interested to know that Chicago's most prestigious firm has a boy as their chief designer…."

"What?" Francis flushed with anger but understood the ramifications of the veiled threat.

"You don't have to start again. Just make a few changes. It won't take much I promise you."

"What do you expect me to do?"

"For a start, get rid of the curved walls. They're ridiculously expensive."

"You want it straightened?"

"Yes, I think that's what I'm saying. And the outdoor core with the elevators. That better go. Big bucks there. Anyway, you're the architect, figure it out. And here's a list of items that will save me bunches of money. It's from the contractor."

Francis took the list and perused it quickly. "I'm not sure I can do some of these items. They would be against the building codes."

"Fuck the building codes. That's why I pay off inspectors."

"I really should go over this with Vance."

"Look, Francis, this is your chance to design your building, to make it yours, not Connor West's. I know you can give me a great building that is within budget, and if your conscience bothers you, work within the codes. Square off the three elements, put the core inside, and get rid of some of these elevators. The mechanical is way too expensive. The hotel does not need central air, do it with exterior wall units. Bottom line, I need it in budget and you're going to be the one to get it there."

"I'll see what I can do." The idea of making the building his own was starting to take hold. Connor would be furious, but he was the head of design, after all. Yes, he would re-design Chicago World Tower and claim his rightful standing in the firm. It would be a good design and one that was in budget.

"We understand each other?"

"Yes, I, I guess so. I never really liked that design. I think I can make it more, well, more reasonable. Anyway, I'll do my best."

"Great, when it's done, call me. And keep Jefferson out of it. I should close on the financing in a week or two and I'll give him the go ahead for the construction documents. All he cares about is collecting money, anyway."

"Okay, I understand." Francis got up and stole one more look at the elegant and original design that he had just agreed to destroy.

CHAPTER 56

Carmine Messina instituted an uneasy peace in Maywood. He let the Player's Club take over most of the town's protection racket allowing them to collect money from the small businesses. But he kept tight control of the much more profitable drug business and still had the two whorehouses and a good group of white hookers. He also controlled the unions and the city officials. No construction took place without the Outfit getting a cut. He would bide his time on retribution for the beatings the two punks had given several of his customers, including Lucca and Vincenzo, Italians he had personally promised to protect. This "infamia" would not, and could not, stand.

All these things passed through his mind as he sat in a dark corner of Villa Roma Supper Club on Cermak Avenue in Cicero. Even though it was just 5:30 P.M., he was hungry. Most days he did without lunch to watch his weight. He swirled his glass of tonic water with his finger, impatiently waiting for his dinner guest. He kept his eyes on the door, seated in the banquette with his back to the heavily brocaded wall. A .38 caliber Smith & Wesson was on the black leatherette seat at the ready. It was unnecessary really. This was the home turf of the Outfit, and he owned the restaurant, which by eight o'clock would be full of only white people— the men in shiny suits and loud ties, the women in silk dresses and ostentatious jewelry, with teased hair and too much makeup. The restaurant was famous for its pasta dishes, particularly the Lobster a la Vodka served over angel hair pasta. Messina usually ordered a strip steak and creamed spinach side. Italian food was too rich for him and gave him gas.

He watched the door open, putting his hand on the piece. Once he saw the maître d' lead a short, chubby man toward him, he relaxed.

It was Donald McFinn, head of the International Brotherhood of Electrical Workers, Chicago Local 134. McFinn walked, waddled really, over to the booth in the corner. The maître d' moved the round table over to one side so the portly head of one of Chicago's most powerful unions could drop down to the banquette, breathing heavily, wiping his brow with a handkerchief.

"Don Messina, good to see you again. You look well."

"Please, Donnie, no 'Don,' just Carmine in here. You okay? You're sweating."

"I always sweat. I'm fine. I just need a beer."

Carmine Messina lifted his hand and a waiter, one of two assigned to his table, instantly appeared. "Bring my friend here a beer. Miller High Life. If you don't mind, Donnie, my friend; let's order. I'm hungry and I want to get out of here before all the jamokes show up and want to kiss my ring, if you know what I mean."

"No problem, no problem at all. I can always eat," McFinn patted his large round stomach; it looked like he had swallowed a volleyball. He continued to wipe his brow and took a drink of the Champagne of Beers. His skin was pasty white, and his grey hair was thinning. But he had deep green eyes and had never needed glasses. Years ago, during World War II, he was much thinner and was a marksman, a sniper in the infantry. He fought alongside Carmine Messina in Italy and they were close friends; though after the war, they went separate ways. When Messina rose through the ranks of the Outfit and became a lieutenant, he ran into McFinn at a jobsite when he was making the weekly collection. Donnie was an electrician on the job. They hugged and had beers. It was not long after that that McFinn got active in the electrical union.

Messina raised his hand again and the other waiter instantly was at their table.

"The usual, Frank. Make sure the steak is medium rare. My friend here will have the house specialty. Put extra lobster in it. And bring him another beer and a bottle of the best Chianti we got."

"Yes sir, right away." Frank hurried off to the kitchen.

"So, besides the pleasure of your company, what's on your mind, Don?"

"I told you to call me Carmine; we go way back," Carmine looked annoyed.

"It's a sign of respect. So, tell me."

"Have you read about the new project planned on the lake, what they call a mixed-use project? You know everything, office, apartments, and hotel all in one big building."

"Sure, I have. All my electrical subs were drooling about it until they saw who the developer was. That dickhead Steel Simpson."

"Exactly. He screwed Cooky's Concrete out of $2,350,000."

"Sorry to hear. I can't get any subs to bid on his warehouse projects in the Western 'burbs except one, Paulie Harris. He adds 20% to every project as vigorish in the event he don't get paid. So far, he's been lucky. I mean the schmuck got to pay someone, sometime or no one would work for him, for Pete's sake. But this project is too big for Paulie. Plus, he don't want to come into the Loop."

"I'm going to get the concrete work on that job. I figure if this Simpson guy gets financing, and my sources say he probably will, the job will start in like six months."

"That don't make sense. Why would you want that contract? You've already been stiffed once."

"Don't worry about me. What I want to know is how we can get to the eventual electrical contractor and have him, say forget stuff, wire the place wrong, maybe use cheap materials and have the inspector pass it all."

Donnie McFinn nodded and finished his Miller. "I see. I get it now. Like I said, the job is too big for most of my boys. There's only two that could handle it; but they wouldn't touch it. Does he have a general contractor yet?"

"No. Too early. But my guess he'll go with blood and hire his uncle, Josef Simpson, even though they hate each other. The three or four big GCs don't want to fool with Simpson. For the same reason your boys won't touch it. He's what, done three, four Loop projects and gone through as many contractors. What is it they say: 'Screw me once, shame on you; screw me twice, shame on me?'"

The salads arrived: two Caesars with real anchovies. Frank uncorked the bottle of wine and poured it, knowing the Don hated all that ceremony of sniffing the cork and sampling the fruit of the vine. If the wine was swill, he'd let Dominic Salvatore, the general manager, know about it in ways he would not like.

"Even if Steel and his uncle kiss and make up, I bet he still has to go out of state for an electrical sub. They'll have to register with the local union, but we won't have much control; if you know what I mean."

"Donnie, I need to set things right with Simpson. No one screws me out of over two million."

"I get it. I get it. Let me think a minute." He stuffed a huge mouthful of salad into his mouth. McFinn did not have the best table manners. Messina tasted the wine. It was good. He took another sip, placing the glass back on the table.

"You know, Carmine, I been meaning to ask you. Why's this place so dark? I couldn't read the menu if I had to."

"You didn't have to. My customers want it to be romantic. But I won't allow candles on the table. Too much risk of fire. So, the lights get turned down. At eight o'clock, we'll dim them even more. But let's get back to business."

"Hmmm. Risk of fire. Lights turned down."

"What the fuck you mumbling about?"

"Any my guys do a bad job, there is a big risk of fire."

"Exactly. That's exactly what I want." Messina was getting agitated. He poked at his salad.

"Yeah and when it's found out it was bad wiring or something like that, my union gets blamed and a good sub goes out of business. If they figure out it was intentional, it's worse. It's a criminal offense."

"Since when has that bothered you, or me, for that matter?"

"But we don't usually get caught when we do. So, the lights get turned down in this place?"

"Yeah, I already said that. What's your point?"

Frank brought the main course, effortlessly set it before the two old friends, now locked in a heavy debate. He cut into the steak to show the Don that it was a perfect reddish pink. Then he ground fresh parmesan cheese onto McFinn's pasta dish and departed quietly.

"What if I talk to Charlie Naughton at the building department? You know, he's the head electrical inspector."

"You mean give him a heads-up were gonna do a bad wiring job?"

"You know, Don, and I say this as a friend: sometimes I'm not sure how you got to be where you are."

"We'll take a trip to the lake. I'll show you."

"Sorry, I meant no disrespect. Let me get to the point. Here's my idea."

"Please, before I lose my appetite…"

"I tell Charlie Naughton that the union is concerned about this guy Simpson trying to do a bad job on such an important building. Everyone knows that hotel he did on Oak Street is crap construction. Paid off all the inspectors. Tell him it's no longer good business for the local if the electrical work is shoddy. You know it reflects badly on us. In fact, I tell him we want his inspectors to be so tough on the out-of-state electrical contractor that they won't set foot in Chicago again. He'll like that. Protect the local interests. Yeah, the IBEW wants, no, insists on rigorous inspections. Shut the job down in fact, if necessary. Check every twist of wire, every junction box, every main feeder panel. Make sure every penetration is fire-caulked. All the stuff his guys ignore because they get a brown envelope from the subcontractor every week."

"They won't like not getting that envelope."

"They'll get one from my union. We'll pay them off to be the biggest pricks any contractor has ever seen. And Mr. Simpson's project and its progress will slow to a crawl. Maybe even get shut down for a week or two. If you want to hurt Simpson, hurt him where it counts, in his wallet. A project this big, he'll be paying some big interest on the borrowed money, and it will be sizable when the electrical work starts—all that foundation work being done, and lots of concrete poured, with the big monthly rentals on tower cranes. Nothing worse than a job stopping when the interest meter's running."

"Donnie, you're a fuckin' genius. I'm gonna order you two tiramisus!"

"Yeah, and you're gonna contribute extra to the union coffers for the vig."

"Done." Messina cut into his steak. It was perfect. He decided he might have some dessert too.

CHAPTER 57

On Saturday, morning Bob Marlow was returning to his apartment after a brisk run in neighboring Lincoln Park and along the lake. It was always a bittersweet time because, while he loved the city and the wide-open expanse of the great lake, he now missed his two boys terribly: taking them to Little League games, swim lessons, or just spending time with them. His wife had severely restricted his visitations to one weekend per month after she had smelled alcohol on his breath after taking the boys to a Cubs game in August. He had protested and threatened to get a lawyer, but it was of no use.

As he entered his building, he saw that the mailman was putting the day's mail into the many resident boxes.

"Hey, Sam, how's it going?"

"Same old, same old, Mr. Bob. Hey, I'm glad I saw you. I've got something for you, registered mail. You need to sign for it. This'll save me the trip up to the 21st floor." Sam handed Marlow the mail with the registered letter on the top. "Sign right there on that blue piece of paper."

Marlow did so with trepidation. The return address on the letter said Morgan, Foy, and Van Ness, Attorneys-at-Law. He thanked Sam and headed into the first elevator that opened and pressed the button to his floor. He felt the letter; it was thick. Marlow did not like the look of it. Entering his apartment, he threw the envelope on the kitchen counter. Marlow had been sober for two weeks. This wasn't going to change anything. He showered, put on fresh clothes and left, going down the elevator and out the building, down to the Egg & Biskit, a greasy spoon diner located on North Wells. His usual stool was empty as the morning rush was over.

"Morning, Mr. M. What will it be, the same?"

"Morning, June. Yeah. The same."

Marlow opened the thin Saturday edition of the *Chicago Tribune*, but his mind could not stop thinking about the envelope and its contents. Had he expected to get a petition for divorce? Probably, but he hoped that it would never happen. He was doing well until that day last summer. *"For Chrissakes, it was a ball game! I had two beers,"* he thought. But that was enough to throw his wife into a rage, swearing he would never see his boys again, that he was a hopeless drunk. If he was a hopeless drunk, she was a contributing factor, always spending money and nagging him when there wasn't enough. And then when he worked long hours to ensure that the all-important Christmas bonus would be large enough to sustain them until at least the summer, she bitched because he was never home. He knew he was connected to booze in a symbiotic way. It eased his pain, but it caused it as well. He hated booze, but he needed it. No, he really loved it.

"Here you go, darlin'. Two eggs scrambled with cheese, three link sausages and a bagel. I'll get you more coffee." June gave him a smile.

"Thanks." This morning Bob Marlow did not care for any of their usual smack talk that always brought laughter to his day. June returned with the stainless round pot of coffee.

"Everything okay, Mr. M?" June could see he was not his usual self.

"Swell, just swell. A lot on my mind, I guess…" He cut the sausage link and put a piece in his mouth.

"Well, I'll leave you to it then. Enjoy." June walked away to tend to another late morning customer.

The Wells St. Beverage Barn was a block beyond where Bob Marlow should have turned to head back to his apartment. But instead of turning, he kept on walking, as if in a trance. He had not committed to buying a bottle. He just wanted to walk past the place. Then a billboard on top of a four-story building caught his attention. It was positioned to face the riders on the L train. A handsome couple was holding large glasses of Seagram's V.O. Canadian whiskey by a fireplace. In the background was a snowy scene of the two happy people tobogganing down a slope. The billboard read:

Seagram's V.O.
For People Who Get the Most Out of Life.

Marlow stared at the double old-fashioned glass held by the man. He proceeded onto the liquor store. He knew then what he was going to do. Yes, there was a half-bottle of Evan Williams that he had not touched in two weeks. But he knew that would not be enough once he opened the thick envelope. Now he was at the front door. The shop window was decorated for the upcoming Thanksgiving holiday with fall colors and bottles of bourbon, scotch, gin and vodka displayed on different shelves. Marlow paused. He turned and walked away, down a half block.

"Oh, fuck it." He changed directions and headed back to the store. In five minutes, he was walking back to the apartment, with two handles of Evan Williams in a brown paper sack.

The architect filled his favorite crystal glass with ice and then his favorite bourbon. He sat down and took a deep drink and opened the envelope. He ignored the cover letter; he went to the legal document: *Petition for Separation and Divorce.* The document had been filed in the Superior Court of Cook County three days earlier. Looking at the document, his breath left him. He choked on the words. Seventeen years of marriage ended by a piece of paper. He scanned the document, taking another drink. Marlow flipped the page, then another until he came to the section noted as "Custody." It read:

Sole custody of the two minor children, Benjamin and Austin Marlow shall rest with the Plaintiff, Joan Marie Marlow. Defen-

dant, Robert Marlow, shall be granted visitation rights as solely determined by the Court and Plaintiff, and only if he enters and successfully completes an alcohol rehabilitation program approved by the Court.

"Fucking bullshit! She can't do that. That bitch can't keep me from seeing my boys." Bob Marlow was talking to no one in particular; he got up and went to the window and looked down at Lincoln Park. It was a beautiful day, but he wasn't going to be enjoying it. He went to the kitchen for more ice and more bourbon.

By Sunday evening, Bob Marlow had been drinking for 18 hours straight, except for four hours when he was passed out. It was eight o'clock and he decided that that he might need some food, so he ordered pizza to be delivered. He didn't want to go out; he had everything he needed right in the apartment, one more handle of Evan Williams.

His head pounded but the only way to stop it was with another drink. The apartment was a mess. He had knocked over a lamp stumbling around and the petition for divorce was strewn all over the living room floor. The toilet was a mess from throwing up; after that were the dry heaves. He needed the pizza, but he needed another drink more. He was on his second drinking glass since he dropped the crystal one onto the tile floor where it disintegrated into a hundred pieces. He had a nice, half-inch cut on his hand to show for his vain effort to pick up the pieces. Now he was using a Welch's jelly jar glass; it was easier to hold onto. He had long ceased putting ice into the whiskey, and anyway the ice trays weren't frozen. He stared down at Lincoln Park; he should be at his real home in Oak Park with his kids.

The doorbell rang; it was the pizza. Marlow managed to find his wallet in the bedroom, yelled "I'm coming" and opened the door. Taking the box from the delivery boy, he handed him a twenty and told him to keep the change. The boy shook his head at the disheveled figure in front of him, and the smell, like a dive bar, but liked the tip. Marlow put the pizza box down onto the coffee table; it cantilevered precariously on the edge. When he opened the box, the pizza slid onto the floor. *"Shit,"* he thought. He managed to slide the pie back into the box in a heap. He separated a gooey slice and after taking a drink, bit into the needed sustenance. Two minutes later, he was hurling food, booze and blood from his mouth. He picked up the large bottle and upended it, finishing the last of it. Then he passed out again onto the floor, mouth covered in blood and tomato sauce, vomit, the half-eaten slice and an empty bottle beside him.

CHAPTER 58

By Saturday afternoon, the floor was strewn with bumwad and Francis Nolan's head pounded. No alteration, no geometry, no revision worked. He felt like he was sinking in quicksand. The more he tried to change the design, the more complicated it got. Every aspect of the curved walls was connected to the interiors of the spaces. As the hours wore on, he began to hate Connor West. How could a young kid right out of school have brought forth such a creative, yet rational design? It had taken him six years at Notre Dame, six years he hated, to get a degree. He had gotten a C on his final design project. A "C!" And West had graduated *magna cum laude*! Nolan went to his desk and found some aspirin. He took three and headed for the elevators and the coffee shop around the block. He needed a break.

As Francis sat at the counter picking at his lunch, he took a paper napkin, and with his Mont Blanc pen, began sketching a crude diagram. Three boxes one on top of the other, each one smaller in size, but perfectly proportioned. A rectangular, not a square base. Nolan was energized but could not admit that this revision bore an uncanny resemblance to his own original design from the schematic presentations. He paid the bill and headed back to the office.

By Sunday night, Nolan was finished. He had hated every moment of the work, yet was satisfied with the result. He told himself that the design was much more practical; more down to earth; more reasonable, as he had told Simpson. What it lacked in grace and excitement, it made up for in being simple. Now, instead of sails there were three rectangular boxes, each with its own pediment—a colonnade of faux columns to identify the lobby portion of each component. The windowless mechanical floors between the components looked heavy, but so what? They served a necessary purpose and that was enough. Form follows function. The base of the entire project had also been turned into a solid rectangular block several more stories in height, faced in metal panels, and punctured with glass only where necessary. The net effect was that Chicago World Tower now resembled three cereal boxes, one on top of the other, from jumbo size, to large, and lastly, regular size. It seemed bulkier than ever. And, as a final dagger in West's back, the "mast" was gone. Finally, he changed the glass on the building to the old window wall system used on Chicago Center, not the all-glass system that had just been developed, where you couldn't see the metal vertical and horizontal mullions. It was safe, as long he didn't mess with the specifications again, and it was cheap.

Francis turned off the lamp above his drafting table. He was exhausted but satisfied. Yet he felt dirty. He had despoiled a beautiful thing. The way he felt he just wanted someone to dominate him, in the same way he was about to dominate Connor West. He looked forward to seeing Ricardo, both for the enchiladas that he was preparing and the whips and leather ties afterwards.

CHAPTER 59

When Connor came to work on Monday morning, he went directly to Bob Marlow's office instead of to his new digs on the east side of the 12th floor. The area set up for the Chicago World Tower project, was just outside of Francis Nolan's office, but in full view of his own. He longed to be back in the large open studio working with Marlow, his guide and mentor. Junior was aloof at best, rude at worst. He knew that Nolan was jealous and resentful that the design picked had been his.

The lights were strangely off and there was no hot coffee in the pot. It wasn't like Marlow to not be there, beating the sluggish young designer to the office on Monday mornings. Marlow told Connor that he made a point of getting into the office early, it helped him to not drink excessively on Sunday evening, evenings always spent alone. He found the coffee can and made a pot for himself. While he waited for the coffee to brew, he nosed around the office and noticed a form from the Department of Immigration titled: "Request for Immigration History and Status, Form USDIN# 53-174." Marlow had begun to fill it out, but it was far from complete. Connor saw that the history that Marlow wanted was for Leo Skoroshod. West dismissed it. Marlow was probably just trying to piece together a reason Leo took his own life. With hot coffee now in his Cubs mug, Connor headed to his drafting and workspace, one that, for a new employee, was quite generous.

Francis Nolan was waiting for Connor to arrive. He knew this would not be pleasant, but it was time for the young kid to get a lesson in the realities of the business of architecture.

"West, got a minute?" Francis was standing at the door to his office holding it open. West was puzzled. Junior never wanted to speak to him, particularly on a Monday morning. To the right of the door was a floor to ceiling tack board where sketches and drawings could be pinned. The wall was full of what looked like a bad dream of his design. He stared in disbelief. This had to be a cruel joke. Nolan saw that West was looking at the new design. *"Let's get this over with,"* he thought. He spoke, voice wavering.

"The design is way over budget. Over twelve million in fact. The developer wants changes made. I made them. It's a…a more honest building. And it's in budget. I'll leave it to you to fine tune some of the details. We'll probably be released next week for the construction documents."

"What is this? What have you done?"

"I modified it. You knew, I knew, that the curved walls were expensive. The outside elevators too. There is a twelve plus million problem with this building. The client can't afford it."

"It's my design! You can't just fuck with it!"

"I can and I did."

"But not this way. This is…it's garbage!"

"Watch it boy. Remember who you're talking to…"

"I know who I'm talking to. Someone who couldn't design a damn outhouse."

"Welcome to the real world, college boy. You're not in your ivory tower at Harvard designing pipe dreams anymore."

"You can't fucking do this! This is shit!"

"It's not your design; it's the firm's design. You don't own it; the firm owns it. I made changes that are necessary. And if we don't get the budget down, it won't be built. And Simpson would probably sue us for breach of contract. So just suck it up and get the rest worked out."

"You had no right! It is my design, no matter what you say!"

"I'm not telling you again. The firm owns this design and as long as you work here, as a designer, you work for me!"

Connor glared at Nolan. "I won't change a thing. You can change it!"

"You, you listen to me, you little shit," Nolan said, voice cracking. He had never had to reprimand anyone, and his body was trembling. "You work for me. Understand? Not Marlow, not Jefferson. You think you can just waltz into this firm, my firm, and design what you want. You're a little bug and I can squash you and your design if I want." Nolan was shaking, but proud he had said what he said.

"A chimpanzee could improve on this!" Connor went to the wall and tore off the sketches. He turned and threw them at Nolan. But he decided that was not enough. He picked up one of the onion skin sketches and turned to Nolan, grabbing him by the throat. He stuffed the drawing into Nolan's mouth. "Eat shit, Nolan!"

Nolan was stunned, and terrified. He spit the paper out of his mouth, but all he could muster to say was: "You fucking assaulted me, West. I'll have your job!"

"You can have it!"

"You'll treat me with respect! I'm the head of design!" Nolan screamed in a whiny voice.

"Yeah, well, that's a fucking joke!" Connor stormed out of the office and headed down the hall to Marlow's office.

Connor was furious. He needed to find Bob Marlow. He looked all over the huge drafting hall. Not seeing him, he called Marilyn and got his boss's' home phone number. After dialing the phone seemed to ring forever. Finally, he heard a voice.

"What? Who is it?"

"Mr. Marlow, it's Connor. Are you all right?"

"No, not really. I think I could use some help. Can you come?"

"I'll be right there. Where do you live?"

"1705 Lincoln Park West. Get the manager to let you in."

West headed directly to the elevator and down to a cab outside. Traffic was light and he got to the new thirty story building facing Lincoln Park in 15 minutes. The building manger sensed West's urgency and was opening the door to apartment 2109 a few minutes later. There was a small entry foyer with a closet blocking the view to the living room. Connor, followed by the property manager, peered into the bedroom on the left, and seeing nothing turned to the right toward the living room. Bob Marlow was lying unconscious in a pool of vomit, blood, booze and pizza. He was barely breathing.

CHAPTER 60

J. Vance Jefferson peered out his 14th floor window across the street to the swirling snow at Grant Park. It was called "lake effect" snow and would play hell with his Friday commute home to Evanston. The week had exhausted him, beginning with the call from young West about Marlow. He had gone straight to Rush Presbyterian; his partner was still unconscious even after they had pumped out his stomach. The blood alcohol level when he was admitted was off the charts at .50. They had started an IV, but he had not yet come to. As he looked down at the ashen face of his partner, he thought, *"This time you've gone too far, Bob."* But then he sensed an opportunity. This was not the first time the firm had sent a partner or senior associate off to rehab. It was one reason John Shaw had retired early. Over the years, the profession ground you down into sawdust, and the only refuge for most was alcohol.

A call to the New Day Clinic in Boca Raton, Florida, was all that was necessary. By the second day as Marlow sat up in bed, head pounding, protesting that he did not need to check into rehab, Jefferson was forced to call Marlow's wife, Joan, who came and promptly told Bob that if he did not go into a program and sober up once and for all, he would never see his two boys again. With that he consented, and a medic and a former professional boxer were at the hospital the following day to escort their new patient to a waiting plane at Midway Airport. Jefferson had spoken to the director, whom he knew, with a strong recommendation that Bob Marlow stay in rehab for at least six months, and that if the director did so, there would be a most welcome donation to the facility by the firm. The response was immediate.

"Vance, if what you tell me about Mr. Marlow is correct, I certainly can see that he will need to be here that period of time to recognize the benefits of sobriety."

And so, it was done. He had six months to change the direction of the firm and exercise total control with Marlow out of the way. Francis, after all, had no balls to stand in his way. Now he just needed to get the green light to begin the construction documents for Chicago World Tower and with that send an invoice for over $4,000,000 to that ass, Steel Simpson. By a conservative estimate, 25% of that would be profit. It could still be a good year with a huge bonus for him if the project could proceed. But phone calls all week to Simpson had never been taken or returned. Jefferson went back to his desk and buzzed Marilyn.

"Yes, Vance?" Marilyn was finishing up work and was ready for the weekend with Connor. She hoped that dinner out at their favorite Italian restaurant, followed by a cozy night in his apartment watching the snow out the window, would brighten his mood, soured by the Monday morning meeting with Francis, Jr., and the desecration of his design effort. That day, after the meeting and finding Bob Marlow blacked out drunk, she had had to talk him off of the cliff. He was ready to quit. For many selfish reasons, she did not want him to. It was a great comfort knowing he was there in the same building when Jefferson put his disgusting hands on her. But she could never tell Connor that. The best she could do was to remind him that he still owed over $20,000 in student loans and that no other firm in Chicago would pay him close to what he was earning at NJ&M. He had grudgingly agreed and had worked all week to salvage something of his design concept from the blatant mediocrity that Francis Nolan had wrought. A pep talk from Jerzy had also helped. The man had almost died of torture and starvation in a German POW camp, so he had to admit that having your design shit upon was a small matter. Jerzy had reminded Connor that he had a life of great designs ahead of him. The week had undoubtedly taken an emotional toll on the young man. Like Marilyn, Connor looked forward to a night of Italian food, wine and snow.

"Did you call Simpson?" Jefferson was agitated.

"Yes, Vance, I did. Three times. Ruth says she will have him call as soon as he is back in the office."

"All right. Are you leaving?"

"Yes, Vance, if there is nothing else?"

"With this snow, I thought we might go over to the Italian Village, grab some dinner, and wait for the weather to clear."

Marilyn sighed. "Vance, I have plans. And you have a wife at home. Please, go home to her."

"Sorry. Just a thought. You know I worry about you…like a father."

"I appreciate that, Vance, but please don't. I have a father, and he worries about me quite a bit." She hung up, and quickly gathered her coat and purse, to escape before Jefferson could reply. Then the phone rang and line one lit up. She was going to let it ring, but then decided that if it was a call for her boss, it would distract him, and she could make her getaway.

"Mr. Jefferson's office."

"This is Steel Simpson. Let me speak to Vance."

In his office, Jefferson lifted the receiver. "Well, well, Mr. Simpson, the phantom developer!" Any pretense at politeness to his client had left J. Vance Jefferson long ago. He had decided to treat Steel Simpson as Simpson seemed to treat everyone, with disdain.

"It might interest you to know Jefferson, that I have been working on more important things than the architecture for Chicago World Tower. Like getting the money."

"That would be novel. Since you owe us one and a half million. And have for some time. Can I expect it soon?"

"Have you made the changes to the building to get in into budget?"

"No, for several reasons. The number one reason is that you haven't paid us. The other that it's going to ruin great architecture. I seriously recommend against it."

"Are you going to finance the twelve million I'm over budget?"

Ignoring the question, Jefferson retorted, "When am I going to get paid? We'll discuss the design afterwards." Jefferson, who had been to Nolan's office and reviewed the design, which he determined was mediocre at best, could not have cared less about the design. He just wanted to collect the fee.

"How about Monday? I'll have a cashier's check delivered to you for, let's see, $1,550,000. I just closed on the financing today. You're authorized to begin construction documents."

Simpson was not lying for a change. He had indeed closed on the construction loan. But only after being lectured by Brad Wentworth about rubber checks and not paying consultants. To get the deal done, though, Simpson had to create an entirely bogus budget for the project that totaled $100 million, not $112 million. He had also assured the banker, as well as Ali Sharif, his partner, that the building was being designed according to the rendering that stood on the easel in Wentworth's office. And lastly, he had submitted a financial statement that was a fantasy. But no one took the time or cared to check. Brad Wentworth's bank collected one-and-a-half points on the loan, $900,000. His year-end bonus would be five percent of that.

Jefferson, though pleased at the news, pressed for more this time. "I want a $500,000 advance on the CDs. Then we'll start."

Simpson was silent, thinking. Finally, he spoke, "Okay, on one condition."

"There's always a condition with you isn't there, Steel. What?"

"Don't ever call my banker again to bitch about not being paid or for any other reason!"

"Then pay me! Goodbye, Steel." Jefferson looked out again at the snow, now falling in greater amounts. He turned and grabbed his coat hanging on the door. "I'll sit this out at the Berghof," he thought, pleased with the idea that come Monday, he would have a cashier's check for over two million dollars in his hands.

CHAPTER 61

Bob Marlow took his first walk around the grounds of the New Day Clinic. The meandering sidewalk went around the large central courtyard where the main building, numerous four-person residences for the "guests," a workout facility, and a classroom building were arranged like spokes in a wheel. The grass was perfectly maintained thick St. Augustine. There were palm trees, bougainvillea bushes and perfectly pruned oleanders, hibiscus and sea grapes. In the center of the courtyard was a large fountain. The sound of the bubbling and cascading water was calming and welcome after the last 48 hours. The last two days had been excruciating; he was shaking when he got off the plane in Palm Beach and had the sweats by the time he arrived at the facility.

There was no check in, only two orderlies in white coats who led him to a dry-out cell. There was a single bed, a metal toilet and a small sink. The walls were padded. He had thought, *"So this is what it's come to, you drunk…a padded cell."* But, in fact, he needed it. He had the chills followed by more sweats; he hurled up his hospital food, and then began the dry heaves. There were hallucinations. He pounded his head on the walls. He crawled up in a ball in a corner and cried until there were no more tears. Then the shaking began again, this time worse than ever before. An orderly brought him some soup, which he was able to keep down, but then his stomach cramped up. Finally, by noon Friday, he lay down on the bed and slept. When he woke at ten Saturday morning, he was weak, but his head no longer hurt.

Once he regained consciousness, Marlow vaguely remembered listening to Connor while in the hospital in Chicago. Something about Nolan fucking with his design. He seemed very upset, but in his condition, all Marlow could offer was: "I'm sorry." Once he was better, he would call Connor and get the whole story, but he could imagine that Francis would indeed mess up a good design.

As he walked around the courtyard, an orderly followed some distance behind. There were no fences, no walls. He could make a run for it. But he decided not to; if you had to dry out this place looked like a good place to do it. The warm air brushed against his face. Between the buildings he saw an orange sun setting. A thirty-day vacation would do him some good, he thought. He turned and walked back to the orderly.

"Hey, where's the bar in this place?"

"They said you had a sense of humor, Mr. Marlow. Sorry, no bar. And there isn't one within several miles."

"Okay, I'm hungry. What time is dinner? And can I get a real room?"

"Certainly, Mr. Marlow, follow me."

CHAPTER 62

On a clear and very cold day on December 13, 1973, the great effort to execute the construction documents for Chicago's greatest building began. Jefferson had indeed received the outstanding monies, and the half a million as promised by Steel Simpson, the previous week. With luck and a few changes, the documents would be complete by late spring. And Jefferson would have made the firm over $1,400,000 in profit.

That evening, Nolan, Jefferson and Marlow had its Christmas party in the famous and overly ornate Crystal Ballroom at the Blackstone Hotel, a location chosen by Marilyn Jones and approved by J. Vance at their dinner at Jacques. It would be the most expensive party the firm had ever had; the frugal Francis Nolan, Sr., would never have allowed such an extravagance, but he was dead. Bob Marlow was in rehab. All Francis Nolan, Jr., cared about was what brand of vodka would be served. Jefferson now had complete control of the company and he wanted a big party. He wanted everyone to know that he alone was in charge and that their future was limitless under his guidance. Generous bonuses would be handed out, the largest to himself. Everyone would be served steak and lobster and get drunk. Jefferson had reserved a junior suite for what he hoped would be a fun night with Marilyn, who would receive another raise and a $1,000 bonus. Connor West would be promoted to senior designer with a raise to $30,000 per year, and a $3,000 bonus. 1974 promised to be a red-letter year for Nolan, Jefferson and Marlow.

Johnny Messina had reserved the Florence Room at the Villa Roma Supper Club for Cooky's Concrete Christmas party. The paisley wallpaper and imposing crystal chandeliers were a bit over the top for him, but his dad had insisted and gave him a special price. The office staff had decorated the room with a big tree and Christmas lights strung outward from the center of the room. There was lasagna, manicotti, a carved roast beef, jumbo shrimp—the works. Johnny Messina toasted his employees. There was beer, red wine, and plenty of booze. Carmine Messina made an appearance and thanked everyone for their hard work.

"When is this job gonna happen?" Carmine had taken Johnny off to the side; it was the real reason for his visit.

"Josef Simpson told me we had the job if I held my price until next summer. He told me that the architect had started the final drawings." Johnny Messina didn't want to talk business at the Christmas Party, but his father seemed anxious.

"Good, go enjoy your friends. They gettin' bonuses?"

"Of course, Pops. We are going to have a great year in 1974."

Billy Flanagan didn't understand why anybody would want to live around Soldier Field. The wind swept in from the lake, and chilled you to the bone, and there was no way to set up a warm, dry place to take shelter. The building had gates everywhere and he couldn't find one that was unlocked. So, he had gone west at least a half mile where trees and buildings blocked the cold wind. There off an alley, he came upon an abandoned bungalow. One of the four rooms had an intact window; it was at least ten degrees warmer than the rest of the house. And there was plenty of wood to make a fire. He could tear off the horizontal wood slats that had long ago held the plaster on the walls. He had even found a mattress in the trash down the street and an old chair that had been thrown out. At a Christmas tree lot, he got a job for a week unloading fresh trees and received $20 and a small misshapen tree. It was now propped up in the corner of his new home. He would have taken a picture of it with his camera, but he had no flash bulb. He built a small fire, sat down and opened the hamburgers he bought from White Castle. The year had begun badly but it was going to be a Merry Christmas for Billy Flanagan.

"What are you doing? Come on; have some champagne." Steel Simpson was in a mood to celebrate. Chicago World Tower would soon be a reality.

"I'm writing a want ad for a maid. Now that you're 60 million richer, I'm going to start living like a wealthy woman for a change."

"Gessus, can you not give it a rest? And we're not rich. That money is needed to build a building."

"Yeah, but you told me you were getting a big development fee."

"Which I have to split with that raghead, Sharif. He's really been a pain in the ass. He wants to know everything. It takes all my day to make up stuff. Here's your champagne. Can we just toast to us? It's Christmas!"

"Fine. To us! Team Simpson." Reese Anne Simpson gave Steel a short kiss on the lips, then took a deep sip of the bubbly. She had to admit, it was good stuff. For now, she'd stick around to see what happened with that big phallic symbol her husband was going to build. She probably was going to have to have sex with the man tonight, a prospect that made her down the remainder of her glass. At least she was getting a buzz.

On Sunday, Marilyn and Jane went all out to set the dining table for dinner. Earlier in the day, Marilyn and Connor had walked to Old Town to the Crate & Barrel store and bought holiday placemats and matching napkins, wine glasses, and a set of new stainless tableware. Jane had gone to the butcher shop and bought a standing rib roast. There would be browned potatoes, carrots and fresh string beans. For dessert, they bought an apple pie from the bakery, to be served with ice cream. Connor and Jane's new boyfriend, Ross, would provide the wine.

The girls bought a tree and decorated it with colored lights, inexpensive glass balls, and strands of popcorn. It was going to be a fun night and Marilyn couldn't wait to see Connor again. She hoped he would like the present she had bought him. Tonight, there was no room for Vance Jefferson, or his hands and filthy advances. She had met Alice Jefferson at the company Christmas party, who stayed until the end, and that ended any chance of her boss hitting on her.

John O'Rourke sat at his desk and Mike Grabowski occupied the guest chair. He had brought out a bottle of Jameson's from the bottom desk drawer and fetched two glasses from the break room. It didn't matter that they were tall juice glasses; they held the whiskey quite well.

"Here's to another year down the tubes." Grabowski lifted his glass to toast his boss.

"Yeah, eleven cases, ten solved…" O'Rourke took a pull on the drink and stared out the window to the alley at the mess of electrical and telephone wires running past.

"What's the matter? That's a pretty good record." Grabowski looked down at his glass. He held it tight, preferring to let the whiskey warm before imbibing.

"I guess. But it ought to be eleven solved."

"You're setting pretty high standards for yourself, aren't you? Plus, the boss closed that case."

O'Rourke stared out at the snow that was beginning to fall. "Just because some people have no standing or suck in this city is no reason not to give them justice."

"Look, we did our best. We couldn't connect Simpson or his driver to the fire. I can't say I disagree with O'Halloran on this one. It was probably accidental."

"Maybe so, but something just doesn't add up. Okay, Simpson was at that alumni event in Evanston. But it doesn't mean his driver took him there. And Jensen's hand was bandaged. Like it was burned."

"John. We couldn't even identify the victims."

"I know and that's what bothers me. There's no closure. There has to be closure. Someone knew those two people; they were someone's sons, brothers, friends."

"You're not going to let this go, are you?"

"No, I'll do it on my own time." He picked up the spent flashbulb. "Maybe we've been approaching this from the wrong angle."

"What do you mean? We ran it into the ground." Grabowski was now drinking deeply of the Irish whiskey and it warmed him; he looked out at the snow that was beginning to fall.

"We've been trying to trap Simpson. But he's too smart. Look, two people died, but there were over 30 people that lived there on the lake. They must live somewhere else in this fair city." O'Rourke rolled the flashbulb in the palm of his hand. "And one of them has a camera. And if he or she has a camera, and used it to take a picture, then that camera is a valuable piece of evidence; if they still have it."

Grabowski reached for the bottle and poured another. "Well, Merry fucking Christmas, boss. I guess I'll be checking shelters, underpasses, railroad spurs, and whatever else, come January 1."

"I appreciate the help. And Merry Christmas to you." John O'Rourke reached for the Jameson and they did another toast.

The haze of smoke from weed hung heavy in the main room of the house on Warren Avenue. The crew was looking at *Fat Albert and the Cosby Kids* on the color TV. For some, the view was partially blocked by the case of Schlitz Malt Liquor on the coffee table, next to a mirror with a rolled Benjamin and a razor blade. All the lines of coke had been finished. Some of the members were at the dining room table filling plates with Kentucky Fried and coleslaw. Others were in corners grabbing ass and kissing their girlfriends. The Four Tops played on the stereo. On the enclosed porch beyond the front door, there was a Christmas tree with a few colored lights. It was the Christmas Party for the Lucifer Player's Club. Everyone was there except for Tiger

Gibson, but his presence was both felt and expected. Then, in an instant, he appeared from the basement, stuffing a knife into his pocket. The room went quiet, and someone turned off the TV.

"Hey, ya'll listen up. LaToya's gonna pour some Cold Duck. We're going to toast." La Toya and Ronnie came through with plastic cups filled with the purplish, fizzy liquid.

In a corner, Quince, a newer member, muttered: "Shit, I don't want no Cold Duck. I want some Martell."

Gibson heard the comment and glared at Quince. "You want to go down to the basement, nigga?"

"No, boss. Just sayin'…no offense."

"Good, now let's toast, which is what proper people do. To the Club, the Organization. To everyone. It was a good year…mostly."

Quince tried to get himself back in his boss's good graces: "To the Lucifer Player's Club." Gibson stared at him still disliking the name.

"Yeah, to the Player's Club." Tiger went along; it was Christmas. "Listen up. Next year we are expanding."

Later, in an upstairs bedroom, Gibson expounded on the meaning of his toast to a half dozen of his senior staff, such as it was. This included Artemus, Biggy, Jerome, Maurice, Tiny, and Quince, who had crawled back into Gibson's good graces with a Christmas gift of a boosted Rolex Daytona 6265. Tiger was drinking Stoli vodka on the rocks.

"Next year, we are taking over the drug market in Maywood and the surrounding towns. I want to get the guineas out of our turf."

"How we gonna do that, boss?" Maurice inquired.

"You let me handle that. But they won't let that business go easy, like they did the protection. Things could get a little…mean. So, keep your damn head on you, Maurice. We can't have you icing no dagos. We do this in a professional way."

"'Bout time we get in that business. Now we all gonna be rich!" Maurice stated, a big smile on his face.

Gibson's eyes narrowed looking at Maurice. "What do you mean 'we'?"

PART FOUR

THE BUILDING
February 1974

CHAPTER 63

FEBRUARY 1974

Since January, the team of 75 professionals had worked diligently on creating the construction documents for Chicago World Tower. Connor, Taubert and Caudy had improved on the crude and poorly proportioned design that was Francis Nolan's brain trust. Though the curved walls and their sail-like imagery were gone, they had created interesting setbacks along the main facades and designed faceted corners that diminished the boxiness of the individual building elements. This was replicated at the base, which was now square once again, but more acceptable in scale and appearance.

As February began, work had become routine. Connor enjoyed his work for the most part and particularly the camaraderie of the team, who often headed to the Berghof on Fridays for beer, brats and hard-boiled eggs. While things were still on an even keel with Marilyn, he had never confronted her about her "other" evenings out. Though these unavailable nights had not materialized through the last month, he still needed to know what was, or had been going on. He decided it was time and, on this Friday, he would beg off going out with the team and take Marilyn to a new restaurant. He thought that he might want to marry Marilyn; but first he had to find out about those clandestine evenings.

"Hey, what are you doing tonight?" West made his voice as cheery and upbeat as possible.

"I thought you'd never ask. Nothing. Oh, wrong. I'm going to watch *Mary Tyler Moore* tonight." Marilyn was toying with her boyfriend, and he liked her wit and spunkiness.

"No, you're not. I'm taking you to a new restaurant. I'll pick you up at seven."

"If you insist. I guess I can wait and watch *Mary* on re-runs. See you then. Oh, what's the dress?"

"I don't know. Nice, I guess."

"You're no help."

"Well, you always look great."

Lawry's Prime Rib had just opened off of Michigan Avenue on East Ontario and though Connor hadn't made a reservation the maître d' took pity on the earnest young man and his beautiful date and found them a table near the kitchen. The place was full, and Connor tipped the man $10 for getting him out of an embarrassing jam. Another surprise was the prices on the menu.

"What's the occasion, Mr. Big Spender?" asked Marilyn thinking that this was the kind of place that Vance Jefferson had taken her to as a routine. But this was so much better; she was with the man she loved, and he would not be groping her under the table. "Connor, let me pay for half of this. I mean the prime rib is $25.00!"

"Nope, it's our one-year anniversary."

"It is not. I didn't meet you until April 27, 1973, at 8:30 A.M."

"Well, I talked to you before then."

"Yes, that was April 20, 1973, at 3:10 P.M."

"Close enough. Just say I wanted to meet you earlier, like February 10. Do you want to get a bottle of wine?"

"Yes, but I think I'd like a cocktail first since I'm going to help pay for this little outing."

After two cocktails, Cosmos for Marilyn and bourbons for Connor, they ordered shrimp cocktails, queen's cut prime rib, twice-baked potatoes and Bibb lettuce salads. They held hands, laughed, and enjoyed the evening.

At an inevitable pause, Marilyn spoke. "Connor, I've been thinking. I'm going to go back to school and finish my degree. I've decided I want to become a teacher. I'm sick of being a secretary, and I certainly don't want to be one forever. I've had my fun living in the city, but it's time I got serious."

"Marilyn, I think you'd be a terrific teacher."

"You wouldn't mind if I left the firm?"

"Of course, I would. I'll miss seeing you every day. But I understand. I mean, Jefferson can be an ass sometimes."

"Yes, he can be. He truly can be."

Connor didn't want to ruin the evening with questions of another boyfriend, or whatever it was, that had distracted Marilyn over the last months. But their future, required an explanation. He finished his glass of red wine and summoned the courage to inquire.

"Can I ask you something? It's important." He looked Marilyn directly in the eyes to try to see her reaction.

"Of course, you can."

"I need to know about all those evenings you were busy and couldn't go out. I have to know. Was, is there another guy? I wouldn't ask you but it's well, been really bothering me."

"Oh, Connor, I'm so sorry. It was nothing, nothing at all."

"That's not an answer. It had to be something."

Marilyn took a swallow of wine. Tears started rolling down her cheeks. Then she took up the wine glass again and took a deep drink.

"Connor, I'm so sorry. I didn't mean to hurt you."

"So, it is another guy. Fine! I thought we had something special!"

"We do, Connor, we do. I love you! It's not what you think but I don't want you to quit Nolan, Jefferson and Marlow." The tears continued, and Marilyn starting crying in low sobs.

"It's another guy at the firm? Under my nose! I bet it's Taubert. I see how he looks at you. I should have called him out long ago."

"No, Connor, no. It's not him. It's not anyone. Well, not anyone I care about."

"You're not making any sense."

"It's Vance Jefferson! He's been making me go out with him to discuss picnics and parties, and flowers for meetings, and marketing proposals, but he just wants to…"

"Jefferson! Wants to what?"

343

"Go to bed with me! Oh, Connor, I feel so dirty!"

"Did you? Did you sleep with him?"

"No! How could you think such a thing?"

"Well what then? What did he do?"

"He touched me. Oh, please don't make me say anymore. I feel so ashamed."

"What do you mean— 'He touched you?' How?"

"Connor, he puts his hands all over me…"

"That son-of-a-bitch! I'll kill him!"

"Don't say that. He's just a dirty old man. Anyway, I think he's lost interest in me. And I'm going to quit anyway. Remember what I told you about when he first hired me, and Mr. Nolan told me to be careful. I guess that's why he's gone through so many secretaries."

"Yeah, Marlow told me he got one of his secretaries pregnant. And I'll still kill him."

"No, you won't, and you can't say anything. He'll fire you. We shouldn't even be dating. Please. Jane told me to stand my ground now that he's had his fun, I will. I promise, I will."

"Had his fun? What's that supposed to mean?"

"Connor, it wasn't anything. He just wanted to toy with me. Connor, I love you. But I needed the job, and at least we got some raises out of it."

"What if he doesn't stop? What will you do the next time he wants to discuss this year's softball game?"

"I blew him off last December one Friday when it snowed. I told him to go home to his wife, and he did. If he asks again, I'll threaten to tell Bob Marlow."

"Fat lot of good that will do. He's in rehab with his own problems."

"I'm sure Dick Schiffels and Norman Weese might be interested."

The two were quiet for what seemed like endless minutes, but Connor's temper was leveling out. Finally, he spoke. "Okay, thank you for telling me. But I wish you had told me sooner."

"Would it have done any good? Were you going to chaperone us?"

West smiled at the image. "No, I guess not. Look, let's get out of here. I've got another bottle of wine at the apartment. You game?"

"With you, I'm game for anything, anytime. I told you that I love you."

Connor squeezed Marilyn's hand. "And I love you." He smiled at her, but still wondered how much J. Vance Jefferson had gotten away with.

CHAPTER 64

Steel Simpson walked past the main reception desk toward J. Vance Jefferson's office.

"Excuse me, sir, may I help you? Sir, you can't go back there." The receptionist became frantic. No one was allowed in the executive area without being announced. She picked up the phone and dialed Marilyn Jones. The red light lit up on Marilyn's phone as she looked up and saw Steel Simpson heading down the corridor to her. She picked up the phone. "Never mind, Rosemary, I've got it."

"Hi sweetheart, I want to see Vance." Steel Simpson peered down at the executive secretary with a smirk. His tone was not of request but of command.

"Mr. Simpson, I don't see you on his calendar. He's a little busy right now, I'm afraid."

"Put me on the calendar. It's March 28."

"So it is. And that means what?"

Simpson walked by Marilyn's desk to the door of Jefferson's office. "He owes me some drawings." He opened the door and went in. Jefferson was reading the *Chicago Tribune*, a Tootsie Roll Pop in his mouth.

"Steel, what a pleasant surprise," he said almost choking on the candy. "I wasn't expecting you. Did you want to bring me our check for March in person?" He looked over at the accounts receivable sheet on his desk. "Well, look at that. You're only 15 days past due. You must have a check."

"Funny, Vance. Hey, aren't you an architect?"

"I'm actually a structural engineer, but why do you ask?"

"Because most of the time you sound like a fucking shylock."

"You're amusing, Steel. Look, this place doesn't run on hopes and dreams. I have 75 people working on your project as we speak."

"And that's why I decided to drop by."

"With a check, right?"

"I don't recognize due on receipt. Everyone gets 30 days."

"It would be quite something if we received a check from you in 30 days."

"Am I up to date or not?"

"Technically, yes. By tomorrow, you'll be overdue. We allow a week for the mail." Jefferson was growing weary of the back and forth. At this moment, he was wishing that he had listened to Francis Nolan and stuck with municipal work.

"Vance, by tomorrow, your drawings will be overdue. You said you'd be done by March 29. I looked at the March 15 progress set. You're a long way from done."

"It didn't help that we had to start over after you demanded that Francis change his original design."

"Don't bullshit me, Vance. Francis couldn't design a doghouse. Your kid Connor designed it. Francis even admitted to that."

The blood drained from Vance's face. He was caught off guard. Recovering after a long pause, he said, "It was a team effort, Steel. Leo Skoroshod, the senior designer who died, had a major role in the effort. It took some time to recoup from his loss as well."

"Nevertheless, the finished CDs are due tomorrow. I have a building to build, and the interest meter is running on all the cash I've laid out, and I'm getting heat from my partner, too."

"We will need another month. It's a complicated project."

"Yeah, yeah, yeah. Spare me the excuses. What? Did you say another month?"

"Yes, I believe I did." Jefferson glared at Simpson.

Simpson turned and headed for the door. "You have 15 days. And no more money until you're finished."

"I might as well stop work then. You've paid $2,000,000. The fee for the construction documents is $4,000,000, which includes the past due invoices."

"Keep drawing, Vance. I might get you a check." Steel Simpson walked out and, as he passed Marilyn's desk, said, "Have a great day, gorgeous."

CHAPTER 65

The meeting room was cheerful and well lit, with a wall of easterly facing windows that bathed the space in morning light. On the walls were motivational posters with words of wisdom for the occupants. Ten chairs were assembled in a circle; one somewhat larger.

"Let's get started. Bob, how are you doing?"

Bob Marlow sipped on his fresh refill of hot coffee from the Palm Coast Dining Room after another great breakfast at the New Day Clinic. In fact, if you had to do rehab, this was the place to do it. The food was great, and so were the desserts, compensation for giving up the booze, he guessed. His room was spacious and included a nice sitting area with TV and a well-sized bath off the entry. There was an indoor and outdoor pool, tennis courts, and even an indoor running track around a regulation basketball court. Over the last four months, he had lost ten pounds, gotten a tan, and exercised himself into the best shape of his life, regularly pumping iron in the gym, followed by a three-mile run.

"Fine, when do I graduate?"

The counselor, John, a balding middle-aged man who was a recovering alcoholic, 15 years sober, was now used to Bob's wit, or was it sarcasm?

"I don't think we ever graduate, now do we? We may be sober, but we're always going to be recovering. You can't change a pickle back to a cucumber."

"I once saw a magician do that." The group laughed. Marlow was in rare form, but more than that, was ready to be gone from New Day, great desserts notwithstanding.

"That's right, but it was magic after all. Tell me, how do you feel about alcohol now, Bob?"

"I never thought I ever say this, but I really don't miss it anymore. I could not have said that when I came here. I know it's not my friend."

"Good, but on the outside, with a bar or liquor store down the street, will you be tempted?"

"I think I'll always be tempted, but I want to see my sons again and make amends to them…and yes, my ex-wife too, for the pain I caused them." Marlow had to admit, he had the BS down. After 72 of these daily sessions, he had picked up some pretty good pointers from the men and the women who had cashiered out of the place. Now he needed to do the same.

"That's good to hear, Bob. Anyone else?"

James, a lanky, thin dude with a thin moustache, who now carried a Bible everywhere spoke: "I don't think I could be at this good place today without the help of Jesus, my Lord and Savior. He has brought me through the darkness into the light."

Marlow silently groaned. *"If I listen to anymore Jesus stuff from James, I'll need a drink again,"* he thought to himself. He tuned out the born-again talk and thought about his phone call the previous evening with Connor West.

"Hey, thanks for sending me the half-size set of drawings on Chicago BS Tower. I have to admit, your revised design is pretty good." Marlow had relished looking at the progress drawings West had sent. He now realized how much he missed architecture. He had even put the drawings up to his nose so he could smell the ink and ammonia that were used to print them.

"You told me that sometimes our job is to make lemonade from a lemon. Or is it, 'Even a blind squirrel finds a nut sometimes.' I have to admit, I was extremely pissed off when Francis messed with my original design."

"Ya think? I mean stuffing the bumwad into Francis' mouth? If the old man had been alive, you would have been fired on the spot. Actually, maybe not. He always liked people who didn't take any shit."

"Yeah, he hasn't spoken to me since, and he stays away from the big room where we're working on the CDs. So, how's rehab? Miss the booze?"

"Fine, I guess. But I need to get out of here. I need to be back in Chicago. Help you guys finish that job."

"I think it's pretty well under control now. Even Muktar can't seem to find any problems with the mechanical rooms anymore."

Marlow chuckled. "Fun, isn't it?"

"Tedious, but fun, I guess. You never answered me about the booze—missing it, that is."

"I'll always miss it. But I've been sober 124 days. That's too much time invested now to fall off the wagon. Plus, I wanna see my sons."

"Bob. Bob. Are you here with us?" The counselor's admonition brought Marlow back into the group session and among the present and accounted for.

"Sorry, daydreaming."

"I wanted to tell you that the director would like to see you after our session. If it's convenient for you."

"No problem. I only had a trip to Boca Bottle Shop planned today. They have a special on Evan Williams."

The room broke out again in muted laughter. The counselor was not amused but managed a weak smile.

"John said you wanted to see me…" Marlow plopped down into one of the guest chairs without permission. It wasn't that he was being rude, but he just felt like an equal to all these doctors, psychologists and counselors. He might be in a different profession, but he was still equal to them, even if he had been a drunk once.

"I did, Bob, I did. You've been here four months. You've done well. John gives me good reports from your sessions, and I guess we've all enjoyed your, shall we say, humor. Humor is good. You'll need it on the outside."

"I think I had it on the outside. I just needed more of it in here." Marlow wanted to ask to be released from the velvet prison that was now known by the inmates as *Happy Days*, a new comedy that had just debuted on TV.

"I have to tell you that your partner asked me to make sure you were 100% well before you are released."

"That's interesting; so nice of Vance to be concerned. John just said in our little group session that we never get 100% well."

"He did? Well, yes, but he is dealing on one plane and I am on another. How do you feel? Ready to go? Can you handle the world without alcohol?"

"Honestly, is anyone ever ready to go? There are no temptations here. We don't walk by a Tiki Bar. There's no on-site liquor store. Hell, you even rip out the booze ads from the *Life* magazines. The biggest temptation is the chocolate éclairs after dinner. In the past, it didn't take much to throw me off the wagon and into the ditch. But I'm physically fit now, and I love that. And more important, I'm on solid mental ground: clean, present, and in the moment as we say. I know I can never just have one drink again. And if I do, I'll never see my sons, and I'll lose my job. And I miss both terribly." Marlow sat quiet, figuring he had just signed up for another two months.

"Good answer. Honest answer. Okay, even though Vance Jefferson won't like it, you're released as of May 3, next Friday."

"And what does Jefferson have to do with it?"

On Monday morning May 6, Bob Marlow walked into Nolan, Jefferson and Marlow, Architects and Engineers to the clapping and cheers of the firm assembled in the great drafting hall. Vance Jefferson was not among the throng. Marlow went to his office, made a pot of coffee, and looked down at the Immigration form he was filling out on Leo Skoroshod. That seemed like a good first task for the day. Later, he'd get with Dick Schiffels for an update on Chicago World Tower. He opened the bottom drawer of his desk, the one where he kept the bottle of Evan Williams. It was empty save for a note:

Go get a Coke.
Glad you're back!

Connor

CHAPTER 66

Tiny labored over the small bags, filling each with white powder. He wanted to be back out on the streets, but Tiger Gibson had decided that he was too small to be a collector; yet his small fingers were perfect to fill the plastic bags with heroin and cocaine. Tiger had found a source from a Mexican gang on the Southside of town, who got him all the product he wanted. And it was 95% pure, better than the garbage being sold by the wops.

The business plan was simple. For a couple of weeks, it would be free and uncut. Then he'd slowly dilute it with corn starch and start to charge, but less than the Outfit was pricing it for, and theirs might be diluted by as much as 40%. With their stuff, you almost didn't get high, but you sneezed a lot.

Tiny and his small group of four continued to open five-pound bricks of heroin, break, chop and dice it and then weigh the individual portions and pack it into nickel and dime bags. Business since the New Year had taken off. Gibson's purveyors got out on the street before noon and demand grew. Hell, it was free or almost free to the "regular" customers. By the time Eddie, Gino and the other associates of the Outfit started work around two, after long lunches at one of several Italian restaurants in nearby Cicero, there were no takers.

Carmine Messina sat in his private office on the second floor of Cooky's Concrete Company. While he would have preferred to be tending his vegetable garden and planting tomatoes on this warm day in May, he felt it was important to show up at the office several times a week. He looked down at the weeks' take sheets that were prepared for him by

Kenny Ito, his bookkeeper. He flipped past the first two sheets; he knew what he wanted to see, the drug sales on the near Westside. They had been declining steadily since the first of the year. And it wasn't just Maywood, but a larger swath. Business was off by $45,000 in the last month alone. He estimated that since the first of the year the Outfit had lost almost two hundred grand. *"Mother of God, this is getting out of hand. Fuckin' nigga gang."* Messina had heard about the talk at the Italian American Club around the poker table about giving away the protection business to the Player's Club. Now this. Some of his lieutenants were thinking he was going soft. He picked up the phone. "Adele, get hold of Eddie. Tell him to meet me at Rocco's in Cicero for an early lunch."

"Yes, sir. Today?"

"Yes, dammit. Today!"

Eddie "White Shoes" Vincente, wearing his ever-present white patent leather loafers, sat in a booth at Rocco's, at the back of the establishment. He knew what the lunch was about, and it was not about the daily special of manicotti. He faced the window so he could see the Don walk in with his bodyguard, Tony. He would switch places when they sat down so that Carmine Messina could keep an eye on the front door. He ordered an iced tea while he waited. As he stirred the tea, he realized that his hand was shaking. He looked up to see Carmine Messina standing over him.

"Don Carmine, it is good to see you. Here, please sit." Eddie got up from his chair and moved around to the chair facing the back of the restaurant. *"Great,"* he thought, *"the last thing I'm gonna see in my life is the door to the men's!"*

"Eddie, it's good to see you too. You look tense. Relax. I'll get us some wine." Messina motioned to Rocco, who came right over. It was rare that his little restaurant had such an important man as a guest. "Rocco, bring a bottle of Chianti. Two glasses."

"Pronto, Don Carmine. Pronto."

"Eddie, how long you been working for me?"

"I don't know, boss, nine, ten years."

"Eleven years, Eddie. Eleven years. And you've been one of my best lieutenants. And a good friend too."

Rocco brought the deep red Italian wine and Carmine waved his hand. "Pour, Rocco, just pour." He pushed the first full glass toward Eddie. Eddie nodded and took the glass.

"Saluti, Don Carmine."

Messina let the title pass. "Saluti, my friend." They drank in silence, and Eddie felt the smooth liquid calming his nerves. But Messina didn't seem upset either. Finally, the Don broke the silence.

"Eddie, we got a problem on the Westside. And Eddie, it's your territory. I had to give up the protection business to the blacks and I hear talk about that at the club."

"Boss, I told you not to do that, remember. I coulda taken out a couple of those nigs and it would be history."

"I know, I know, but you know I hate violence. And now they're taking over the drug business. I thought it might just be in Maywood, but it's all over the Westside. Whadda you know about all this? I thought at first, in January, it was just the time of the year. But no…"

"Don, me and Gino haven't done anything different. We always sell in the afternoon when the joneses hit the drug heads. But this Player's Club started handing out bags in the morning, at the beginning. For free! Now they're charging but the cost is less than our junk and its better quality. I know. I tried it."

"How much you cuttin' our product?"

"I don't know, 25, maybe 30 percent."

"And now no one wants it…" Carmine realized he had a problem.

"Shit, boss, it's like I can't give it away. By the time I get to them they're already higher than a moon rocket."

Messina took a drink of wine. He looked up at a poster of Rome on the wall. "I was there once, after Sicily, on leave. I'd like to go back someday."

"Boss, whadda ya want me to do about this situation? About the Player's Club?" Eddie ignored the travelogue.

"Nothing, right now. They've gained the upper hand. But reduce our prices and make our stuff pure. Once they have a taste, that's what they'll want."

"I'm sorry I let this happen, boss. Truly, I am. I could make an example of one of their runners. There's a punk, Maurice, I'd like to take off the streets."

"Is he the one beat up Lucca, Vincenzo, and the barber; what's his name?"

"Carl Johnson. Good guy; gives a good haircut too. Yeah that's who I think did it. This kid Maurice and a smaller kid called Tiny."

"I guess they got nicknames too, eh White Shoes?" Messina chuckled.

"Just say the word boss. I'll make an example of 'em."

"Violence isn't good for business, Eddie. We gotta be patient." He put his hand on Eddie's sleeve, squeezing it gently. "Soon, I'll make the example of this 'Tiger' Gibson and his Players. Hey, sorry, but I gotta go. Enjoy the manicotti." Messina rose from his chair and walked toward the door. Then he turned. "See ya, Eddie."

His lieutenant raised his hand in a wave and then he began to look at the menu. He took another drink of the Chianti. He realized he had worked himself up into a lather for nothing. Then he glanced up. The door to the men's was opening. He looked up and saw his partner, Gino, and the barrel of a gun with a silencer. Two quiet pops echoed in the restaurant. Eddie's head blew open and what was left of it dropped to the table. Rocco was ready with towels and a blanket. With luck, he'd have the place cleaned up before the lunch rush.

CHAPTER 67

"Fine, Steel, I'll release the drawings, but I'd better see a check for our last two invoices by the end of the week. By May 15. Goodbye."

Vance Jefferson put the phone back in the receiver hard. He looked out the window and ran his hand through his ever-graying, long hair. *"This better pay off,"* he thought. Issuing the stamped and signed construction documents before he had been paid over a million-and-a-half dollars was something he had promised Bob Marlow that he wouldn't do. But since his return from rehab, two months too early to his chagrin, he had kept Marlow out of the loop on the affairs of the company.

Jefferson picked up the phone and dialed the three-digit extension for Dick Schiffels.

"Yes, Vance? What's up?" Schiffels was always even-keeled, polite and businesslike.

"Are you finished with the Chicago World Tower drawings?"

"I'm just checking the final set now. They look good. I'd say by tomorrow, Friday at the latest. We really made great progress this last month. Authorizing the overtime helped a lot."

"Then send them out Friday after you've stamped and sealed them. Send 25 sets to Simpson Construction." Jefferson thought about the overtime: over $48,000 taken from their profit on the job. He reached for a Tootsie Roll Pop; he really wanted a drink.

"That's a lot of drawings to reproduce. I'll call Chicago Repro and tell them to work all weekend so Simpson will have them on Monday."

"That works. Thanks." Vance put down the receiver. He would call his friend at the *Chicago Tribune* and let him know that Chicago's biggest project would soon be under construction. The positive press would even out any delays in payment or lost profits. The firm would probably get several new jobs because of it. He only had one more task to ensure NJ&M would get paid. He picked up the phone again.

"Records, this is Fred."

"Fred, I need to see the shop drawings for the curtainwall system on Chicago Center."

"You mean the drawings where we noted the mullions and glass tolerances incorrectly?"

"Yes, those. Exactly those."

Bob Marlow had never been so bored in his life. Since he had returned from rehab, there had been little to do. Dick Schiffels was in charge of the firm's biggest project, and only a handful of new ones had begun in design, which needed minimal input from him. He picked up an old *Architectural Record* and flipped the pages. At least he felt great and was proud that after five months, 153 days exactly, he was still sober, but better yet, had little desire to drink. He lifted his coffee mug and as he did, saw the mail cart. He took a small pile of mail and magazines from Simon, an old black man who had been with the firm for years. On the top of the stack was a return address he instantly recognized. It was a response from the Immigration Service. He reached for his letter opener and slid it along the flap. He read the legal mumbo jumbo until he scanned down to the important part:

> *Renewal of Visa was denied by the Department because Appli-*
> *cant's employer, Nolan, Jefferson and Marlow, Architects and*
> *Engineers, indicated that Applicant's employment was to be ter-*
> *minated in the near future. Since the original visa was granted*
> *based upon applicant having gainful employment in the United*
> *States, lack of a means of monetary support compels the Depart-*
> *ment to deny the request.*

"Son of a bitch!" Marlow murmured under his breath. "Jefferson! He fucked Leo! How could he…?" He put down his coffee mug as the anger rose inside.

"Hey, Bob, got a minute?" Marlow looked up; it was West. He sighed. Not a good time, but he hadn't talked to Connor in a while. Marlow opened his center drawer and slipped the letter inside. West noticed.

"If this is a bad time…"

"No. It's fine. How's the big project? Are you done?"

"As a matter of fact, we are. The drawings went to the printer today. They're going to have to work all weekend to print the 25 sets. Each set has 307 sheets. Can you believe that?"

"Wait, we're printing 25 sets just for review?"

"No, they're issued for construction. The check set was reviewed a week ago. Mr. Schiffels stamped and signed the architectural drawings, and after Jerzy approved the structural, Dick signed off on those. Mr. Oliveri stamped the MEP drawings. Is something wrong?"

"Yes, lots. I was supposed to stamp and sign those drawings and only when…well never mind. So, now what are you going to do?"

"Monday, Mr. Schiffels wants me to go up to Evanston to Simpson Construction and do a review with Josef Simpson, the president. I assume there's some relation between our terrific client and the construction company that bears his name. Does he own it?"

"No, I don't think so. But I think his father started it."

"They must be a pretty large company to handle this job."

"Actually, I think it's a pretty big job for them. Back during the war, they were really big, but not in the last few years. Maybe you can find out what you can about them. I heard Steel Simpson negotiated the project. No bond."

"Is that bad?" Connor asked knowing little about the intricacies of bidding, bonding and insurance.

"It could be for Simpson, or more to the point, the lender. Anyway, what's next for you? I seem to be out of the loop lately."

"I think I'm being assigned to designing space plans for a couple of floors in the Equitable Building. From a 75-story building to rearranging offices."

"Such is the life of the architect, Connor, my boy. Now, if you'll excuse me, I need to go talk to the senior partner, Mr. Jefferson."

"I'm glad you mentioned that. I need to tell you something. When you were in Florida…well, I couldn't mention it on the phone, but I need to tell you now."

"Tell me what? Are you quitting?"

"No. I don't really know how to say it, so I just will. Mr. Jefferson has been hitting on Marilyn." Connor fidgeted in his chair. He was glad it was out, but he thought he might be signing their termination papers.

"Hitting? Not again, that S-O-B." Marlow's blood was rising now on this third piece of information on his partner.

"Marilyn won't exactly say, but he's been insisting on going to dinner with her to discuss business. Then he puts his hands all over… well, let's just say he puts his paws where they shouldn't be. She's sick of it and doesn't know what to do. She's afraid if she speaks up, she'll lose her job."

"Okay. Thanks for telling me. I'll handle it." Suddenly, Bob Marlow once again felt the urge for a drink.

CHAPTER 68

"Robert, come on in. How are you feeling? I'm sorry we haven't had a chance to visit much since you got back from Florida. My, you look good. You even seem to be maintaining that tan!"

"Spare me the niceties, Vance." Marlow's sturdy, muscular body lorded over Jefferson seated behind his granite desk. "We have a few things to discuss. First, I understand you gave yourself a $50,000 year-end bonus. Where's mine?"

"Bob, you think that lovely facility in Boca Raton is cheap? The firm paid for your four months there. That totaled almost $25,000. And let's face it; you weren't very productive the last part of last year."

"Bullshit. I was as productive as ever. So, write me a check for the balance, $25,000. And what did you have to do with keeping me there as long as I was? I should have been back by the end of February."

"Robert, Bob, I was in regular consultation with the doctors there. That's all. I, we, wanted to make sure you were ready this time to re-enter society. You gave us all quite a scare, you know."

"OK, fine. We'll let that go. Just know I plan on staying sober and maintaining my rightful place in this firm. But since I've been back you seem to be keeping me out of the loop on a lot of stuff. I don't like it. I am the partner-in-charge of production, not Dick Schiffels."

"Again, Bob, I am only trying to let you ease into work again. I didn't want to tax you."

"Well JV, you just go ahead and tax me!"

Jefferson was getting annoyed. He stood up so he could be eye to eye with Marlow. "Why? So you can fall off the wagon, Bobby? I saw you in your apartment in a pool of vomit and blood and then in a coma in the hospital. And what company will shell out all the money we did to get you sober? So, excuse me if I didn't put you back into the game right away."

Marlow had to admit that Jefferson was probably right. And he wasn't playing from a position of strength. He decided to move on. "Have you been paid by our wonderful client? I understand you let the sealed construction documents out the door."

"I expect a check any day now. Steel promised me. He only has to get a pay request processed through the bank."

"Just great, Jefferson! Our only bargaining chip is gone. I can't believe you let Schiffels sign them, drawings that I'm supposed to sign! And, at this point, you'd trust that asshole, Simpson to pay us. How much does he owe us?"

"It's not substantial. And we've made a handsome profit on the job. So, just leave me to manage the business affairs of the firm. I assure you that soon you'll have more new projects to handle than you know what to do with. If there's nothing further, I have some new proposals to put together." Jefferson opened the door of his office to indicate that the meeting, having turned sour, was over.

"We're not done yet, Vance. Let's talk about Leo."

"What about Leo?"

"You're the reason he committed suicide." Marlow was now face to face with Jefferson; his anger was rising exponentially. He had been screwed out of his bonus; was incarcerated for months in Florida; and there was no good excuse for sending out the completed construction documents without being paid and without his signature. God only knew how much the firm was owed. He rolled into Jefferson. This was a punch he was determined to land.

"I found out from the Department of Immigration that the reason they did not extend Leo's visa is because you told them he was going to be terminated. Way to sign a death sentence. You knew if he got deported that he was going to some gulag in Siberia!"

"That's ridiculous! I'm not responsible for his death! I had no way of knowing his wife had been sentenced to prison. It must have depressed him. I only told Immigration that Leo's status was not long term…"

"Not long term? Bullshit. You told them he was going to be terminated. Why? He was one of our best designers."

"Oh? And what did he contribute to Chicago World Tower? Nothing! If it hadn't been for young West, we'd have had two mediocre designs."

"You signed his death warrant well ahead of securing that project and you know it."

"Correct. After the offer we made to West, I had to make…adjustments to the payroll."

"You're so full of shit, Jefferson. Leo's dead and even if your notice to Immigration wasn't the last straw, it was the first. He knew what was in store for him if he went back to Russia. So, he hung himself! God, I wish Francis Nolan were still here!"

"What's that supposed to mean, Marlow, you sorry-ass drunk? We're done here! Now get the hell out of my office."

Marlow brushed past Vance Jefferson; his fists clenched. Then he remembered his promise to Connor. He turned and faced his partner one more time, grabbing his coat with both hands.

"And keep your hands-off Marilyn Jones or I'll destroy you! You've wrecked the lives of enough women around here!"

Bob Marlow headed down the hall back to his office. Vance Jefferson's face turned pale. From the other direction, seated at her desk, Marilyn heard the last of the argument. She smiled.

CHAPTER 69

The courtyard of the consulate of the Kingdom of Saudi Arabia was in full bloom with azaleas, tulips, and daffodils. Steel Simpson admired it from the large office that was the domain of Ali Zyiad Sharif, Consul to the State of Illinois representing the interests of his foreign country. In one corner, Sharif had installed a large oak table so he could look at the latest drawings of Chicago World Tower. In another, there was the original rendering of the building, the masterpiece that Connor West had designed, that his partner had now mangled. Simpson paced around the room. He had been in there over ten minutes and Sharif had not shown his face. He didn't like being treated in the same way that he treated people. Then the door opened.

"Steel, it's been a while. Too long really. I'm not doing my job and monitoring this project as much as I should."

"Ali, nice to see you, too. Not to worry. I have it all under control."

"Do you?"

"Of course. Look, you have the stamped construction documents. We're ready to begin construction as soon as we get the building permit from the city. And I've greased the skids at City Hall to ensure that. Cost the project a lot, but it will be worth it."

"I'm not surprised. This is Chicago after all. But what you're permitting is not what the House of Saud approved. I've looked at the plans. It's not at all the design we wanted. My father is quite upset."

"Ali, my friend...this design," Steel pointed to the rendering, "was not feasible. It cost way too much."

"Your estimate that you provided to Brad and me at the closing of the loan indicated that it was in budget."

"I know. That's what I was told by my uncle." Simpson had lied so much that the lines of reality and fiction were blurring. "Then as the design progressed, he kept getting higher costs from his subcontractors. Ali, the original design was 12 million over budget."

"And you should have informed me of that. We expected an overage. It always happens. We could have funded that much in a minute."

"And how much ownership in the project would it have cost me?"

"We would have been happy to fund it and become 50-50 partners." Ali was flipping through the drawings, shaking his head.

"Ali, I don't want a 50 percent partner. And what you don't understand about real estate development is that the hotel operator, the office tenants, the condo buyers, the public don't give a rat's ass about beautiful design. It's location, location, location."

"Steel, do not lecture me about real estate. Design does matter. And it matters to my family."

"Not for 12 million, it doesn't."

Ali looked up at his partner. "This is not nearly as exciting as the original concept; it's serviceable, but boring. I guess at this juncture we have no choice but to go along with it. Are you paying everyone?"

"Like clockwork."

"Don't jerk with me, Steel. I know how you do business."

"Ali, don't tell me how to run my business. I pay when I'm satisfied."

"Which is rarely."

"Ali, let's not argue. We are partners. Even with the revisions it's a great project and now it's about 50% pre-leased. I've even got the groundbreaking ceremony set up. We'll have a big tent, champagne and Eggs Benedict. The senators and the governor are invited. You should get your invite today."

"It will certainly be on my calendar. And I promise you, my friend, that before this is over the House of Saud will be majority partner if you fuck up just one iota."

Steel Simpson headed his Mercedes in the direction of Glencoe. He wanted to check on the progress of the new pool, cabana and two-bedroom guesthouse he was building. The total cost was over $350,000 which included formal gardens and fountains. Chump change he had skimmed off the construction loan by billing non-existent costs. And Reese Anne had her maid now, plus a gardener. For the first time in their marriage, she seemed happy. Well, maybe not happy, but placated. And if he had enough time left in the day after his visit to the North Shore, he would check out that new condominium building along the Gold Coast. He needed a larger in-town aerie. He could find the $450,000 purchase price from other miscellaneous costs in his budget. Simpson put his foot on the gas, and with the top down, headed up Lakeshore Drive.

CHAPTER 70

On Monday afternoon, Connor took the "L" all the way up to Davis Street in Evanston and found the office of Simpson Construction easily; it was literally across the street from the station. A pleasant, middle-aged secretary ushered him into a nondescript conference room. The only notable feature was a portrait of a distinguished looking man with a moustache and stern expression. Based on the three-piece suit, period tie and gold watch chain across the vest, the painting looked like it had been done in the 1940s.

"Connor, nice to see you again. This is some set of drawings. Several hundred sheets, I imagine." Josef Simpson was cordial to the young architect. He had no reason not to be. There would be plenty of time for conflicts and arguing change orders in the future.

"To be exact, 307 sheets. It's quite a project. Are you sure you're up to building it?" West probed.

"It is the biggest job we've ever done, but it's all in the organization of the job. And you're only as good as your worst subcontractor and ours are top-notch. I have a couple of experienced superintendents who'll direct the effort, and we will continue to do the carpentry. It's in our blood. My older brother was a carpenter, after all."

"Did he start the company?"

"Yes, he did. That's him on the wall."

"Was he born here?"

"Oh no, my family comes from Norway. Lars sent for me and my mother when I was 10."

West stared at the painting. He wasn't sure he heard Josef correctly. "What was your brother's name?"

"Lars. Lars Simpson. He came to the United States when he was just 16. On the *Olympic*, you know the sister ship of the *Titanic*. If our father hadn't died in 1911, Lars wasn't going to come over here until 1914. Then he would have been on that ship and drowned."

Connor West looked down. He thought about the words his father spoke on his deathbed. *"Lars Sim…, that son of a bitch didn't give me a job and I saved his life on that boat…"* The words repeated over and over in Connor's mind. He looked up at the painting again. "Did your brother ever talk about the voyage on the ship?"

"Now that you ask. He said he almost died when a large timber, the kind they keep on ships in the event the ship's hull is damaged, almost fell on him. He said a coal stoker deflected it and saved his life. Why do you ask?"

Connor couldn't speak, and then finally said: "No reason. It must have been tough in those days…"

"Indeed, it was. But Lars was a hard worker and made something of himself. He supported our whole family for years after our dad died."

"Is Steel Simpson your son?"

"Oh no. Lars is Steel's father. In many ways, they're both alike, not always in a good way. Well, let's get to these drawings, shall we? There's a lot to cover and I hope this time the building is in budget."

"Your nephew made sure of that." Connor turned to the first plan sheet of Chicago World Tower. His hand was trembling.

"I'm fine, Mom." Connor listened into the receiver. "Yes, I know I've been bad about calling but we just finished the drawings on Chicago Tower. I've been pretty busy."

He was silent again. "Marilyn's fine. She's great." Pause. "No, I don't know if I'm going to marry her. I haven't had time to think about that. Look, I have to ask you something."

Pause again. "I know. I will. Listen, do you remember the name of the man Dad went to see here in Chicago about a job?"

Connor listened. "Yes, the man who didn't give him a job. Just before Dad died he said he saved the man's life and the man acted like he didn't know him."

Now Connor strained to hear as his mother's voice trailed off. "What did you say?"

He listened again. "Lawrence? What? Lars...Lars, are you sure? Do you remember his last name?" Pause. "Simpson? S-I-M-P-S-O-N," Connor spelling it out. "Are you positive?" Pause. "Okay, look I have to go. Love you, and I'm sending you tickets to come see me soon." Pause. "Yes, you can leave New York. Love you. Bye."

West put down the receiver. Since the moment he set foot in Chicago, with the exception of meeting and falling in love with Marilyn, his life had been tossed around like a rowboat on the ocean. He got up and went to the cupboard and found a bottle of Seagram's and a glass. He realized he was becoming like his father, and suddenly Connor didn't really care.

CHAPTER 71

The Friday morning in late May broke dark and ominous. The sky was putty and charcoal grey. A white mist of low clouds hung over the tops of the neighboring buildings. The front was moving in from the west, a Midwestern spring storm that promised to foul the traffic into the Loop, and the moods of commuters and vacationers alike.

"Shit, I've spent over $25,000 on this groundbreaking party and look at the weather!" Steel Simpson was in a bad mood.

"It's a good thing you ordered a tent." Ruth looked out the window to the land along the lake and shook her head. "Here, I made you coffee. Oh, and what about the extra champagne? Do you still want me to get it?"

"Fuck the champagne. I'll be lucky if they drink six bottles. And look at this. The governor has backed out, and that ass of a senator, Goodman, sends his regrets. And he's a Republican, for God's sake."

"It will be fine. By my count last night, you had 153 RSVPs including the mayor and the congressman. You better get going. Lothar just called. He's waiting for you downstairs in the garage."

Even though the site of Chicago World Tower was just a few blocks from the Wrigley Building, it took Lothar over a half hour to get there. Rain had begun to fall in earnest and the two-lane side streets were snarled in the morning rush. Simpson was beside himself and only took comfort in the fact that his assembled guests were going to be cooling their heels waiting on him. As he got out of the stretch Mercedes that he had rented for the occasion, the wind picked up and the rain came down in hard, cold droplets. "Fucking Chicago weather," Simpson muttered waving away the umbrella that Lothar had brought out to shield his boss from the elements.

Simpson's mood changed, however, as he entered the tent, warmed by propane space heaters. The ceiling was festooned in hundreds of lights and there were large fichus trees placed at all four corners. Around them circled high-top tables with white table-cloths; green Astroturf was on the ground. To one side, was a long buffet table with steaming serving dishes. There would be Eggs Benedict, French toast, waffles, mounds of bacon and sausage from Wisconsin, and fresh fruit. On the other side, were two bars serving Bloody Marys', Mimosas and French 75s. A 15-foot-high detailed model of Chicago World Tower, complete with interior lighting, stood prominently in the center. Eight large renderings of the building and the interiors flanked the model. Hefty color brochures were stacked on the reception tables. This event was as much about selling as about showing off and celebrating a milestone: one Simpson had dreamed about for over two years.

Finally, at the front of the tent was a mounded pile of imported black topsoil, nothing like what lay beneath the feet of the invited guests. It was soft, fine and free of impediments; embedded in it were seven gold shovels. The groundbreaking ceremony would start at 10:00 A.M. sharp, provided the growing wind and now incessant rain did not blow the tent away. Simpson moved about the space like a tourist in an exotic marketplace. He wished he had postponed the event for a more accommodating month like July; he still did not have the building permit. He ordered one of the waiters to bring him a Bloody Mary, extra vodka. With drink in hand, he caught the eye of the mayor, who was sipping on champagne. He approached him, anxious to get information on the building permit.

"Ah, it's the man of the hour. Steel, good to see you as always."

"Jack, so good of you to come."

"Steel, we're very impressed," Jack intoned. "This is a big deal for Chicago. I didn't think you could pull it off, but you did."

"Not quite, Mr. Mayor, I'm still waiting on a building permit. What's going on with that?"

"Steel, I have no idea. I've a big city to run. I can't keep track of every department, much less what they do every day. Oh, and you may have heard, I'm running for re-election."

"What the fuck, Jack, don't tell me you don't know what's going on with the permit. It's the biggest project in the city, and your people are sitting on it. Something about the electrical department flyspeck-ing each detail." Steel wasn't holding anything back. He had already paid over $10,000 in bribes, to no good effect.

"You seem to know a lot more about the situation than me. I could make a call to Charlie Naughton over there. Did I mention, I'm running for re-election? Campaigns are expensive you know."

"How expensive?"

"How bad do you want that building permit?"

"You SOB, first you rob me on the land sale, and now what do you want?"

"Steel, now that was a legit commission to the real estate agent acting on your behalf. But since you asked, I've just signed up for a new slate of TV advertising. It's pretty expensive. I would be very grateful for your support. Say $10,000?"

"$10,000! Seriously?"

"I bet the interest meter is running pretty fast on this project right now."

"Fine, but for the ten you not only make the phone call, you get me that fucking permit! My uncle is ready to start digging Monday."

"Monday is a little aggressive, but if you get me a check by then, I think I can facilitate things with Charlie. Now, I think I'll get some breakfast before we have the ceremony. Hopefully, we'll still have a tent over our heads. And again Steel, congratulations." The Mayor strolled off, smirking.

After a round of speeches by Tommy Keane, the long-time alderman for the 42nd Ward; Mayor Jack Malone; 7th District Congressman Daniel O'Shea, and the lieutenant governor of Illinois, whose name no one knew, but stood in for the governor, all heaping effusive praise on Steel Simpson and what he was about to accomplish, the five men gathered behind the gold shovels. There they were joined by J. Vance Jefferson and Ali Zyiad Sharif, both of whom declined an invitation to speak at the dais. Jefferson and Sharif were at each end of the line of the dignitaries, reflecting their status in the pecking order of importance, though without an architectural design and $40,000,000 in cash to build it, the event would not be taking place. Simpson was next to Jefferson, so the politicians could grab center spotlight. As the wind howled outside the tent, he leaned over to Jefferson. He snarled in a low voice, barely audible above the flapping canvas walls and pounding rain.

"I hope your design took these winds into account, Vance."

"Pay me and we'll find out."

On cue, with TV cameras running and reporters from the *Tribune* and *Sun-Times* taking pictures, as well as the national media outlets, the seven dignitaries dug into the soft dirt and flung it forward into the air. As flashbulbs popped, the assembled guests clapped and cheered. Outside, the wind rushed through the canyon of the Chicago River, and the rain fell in an onslaught of horizontal shards. The tent could bear no more. A side between two of the aluminum poles began to tear and give way. The canvas yielded to the battering storm, blowing over trees, tables, and brochures. The model of the building swayed but held its own.

Ali Sharif made his way over to his partner. "This is a bad omen, my friend."

"I don't believe in omens, Ali."

CHAPTER 72

"Chicago Consultants." The voice was crisp and professional.

"Good morning, this is John Messina. Is Abe available?"

"Let me check, Mr. Messina. I believe I saw him come in." Johnny Messina sipped on his Coke and looked at the construction schedule that had been sent to him by Josef Simpson.

"Hey, John. How are you? I hear we're going to be testing your concrete on the World Tower. That's a big job." Abe Goldman was the senior vice president at Chicago Consultants responsible for the soil testing for Chicago World Tower. Now they would follow through and test the materials that would be put in place at the project.

"Yes, Abe, it is a big job. Really big." Johnny perused the lengthy schedule. He'd be pouring concrete all year.

"Let's hope we get paid this time."

"Abe, I surely hope that we do. Truthfully, I didn't want to do the job, but it's too big to pass up. Joe Simpson has promised me we'd be paid in a timely fashion, so we'll see. I have a favor to ask you."

"Sure, if I can," Abe raised an eyebrow. The relationship between his firm and the concrete supplier had to be arm's length.

"I need a job for a friend. He's an old man and he just got out of Statesville for something stupid he did when he was, well, less old."

"Really. What was that?" Abe's interest was piqued but he knew where this was headed and didn't like it.

"He robbed a bank. That's it. He hit on hard times and did a stupid thing. One bank. Just got paroled after doing seven. He was a model prisoner. He's old now. My dad knows him. I told him I'd make some calls. Maybe you'll need a driver to pick up the cylinders from the World Tower site and take them to the testing lab. The guy's not gonna touch any money, just cylinders of concrete."

Abe was silent. Johnny Messina had brought up his father and he understood the implication. He knew all about Carmine Messina and it wasn't a good idea to mess with him. "Just drive the truck, huh?"

"Yeah, what else can he do, test concrete?" Messina offered a weak laugh. "The guy's got an 8th grade education, but he used to drive a cab here in the city. Knows all the streets. He's gonna get the cylinders to the lab on time. I promise you that."

"What's his name?"

"Enzo Liguria. What do you say, Abe? He's old, he's harmless."

"Geez, another wop," Abe thought. *"All I deal with in this city are the Italians and the Irish."* He hesitated but knew that John Messina, unlike his father, was a straight shooter, and that Cooky's Concrete was the only company in Chicago whose mud would meet his firm's high standards.

"Have him come to our office and see Stanley Levine. He'll get him set up; he'll need to start right away."

"Hey, Abe, I really do appreciate it. Oh, by the way, what kind of trucks you drivin' now, stick or automatic? So I can tell Enzo. He might want to know."

"We just purchased three new Ford F-250 trucks. They weren't cheap either. But we got them with automatic transmission, and in our company colors of dark blue, which was a special order. He'll have one of those. We bought one just for your job."

"Great. Thanks."

"Look, send Mr. Licorice around; we'll hire him. Regards to your dad."

"Abe, thanks so much. I look forward to working with you." Messina hung up the phone and buzzed Adele.

"Adele, get me Eddie Lambert at Al Piemonte Ford. Yeah, in Melrose Park."

By the end of the day Cooky's Concrete was the proud owner of a brand new, dark blue Ford F-250 pickup truck with automatic transmission. And it even had an FM radio.

The phone calls always began in the same way.

"Talk to me, Johnny." Carmine Messina was getting antsy. He knew construction could be slow, but the Chicago World Tower project seemed slower than most.

"Dad, relax. I know why you're calling. I got everything under control."

"If that's the case, why's it taking so long to pour some mud at your fucking job?"

"Well, thanks to you and your friend McFinn, the job's already been shut down twice by the electrical inspector."

Messina smiled. "I don't know what you're talkin' about…"

"Look, Dad, I got the news you want. We start pouring next week."

"Pouring what?"

"Why do you care?"

"Just answer the question."

"Sorry. No disrespect. The caissons. There's 14 of 'em."

"I bet they're big."

"Oh, yeah. Each caisson is gonna take 21 yards of concrete and because there are 14 of those huge pipes so we'll be pouring over three nights, 28 loads every night in seven trucks. We'll start at midnight and end about 6 A.M. No traffic then. I've talked to the boys in blue. They'll have local streets blocked."

Messina whistled under his breath. "Yeah, that is a lot of mud. Back in my day a big job was one full truck of 9 yards. But you're talkin' what?"

"810 cubic yards of seven thousand PSI concrete at $35 a yard plus night pour premium, another five bucks a yard or $32,400."

"What if you don't get paid? And more to the point, how you gonna fuck this guy, Simpson?"

"Like I said, Dad, I have everything under control. Well, except one thing."

"What's that?"

"I promised Marie I'd take her to Lake Geneva next week for our seventh wedding anniversary. Her mom's gonna look after Robert and Anthony. These electrical delays have set the job back. I should have had this big pour done by now. But now its next week and I've made reservations and Marie is all excited, and…"

"Hey, relax. Her mom's takin' care of my grandsons, which I'm glad I ain't doin'. So I'll handle the night pours. Piece of cake."

"Dad, that's terrific. I owe you. Hey, I can handle Wednesday night. We don't leave until Thursday, so you just have that night and Friday. I've got seven of my best drivers scheduled."

"Hey, we're family. Take your beautiful wife to that resort; have dinner on me. I'll handle the two nights. Look, I gotta go. Ciao, son." Messina put down the receiver and opened his desk drawer. He pulled out another phone and dialed.

"Gino, it's on for next Thursday. Let the boys know. And bring plenty of guys and firepower. I don't want any fuckups."

"Chicago Plumbers Local 130."
"Ray O'Brien, please. This is Carmine Messina."

"Chicago Sheet Metal Workers Union, Local 73."
"Bobby Neil, please. This is Carmine Messina."

"Pipefitters Local 540. Who's calling?"
"Let me talk to Sal Campania. You know who this is…"
"So sorry, Mr. Messina. Right away!"

"International Union of Elevator Constructors, Local 2. Who can I connect you with?"

"Donald. He still in charge? This is Carmine."

"Right away, Mr. Messina, right away."

"International Union of Operating Engineers Local 399. How may I direct your call?"

"Let me talk to Manny." There was no response so Messina waited.

"Manny Santiago."

"Manny, it's Carmine."

"How ya doin,' my friend? Long time."

Messina was tired so he got right to the point, even though this was his most important call. "Manny, I need a favor. Who's working the crane at Chicago World Tower?"

"Sure, Carmine, anything for you. Let's see. I got the assignments somewhere here on the desk." Messina could hear papers rustling. It was a wonder that unions stayed in business with the jamokes who ran them, he thought.

"Here it is. Roscoe Brown. He's our first Negro, I mean black guy. But he's good, very good. Came up through the Disadvantaged Apprenticeship Program. Why?"

"Because you need to give him a night off next Thursday. I want Sallie Como working the rig that night. He's one of my associates."

Manny knew not to ask any questions. "Hey, come to think of it Roscoe been asking me for a day so he can go see his sick mother in Gary. I'll take care of it. Sallie it is. It's night work, right? Big pour, I hear. The caissons."

"Yeah, I guess. I don't know. Johnny just said it would be a busy night and he wanted a seasoned guy. Thanks, Manny, I got to go." He hung up the phone, placed it back in the drawer and locked it. The number was private and untraceable. He leaned his chair back and rubbed his eyes.

The afternoon calls had finally ended; they had been more than productive. Carmine Messina had been reluctant to call in favors until the Chicago World Tower project began, but now that concrete was going to be poured, he made the calls to the strongest unions in the city. The lack of effort, the unintentional mistakes, the walkouts and strikes by these unions and their members would take a toll over time on the project, costing precious time, and great amounts of money. And no one would know why or could place any blame. It was just one of those things. Some jobs were just jinxed.

Tired, but savoring the sweet taste of revenge, Carmine called for his car. Then he called Benedetta at the house and told her to open a bottle of '62 Sangiovese, and make his favorite dish, veal ravioli in red sauce. He would have dinner on the patio and listen to *Turandot* by Puccini. It had been a good day. And next week would be better. He would finally settle accounts.

CHAPTER 73

Grabowski kicked the flap of the makeshift tent. Unlike a cop, he didn't carry a baton, and he had no desire to touch the badly soiled, ripped fabric of the door to this humble abode. "Hey, anyone in there? Wake up!"

He was under a railroad overpass of the Chicago Northwestern, just west of the Loop. At that moment, though, he wished he were checking out burned out remains of buildings. Three months of searches had yielded nothing but a couple of minor drug busts and a disorderly conduct rap when one of Chicago's homeless kicked him in the family jewels. He heard garbled muttering from within.

"Well, someone's alive." Amy Kolska took out her flashlight and without regard for the lack of cleanliness of the tent, stuck her head inside. The beam came down on a dirty bald head. "Hey, my friend, mind if we ask you a few questions?" Amy Kolska was from Community Relations. John O'Rourke had sweet-talked her boss into letting her spend afternoons with Mike G. He thought her experience and expertise with the local homeless population would be more successful than the matter of fact and sometimes heavy-handed, Polack who worked for him.

"What the heck..." came the voice from the tent. "What is this? Why are you waking me?" The man inside lifted his head and shielded his eyes from the beam of bright light.

"Relax, no hassles, we just want to ask you some questions. So, if you're dressed—come on out. Might even be something in it for you." Amy's voice was smooth and matter of fact, not threatening. She moved back and instinctively dusted off her dark blue suit. Under it was a white blouse, no jewelry. Her only nod to her job was some black, ankle-high, lace-up boots.

"Maybe this one. We have to hit pay dirt sooner or later. This shit's getting old," Grabowski said within earshot; he had skipped breakfast and was hungry. He was ready to buy this vagrant a meal if he could help in any way.

"Relax, we're meeting our fellow citizens." Amy's comments were always upbeat as she turned and spoke to her temporary partner. He looked intently at her. She had vivid green eyes and brown hair, cut in a 1920s style. Her body, even under the simple blue suit was tight and shapely. Hopefully, the relationship with her wouldn't end when they found the Ansel Adams of the lake.

The occupant of the makeshift tent, one of several residences made of cloth, cardboard or shipping crates under the tracks, emerged, rubbing his eyes. "How can I help you today, officers? I assume you are the city's finest, that is?"

"Well, at least he's fluent in the language," Grabowski said.

"Shut up, Grab. Sir, what's your name?" The interview had begun. "Joe."

"Got a last name to go with that?"

"Smith."

"OK, Joe…Smith, we'll play it your way. How long have you been living here?"

"I don't know. Four months? No. Incorrect. Six months. Yes. I established residency last November. It was a cold winter."

"Where'd you live before that?"

"I had to move around a lot. I had a really nice studio on the lake for over a year. But some dastardly person burned it down."

Amy glanced back at Grabowski who stopped midway into lighting a cigarette. He smiled and almost lost his Camel.

"You lived on the lake, by the Chicago River? Near Lakeshore Drive?"

"Yes, it was better than the Gold Coast. Why they let that place exist for so long…well, I'm amazed. But it was nice. I had a real tent that I used to own before I came upon hard times. And it was a community there. Everyone knew everyone and we looked out for one another. Now I'm here at this shithole. Oh, pardon the French, madam."

"No offense, Joe. Say, you hungry? Looks like you could use a good meal."

"Why, that would be delightful, but I'm not sure I can be of much help."

"Maybe a good meal will bring back some memories. You don't mind riding in the black and white, do you?"

"Not as long as you don't cuff me."

"Joe, we would never do that. Here, this way."

"Okay, I like you. You're a nice person."

"And so are you Joe, so are you."

They reached the Crown Victoria and Joe settled into the back seat. Grabowski at the wheel located a greasy spoon about seven blocks away. It was a breakfast/lunch place that was about to close at two. They got out and entered, and Mike flashed the cashier his badge. The employee gave up any thought of an early close. Mike looked at the special of the day written on a chalkboard. It was pot roast, gravy and three sides. Perfect. He looked toward the only waitress, a large black lady in a stained, white outfit.

"Any specials left?"

"Lordy, lordy, you come in at closin' wantin' the special! Well, you be in luck. Maybe two."

"Fine, bring us those and my partner will have..." Grabowski looked at his svelte partner. He assumed the blue-plate special was not a part of her daily caloric regime.

"Please bring me a bowl of your chicken noodle soup. And saltines and a Coke."

The three sat down in a faded booth of red vinyl, Grabowski and Kolska on one side and Joe on the other. Joe looked over the place and whistled.

"This is a fine establishment. Not Chez Paul, but it will do."

Grabowski looked at Amy with a surprised expression. The guy might have some stories to tell. However, now that they were out of the fresh air, Joe's lack of daily hygiene was becoming omnipresent. He hoped it wouldn't ruin his appetite. Amy, sensing the less pleasing aromas now, continued.

"Tell me, Joe, do you own a camera?"

"Oh yes. I have a Nikon and all the lenses. Are you serious?"

"Did someone at the lake camp have a camera?"

"Hmmm, the memory isn't what it used to be. But now that you mention it, one guy did. It was around his neck at all times. It wasn't a Nikon though."

"What type was it?" Grabowski's interest was piqued, and he wanted to move faster. Joe Smith looked at him and frowned. He liked talking to the pretty lady cop. This guy was so typical of a gumshoe.

"I don't know. Like a Brownie camera. The kind you look down into to see what your picture's going to look like. The guy was a little nutso. He thought he was the king of Ireland. Said all his enemies were captured and imprisoned in the camera."

"You know where we might find him, Joe?"

"Oh yes, let me get out my address book."

"Don't get smart with us, Joe. I can cancel the pot roast," Grabowski growled, getting annoyed as his stomach was grumbling more, and Joe's aroma was becoming more noxious.

"Sorry. Look, after the fire, we all scattered like cockroaches. That's what we are to the city anyway—cockroaches."

"The fella with the camera. Do you remember his name?" Amy was back in her calm soothing voice. Joe smiled at her, looking away from the cop.

"I do know that the two guys who died were Mouse and Pat."

"Do you know their real names?"

"Oh my, you're making my head hurt. Let's see. Mouse told me his name once. Yes, it was Jimmy…Jimmy Anderson. Pat, well, Pat was I think short for Patrick. His last name was Walsh. I saw it on his army duffel bag. Yes."

"And the guy who owned the Brownie camera?"

Joe looked up at the ceiling rubbing his chin. "So many questions. I hope the pot roast is good. The guy with the camera was, a Bobby. No that's not right. Starts with a 'B' though. Wait. Wait. Billy! Yeah, Billy Flanagan was his name. Makes sense he was Irish, thinking he was the king of Ireland. Yes, he never let anyone touch that camera. Said it was his badge of authority, something like that. The fellow was a little confused, but harmless. He had lived there a long time, I think, because he really had a lovely place."

The black waitress brought their lunches. The gravy looked like wallpaper paste; the pot roast had a silvery appearance. There were mashed potatoes, green beans and aromatic creamed corn. Grabowski suddenly lost his appetite. Joe dug in like a wolf that hadn't eaten in weeks.

"May I get some bread or rolls, if it's not too much trouble? This is great food!"

The waitress looked at him, smiled and nodded.

"Joe, have you run into Billy since you had to leave the lake? You know at some other…encampments?'

"Matter of fact, I did one time. Down by Soldier Field. We heard there were good places to sleep under the bleachers. But we could never get under the bleachers. There's a big fence around the whole place. Place is shut tighter than a cat's ass! Oh sorry…"

Amy rolled her eyes. "It's okay Joe, I've heard it all. When was that that you saw Billy?"

"A…well, it was just before I moved to my present abode, so last November. It was cold, I know that. And before a game against the Packers when the cops rousted us. I headed toward Grant Park. I saw Billy walking straight west. That's all I know. Hey, ma'am, do you have any pie?"

"All gone, honey, but we got chocolate cake. Want some?"

"Yes, please, and a dollop of vanilla ice cream would be heavenly."

Mike looked at Amy and smiled. Joe Smith, if that was really his name, was a piece of work. *"There but for the grace of God, go I,"* he thought.

"Anything else, Joe?"

"I could use a little spending cash if it's not too much trouble."

"OK, on one condition. What's your real name?" Amy being curious.

Joe looked out the window of the restaurant into a far distant past. "Joseph Halstead Buckingham."

Mike stared at Joe. "Buckingham?"

"Yes. The fountain at the lake is named after my grandfather."

CHAPTER 74

Connor sat at his drafting table looking down at shop drawings for Chicago World Tower. No one had told him that architecture could be so boring and tedious. The only break in the day was having coffee with Bob Marlow in the morning or a walk out to the park in the afternoon for a Coke and fresh air. He stared at Tomlinson's postcard from Key West. On his worst days he wished he was there; and ever since that day at Simpson Construction most days were pretty bad. He was consumed with anger. He had designed a building for a man whose father had ruined his father's life and Connor had suffered those consequences since childhood. His design had been bastardized and, finally, his boss was molesting his girlfriend. He realized he was drinking too much. Even Bob Marlow commented one morning the previous week on his appearance.

"Man, you look like shit."

"That noticeable, huh?"

"Yeah, you look like me from a while back. I don't know what's eating you, but the answer isn't at the bottom of a glass. Believe me, I know."

"I know. I'm just trying to work through some stuff right now. I'll be all right."

"Has Jefferson been leaving Marilyn alone?"

"I think so. It's not her. It's all me."

"Look, don't become one of those talented but tortured geniuses who end up dead from cheap bourbon. If you go out, make it the 15-year-old stuff."

Connor laughed. "What would I do without a mentor like you, Bob?"

Marlow walked away. "Mentor, huh? That's quite a compliment. Your mentor advises you to lay off the sauce."

The conversation resonated in Connor's head, which was beginning to hurt. *"Fuck it. Time to get even,"* he muttered to himself. He headed for the stairs and went down to the records department where the old files were kept.

"Well, Mr. Connor, what brings you down here to the morgue?"

"Hi, Fred, how ya' doing?"

"Same shit, different day. Is it nice outside?"

"Yes, it is, and we should both leave this place for the rest of the day."

"I like that idea, son. What can I do for you?"

"I'd like to see the shop drawings for the curtainwall on Chicago Center."

"My, my, those have been popular lately."

"Oh, how so?"

"Mr. Jefferson checked them out. Let's see April 26."

Connor stared at Fred. Lying, he said: "Oh, yeah, he told me he looked at 'em. He told me to study them, so we didn't make the same tolerance errors on Chicago World Tower. We're using the same system."

"That's a good idea. I heard that mistake could have cost the firm millions. And if the glass had popped out, people could have been hurt, even killed. I guess he still has them. Sorry."

"Oh, OK; I'll go check with him then. See ya later."

West returned to his desk, deflated. His boss was going to make sure that the curtainwall system was within tolerances. He couldn't mark them up like Junior had done a couple of years ago causing the glass to leak, or worse, fly out of the aluminum frames when the wind and atmospheric pressure changed dramatically.

"What the hell are you thinking, Connor?" he wondered to himself. *"You're going to destroy your career and maybe kill people from falling glass!"* There had to be a better way to get back at Simpson and Jefferson, if indeed he had the stomach for revenge.

He looked at his watch. 2:45 P.M. He got up, grabbed his sport coat and headed for the elevator. It was time for a Coke in the garden of the Art Institute. The shop drawings could wait. He knew he wasn't going to return today. He had to get some things decided. He could no longer go on in this limbo of despair, hatred and personal misery.

At 4:00 P.M., West headed for the bus stop. He made no progress with his decisions, other than to go home and change clothes. He took a run in Lincoln Park, and called Marilyn to see if he could come over for dinner. He knew the answer would be *yes*. After that, he didn't know how the day would end but he had hopes.

"Hey, what's up? I just finished a run in the park."

"You big shots always get to leave the office early while we peons have to stay until five."

"I decided that the shop drawings for the toilet partitions could wait until tomorrow. Can I come over?"

"No, I have a hot date with Taubert tonight."

"Funny. Please. I'm lonely."

"Okay, I might even give you dinner. I'm making spaghetti."

"Thank God Jane taught you to cook. I'd be eating pizza forever otherwise. Spaghetti, huh? That calls for a nice Chianti. I'll see you in thirty. Bye." Connor's mood brightened. He might even get to sleep over.

Over dinner, Connor told Marilyn about Lars Simpson and his father. It felt good to tell someone, and though it struck her as only an amazing coincidence and not the life-altering event as Connor saw it, she was sympathetic and kissed him on the head after he finished. Then Connor looked up and kissed her hard on the mouth. She opened a second bottle of wine.

Later, they made love over and over again. In the sweat, moaning, cries of pleasure, panting, deep kisses, hands everywhere, arched backs, thrusting body parts and mutual orgasms, Connor West exorcized his demons. When it was over, Connor laughed until he began to sob deeply. Marilyn cradled him in her arms, holding him tight, not fully understanding what was happening, yet loving him more and more in all the mystery and confusion. Then Connor looked up at her, eyes wet with tears.

"Will you marry me?"

"Oh yes, Connor, I'll marry you. Oh yes. Oh yes! I love you so much!"

Then Connor cried again until he laughed. It would all be OK now.

CHAPTER 75

At sundown they drove up in two Caddies and a white van to the house at 2017 Warren Avenue in Maywood. Gino DiLaurenti had assembled a small army. There was Caesar, Buddha, Aldo "the Neck," Julio, Cufflink, Vito, Tommie "Hiccups," Tony, and several other associates. The cars parked down the street; the van was in the alley at the backdoor.

The Outfit's best muscle pulled nylon stockings over their heads and surrounded the house. When the men at the rear door heard the door break open at the front, they did the same. They rushed into the front room where the crew from the Lucifer's Players Club was smoking weed, snorting coke and drinking malt liquor. Their bitches were in their laps or spread out on the floor. *The Price Is Right* was on the TV. Tiger, Artemus, Biggy, Jerome, Tiny and the rest tried to pull their weapons, but they fumbled and slipped, and the girls got in their way. Guns were at heads in a heartbeat. Other associates aimed several shotguns at the entire gathering. To send a message, Gino put a bullet into Jerome's head, splattering the wall with blood and red matter. He would be the lucky one. First a couple of girls screamed, but then they were all still.

The women were lined up against the wall, shaking and crying, and the members of the Club were bound with plastic electrical straps, both hands and feet. Their mouths were sealed with duct tape. One by one, they were carried out to the white van and stacked like so much cordwood. Tiger Gibson was the only one who twisted and fought. Gino took out his switchblade and ran it across Gibson's cheek. Blood gushed out, and Tiger began to behave himself, not even crying out from the pain. When all nine of the members were in the van, it sped off.

Back inside the house, while Caesar took Polaroid's of the faces of each of the girls, Gino asked who Tiger's girlfriend was. No one answered. He put a gun to one of the girls' head and began to count to three. At "2" she sputtered out "LaToya," nodding in her direction. Buddha grabbed LaToya from the lineup and placed her in the center of the room. Photographs all taken, Gino went up to LaToya, raised his gun outfitted with a silencer and shot her three times in the heart. She dropped like a stone and the girls screamed and sobbed. One went down on her knees to LaToya, but Gino grabbed her by the hair and punched her back against the wall. He was breathing hard.

"Now, we got all your Polaroids. You didn't see nuthin' here, right? If you tell the cops, or anybody, your momma or daddy, we will hunt you down. We will find you, be sure of that. And we will kill you in worse fashion than this bitch died. Capisce?" He nodded; the muscle began to depart, pulling off the stockings as they left and holstering their weapons. As Gino walked through the door he turned. "You probably want to find new boyfriends, too."

The van headed directly to Cooky's Concrete Company and the gate opened as it approached. Carmine Messina was standing in the rear lot waiting. There would be seven trucks doing four runs during the night. He had substituted three of the newer drivers, who knew nothing of the history of Cooky's, with three of his own older drivers, Julius "Emperor" Nero, Eddie "Fast Shoes" and Louie "the Comedian" Guilia. He looked around the yard. The security was all seasoned guys, longtime associates. The rest of the boys would be along shortly. Then he noticed a small figure over by one of the trucks washing it. He walked over. He was just a kid.

"Who are you? What are you doin' here?"

"I'm Donnie. Donnie Romeo. I wash the elephants."

"What? Elephants?"

"Oh, that's what I call the trucks. They're kind of like elephants, don't you think? Johnny, I mean Mr. Messina hired me to come after school. Says the trucks have to always look clean."

"Yeah, I see. You know who I am?"

"Sure, you're Mr. Messina's daddy. He says you're retired."

"Sort of. Listen, Donnie, can you keep a secret?"

"Sure."

"OK, what you see tonight you never saw. Don't even tell my son." Carmine dug into his pocket and pulled out his wad of bills. He peeled off a Benjamin and handed it to Donnie. "Here, this is for you. But you got to blood swear you'll never tell anyone about this. If you do, well, it won't be good."

"I swear, Mr. Messina, I swear."

He patted Donnie on the cheek. "Good, then we have an understanding."

The rest of the small army had arrived back in the Caddy's. The van parked over by the washout pond. Each one of the members of the Player's Club was dragged out of the van and then tossed into the pond. They tried to scream through the duct tape and with their feet bound, tried as best they could not to sink underwater. After struggling, most managed to crawl up the side of the small embankment exhausted, trying to breathe. They were covered in the grey sludge and shortly it would harden on them. As the heat and chemicals of the aggregate penetrated their clothes, they would want to scratch everywhere. Their pathetic existence would get even worse. This was just the beginning.

"Who's Tiger Gibson?" Carmine Messina was dressed simply in blue jeans, a black polo shirt and light rayon jacket with epaulets. It too was black. Gino went over to the leader of the Player's Club, pushed him out of the lineup and ripped off the duct tape. Gibson grimaced, and the blood started flowing again from his cheek, turning one side of his now grey face red. Carmine walked over to him. "Latrice. May I call you by your proper name? Well, never mind. I brought you here to settle some business. I got a stone in my shoe. And it's you."

"Fuck you talkin' about, 'stone in your shoe?' All I did was take what's mine in MY neighborhood. A hood you got no business in!"

"Eh, eh, eh," Carmine wagged his finger in Tiger's face. "But you never came to me and asked me nicely if you could share. I was in your neighborhood before it turned dark. So I'm sure some equitable arrangement could have been worked out. I have many black associates in my organization. But you just took the business; and beat up my loyal customers and some almost died. So, I let you have the protection. I'm a reasonable man, even though it made me look weak. But then the drugs. No, no, no that crossed the line."

"So, fine, you gave us our mud bath and scared my boys. You can have the drugs back. Just let us go!"

"I'm afraid, my friend, it's a little too late for that."

An associate was loosening the bolts that held the oval cover plate that gave access to the drum on one of the concrete trucks. It was large enough for a man to fit in for periodic cleaning. Gibson looked over and saw that the man had pulled back the cover, exposing the inside of the drum.

For probably the first time in his life, Tiger Gibson was terrified. He suffered from claustrophobia and hated small spaces. "Look," his voice shaking, "this has just been a big misunderstanding. I'll give you back the protection business, too. I'll even give you half the profits of my cathouse. Just let us leave now."

"Mr. Gibson, you should have shown me this respect a long time ago. Goodbye." He nodded. Messina's associates quickly surrounded the nine men. A ladder had been placed up to the opening on the drum of the concrete truck. Though they struggled, each one was taken by one of Messina's men and they were quickly forced into the dank round space of the concrete mixing chamber. Latrice, "the Tiger" was the last one in. As he went in, he screamed, "You mutha fucka, fuck you!"

The top was put back in place. The first four trucks had been loaded earlier from the large and towering mixer that created the raw and wet concrete. They began to leave the yard; it was still daylight, but the sun was about to set. The other two trucks were loaded up with concrete. The last contained the human cargo. The second group would arrive well after dark and there would only be floodlights at the jobsite. He looked in the direction of the young boy Donnie. He was hoping he was minding his own business and fortunately for Donnie, he was.

The boy was filling test cylinders from a different batch of material made in a smaller secondary mixing rig and placed them in a brand-new Ford F-250 pickup, a bright blue one. He didn't recognize the driver but shrugged. Maybe Johnny preferred to take the test cylinders to the job directly because it would have a better strength, though the inspector usually needed to witness the material coming straight from the truck's chute. So, he thought, Johnny might be paying off the technician at the jobsite to use these cylinders; he didn't raise a fool, after all. The caravan slowly moved out of the yard. Messina smiled and offered a salutary wave. "See you in hell, Mr. Gibson."

CHAPTER 76

Erwin Manfred Strauss was sitting in Simpson Construction's job trailer reading a copy of *Field and Stream*. A longtime security guard for the company, he had been assigned by Josef Simpson to this most important project. He hated coming downtown, preferring the boredom of the company yard in Evanston, but it was more interesting with all the activity that went on at night. It sometimes reminded him of when he was a guard at Dachau during the war. The camps ran 24 hours a day. Carmine Messina knew this of course, having checked up on who would be at the jobsite on this Thursday night. An Ex-Nazi didn't worry him. He probably liked to drink as much as old Hans Dieter, his associate who worked protection in the German neighborhoods.

The door to the construction trailer opened. Manfred wasn't used to company; his feet were propped up on a desk, and a bottle of schnapps nearby. He quickly stood up, standing at attention and looked at Hans. "Yes, can I help you? Who are you?"

"I'm sorry. I'm from Cooky's Concrete. I'm advance fellow. We have big pour tonight. I must make sure everything is ready. I should come in and introduce myself, I think. I am Hans Dieter."

"Oh, so sorry, I'm not used to visitors. I mostly work at the main office." As he spoke, he tried to push the bottle of schnapps out of the line of sight. Hans noticed the move and the shaking hand. He had his opening.

"Hey, it's good; you're fine. I don't care what you do at night here. Look, I have even got flask myself." Hans pulled a rather large leather flask from his back pocket and held it up proudly. He continued: "After all, there isn't a lot for me to do once the concrete starts pouring. Say, you look familiar. Do we know each other?"

"I do not think so. My name is Strauss; that is Fred Strauss." A slight accent betrayed his fabricated American name.

"You're German, aren't you?! So am I. I'm from Stuttgart. We are I think the same age. Did you fight in the war for the Fatherland?"

"Ah yes, I, I was in the...a 137ᵗʰ Infantry Division under General Geyer. I fought on the Eastern Front." Strauss was lying through his teeth. He was in the SS and spent most of his time during the war killing Jews.

"I don't believe it. I was in the 8ᵗʰ Infantry with General Heitz, and I too fought those Russian bastards! We should toast!"

And so it began. One toast. Two toasts. War stories, memories of the old country. More toasts. Buddha would not have any problem getting to the main electrical panel located right by the trailer unnoticed.

The first of Cooky's shiny white concrete trucks was slowly lumbering down the temporary construction road that had been built for the project. It pulled up alongside a Liebherr truck-mounted crane, being used until the two permanent tower cranes could be installed. The foundations for those cranes would be poured the following night. The driver, Julius "the Emperor," climbed down out of his rig and walked over toward the large wheels of the mobile crane. Sallie Como was waiting for him.

"Julie, how ya' doin'? I heard we got a special pour tonight."

"Yeah, Sallie. These first four trucks are just concrete. Then the special cargo comes. After that two more trucks of mud. Where we pouring?"

"You just pour the shit into the bucket. I know where it's goin'. You think this is my first poker game?"

"Hey, no offense. Into the bucket it all goes."

"Gimme a minute. I gotta get used to this rig. We hooked up an extra-large bucket tonight for our special cargo."

"Boss thinks of everything, don't he?"

"He ain't the boss for nuthin..."

Julius looked over at a Ford F-250 pickup truck and a young technician readying a line of concrete test cylinders to be filled. At the wheel of the new dark blue pickup, turning the dial on the FM radio, was Enzo Liguria. "Whadaya goin' to do about those guys?"

"Relax, the driver's ours. The other kid, well, we're pouring concrete tonight, aren't we? Just wait."

By the time Sallie was ready all four trucks had shown up, and he could make out the last three, lights piercing the new darkness, coming over the construction road. Construction workers, all low-ranking members of the Outfit, were positioned on the edge of the caissons to center the bucket with the caisson below and then pull the lever on the bucket to release the mud into the huge forms. Others had hand-carried vibrators that would be placed into the poured concrete and used to eliminate any air voids in the wet mix and the reinforcing in the caisson. Concrete workers affectionately called them "dicks" because of their particular appearance at the end of a long cable. Everything was ready.

With the lighter traffic, the ride from Milwaukee Avenue to the jobsite had taken less than 30 minutes. It was now almost nine o'clock. But it had seemed like an eternity in hell for Tiger Gibson and his crew. The drum was like an oven even on the cool night. Soon the smell of urine and soiled underwear caused by the terror they experienced fouled the dank, interior air. Gibson had done his best to tear off the duct tape from several of his guys, but that only made matters worse. Most of them were screaming for their mothers or cursing him for their situation.

Louie the Comedian had also decided on his own that it would be a nice touch to have the drum turn; something a driver did at times to keep the mixture inside from setting up too quickly. The human cargo fell over each other, tossed about like rag dolls, heads banging into the steel sides. With their feet and hands bound, they were unable to get any footing, but it didn't matter, the floor beneath them just kept moving. Finally, the truck slowed, and the drum ceased to turn. The nine Players moaned, and some cried in loud sobs.

"Shut the fuck up, y'all! We die, we gonna die like men." Gibson's fear had now turned into defiant resignation; he had lived The Life for a couple of years. He wasn't ready to go, but he realized more than the others, what a dangerous game he had played. And he had lost. So, what? He would die with dignity.

Sallie had deposited the concrete from the first four trucks evenly into the three caissons. The young technician, Ben Rosenstein, fresh out of the same program at Chicago Circle campus that Johnny Messina had attended years before, dutifully filled the containers, four for each truck. He had placed them into the bed of the blue pickup truck and was ready to take samples from the next truck. Louie pulled up by the crane and got out. He walked up to the young technician. "Hey, you from the testing agency?"

"Yeah, I'm Ben. And I need to take the samples after you add water to it. I need to have it like it is poured. So, don't even argue with me."

"Yeah, yeah, I know. I know. But what I come to tell you is before I left the yard, I had problems with the drum. The hopper is stuck. So, I need a couple a minutes to work on it."

"How long?"

"Gimme 15, 20. I should get it working by then. Okay?"

"Well, I guess that'll be all right. I was ready for my break anyway." He walked off in the direction of a small trailer that contained one office and a storeroom for empty cylinders and on-site testing equipment.

Buddha had watched the conversation over by the main electrical panel. Once the technician was out of sight, he flipped a half dozen of the breakers and the site went dark. The lights around him and in the trailer went out too, but he quickly reset the breaker to restore power in the trailer. Erwin, on his fifth schnapps, barely noticed. Louie kept the parking lights of the concrete truck on so there was some illumination. He climbed onto the truck's catwalk and quickly removed the four bolts that held the cleanout cover and the cargo inside. He didn't worry about having to go in and pull the hostages out. After their miserable incarceration, they couldn't get out fast enough, legs wobbling, bloodied heads, covered in sludge, urine and feces.

"Geesus, you guys look bad." He laughed, but there was no time to waste.

Sallie lowered the concrete bucket by Louie's truck. Tiny, Maurice and Artemus were thrown into the bucket. Tiny began to scream. Enzo in the Ford had found a classical music station playing opera. It was "La Traviata." He turned the volume up. The last two trucks began to rev their engines and their drums began to turn. No one could hear Tiny, particularly his mother, or God.

From the cab of the crane, Sallie pulled back a lever and the bucket began to rise. In unison, he began to turn the crane toward the caissons. In the dark, he realized that on this moonless night, he could use the illuminated Wrigley Building in the distance as a backdrop, and the bucket would be silhouetted by its bright floodlights. He positioned it as best he could and began to lower it. When it was a few feet above the giant tube, a construction worker grabbed hold of the large round bucket and grabbed the lever. "Bye, bye, fuckers." He pulled the lever. The three tried to resist gravity, but it was to no avail. First Artemus fell square into the hole, landing into the concrete that began to suck him in. Maurice planted his bound feet against one side of the bucket, but was quickly bludgeoned with a concrete "dick" and finally gave up. He landed on top of Artemus who was trying to keep his head above the grey quicksand. They both sank, concrete rushing into their open, crying mouths. Finally, Tiny, still screaming, had freed himself from the electrical ties because of his small hands and wrists. He held onto the rim of the bucket. This didn't last. The worker who had pulled the lever stomped hard on Tiny's fingers. Tiny screamed even more, but it was over in an instant. The flailing arms caused the bucket to move sideways, he fell onto the reinforcing. It pierced his side going through his heart. He was suspended above the concrete, crucified. He was lucky. He died instantly.

The pour was repeated quickly one more time, three of the Players in each caisson per Messina's orders; he wanted to spread the damage throughout the structure. The last pour was saved for Biggy, Quince and Tiger Gibson. Seeing what had happened to the other six members of their gang, they fought mightily but were overcome with the workers amassed against them. Sallie decided that he would lift Tiger separately. He had a special end in mind for him. Once Biggy and Quince were dropped into the third hole, Louie checked the bindings on Tiger to make sure they were secure, and he was thrown into the waiting bucket. Before he could escape, Sallie lifted the bucket high into air; a worker rode along on the outside. When he determined that the bucket was at least 30 feet above the hole, he stopped. He was risking missing the hole below, but it was worth it. The lever was pulled and Latrice "El Tigre" Gibson fell like a rock. It was a perfect shot, almost. Tiger's legs hit the solid steel framework of the caisson and broke. The impact flipped Gibson over and he hurtled head-first into the waiting wet darkness below.

Pain seared through his knees that took the full impact of the fall, and Gibson struggled with every fiber of his wrecked body to right himself. Submerged in the wet, thick concrete, he couldn't breathe. He tried to turn himself upright. He had only his hands to use as small paddles. His lungs screamed for air. Slowly, for what was an eternity, he finally sensed that he was rising. He paddled and squirmed furiously. This was not how he was going to die. Gun, yes. Knife, OK. But not by suffocating in concrete. At last he felt his forehead break above the surface. Then there was air! He gasped. It was heavy and dense, smelling of aggregate, rock, steel and grease.

He could make out the form of Biggy next to him, impaled above on the reinforcing, moaning and gushing blood. He assumed that Quince had already drowned below. He leaned back and with his hands, found some reinforcing, his face submerged again. He grabbed on as best he could to the half-inch-thick bars and began to rub the plastic bindings against the rough reinforcing. Every time he moved his hands downward, his head dipped into the disgusting mud. Then with all of his strength, he moved upward again. Finally, on the fifth attempt the bindings ripped in two. Now his arms could move freely! He grabbed a bar with one hand and turned himself around, fighting the heavy mixture that surrounded him. He began to shimmy up the steel, his legs throbbing with pain and useless in the effort; his strong biceps did all the work. He looked up. It was over five feet to the top. If he could get up there, then it might be possible to crawl over and then just fall to the bottom of the excavation below. He had no idea how far it was. He might break more bones, but he would not have drowned inhaling concrete.

As Tiger inched closer to the top, the construction lights came back on and illuminated the sky above him. He thought he heard Italian music playing. There were loud voices. He shimmied faster. He might make it after all! One hand over the other, his body two times his normal weight, clothes and boots weighed down by the concrete, he placed one hand over the other. *"Kiss my black ass, you fucking dago asshole,"* he thought. *"I'm gonna beat you!"*

Gibson was nearing the top. One more effort and he might be able to grab the rim of the caisson. He heard the whirr of an engine. The light was brighter above. He looked up; moving directly above him was the giant concrete bucket. He moaned and suddenly Tiger had no more strength left. He dropped his head. "Shit!"

The bucket was opened, and five cubic yards of concrete hit his head hard, cutting it in several places. He let go of the reinforcing with one hand, and barely hung on with the other. Blood ran down his face and he felt the warmth of it against his cheek and mouth. Now the muddy grave was up to his neck. The bucket moved away. He took a deep breath and regained his hold on the reinforcing with both hands. There were only minutes before the next load would come. He had to climb out. With all the power that he had left, he climbed on, slowly out of the grey goo. He reached for the edge of the caisson; missed. With a last great effort, he reached again. He could feel the smooth rounded steel rim in his hands. He would make it!

He let himself sink in the mud, and then pulled himself up in one last great effort. His waist was at the precipice. He pulled again, but he could not kneel on his smashed knees. He could only try to pull himself over and fall to the ground below in one move. The sound of grinding gears began again, and the shadow of the bucket suddenly loomed over head. Seeing the bucket above, he sucked in air and held his breath.

Sallie could make out a dark hulk on the top of the caisson. "Shit! That fucker is escaping!" He turned the crane slightly left; now he was directly above Tiger Gibson. The worker on the bucket waved at him. He stopped the crane. The bucket opened and Gibson fell back into the hole, one hand still grasping the edge of his now circular prison. The worker on the bucket motioned Sallie to lower him and he jumped off onto the top of the foundation. He carefully walked over to an exposed hand and reached in his pocket for his switchblade.

Tiger was completely submerged in the concrete. He knew the caisson was full, so he had to pull himself up through the cold, wet concrete, and over the rim. And he had to do it before his lungs gave out. Then he felt another hand grab his. It was rough; maybe someone was going to pull him out and he would live, his lesson learned! Then there was nothing but an unbelievable searing pain. Gibson instinctively opened his mouth to scream. The concrete rushed in. Messina's goon began to cut away at the exposed hand. It twitched and tried to pull away to no avail. Finally, it was free. Blood bubbled up though the wet concrete. The hand might make a nice gift for the Boss.

After the pour was done, cylinders of concrete placed in his new truck, Enzo Liguria headed for Lower Wacker Drive. He drove until it turned south. At eleven o'clock on a Thursday, it was empty of traffic. He began to slow down; the previous night he had missed the small turn into the service drive that contained a loading dock. There were two doors, one unmarked and another one stating in florid writing above it, "Messina's Flower Shop." Alongside the dock was a brand-new Ford F-250 pickup truck, dark blue. He put his own truck in park and climbed into the cab of the other. First, he had to find that classical station he was listening too, and then he would go onto the lab with cylinders full of 7,000 PSI concrete, poured earlier at Cooky's yard.

Another of Johnny Messina's men would drive Enzo's pickup to a dump by the river on the Southside and dispose of the cylinders that contained 4,000 PSI material that came from the jobsite. This would be repeated for months on end, each batch of concrete poured into Steel Simpson's monument to himself and his ego, 3,000 to 4,000 PSI less than required. The test reports would show differently, coming in all above strength. Johnny Messina had taken out his slide rule and determined that the building would not fall down. However, over time, hairline cracks would appear in the columns and beams of the structure. Costly repairs would be needed in the way of steel plates around hundreds of columns. And no one could question the strength of the concrete. It would all pass muster in the reports. If there were problems with the structure, blame the architect.

The concrete began to set around the bodies of the now defunct Lucifer's Player's Club. Three mighty caissons of Chicago World Tower were the graves of Tiger, Maurice, Tiny and six others. Carmine Messina would move quickly to restore hegemony and order in Maywood. The Outfit would be firmly in charge, and the mutterings at the Italian American Club would be silenced. In fact, the fear of Carmine Messina increased tenfold.

The steel formwork was removed; there was no evidence of the inhabitants within the columns; the construction workers had used the vibrating dicks effectively around the perimeters, eliminating any voids. However, inside the reinforcing cage the bodies began to decompose. Over time the corpses would turn to bone and then to dust creating great voids in these most important building elements. Carmine Messina hadn't used a slide rule or done any calculations. In fact, he didn't even own one. Let the building fall; he didn't care. Nobody stole from him.

CHAPTER 77

D E C E M B E R   1 9 7 4

J. Vance Jefferson walked backed to the Santa Fe Building in what had become a sudden and aggressive lake-effect snow, heavy but probably brief. He raised his collar against the wind, and was warmed by his last martini, a fourth. It had taken that many to cajole Asa Morton to lend him another $250,000 to make the firm's payroll. He recalled the meeting. He had to grovel to get the money. He had never done that before. Grovel. Beg! It was insulting. Fucking Asa Morton. Over the years there was no telling the amount of money NJ&M had run through his bank. *"And then he acts like he's doing me a big favor,"* he thought. *"OK. Well, fine. Time to institute my insurance policy."* He picked up his stride but found himself weaving and sliding on the new snow.

Once back inside the warm confines of the Santa Fe lobby, Jefferson pressed the elevator button to the 12th floor, not the usual 14th executive floor. In the corner office of the great drafting room Dick Schiffels was checking shop drawings, white swirls of smoke rising from his pipe. Connor noticed the senior partner brush against and then run into several drafting tables on the way to his destination. He put his head down and ignored the man.

"Dick…"

"Oh, hi, Vance. How are you?"

"Have the ship, shop drawings for the curdin wall for the whirled tower come in?" slurring his words and ignoring any pleasantries.

"Ah, yeah. Just came in today. They're next up. You okay?"

"Fine. Let me have them."

"But I'm about to check them."

"We can't have a fuckup like last time. I'm checking 'em myself personally. Now give them to yours truly."

Dick was about to protest. He didn't intend to make the same mistakes Francis had and Jefferson knew that. But then he relented. One less tedious chore to attend to. Maybe he'd leave early; it was bound to be a hellacious rush hour anyway.

Schiffels looked hard at Jefferson. "Sure thing, Vance. Knock yourself out. Big marketing lunch?" handing the drawings to his unsteady boss.

"Mind your own damn business." Jefferson took the drawings, turned and swayed down the aisle way.

"*Well, fuck you, too!*" the senior project manager thought. "*I think I'll go home right now…*"

Jefferson passed by Marilyn's desk. She was planning on leaving early and going shopping at Marshall Field's, then have an early dinner at the Walnut room with Jane. As such, she had just freshened her makeup and splashed on a nice perfume by Yves St. Laurent. Today she wore a pink blouse, cut low at the front, revealing a slight amount of cleavage. Jefferson stopped and leaned over, glaring at the hint of exposed breasts. The perfume hit him like an aphrodisiac. Suddenly he was horny as hell.

"Marilyn my love, you're not going anywhere are you?"

"Well yes, Vance, I'm meeting a friend for dinner."

"No, sorry, honey, we have a big proposal to do. Tell your boyfriend you'll be late."

"Sir, it's a girlfriend. Really? What if I come in early tomorrow?"

"No, tonight. I need you tonight. Give me 10 minutes and then come into my office. Bring the normal materials."

Marilyn wanted to cry. She got up and headed for the closet where the marketing materials were kept. Vance ambled to his office and hit the door jamb as he went in. He removed his coat and opened the credenza, taking out a crystal decanter containing gin and a glass.

"Fuck, I don't need ice." He poured three fingers of gin into the glass, downed it, and poured another. He could still smell the perfume. He pulled off his tie and stumbled into his chair. Today, he would have Marilyn Jones. Fuck her boyfriend, Connor.

Marilyn was at the open door, arms full of brochures and individual sheets highlighting projects the company had done. It was very strange. Jefferson had lunch with Asa Morton, his banker. What new client?

Seeing Marilyn, he jumped up, teetering slightly. He took a big sip from his glass and then went over to her. "Here let me help you, hon." He took the stack of materials from her and placed them on his desk and quickly returned to shut the door. Marilyn stood there ramrod straight, fear beginning to rise up in her. She had thought all of Vance Jefferson's advances and gropes were a thing of the past.

"How about a little cocky-tail before we begin? It's almost five, and what is that perfume? I love it!"

Marilyn remembered what Jane had said: *"Don't take any shit from him. Let him know you're in control; he'll back down."*

"Vance, I don't want a drink. I want to leave. You're drunk. We can do this proposal tomorrow!" There was tension in her voice.

Jefferson ignored her, and pulled out a martini glass, shaker and a bottle of vodka. He was searching for the small bottle of cranberry juice he had purchased long ago in the event this night ever came to pass. "Ah, come on, baby, have a Cosmo. I can make a really excellent one."

"No! I'm leaving. Understand? I'm leaving. I have another engagement." Her voice was firm, as she tried hard to avoid it trembling.

"You can see little Connor any time. What you want is a real man." Jefferson went over to the door and locked it. He turned to her, eyes filled with lust and desire.

Marilyn's heart beat faster. She had never seen Vance Jefferson drunk, not this drunk anyway. And she had never seen the look that was now on his face. It was a sick, mean smile, a smile of pending conquest. She watched as he poured vodka into the triangular glass, forgetting any other ingredients. The liquid sloshed over the rim onto the floor as he carried it over to her. He grabbed her wrist and she refused to take the glass. He put it against her lips and tried to make her drink it.

"Stop it. You're hurting me!" Marilyn tried to break away, but Jefferson grabbed her chin and tried to pour the alcohol into her mouth.

"Drink it, it will relax you!"

"Let go of me! I don't want it!"

Jefferson forced some of the liquid into her mouth and she spit it out and lashed at the glass. The drink fell onto the floor; the glass shattered.

Jefferson sneered. "OK, so that's how it's going to be!" He grabbed his prey by the shoulders and pushed her toward the couch. Marilyn tried to resist, but he was too strong, and she had begun to panic; she didn't know what to do. This was now unchartered territory. Then, suddenly, she was lying on the couch and he was on top of her.

"No! Stop! Get off of me, you bastard!" Marilyn Jones was now fighting for her honor, and perhaps her life. Then she felt his hand under her clothes madly groping and then finding her panties. He pulled hard and they ripped in his hands. He put his hand between her legs and forced several fingers into her. She screamed and tried to raise her arms to push him off, but he only needed one hand to hold her down. It was around her throat and she could feel it tightening, choking her.

"It doesn't have to be this way, Marilyn. Remember Chez Paul? And Jacques? Then you were grateful to me. You let me touch you. I want you so much. Quit fighting! Relax and enjoy it."

Marilyn began to gasp for air. She made a hollow sound. "No, please, don't." Then she felt his manhood stiffening against her. He pulled his hand out of her and began to undo his belt, then the button on his trousers. He went back to her pussy, rubbing harder and feeling her inside. Tears poured down her cheeks, and Marilyn tried to move her head from side to side, and tried to breathe. He could tell she was choking, and he moved his hand away from her neck to the inside of her blouse. Finally, he was touching what had been the object of his desire for so long, her ripe, round breast. The nipple was taut from fear. With his other hand, he pulled down his pants and boxers.

"Please, let me love you. Let me pleasure you. I want you so much and I know you want me." Jefferson was whispering in her ear. Marilyn could not believe what she was hearing. He was going to rape her and he was convinced it could be mutual. She squirmed and fought.

"You bastard, let me go! I hate you! I don't want you. Stop, stop, please, stop!"

Then she felt his hand on her again pushing his hard cock into her. She quit fighting, tears running down her face. She laid still and thought of Connor. Where was he? She felt Jefferson moving in and out of her. Then she blacked out.

Marilyn awoke and Jefferson was gone. The empty glass was on his desk, the brochure materials still where he had placed them. She got off the couch, straightened her skirt and put her ripped panties into the small skirt pocket. She ran her fingers through her hair to straighten it and walked out of the office. But there was no one there to see her. At her desk, she grabbed her coat and handbag and left the building. The snow had stopped and Marilyn Jones didn't know where to go.

"Bob, how's it going?" Connor was at Marlow's doorway. He was sporting a new haircut and didn't look as disheveled as in the recent past. His eyes were clear and bright. He was wearing a new rep tie and crisp blue shirt.

"It's must be the prodigal son returned. My, you look sharp tonight. Date with Marilyn?"

"No, she's over at Marshall Field's shopping and dining with Jane."

"You look a lot better than you did last week. Maybe it's just the haircut."

"So, listen, I want to apologize for being, well, distant lately."

"Moody?"

"OK, yeah, moody."

"Hungover?"

"Fine. That, too."

"An asshole?"

"I wouldn't go that far! But I just want you to know I've worked some stuff out. I'm better now."

"Good, because I was ready to give your job to Taubert."

"Ouch. That stings. I was wondering…if you're ready to leave, maybe we go back to the Top of the Rock and have dinner. My treat. I'll explain what's been going on."

"If I recall last time we did that, I was drinking a lot."

"Just iced tea. Or tonic. Or water."

"I just happen to be free. Let's blow this pop stand and do it."

"Great, because I'm feeling great, and I want to tell someone."

"You can tell me, then. I'm all ears."

CHAPTER 78

"Brad, come in. To what do I owe the pleasure?" Given all of the problems of late surrounding the Chicago World Tower project, Steel Simpson was not surprised to see his lender. He had hoped that Wentworth would be too busy doing other deals to worry about a project so far down the road under construction.

"I must say, you have a bird's eye view of all the construction from here," Wentworth said, looking out the window. In the distance the building had risen above its foundation up to the third floor of the base, which was being poured. Light flakes of snow swirled outside the window. Christmas decorations adorned lamp posts on Michigan Avenue.

"Yes, I can watch the progress every day. I get a woody every time I look over there."

"Really? I'd think it would be kind of deflating. Let's see, you started construction in June. I see the base isn't even finished. You know I'm hearing a lot of bad things."

"Just the normal startup problems. We're hitting our stride now."

"I hear the job has been shut down now for the third time because of substandard electrical work."

"There's nothing substandard about the work. The inspectors have been real pricks, that's all. They have it out for my electrical contractor just because he's from Indiana. Hell, I couldn't get the local guys to bid it."

"Imagine that." Wentworth's sarcasm was clear.

"What's that supposed to mean?" Simpson looked up from papers he was not reading.

Wentworth ignored the question. "I got another call from Norman Weese at Nolan Jefferson. He says they haven't been getting paid…"

Simpson went into his defensive mode. "You see the pay requests. They're funded every month…"

"But are they paid?"

"Of course they are. Well, mostly. The first change order was their entire fault. It cost me over two hundred grand!"

"The architect can't be held responsible for site conditions they are not aware of. Nor is the contractor. That's why there is a contingency. And what about all the other change orders? Are they their fault too, Steel?" Wentworth was boring in.

"Mostly. Their drawings are crap, and I have to pay for the extra costs. Well, they can share in the pain."

"I'm not sure that's in their contract, either. When are project delays and labor problems the architect's fault? They aren't at the jobsite since you're too cheap to have an on-site architect's representative."

"We didn't have that in the budget," Simpson lamely replied.

"Well, you should have. Let's see if I've got this right. A cable broke on the tower crane causing the load of scaffolding to fall through two floors. Two-week delay. A fire started in a supply room where flammables were stored. I hear it took an entire day to put the fire out, and then the job was shut down three weeks to check the structure. And then there's the sheet metal workers who walked out over unfair labor practices."

"What's your point, Brad? Okay, we've been a little snake bit. But it's all behind us now."

"My point is that you're almost out of contingency, which I thought was plenty, and you're less than a quarter of the way done. I'm getting pressure from the boys upstairs to audit this job, and I'm about to do it. So, get your act together. Make peace with your uncle, the unions, your contractors, whoever. I don't care! And for God's sake, quit jerking the fucking architects around and get them paid. I'm tired of hearing from Norman Weese!"

"Brad, there is no need to audit. I'm getting extra funding from Ali Sharif as we speak. Everything will be fine."

"Good, Steel. Good. And you had better get it or I'll stop funding this fuck-up of a development! Later." Brad Wentworth picked up his hat and exited Steel's office. Simpson slumped in his chair and after a minute, buzzed Ruth.

"Yes, sir?"

"Ruth, call up the Lakeview Condominiums and tell them I want my deposit back. Tell them to cancel the sales contract."

"Yes, sir."

Simpson stared out the window. A small part of him wanted to be building warehouses again on the west side. No one gave a shit about them, or whether anyone got paid. He reached into his side drawer for the bottle of Bufferin. Maybe his fucking Arab partner was right; the job was jinxed. But it would be a cold day in hell before he asked that pretentious Muslim for any more money.

"Steel, this is Ruth." She was on the intercom.

"For God's sake, I know that. What!?"

"Lakeview Condominiums said it's too late to refund your deposit. The deadline was last Friday. And they said the contract calls for another $150,000 payment by next week."

Simpson rubbed his temples. He picked up the bottle of painkillers; he would need three.

CHAPTER 79

Since Mike and Amy's fortuitous meeting with Joseph Buckingham, Billy Flanagan's trail had gone cold. And there were other more pressing and important arson cases. Amy had gone back to Community Relations, and Grabowski was dating her.

The two had searched all over the lower west side beyond the lakefront and Soldier Field. One day, they had even driven down an alley and missed a sidewalk off of it that led to an abandoned bungalow, a large shed really. They asked around the local populace if they had seen a bum with a camera around his neck. Amy was warm and encouraging but memories were short or non-existent. The two comrades had checked every flop house, underpass, and abandoned building. No Billy Flanagan. He had vanished or died.

"Another year down the tubes, my friend." John O'Rourke had brought out the bottle of Jameson and looked at his partner with the expression, "Want some?"

"By all means. It's Christmas." Grabowski looked over to the small artificial tree decorated with little ornaments sitting on top of the file cabinets.

"You know, we need some new decorations."

"Wait until January, you won't care." O'Rourke poured two decent shots and handed a glass to Mike. "We did this last year, didn't we?"

"We've done this every year for the last five years…" Grabowski took a pull on his holiday party drink.

"No. I mean sit here with the case of Mouse and Pat not being solved." He looked down at the flashbulb still sitting in the inbox on his desk.

"God, will you give it a rest! I spent most of the year looking for Billy Flanagan. What did it get me?"

"It got you Amy. I'm quite the matchmaker, I must say."

"You have me there. But I don't think she's that crazy about me…"

"I can't imagine why. A great catch like you?"

"Screw you, and Merry Christmas!" Grabowski finished his drink and poured another. The phone on O'Rourke's desk rang.

"Arson, O'Rourke." His voice betrayed an annoyance at the call. "Why do you think its arson?"

Grabowski was eavesdropping and knew that the call would screw up his night too.

O'Rourke reached for his pad and scribbled down the address. "I see. OK, we'll be there shortly."

"What's up?"

"A bungalow just went up like a bonfire. Down in the neighborhoods where you were looking for Billy. They have a suspect." He reached for his coat and began to head for the stairs, his partner right behind. Then he turned back sharply and went back to his desk. He leaned over to the "In" basket and grabbed the flashbulb. Grabowski shook his head.

"Hey, this could be our lucky day." O'Rourke patted Grabowski on the shoulder and smiled.

———————

The scene off Lawndale Avenue wasn't exactly out of Currier and Ives, but it did have its holiday moments. There was a flickering of flames from the burnt-out house.

A considerable amount of smoke was still rising, contained by the confines of the small walkway area. O'Rourke waved his arms for visibility and held a handkerchief to his mouth. He saw a firefighter and made his way across hoses and debris.

"Who's the man in charge?"

"Lieutenant Ryan." The firefighter, face smudged with soot, nodded to a clearing where his boss was standing over a slight figure sitting on the arm of a burnt-out chair.

O'Rourke walked that way and Grabowski followed. "This shouldn't take long. Looks like they found the dirt bag that started this fire." In a moment, they were by the side of the lieutenant.

The firefighter, no more than 25, looked at the two quizzically, and then said: "You guys from arson?" O'Rourke flashed his badge. He shook his head, and then looked down at the pathetic figure on the chair. The little man had a Brownie Starflash Camera around his neck. He looked at O'Rourke and Grabowski and smiled.

"I'm sorry. I'm sorry. I didn't mean to. It was my house. I was cold. I was cold." Billy Flanagan was shivering, face and hands covered in dirt and soot. He held a steaming cup of coffee in his hands but wasn't drinking it. He hated coffee.

"Sorry to ruin your night. This bum did it. Open and shut case. I'll have one of the officers take him down to central booking."

"No, that won't be necessary. We'll take him."

"But he needs to be booked."

"Don't worry about what needs to be done. We've got it. Maybe you should finish putting out that fire, huh, Lieutenant?"

"Sorry, Inspector. You're in charge."

"That's right. I'm in charge." He looked down at Billy. "Billy. Billy Flanagan?"

"You know my name. You know my name."

O'Rourke was almost giddy with excitement. Two years of searching was over; the solving of the fire by the lake was as close as a foot away and it was hanging around Billy's neck. "Hey, Billy, you hungry? I bet you'd like a nice turkey dinner with all the trimmings. How'd you like that?"

Grabowski shook his head. Why were all his partners social workers? Grab the camera and leave the bum.

"I like turkey. I like dressing and peas. Am I under arrest? Am I under arrest?"

"No, Billy; it was an accident. I'm sure. Come on. Let's get you warm and fed." He looked at Grabowski. "I know of a pretty good Greek place close by down on Cermak Avenue. I think it's called Alexander's."

"Fine, I was getting hungry. I might have a gyro." He grabbed Billy's coat by the shoulder. Billy screamed.

"Grabowski, take it easy!" O'Rourke scowled at his partner. He knew it wouldn't be easy to get the camera from his captive. "Sorry, Billy; don't mind him. You come on, this way."

"I think that was the best gyro I ever had," Grabowski spoke, his mouth still half full.

"I think Billy liked his dinner, too…" O'Rourke was watching Billy finish a piece of coconut cream pie. "Billy, who's in your medallion?" pointing to the Kodak camera.

"Bad people."

"What kind of bad people?"

"People who want to take my throne away. I'm the king of Ireland. The king."

"Anyone else?"

"People who burn down homes. My home. They killed my friends."

"What friends?"

"Mouse and Pat. They were burned. Mouse and Pat were on fire."

No matter how O'Rourke sweet-talked Billy, he would not part with his camera. He was getting frustrated as he sat in the interview room. He could just have Grabowski hold Billy's arms and grab the camera, but he felt badly for Billy. It was evident that the camera meant everything to the poor man. In a last-ditch effort, he decided to call Amy Kolska. She arrived within a half hour.

"Billy, I bet you'd like a hot shower. Would you like that?" Amy's voice was calm and sweet.

"Yes, yes. I would. I would."

"I'll keep your camera for you. I'll take good care of it." Amy touched his hand and squeezed it gently.

"It's my chain of office."

"Sorry, yes. Your chain. I'll take good care of it, I promise." She took Billy by the hand and led him up the stairs where the locker room was. O'Rourke and Grabowski shook their heads. In a minute she was back with the Starflash camera in hand. O'Rourke took out the spent flashbulb and placed it in the round hole at the center of the silver bowl. It fit perfectly.

"Grab, I've got a good feeling about this. I'll take this talisman down to the lab. I bet there's film in it."

O'Rourke paced outside the darkroom. Why was it taking so long? One stinking roll of film. Finally, the lab tech opened the darkroom door just slightly. "You better come on in here." O'Rourke practically shoved the tech aside and entered the darkroom, the door swung open. The tech was right behind him and shut the door. O'Rourke couldn't see anything, and then his eyes adjusted to the low wattage red light. Hanging from a clothesline were strips of negatives.

"You could have ruined the print when you opened that door." The technician was dressed in what looked like a hospital gown and black rubber gloves. He reminded the detective of Dr. Frankenstein. O'Rourke looked down into the pans filled with solution. Floating in the middle pan was an 8x10 sheet of photographic paper. It was blank. Then an image began to appear. The head of the arson squad squinted in the dimness. The image grew more distinct. He was mesmerized as it came into full resolution. It was now almost fully developed. Below him was a photo of a large man holding a gas can. It was Lothar Jensen; he was sure of that.

"Bingo!"

CHAPTER 80

Jane was waiting at the door to the apartment when Connor got off the elevator. He had literally run past the lobby security desk, ignoring the guard, who recognized him and buzzed Jane's and Marilyn's apartment. He kissed her lightly on the cheek and went right into the living room expecting to see Marilyn on the couch with a glass of wine. He stopped in his tracks. Marilyn's mother Sarah, and her father Paul, were sitting on the couch.

"Mr. and Mrs. Jones? Where's Marilyn? Is she all right?"

"She's sleeping, Connor," was all that her mother could say.

Jane came into the room and interrupted. "I gave her a sedative. She was pretty shaken up."

Marilyn's dad spoke up in an accusatory fashion. "You were with her tonight; what happened? Did you two have a fight?"

"No, Jane was with her. Weren't you? You guys were supposed to meet at Marshall Fields, right?"

"She never showed, Connor. I called the office, and then here at home. She didn't answer. I just assumed you two had gotten together at the last minute. I was disappointed, so I came home."

"I had dinner with my boss, Bob Marlow. At the Top of the Rock. I wanted to tell him some things that were on my mind. He's like a father to me."

Marilyn's father continued. "Really, so you weren't with her?"

"No! I just told you that! Where did you find her?"

Jane tried to reduce the tension in the room. "Marilyn was over at the next building. She was disoriented. She thought she lived there because the lobbies look alike. But the man at the front desk didn't recognize her. She kept insisting she had an apartment there. So, he buzzed the other doormen around in the adjacent buildings. Bill downstairs asked for a description. He knew then it was Marilyn. He went over and got her and brought her home."

Connor looked surprised. "What did she say?"

"Not a lot. She looked like she was in shock, honestly. All she said was: 'Connor didn't save me.'"

"I want to see her..." Connor turned toward the bedroom.

"Connor, let her sleep. I gave her a pretty strong sedative."

He slumped into a chair acquiescing to Jane's advice. Paul Jones got off the couch and went over to him.

"Tell us what really happened, Connor," Marilyn's father was staring hard at the young architect. He reached in his pocket and pulled out Marilyn's ripped panties and held them out for him to see. "We won't press charges, I promise."

Connor's face flushed red and he grabbed the article of clothing. He looked hard at it.

"That son-of-a-bitch! I'll kill him!" He looked at the three of them and then ran for the door.

Jane tried to stop Connor, grabbing his arm but he broke free and was gone. She looked at Marilyn's parents.

"What son-of-a-bitch is he talking about?" Paul demanded.

"I need to tell you something. First, Connor would never hurt Marilyn. You just saw him. He loves her. She told me that he had asked her to marry him two nights ago. I'm sorry to tell you that now, under these circumstances, but you need to know how much Marilyn means to him." Jane was trying her best to explain.

"Then who is this other man?" her Dad was confused.

"Her boss, Mr. Jefferson. He's a creepy old man and he's been hitting on her."

"Hitting on her? What does that mean?"

"Oh, for God's sake, Paul, you know what it means," Sarah said indignantly.

Jane responded. "He makes her go to dinner with him to discuss office stuff, like planning parties. Then he gropes her. Under the table. He even gropes her at her desk. She's resisted and she thought he had moved on."

"Why didn't she just quit?"

"She was planning to; she wants to go back to school. But first, she was worried that Connor would be fired by Jefferson to get revenge, simply because employees are not allowed to date."

"That's a sane policy," Paul muttered.

"Paul, really. Jane, what do you think happened tonight?" Sarah Jones' voice was worried.

"Something really bad, I think. I told her to be strong and not take any more shit from him, I'm sorry. But he may have crossed the line tonight." Jane knew deep down that Jefferson had pushed the relationship beyond the boundaries…to rape.

"I told you we should have never let her move into the city." Paul Jones was glaring at his wife.

"Oh, stop Paul. You can't keep her locked up in Oak Park. She has to have a life!"

"She's coming home tomorrow. Anyway, Jane can't care for her and work too. I'm sure after a few days, Marilyn will be all right. Then she can find work in the suburbs."

"You should apologize to Connor, accusing him of hurting Marilyn," Jane said voice trembling.

"I'll do no such thing. He's probably been sleeping with her, which is almost as bad as what this man Jefferson did. And I won't let him see her either. This whole 'I want to live in the city' thing has been a big mistake."

Jane shook her head. "I'm very proud of Marilyn and how she has put up with a pig like Jefferson. And Connor is a wonderful and very talented guy. He designed a 75-story building right out of school. You should cut him some slack."

"Jane's right. You're so rigid, Paul. So what if he has long hair? He went to Harvard, after all."

"He's just a free love hippie as far as I'm concerned. She'll find other well-suited boys in Oak Park."

Jane was angry now. "If you want to come back for Marilyn tomorrow, fine. But you can't stay here tonight. This is my home, and with your attitude, Mr. Jones, you're not welcome to stay."

As the cold late-night air hit Connor in the face, he realized that he wouldn't find J. Vance Jefferson in his office reading the *Tribune* with a lollipop in his mouth. He would go into the office tomorrow. He had scores to settle. He slowly walked a block to his building and went up to his studio and a waiting bottle of bourbon.

CHAPTER 81

"Hey, Tiffany, have a courier pick up these shop drawings. Here, I wrote down the address: Great Lakes Glass and Curtainwall. They're up in Kenosha, Wisconsin, but I want a courier to take them up there today."

"Yes, Mr. Jefferson. Anything else?"

"And this. Mail it to the *Tribune* and *Sun-Times*."

"Yes, sir, right away."

The comely blond-haired receptionist looked down at the neatly handwritten piece of paper: "Executive Secretary Wanted."

Vance Jefferson headed back to his office. His head hurt from the umpteen drinks he had the day before. He was sure Marilyn Jones would never return. But it was all her fault, he thought. She would have been so successful at the firm. He would have put her in charge of administration with a big raise. There would be evenings out; dinners at Jacques; beds with satin sheets at the Palmer House. Yes, it was all her fault. When he got back to his office, he opened the Tribune. "Marilyn, I need coffee," he shouted. Then he remembered that there was no Marilyn. He got up and headed for the kitchen.

Connor exited the elevator moments later. "Hey Tiffany. Say, is Mr. Jefferson in?"

"Oh yes, he was just up here. How are you today? Say, I didn't know Marilyn was leaving?"

"What?

"Mr. Jefferson just gave me this." Tiffany handed the want ad to Connor.

"Yeah. She found a better job." Connor feigned knowledge but put the pieces together, thinking: *"Rapes her and then fires her. What a monumental scumbag."* He headed to Dick Schiffel's desk, knowing he would not be there as he never showed until 9:30 A.M.

Among the morass of plans and folded-up shop drawings, Connor found what he was looking for: Submittal for Pre-Fabricated Stair Assemblies and Miscellaneous Structural Supports. It was from the Hammond Iron Works in Indiana. He took the thick roll of drawings and went back to his desk, finding a red marker pen. In an hour and a half, he was done, having added an additional riser and tread to each of the stairs for each of the three major components of the project, the office, hotel and residential. He stamped the drawings "Revise as Noted. Re-submittal not required." Then he initialed them. Checked by: "FN,Jr."; approved by: "JVJ." He thought to himself: *"Perfect. No one gets hurt. The stairs get delivered to the job and only then will they find out they don't fit. Back to the fabrication shop. A big change order for extra charges and time lost, and a lawsuit for Vance Jefferson to handle for Errors and Omissions. Fuck you, Nolan, Jefferson and Marlow, and Mr. Steel Simpson."* He took the drawings back to the front desk.

"Tiffany, have these delivered by courier today to Hammond Iron Works, ASAP!"

"My, we have a lot of expensive personal deliveries today. Okay, you're the boss. What job shall I charge it to?"

"Chicago World Tower to Mr. Jefferson's account. Is he still in?"

"As far as I know."

"Thanks, have a great day."

"You, too, hon. And I'm sorry about Marilyn leaving."

"Yeah, so am I." Connor headed for the executive wing and took a deep breath when he arrived at the closed door of the senior partner. He didn't bother to knock. Jefferson was standing at the window looking out to the lake; he turned and saw Connor West.

"Well, young Connor. Don't you know how to knock?"

"Fuck you, you degenerate bastard!" Connor crossed the room in an instant raised his arm, hitting Jefferson squarely in the jaw. The older man staggered and stumbling found purchase at his granite desk. Connor punched him again, this time in the gut. Jefferson gasped for breath.

"You're...you're fired! And I'll have you arrested for assault!"

"Good! I'll trade that for your being charged with rape!"

"She loved it. She had a real man for a change!"

West saw his opportunity. Jefferson was leaning back against his granite desk, his lower buttocks against the top. Connor raised his foot and smashed it into Jefferson's manhood. Jefferson doubled over in pain and hit the floor, grabbing his crotch. West kicked him again in the chest. Jefferson groaned.

"I should kill you for what you did to Marilyn, you scumbag! But I think I'll see you rot in prison instead." Then he grabbed the crystal bowl full of Tootsie Roll Pops and poured the contents onto Jefferson. He took three of them and crammed them into his boss's mouth, still struggling for air. He looked down at his prostrate boss. Connor swung his leg back and delivered one final kick into Jefferson's balls. Jefferson tried to scream but couldn't; he could only whimper through the lollipops. West turned and headed for the door.

"Oh, by the way, I quit!" He headed for the lobby wanting to make a quick exit. Then he remembered two important items. He took the elevator down to 12. He went to his desk, retrieving his Mont Blanc pen and the postcard from Key West sent by Rat Tomlinson. As he entered the elevator, he was still consumed with rage. Now he would go and find Marilyn.

CHAPTER 82

John O'Rourke entered the main dining room of Johnny Lattner's. This was the day he had anticipated: the meting out of justice. The courts and the attorneys would drag out the legal process, but he loved to see a man's face when he is arrested, cuffs placed on him, and read his Miranda rights. To see the confusion, the fear, the panic. And to do it in the presence of the public and business partners. Nothing was sweeter. At the same time, Mike Grabowski was down in the parking garage to arrest Lothar Jensen. In an abundance of caution, he had brought three uniformed police officers with him.

"Hello, Mr. Simpson. John O'Rourke, remember? We spoke on the phone." He flashed his gold badge so Simpson's companions at the table could see that this was not a social call.

The two guests, interested in leasing a full floor of space in Chicago World Tower, put down their drinks, and looked at each other.

"O'Rourke? What's all this about?"

"Mr. Simpson, you'll need to come with me."

"What the hell? What for?" Simpson's lunch companions now wanted to know too.

"If you insist. Steel Simpson, you're under arrest for the murder of Patrick Walsh and James Anderson aka Pat and Mouse. You have the right to remain silent. Anything you say now will be admissible in a court of law. You have the right to counsel. If you can't afford counsel, which I doubt, Cook County will provide you one."

"Who the hell are Patrick and what?"

"Patrick Walsh and James Anderson. Homeless people who were burned to death in a fire you intentionally set on your land at the lake. Am I ringing any bells now?"

"Steel, did you set that fire at the lake?" His lunch guest spoke and took a deep pull on his drink.

"No, Murray, I didn't set any fire. Look, Inspector O'Rourke. You have the wrong person. I never set any fire."

"No, Lothar Jensen did, and you told him to do it. And he's under arrest too. Please come along now…"

Simpson was shaking and beads of sweat were forming on his head. This could not be happening. He had been told the investigation had been dropped. He got up, steadied himself against the table, his head spinning.

"Where are you taking me?"

"Central booking. I'm sure your lawyer knows where it is."

Simpson looked at his two lunch guests. "This is a big misunderstanding, gentlemen. I'll get this straightened out. I'll get the lease over to you tomorrow."

"I don't think that will be necessary, Steel. The deal is off."

───────────────

Connor rang the doorbell at the two-story colonial house in Oak Park. Finally, Paul Jones opened the door.

"Connor, this is a surprise."

"I've come to see Marilyn. Is she all right?"

"She's resting now. I'm afraid this isn't a good time."

"May I come in? I'll wait until she's awake; I need to see her."

"Connor, I'm sorry to tell you this. But she doesn't want to see you after what happened the other night. I think you should leave. She doesn't want anything to do with you or your architectural firm."

"I don't believe that. I don't believe you! We love each other!"

"I seriously doubt that."

"What the fuck would you know about us?"

"Young man, we are leaving later today for Marilyn to get some rest. We'll be gone awhile. Perhaps when we come back, she'll want to see you. I doubt it, and I won't encourage it, but you never know. Now, goodbye." Jones closed the door firmly.

Sarah Jones was waiting in the foyer. "Paul, I can't believe you didn't let him in. He's a good boy and he loves her. What is wrong with you?"

"Is the car packed? We need to get to Sturgeon Bay by nightfall. The innkeeper said he'd wait up for us. A month at the cabin will do us all good."

"Running to Wisconsin and keeping Marilyn from seeing Connor is no solution." Sarah was protesting but knew it was of no use.

"I just want to get her away from Chicago. And get her checked out by a doctor. For all we know, she's pregnant, by God knows who!"

———————————

Bob Marlow sat at his desk enjoying his new vice, fresh brewed coffee from the deli downstairs. There was a new project to do, albeit a small one, an office building out in Oak Brook. He was reviewing the schematic documents prepared by Gerhard. The phone rang.

"Hi, Bob. This is Ed Connelly at Great Lakes Glass."

"Oh, yes, how are you doing, Ed? We worked together on the Chicago Center job. You helped us dodge the bullet on that one."

"Bob, that's why I'm calling; you guys have done it again."

"Done what again?"

"I just got the shops on the Chicago World Tower job. It's the same system and you changed the tolerances from three-quarters of an inch to one-quarter of an inch on the rubber gaskets. It won't work and we won't warrant it."

"Wait. You got shop drawings that show those changes?"

"Yes, and the initials of CJW are there under 'Reviewed' and RJM are in the box for 'Approved.' I assume you're RJM, but I don't know who CJW is. I know you guys want as much glass to show as possible, but the system could leak at best, and the windows will blow out in strong winds at worst. You need to switch to the Ultra Thin 540 System if you don't want to see any gasketing. And that's going to cost…"

"Hold on. Hold on. I didn't approve any shop drawings for the curtainwall on that project. I haven't even been involved with it."

"Then who is CJW?"

"He's a young designer on staff, but even he wouldn't take it upon himself to…at least I don't think he would. Look, send the shops back just like you got them. I'll look into this. And thanks for the heads up."

"Hey, no problem, but you guys have got to stop screwing around with our systems. We're the curtainwall experts."

"Got it and thanks. I'll get back to you."

"Hey, Bob, one other thing. Weird, but when I was going through the drawings, I found a Tootsie Roll wrapper between the sheets."

"I see. Get those drawings back to me. With that candy wrapper."

Bob Marlow set down the receiver and headed for Connor's cubicle. On the drafting table, held down by the parallel bar was an envelope addressed to him. He opened it.

Dear Bob,

I just thought you'd like to know that I have resigned from the firm. Marilyn has quit as well since she was raped by that pig Jefferson. If you visit him, he won't be in very good shape, but at least I didn't kill him. Thanks for everything and for being a great mentor. You and Marilyn are the only good memories I have of this fucking place. I'll be in touch.

All the Best,
Connor

Marlow read and re-read the words "raped by that pig Jefferson" again and again. His anger grew. Not only did Jefferson rape Marilyn Jones, but he doctored up the curtainwall shop drawings and tried to blame Connor and himself for it. But why? Why put the firm at risk for a lawsuit by screwing up the drawings? He knew one thing: Jefferson was either going to jail for rape or for fraud and reckless endangerment.

CHAPTER 83

Everything about the Cook County Jail was grey. Grey walls, grey blankets on the cots, grey bars, and grey uniforms. Steel Simpson dressed in his grey one-piece jumpsuit sat and stared at the glass between him and his visitor. Irving Montlick had just sat down, simultaneously picking up the phone. He wanted this to be quick. He looked at his frightened client, who looked like he had aged ten years overnight.

"Hello, Steel. How they treating you?"

"Oh, just great. I get room service every day. Why haven't you gotten me out of here?"

"The bond hearing is set for Tuesday."

"That's four fucking days from now. You need to get me out now!"

"No can do. I don't set the docket. It could have been a week. This is a capital case after all, my friend. It's not bribery, fraud, theft or embezzlement: all your specialties. It's felony murder. Try the steak tartare. I hear it's excellent here."

"You seem to be enjoying this, Irving..."

"Not really. I'm probably going to lose my best client. I told you that if you had anything to do with that fire on your land, you could find another lawyer. But since this seems pretty much like an open and shut case, I'll take it."

"Open and shut? I never set that fire."

"But your guy, Lothar, did."

"I never told him to do that. Anyway, they have no proof."

"Tell that to the jury; I'm sure they'll believe you. Oh, and yes, they have proof. A black and white photo of him holding a gas can in front of a trail of burning grass."

"Oh, shit!"

"Oh, shit indeed."

"Did you say felony murder?"

"Yes, second degree. But with luck, a lot of luck, I may be able to plead you down to involuntary manslaughter. It depends on the prosecuting attorney, and the judge. But don't hold your breath. After all, there was no compelling reason for you to have Lothar set that fire in the first place."

"What am I looking at?"

"For murder, let's just say you'll have lots of time to earn your own law degree. For man two, fifteen years minimum..."

"Oh, God! I can't do fifteen years!"

"Adjust your thinking."

"But what about Chicago World Tower?"

"That's the least of your worries. I'd be worrying about whether I prefer being a bitch for the Crips or for the Aryan Nation at Statesville."

"Fuck you, Irving. This is not funny. To tell you the truth, I'm scared. I didn't mean to kill anyone. I just wanted that shanty town gone from my property. You have to help me."

"Steel, that's what so amusing. It wasn't even your property when you had Lothar set the fire. Pretty stupid, I'd say."

"OK, maybe so, but can't you get me probation? It's my first offense."

"Forget probation. Look, I never liked you, Steel, but I'll do what I can. I admit I'm my own type of sleaze ball, but at least I help people, even scumbags like you. But you just take and take, and treat everyone like they're shit. You have no respect for humanity, or more simply, for any other human being. People are all a means to an end...your end."

"Maybe I learned all that from my father, cold-hearted bastard that he was."

"I never met your father, but I heard he was honest, and hard working. Anyway, to the bad news..."

"How could there be any more bad news?"

"The bank has stopped the tower project and audited the books. They found some, shall we say, serious discrepancies. It seems like a lot of funds have been going into your own pocket. They'll probably press additional charges. In the meantime, they've appointed Zyiad Ali Sharif as administrator of the project while they sort through the mis-spent funds. He's been authorized to pay all the past due legitimate bills. Let's see, what else? They have moved to seize your house in Glencoe, and your condo."

"God. Anything else?"

"Oh yes, one other thing. Reese Anne is filing for divorce. I'll see you next Tuesday. The judge is Earl Cromwell. He doesn't like to grant bail to flight risks."

"But I'm not going anywhere."

"Really, if I were you, I'd be on a plane to Rio. Goodbye, Steel." Irving Montlick hung up the phone, got up and left.

Steel Simpson slowly rose, tears welling up in his eyes. He struggled to breathe, and his knees felt like Jell-O.

CHAPTER 84

Donnie Romero stood at the door; his hand was shaking. Finally, he knocked. He heard the voice on the other side say: "Come on in for Chrissakes!" The door opened slowly.

"Mr. Johnny…"

"Hi ya, Donnie. What's up? How're my elephants today?"

Donnie walked in slowly up to Johnny Messina's desk. He stood there, hands holding onto his Sox baseball cap.

"I got to tell you something that's been bothering me. A lot."

"Sit down, son. What is it? You want a Coke?"

"No, thank you. This is kind of like going to confession."

"Well, you need to see Father Silvio if you been beating off again." Johnny laughed at his crude joke, but Donnie just turned red.

"No sir, nothing like that. In fact, I didn't do nothing wrong, but it's been bothering me."

"What's been bothering you?" Johnny's interest now piqued.

"But your father, Mr. Messina told me not to tell you."

"Tell me anyway. I'll cover it with my father. You won't be in trouble."

"I'll even give back the $100 he gave me to be quiet." Donnie reached into his pocket and pulled out a crumpled bill. "See, I didn't even spend it, though I wanted to."

Johnny was getting impatient. "Donnie, what is it you want to tell me? Now!"

"Well, remember about four months ago when you were gone and your Dad was in charge of the night pours?"

"Yeah, back in September. It was my anniversary."

"That night, a van drove up. It was filled with a bunch of black guys. They were tied up and some of our guys and others I don't know threw them into the pond and then they were put into one of the cement mixers."

"You mean the mixing silos?"

"No, into the elephant...a concrete truck. Into the opening where a guy goes in to wash out the tank. Then it drove off with three other trucks that were filled with concrete. Am I in trouble? I promised I wouldn't tell, but it's been bothering me. Those black guys looked scared."

"Jesus Christ! No, Donnie, you did the right thing. Keep the money. And don't worry about my father. I'll deal with him."

Johnny Messina calmly walked into his father's office on the second floor of Cooky's Concrete.

"Dad, you got a minute? We need to talk."

"Sure, Johnny, what's up? Hey, I see they arrested that scumbag Simpson for murder. I guess that's good news and bad news. The project's stopped, right?"

Johnny Messina ignored the editorial. "Dad, what did you do with the black guys you loaded into one of my concrete trucks when you held down the fort for me in September?"

"Fuckin' kids! Never trust them to keep their mouth shut."

"Dad?"

"Look, the less you know about my business, the better. You know that. Let's just say I had two problems I had to correct. One was that douche bag, Simpson."

"I told you I was taking care of him."

"How? By making sure all the concrete you poured at his job would make strength by pouring it here at the yard? How's that gonna get back at that scum that robbed you and me?"

"What the hell are you talking about? All of those cylinders from the yard were substituted with the ones taken at the jobsite. Every bit of concrete poured on World Tower is two to three thousand PSI below required strength!"

Carmine Messina felt the blood draining from his face. "Oh crap. So, what's that mean? Is the building gonna fall down?"

"I'm not that stupid. No, it won't fall. It will develop cracks over time. All the test results, the false test results, will show the concrete at the required strength. They'll blame the structural engineer, not us. Now what did you do with those hostages?"

"Let's just say they're part of the reinforcing in the caissons..." Carmine looked at the floor.

"Oh, my God! How many caissons?" Johnny Messina stared at his father. The building was almost up to the plaza level when he got the news that the project was on hold indefinitely. At least he had been paid.

"We spread it around. Three is what Gino told me."

"Which three?"

"I dunno. Three big ones. The ones scheduled for that night."

"Which night?"

"The first night you were gone. Thursday, right? Yeah, Thursday. Is the building gonna fall down now?"

"Maybe. Shit, those were three critical caissons. This is bad."

"Aw, forget about it. Three little niggers in each caisson, that's all. They'll still hold up."

"Not with 4,000 PSI concrete instead of 7,000 PSI. You compounded the problem. Why couldn't you just whack those jiggaboos the old-fashioned way, and bury them in a cornfield in Kankakee?"

"That's a lot of gas to go to Kankakee," Messina said, trying to make a joke to lighten his son's mood.

"It's a good thing the job got stopped. But I don't know for how long..."

"The paper says he's charged with murder two, so maybe we got lucky."

"Dad, someday that building is going to start again and then we may be charged with murder two when it falls down!"

"Ah, you worry too much, kid. They'll never prove nuthin."

CHAPTER 85

Carmine Messina, the head of the Outfit, sat in his usual booth at the rear of the Villa Roma Supper Club. A month had elapsed since he and Johnny Messina had realized that they had double screwed Steel Simpson and in doing so, themselves as well. The phone call was one of many Carmine Messina handled every day. But it intrigued him and he knew it was worth a meet. Messina had dismissed his two bodyguards to the kitchen, not wanting to make his guest uneasy, or show that he was in need of such protection. He was after all, just an honest businessman in the concrete supply business.

The snow was swirling outside in a late March snowfall and it was still colder than his arthritis liked. Messina was enjoying a rare Manhattan, straight up, thinking about how Steel Simpson might be enjoying prison. The asshole's lawyer, a Jew, had cut a quick deal with the State's attorney. Man three, ten years, with parole for good behavior after doing a solid seven and a half. Simpson's Glencoe house was seized and the proceeds, along with all his other assets, went back to Chicago Bank & Trust. The condo, owned by Simpson outright, went to Reese Anne and she had moved in, re-decorated and began her new single life as a Rush Street cougar, frequenting Mr. Kelly's and Gibson's.

But Chicago World Tower stood abandoned and empty like the ruin of a long-gone civilization along Lake Michigan. In spite of the very low bid that Cooky's had provided to Josef Simpson to provide the concrete, they had delivered only a third of it. They would lose a lot of money. Johnny had even laid off a handful of workers.

As he took a sip of his cocktail, he saw Frank, the maître d', lead a distinguished dark-skinned man in the direction his table. The man was young and elegantly dressed and was wearing some kind of headdress in red and white. It was the kind those Arabs wore in *Lawrence of Arabia,* one of his favorite movies from long ago. Normally, he did not stand up to greet a guest, but this time Messina decided it was the right thing to do.

"I'm Carmine. Should I call you 'Your Excellency?'"

"Should I call you 'Don'?"

"Naw, I hate that. Not true either. Just Carmine."

"Ali is fine. I'm not here in any government capacity. This is family business."

"Hey, we say that all the time too. You know, it's just family business. Please sit. Can I get you a drink?"

"No, thank you. Muslims are not allowed to drink, although I have violated that rule many times."

"Yeah, well I'm Catholic. Drinking is not only allowed, it's kind of encouraged."

"I know. I may convert yet. Just a Coca-Cola is fine."

Messina nodded at the waiter who had appeared.

"A Coke for my friend." The waiter nodded back and left.

Ali Zyiad Sharif Al Saud looked around the environs of the Villa Roma. "I must confess that I don't get around to this part of Chicago very much. It's very, well…Chicago, isn't it?"

"I own a piece of this joint; it's been around a while. Needs some renovation but the customers seem to like it the way it is, so who am I to argue? I have to confess I didn't expect to get a call from you."

"Well, I asked around, and they said you are a man of considerable influence in the building trades. As I told you, I was a partner with Steel Simpson on the Chicago World Tower project."

"You should pick your partners more carefully. Someone once told me, 'Why do I need partners? I can get in enough trouble all by myself.'"

Sharif laughed and looked at the Manhattan, wishing he could order one. Maybe Mafia guys were not such bad types.

"He came to me. To my family. We wanted to get more involved in real estate. We have, shall we say, excess capital to spend. But you are right. Mr. Simpson and I went to Northwestern together; he turned out to be most unscrupulous. So we were, we are, the one providing equity in the project. And you are providing the concrete. Two necessary ingredients for a building, wouldn't you say?"

"I guess that's true. So, what do you want from me? As you say, I was providing the concrete. That's all."

"Oh, I think you were doing so much more."

"I don't know what you mean…"

The waiter appeared with the Coke. Ali looked up. "Can I get a couple of cherries, please?"

"Sure you don't want a Manhattan?"

"No, thank you. So, let's be candid with one another, Mr. Messina."

"Carmine, please."

"Sorry, Carmine. Let me get to the point. It has taken three months, but I have finally unraveled the mess that Steel Simpson left behind. Chicago Bank and Trust was the lender, and was providing sixty million in financing, but after what Simpson did, they made unreasonable requests, and we, my family, were painted with the same dirty paint brush, because we were partners. My family has decided to finance the entire project ourselves."

Messina whistled and raised his glass. "Tu saluti, my friend." What is that, over a hundred million?"

"Yes, well over that when the project is done. But it won't get done with problems from overzealous electrical inspectors, jobsite accidents that shouldn't happen, and frivolous strikes. And that's where I think you can help me. I can't, I won't do anything to erase whatever financial losses you suffered from Mr. Simpson in the past. I was not a part of that and you're a grownup, just like me. But I can make sure you are paid for your concrete in a timely fashion on this job. Chicago World Tower is going to begin again soon."

"How soon?"

"As soon as the plans are re-drawn. You see, Simpson also bastardized the original design which was fabulous. It was cutting edge, forward, exciting. But he had it changed to save a few lousy million. You do appreciate good architecture, don't you, Carmine?"

"I admire the old architecture…the Pantheon, the Colosseum, St. Peter's. They didn't do any cost cutting on those projects. Hell, they're still standing!"

"We'll probably get laughed at, but we're starting over from scratch with the original design by the architect. And I need your help."

"How's that?"

"We can't put the structural grid of the original design over what has been built. It's different, so I need to tear everything down. It will cost a lot, but my family has the resources. And the time, well, what's six months in the grand scheme of civilization? Like you said, look at the Colosseum."

"You're gonna tear everything down?" Messina was incredulous.

"Exactly."

"Including the foundations?"

"Everything, Carmine, everything. The hole in the ground can stay, of course." Sharif took a sip of his coke, looking at the Manhattan.

Messina's heart skipped a beat. He smiled. "I think I know a good demolition contractor that can help with that. And I'll make sure you get a great price."

"And all the other shenanigans that have been taking place?"

"I'll make some calls. The job will run smooth; I can promise that too, but under one condition."

"There's always a condition with your people, isn't there?" Sharif realized the comment might offend, but it was already out there hanging in the air.

Messina took no offense. "If you mean business people, yes, there always is a condition with smart business people. My condition is this. Cooky's Concrete gave a crazy low price to get the contract, for reasons that are of no concern to you. Since then, we have had two increases in the price of aggregate and stone. I'll get your building torn down, completely demolished, under a contract direct to me, at a dirt-cheap price, and you let me give you a new price on the concrete. It will be a fair price, but one where I make a little upside to take care of my, I mean, your problem of the building structure that don't work. Capisce?"

"I capisce."

Messina looked over the waiter, standing in the wings. "Bring my friend here a Manhattan with three cherries."

Sharif nodded and smiled. He put out his hand to Carmine Messina to seal the deal. It was a handshake deal. The best kind.

CHAPTER 86

AUGUST 1975

The cool breeze hinted at the Wisconsin autumn that was just around the corner. Some of the leaves of the chestnut and oak trees were already turning color and falling to the ground of Saint Margaret's Home for Women. As they did every Sunday, the group of thirty or so young women, all simply dressed and all pregnant, made their way from the three-story residence hall to the stone chapel for evening prayer, and a homily from the Mother Superior. Marilyn Jones dreaded it, but it was required. One more month and she would be able to leave. Leave this wretched episode of her life in the past. Leave the hated baby growing inside her with the nuns who would find parents that would love it and never know that it was the spawn of a rape.

Covering their heads with lace, they entered the cool, dark sanctuary and sat down in the hard, wooden pews. Marilyn's back ached from the weight she carried inside her. The hard pew didn't help. She didn't care whether it was going to be a boy or a girl; in fact, she didn't even have to know. She would be told only if asked, and would never lay eyes on it—the nuns whisking it away along with the mortal sin that brought it into this world. Marilyn Jones knew she had committed no sin; she was raped by Vance Jefferson. Yet, she felt guilty, nonetheless. It really didn't matter to Mother Superior. All these young women had sinned one way or the other. Even the ones who had been raped shared in the blame because of their arousing dress, their painted faces, and their lustful smiles.

Sister Mary Blanche stepped up into the pulpit, her full tunic, starched bodice and rigid headdress making the climb more difficult. But it did not matter. Life was meant to be one of difficulty and sacrifice. She looked down over her charges and the other sisters sitting off to the side of the nave. She cleared her throat and began.

"My children in Christ, you are here because Jesus showed us that even though you have committed the sin of fornication, you can be forgiven as He forgave Mary Magdalene, a whore and a prostitute. We have taken you in and shown you His great mercy."

Marilyn squirmed in her seat. *"I was raped, you bitch,"* she thought. No matter how she turned, she could not get comfortable. She felt the baby move inside her.

Mother Superior continued. "We have cared for you within these walls. Our priests have heard your confessions of your grave sins, born of lust and desire. Now many of you are approaching the hour where you shall give birth to a child. A child of Christ. His child, not yours. You may bring the child into this world, but only through His resurrection will the baby be given life. And that child belongs to our Savior."

"How many more times must I hear this garbage?" Marilyn thought. Then there was a sharp pang, and the feeling of her body contracting. She felt the bench getting wet. She looked down. Her long skirt was wet.

"Many of you have asked: 'Will I been given a sedative when I am in labor, something called an epidural. Something to ease the pain?' The answer to that, my children, is no. You shall offer up your pain to God to atone for your mortal sin, to purify your body so that it will be chaste again. Just as Christ endured the pain of His crucifixion."

Another contraction came. Marilyn screamed. She didn't want to hold it in. She screamed for herself, for what she knew she was about to endure. She thought, *"How can I be in labor already? It's only been eight months. The baby is so big, maybe that's why. Please God, let this be over quickly."*

The nuns rushed over to her and saw that her water had broken. One rushed to the side aisle and found a wheelchair. Marilyn was lifted into it and she was taken out the door into the bright sun and the cool breeze. She felt another contraction. She looked up at the swaying branches and the reddening leaves. Her mind was swimming. As the contraction sent pains through her waist and down her legs, she forced herself to think: *"Eight months. Just eight months. Unless it is really nine months? Unless the baby isn't Jefferson's. No, could it be? Could it be Connor's?"*

"Push my dear. Push harder," Sister James urged Marilyn. "There I see the head. Once more!"

Marilyn pushed again and felt the new life slide out of her. She heard a slap and then a cry. "I want to see my baby."

"That's against the rules, my dear. You know that."

"Is it a boy, then?"

"If you must know, yes. A boy."

"I want to see him."

"I'm sorry."

"Listen, you penguin, I have to see him! For the love of God, let me see my baby!" Marilyn screamed. "You bitch, give me my baby!"

Sister James was shocked. But being accustomed to taking orders, she reluctantly handed the newborn to Marilyn. "Only for a minute then. I could get into serious trouble."

Marilyn looked upon the new life she had created. She knew instantly. It was Connor's child.

"I'm keeping my baby. No one is taking him away from me!"

CHAPTER 87

September 1975

Bob Marlow walked down the steps of the small twin-engine plane he had boarded in Miami. The Key West heat hit him like a blast furnace, but he didn't care. He instantly felt like he was in another country even though it was still the good old USA. There was something about the air and the water he spied in the distance. He knew why Connor might have gone here. It was just a hunch, but he couldn't find the postcard from Connor's friend at his desk. And it had been a staple there for the two years they worked together. He often caught Connor staring at it, daydreaming.

Marlow got in a cab and asked for the marina, not sure if there even was one. Once there, he walked from fishing boat to fishing boat asking if anyone knew Connor West. The skippers were as varied as the boats. Some were old with knarled hands; others young and professional; a few hippie types with long Rasta hair. He had about given up hope when at the end of the marina, in one of the worst slips he found a newer boat called "Daddy's Money." A sign on a stand by the vessel said "Half and Full Day Fishing Charters." A handsome young man of patrician bearing came out from the cabin.

"Hey, maybe you can help me."

"Sure, if you want to fish."

"No, I'm looking for someone. Do you know a Connor West?"

"Sullivan, sure I know him."

"I'm sorry. His name is Connor. Connor Jones West."

"Yeah, Sullivan. Oh, that's his nickname. Yeah, he's the first mate on this boat. I'm Rich. Rich Tomlinson. This is my boat."

"Nice. You must be 'Rat' then?"

"Oh yeah, that's my nickname. I went to school with Connor. I don't think I was cut out for architecture though."

"Apparently, neither does Connor. Know where I can find him?"

"It's his day off. He's probably at Captain Tony's. Drinking, I'm sure. You from Chicago?"

"Yeah, he used to work for me."

"What did you do to him up there? Fucked his head up pretty good."

"Yeah, I guess we did. Hey, thanks for the info."

Bob Marlow found Captain Tony's just off Duval Street. It took a moment for his eyes to adjust to the dim light inside. On one side was a long bar interrupted by a wall and then another bar. On the opposite side was a small stage where a guitar player was trying his best to rouse the afternoon crowd. Fortunately, as Marlow entered, he finished a song and went on break. There were two old guys at the first bar close to the street, so he proceeded to the rear bar. There was a sole occupant—young, long hair tied in a bun and a tanned face. Probably a five-day growth of beard. It was Connor. He walked up slowly, not wanting to be discovered. Connor was staring blankly at the one TV above the cash register. The Cubs were playing the Atlanta Braves.

"You like the Cubs' chances?"

"Well, even though they have Madlock and Cardenal, it isn't making any difference." West turned and realized it wasn't just another barfly trying to make conversation. "It's you. What are you doing here?"

"What is it they say in that movie, 'Of all the gin joints in all the towns, in all the world...' I'm looking for you, that's what I'm doing here. How are you?"

"Bob Marlow. Boss. Good. I'm...good. You?"

"Still sober."

West nodded to the bartender. "A tonic and lime, and another bourbon rocks."

"Still trying to find all the answers at the bottom of that glass?"

"Don't lecture me. I don't work for you anymore. Anyway, a few more, and I'll gain all the insight I need into the true meaning of life."

"Have it your way."

"How did you find me?"

"Just a hunch. I met your new boss. Seems like a very nice young man."

"Yeah, Rat and I go way back. He hired me. Pay is shit, but soon I'll have my own captain's license."

"Why don't you come back to Chicago?"

"What, and work for the man who raped my girlfriend?"

"He's no longer with the firm. He doctored up the curtainwall documents and I told him he could either retire or he'd be arrested for trying to screw our insurance company."

"Why did he do that?"

"When Simpson wasn't paying us, he figured that if the curtainwall leaked, Simpson would go after the E&O insurance and make a claim. But Jefferson knew they wouldn't look at any claim from Simpson until all outstanding invoices from the firm were paid. The firm was broke, and it was his last-ditch effort to get some money."

"But he got off scot-free for raping my girlfriend."

"Unfortunately, yes. On that they couldn't prove anything."

"I would have testified."

"If Jefferson had been arrested for rape, it would have been 'he said, she said.' He would have called witnesses who saw them at all those restaurants. It would certainly look consensual."

"It still sucks."

"Yeah, it does. But if it makes you feel better, I sent a check to Marilyn's parents for $50,000, and Steel Simpson was arrested for manslaughter, or at least pleaded to it. His partner took over the project, and paid us everything in arrears."

Jones head was spinning. "What? Simpson was arrested for manslaughter?"

"Yeah, he had a homeless village burned to the ground on the property. Two homeless guys were burned to death. It was before he hired NJ&M. He's in good ol' Statesville right now, serving ten years."

"Why did you send Marilyn fifty thousand dollars?"

"Why not? It was the right thing to do. A way to make amends, I guess."

"Where is she?"

"Honestly, I don't know. Her parents hang up on me when I call. So, I just sent the money. They haven't sent it back though. Something tells me she's still in Oak Park."

"What about Nolan, Jefferson and Marlow?"

"Well, it's Nolan and Marlow now. Turns out Junior has a pretty good head for numbers and accounting and all that boring shit. He's even a fairly good marketer. I'm doing the same stuff. We just need a chief designer. Interested?"

West ignored the query. "What happened to Chicago World Tower?"

Marlow motioned to the barman for another tonic. "I almost forgot. The Saudi partner, Ali Sharif, took over the project. Demoed everything down to the ground and started over. He's building your original design. Rotating Observation Deck with glass floor and all. They're pouring the foundation caissons again. Taubert and Caudy have handled it in your absence."

"I'm sure they did a good job."

"I bet they won't screw up the stair shop drawings, I'm sure of that."

"Oh yeah. Sorry about that, but I was pretty pissed. I needed to get back at Jefferson, the firm, and Simpson. I figured it would cost the firm and delay the project big time. But no one would get hurt."

"I guess I can understand your motives. Fortunately, when the job was stopped, Gary Ironworks sent a set back to us. Said we had returned too many sets. The firm always keeps a copy. I looked them over and saw Nolan's and Jefferson's initials. But Francis never puts 'Jr.' after his initials. So you and Jefferson have a lot in common."

"Don't say that. I don't rape women."

"Sorry, that was below the belt."

"With a lot of time to think about it down here, I was worried, and ashamed about what I did. Not too smart."

"I guess under the circumstances, I can understand why you did it, stupid as it was. Anyway, I never accepted your resignation. Let's say you've been on an extended leave of absence. I didn't know where to send your paycheck so here it is. Eight months' pay."

Connor took the envelope and opened it. "$15,530. I don't know what to do or say."

"Well, you could buy a boat and fish, I guess. But I hope you'll say that you'll come back. Let's start again. Go find Marilyn. Marry her."

Connor looked at himself in the mirror behind the bottles arrayed on the bar. "I miss her so much." Tears welled up in his eyes.

"I need a new partner."

"It's a pretty tempting offer."

"And I think the firm's chief designer should get $50,000 a year. But you'll need to stay off that," pointing to the now empty glass of bourbon.

"You don't know where she is?"

"Come back, you'll find her." Bob Marlow looked around Captain Tony's. He inhaled the smell of the whiskey, the peanuts, the wood, leather and pool chalk.

"You know, I always liked bars."

Connor nodded and smiled. "I'll drink to that."

THE END

About the Author

R. J. Linteau has spent his entire career, 44 years, in architecture, construction management and real estate development. He knows the industry, and he knows where the bodies are buried. This is his first novel.

He is currently completing his second novel, *The Black Orchestra*, a World War II thriller, that will be released in the fall of 2020.

Linteau has previously written two screenplays, one of which was a finalist in an industry contest. He also wrote a lot of short stories in high school, that he sold to classmates for a senior English assignment. It was lucrative and he didn't get caught.

Linteau lives in Marietta, Georgia with his wife. He has two children and two grandchildren. In his spare time, he and his wife of 37 years love to travel and spend time in Key West, Florida, and St. Simon's Island, Georgia.

Please e-mail him with your comments: RJLinteau.author@gmail.com

Thank you!